Dame Ngaio Marsh, a tall, vigorous New Zealander, published her twenty-seventh novel in 1972—at the age of seventy-two. Her best-selling whodunnits are in the classic tradition of Dorothy Sayers and Agatha Christie.

Dame Ngaio, in common with many white New Zealand children, was given a Maori name. (The 'g' is silent.) It is a 'portmanteau' word which can mean 'light-on-the-tree', or a type of tree with a white flower which she describes as 'undistinguished'. It can also mean 'clever'.

Despite her enormous output, the writing of crime fiction is only her second love. The first is the theatre, and she developed the New Zealand public's interest in live theatrical performances almost single-handed. Now the University of Canterbury has a theatre named after her. Almost as splendid an honour as what she likes to call 'me damery'.

NGAIO MARSH

Overture to Death

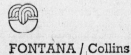

FONTANA / Collins

First published 1939
First issued in Fontana Books 1962
Second Impression, February 1967
Third Impression, October 1972
Fourth Impression November 1972
Fifth Impression April 1973

Printed in Great Britain
Collins Clear-Type Press London and Glasgow

For The Sunday Morning Party:
G. M. LESTER
DUNDAS AND CECIL WALKER
NORMAN AND MILES STACPOOLE BATCHELOR
& My Father

CONTENTS

CAST OF CHARACTERS

Jocelyn Jernigham *of Pen Cuckoo*
Henry Jernigham, *his son*
Eleanor Prentice, *his cousin*
Taylor, *his butler*
Walter Copeland, B.A. OXON., *Rector of Winton St. Giles*
Dinah Copeland, *his daughter*
Idris Campanula, *of the Red House, Chipping*
Dr. William Templett, *of Chippingwood*
Selia Ross, *of Duck Cottage, Cloudyfold*
Superintendent Blandish, *of the Great Chipping Constabulary*
Sergeant Roper, *of the Great Chipping Constabulary*
Mrs. Biggins
Georgie Biggins, *her son*
Gibson, *Miss Campanula's Chauffeur*
Gladys Wright, *of the Y.P.F.C.*
Saul Tranter, *poacher*
Chief Detective-Inspector Alleyn, *of the Criminal Investigation Department*
       Detective-Inspector Fox, *his assistant*
       Detective-Sergeant Bailey, *his finger print expert*
       Detective-Sergeant Thompson, *his camera expert*
Nigel Bathgate, *journalist, his Watson*

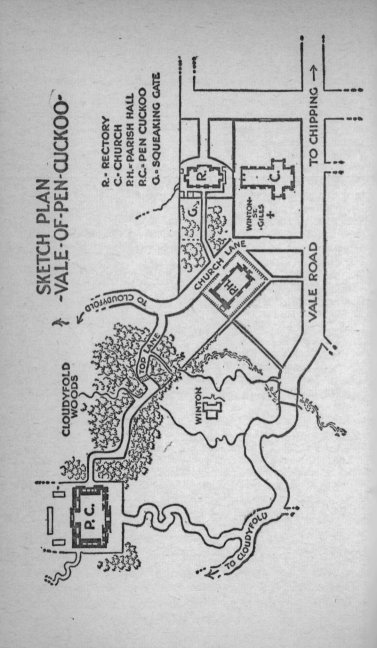

SKETCH PLAN
-VALE-OF-PEN-CUCKOO-

R.= RECTORY
C.= CHURCH
P.H.= PARISH HALL
P.C.= PEN CUCKOO
G.= SQUEAKING GATE

TO CHIPPING →

VALE ROAD

WINTON-
ST.-
GILES

CHURCH LANE

TO CLOUDYFOLD

TOP LANE

CLOUDYFOLD
WOODS

WINTON

TO CLOUDYFOLD

P.C.

CHAPTER ONE

The Meet at Pen Cuckoo

JOCELYN JERNIGHAM was a good name. The seventh
Jocelyn thought so as he stood at his study window and looked
down the vale of Pen Cuckoo toward that precise spot where
the spire of Salisbury Cathedral could be seen through field-
glasses on a clear day.

"Here I stand," he said, without turning his head, "and
here my forebears have stood, generation after generation,
and looked over their own tilth and tillage. Seven Jocelyn
Jernighams."

"I'm never quite sure," said his son Henry Jocelyn, "what
tilth and tillage are. What precisely, Father, is tilth?"

"There's no feeling for that sort of thing," said Jocelyn,
angrily, "among the present generation. Cheap sneers and
clever talk that mean nothing."

"But I assure you I like words to mean something. That
is why I ask you to define a tilth. And you say, 'the present
generation.' You mean my generation, don't you? But
I'm twenty-three. There is a newer generation than mine. If
I marry Dinah——"

"You quibble deliberately in order to lead our conversation back to this absurd suggestion. If I had known——"

Henry uttered an impatient noise and moved away from
the fireplace. He joined his father in the window and he too
looked down into the darking vale of Pen Cuckoo. He saw
an austere landscape, adamant beneath drifts of winter mist.
The naked trees slept soundly, the fields were dumb with
cold; the few stone cottages, with their comfortable signals
of blue smoke, were the only waking things in all the valley.

"I too love Pen Cuckoo," said Henry, and he added,
with that tinge of irony which Jocelyn, who did not understand it, found so irritating: "I have all the pride of pros-
pective ownership. But I refuse to be bully-ragged by Pen
Cuckoo. I refuse to play the part of a Victorian young
gentleman with a touch of Cophetua thrown in. I refuse
to allow this conversation to run along the lines of ancient
lineage. The proud father and self-willed heir stuff simply
doesn't fit. We are not discussing a possible misalliance.
Dinah is not a blushing maid of inferior station. She is

part of the country, rooted equally with us. If we are going to talk about her in county terms, I can strike a suitable attitude and say there have been Copelands at the rectory for as many generations as there have been Jernighams at Pen Cuckoo."

"You are both much too young——" began Jocelyn.

"No, really, sir, that won't do. What you mean is that Dinah is too poor. If it had been somebody smarter and richer, you and my dear cousin Eleanor wouldn't have talked about youth. Don't let's pretend."

"And don't you talk to me like a damned sententious young puppy, Henry, because I won't have it."

"I'm sorry," said Henry, "I know I'm being tiresome."

"You're being extremely tiresome. Very well, I'll speak as plainly as you like. Pen Cuckoo means more to me and should mean more to you, than anything else in life. You know as well as I do that we're damned hard up. There are all sorts of things that should be done to the place. Those cottages up at Cloudyfold! Winton! Rumbold tells me that Winton'll leak like a basket if we don't fix up the roof. The point is——"

"I can't afford to make a poor marriage?"

"If you choose to put it like that."

"How else can one put it?"

"Very well, then."

"Well, since we must speak in terms of hard cash, which I assure you I don't enjoy, Dinah won't always be the poor parson's one ewe lamb."

"What d'you mean?" asked Jocelyn, uneasily, but with a certain air of pricking up his ears.

"I thought everybody knew Miss Campanula has left all her filthy lucre, or most of it, to the rector. Don't pretend, Father; you must have heard that piece of gossip. The cook and housemaid witnessed the will and the housemaid overheard Miss C. bawling about it to her lawyer. Dinah doesn't want the money and nor do I—much—but that's what'll happen to it eventually."

"Servant's gossip," muttered the squire. "Most distasteful. Anyway, it may not—she may change her mind. It's *now* we're so damned hard-up."

"Let me find a job of work," Henry said.

"Your job of work is here."

"What! with a perfectly good agent who looks upon me as a sort of impediment in his agricultural speech?"

"Nonsense!"

10

"Look here, Father," said Henry gently, "how much of this has been inspired by Eleanor?"

"Eleanor is as anxious as I am that you shouldn't make a bloody fool of yourself. If your mother had been alive——"

"No, no," cried Henry, "let us not put ideas into the minds of the dead. That is so grossly unfair. Let's recognise Eleanor's hand in this. Eleanor has been too clever by half. I didn't mean to tell you about Dinah until I was sure that she loved me. I am not sure. The scene, which Eleanor so conveniently overheard yesterday at the rectory, was purely tentative." He broke off, turned away from his father, and pressed his cheek against the window pane.

"It is intolerable," said Henry, "that Eleanor should have spoilt the memory of my first—my first approach to Dinah. To stand in the hall, as she must have done, and to listen! To come clucking back to you like a vulgar hen, agog with her news! As if Dinah was a housemaid with a follower. No, it's too much!"

"You've never been fair to Eleanor. She's done her best to take your mother's place."

"For God's sake," said Henry violently, "don't use that detestable phrase! Cousin Eleanor has never taken my mother's place. She is an ageing spinster cousin of the worst type. It was not particularly kind of her to come to Pen Cuckoo. Indeed, it was her golden opportunity. She left the Cromwell Road for the glories of 'county.' It was the great moment of her life. She's a vulgarian."

"On her mother's side," said Jocelyn, "she's a Jernigham."

"Oh, my dear father!" said Henry, and burst out laughing.

Jocelyn glared at his son, turned purple in the face, and began to stammer.

"You may laugh, but Eleanor—Eleanor—in bringing this information—unavoidably overheard—no question of eavesdropping—only doing what she believed to be her duty."

"I'm sure she told you that."

"She did and I agreed with her. I am most strongly opposed to this affair with Dinah, and I am most relieved to hear that so far it is, as you put it, purely tentative."

"If Dinah loves me," said Henry, setting the Jernigham jaw, "I shall marry her. And that's flat. If Eleanor wasn't here to jog at your pride, Father, you would at least try to see my side. But Eleanor won't let you. She dramatises herself as the first lady of the district. The squiress. The chatelaine of Pen Cuckoo. She sees Dinah as a sort of rival. What's more, I believe she's genuinely jealous of Dinah.

11

It's the jealousy of a woman of her age and disposition, a jealousy rooted in sex."

"Disgusting balderdash!" said Jocelyn, angrily, but he looked uncomfortable.

"No!" cried Henry. "No, it's not. I'm not talking highbrow pornography. You must have seen what Eleanor is. She's an avid woman. She was in love with you until she found it was a hopeless proposition. Now she and her girl friend the Campanula are rivals for the rector. Dinah says all old maids always fall in love with her father. Everybody sees it. It's a recognised phenomenon with women of Eleanor's and Idris Campanula's type. Have you heard her on the subject of Dr. Templett and Selia Ross? She's nosed out a scandal there. The next thing that happens will be Eleanor feeling it her duty to warn poor Mrs. Templett that her husband is too fond of the widow. That is, if Idris Campanula doesn't get in first. Women like Eleanor and Miss Campanula are pathological. Dinah says——"

"Do you and Dinah discuss my cousin's attachment, which I don't admit, for the rector? If you do, I consider it shows an extraordinary lack of manners and taste."

"Dinah and I," said Henry, "discuss everything."

"And this is modern love-making!"

"Don't let's start abusing each other's generations, Father. We've never done that. You've been so extraordinary understanding in so many ways. It's Eleanor!" said Henry. "It's Eleanor, Eleanor, Eleanor who is to blame for this!"

The door at the far end of the room was opened and against the lamplit hall beyond appeared a woman's figure.

"Did I hear you call me, Henry?" asked a quiet voice.

I I

Miss Eleanor Prentice came into the room. She reached out a thin hand and switched on the lights.

"It's past five o'clock," said Miss Prentice. "Almost time for our little meeting. I asked them all for half-past five."

She walked with small mimbling steps towards the cherry-wood table which, Henry noticed, had been moved from the wall into the centre of the study. Miss Prentice began to place pencils and sheets of paper at intervals round the table. As she did this she produced, from between her thin closed lips, a dreary flat humming which irritated Henry almost beyond endurance. More to stop this noise than because he wanted to know the answer, Henry asked:

" What meeting, Cousin Eleanor? "

" Have you forgotten, dear? The entertainment committee. The rector and Dinah, Dr. Templett, Idris Campanula, and ourselves. We are counting on you. And on Dinah, of course."

She uttered this last phrase with additional sweetness. Henry thought, " She knows we've been talking about Dinah." As she fiddled with her pieces of paper Henry watched her with that peculiar intensity that people sometimes lavish on a particularly loathed individual.

Eleanor Prentice was a thin, colourless woman of perhaps forty-nine years. She disseminated the odour of sanctity to an extent that Henry found intolerable. Her perpetual half-smile suggested that she was of a gentle and sweet disposition. This faint smile caused many people to overlook the strength of her face, and that was a mistake, for its strength was considerable. Miss Prentice was indeed a Jernigham. Henry suddenly thought that it was rather hard on Jocelyn that both his cousin and his son should look so much more like the family portraits than he did. Henry and Eleanor had each got the nose and jaw proper to the family. The squire had inherited his mother's round chin and indeterminate nose. Miss Prentice's prominent grey eyes stared coldly upon the world through rimless pince-nez. The squire's blue eyes, even when inspired by his frequent twists of ineffectual temper, looked vulnerable and slightly surprised. Henry, still watching her, thought it strange that he himself should resemble this woman whom he disliked so cordially. Without a taste in common, with violently opposed views on almost all ethical issues, and with a profound mutual distrust, they yet shared a certain hard determination which each recognised in the other. In Henry this quality was tempered by courtesy and by a generous mind. She was merely polite and long-suffering. It was typical of her that although she had evidently overheard Henry's angry reiteration of her name, she accepted his silence and did not ask again why he had called her. Probably, he thought, because she had stood outside the door listening. She now began to pull forward the chairs.

" I think we must give the rector your arm-chair, Jocelyn," she said. " Henry, dear, would you mind? It's rather heavy."

Henry and Jocelyn helped her with the chair and, at

13

her instruction, threw more logs of wood on the fire. These arrangements completed, Miss Prentice settled herself at the table.

"I think your study is almost my favourite corner of Pen Cuckoo, Jocelyn," she said brightly.

The squire muttered something, and Henry said, "But you are very fond of every corner of the house, aren't you, Cousin Eleanor?"

"Yes," she said softly. "Ever since my childhood days when I used to spend my holidays here (you remember, Jocelyn?) I've loved the dear old home."

"Estate agents," Henry said, "have cast a permanent opprobrium on the word ' home.' It has come to mean nothing. It is a pity that when I marry, Cousin Eleanor, I shall not be able to take my wife to Winton. I can't afford to mend the roof, you know."

Jocelyn cleared his throat, darted an angry glance at his son, and returned to the window.

"Winton is the dower-house, of course," murmured Miss Prentice.

"As you already know," Henry continued, "I have begun to pay my addresses to Dinah Copeland. From what you overheard at the rectory do you think it likely that she will accept me?"

He saw her eyes narrow but she smiled a little more widely, showing her prominent and unlovely teeth. "She's like a French Caricature of an English spinster," thought Henry.

"I'm quite sure, dear," said Miss Prentice, "that you do not think I willingly overheard your little talk with Dinah. Far from it. It was very distressing when I caught the few words that——"

"That you repeated to Father? I'm sure you were."

"I thought it my duty to speak to your father, Henry."

"Why?"

"Because I think, dear, that you two young people are in need of a little wise guidance."

"Do you like Dinah?" asked Henry abruptly.

"She has many excellent qualities, I am sure," said Miss Prentice.

"I asked you if you liked her, Cousin Eleanor."

"I like her for those qualities. I am afraid, dear, that I think it better not to go any further just at the moment."

"I agree," said Jocelyn from the window. "Henry, I won't have any more of this. These people will be here in a moment. There's the rectory car, now, coming round

Cloudyfold bend. They'll be here in five minutes. You'd better tell us what it's all about, Eleanor."

Miss Prentice seated herself at the foot of the table. "It's the Y.P.F.C.," she said. "We badly want funds and the rector suggested that perhaps we might get up a little play. You remember, Jocelyn. It was the night we dined there."

"I remember something about it," said the squire.

"Just among ourselves," continued Miss Prentice, "I know you've always loved acting, Jocelyn, and you're so good at it. So natural. Do you remember *Ici on Parle Français* in the old days? I've talked it all over with the rector and he agrees it's a splendid idea. Dr. Templett is *very* good at theatricals, especially in funny parts, and dear Idris Campanula, of course, is all enthusiasm."

"Good Lord!" ejaculated Henry and his father together.

"What on earth is *she* going to do in the play?" asked Jocelyn.

"Now, Jocelyn, we mustn't be uncharitable," said Miss Prentice, with a cold glint of satisfaction in her eye. "I dare say poor Idris would make quite a success of a small part."

"I'm too old," said Jocelyn.

"What nonsense, dear. Of course you're not. We'll find something that suits you."

"I'm damned if I'll make love to the Campanula," said the squire ungallantly. Eleanor assumed her usual expression for the reception of bad language, but it was coloured by that glint of complacency.

"Please, Jocelyn," she said.

"What's Dinah going to do?" asked Henry.

"Well, as dear Dinah is almost a professional——"

"She *is* a professional," said Henry.

"Such a pity, yes," said Miss Prentice.

"Why?"

"I'm old-fashioned enough to think that the stage is not a very nice profession for a gentlewoman, Henry. But of course Dinah must act in our little piece. If she isn't too grand for such humble efforts."

Henry opened his mouth and shut it again. The squire said, "Here they are."

There was the sound of a car pulling up on the gravel drive outside, and two cheerful toots on an out-of-date klaxon.

"I'll go and bring them in," offered Henry.

Henry went out through the hall. When he opened the
great front door the upland air laid its cold hand on his
face. He smelt frost, dank earth, and dead leaves. The
light from the house showed him three figures climbing
out of a small car. The rector, his daughter Dinah, and a
tall woman in a shapeless fur coat—Idris Campanula. Henry
produced the right welcoming noises and ushered them
into the house. Taylor, the butler, appeared, and laid expert
hands on the rector's shabby overcoat. Henry, his eyes on
Dinah, dealt with Miss Campanula's furs. The hall rang
with Miss Campanula's conversation. She was a large arrogant
spinster with a firm bust, a high-coloured complexion, coarse
grey hair, and enormous bony hands. Her clothes were
hideous but expensive, for Miss Campanula was extremely
wealthy. She was supposed to be Eleanor Prentice's great
friend. Their alliance was based on mutual antipathies and
interests. Each adored scandal and each cloaked her passion
in a mantle of conscious rectitude. Neither trusted the other
an inch, but there was no doubt that they enjoyed each
other's company. In conversation their technique varied
widely. Eleanor never relinquished her air of charity and
when she struck, the blow always fell obliquely. But Idris
was one of those women who pride themselves on their
outspokenness. Repeatedly did she announce that she was a
downright sort of person. She was particularly fond of
saying that she called a spade a spade, and in her more
daring moments would add that her cousin, General Campanula, had once told her that she went further than that
and called it a " B. shovel." She cultivated an air of bluff
forthrightness that should have deceived nobody, but actually
passed as true currency among the simpler of her acquain-
tances. The truth was that she reserved to herself the right
of broad speech, but would have been livid with rage if
anybody had replied in kind.

The rector, a widower whose classic handsomeness made
him the prey of such women, was, so Dinah had told Henry,
secretly terrified of both these ladies who loomed so large in
parochial affairs. Eleanor Prentice had a sort of coy bedside manner with the rector. She spoke to him in a dove-
smooth voice and frequently uttered little musical laughs.
Idris Campanula was bluff and proprietary, called him " my
dear man " and watched him with an intensity that made him

blink, and aroused in his daughter a conflicting fury of disgust and compassion.

Henry laid aside the fur coat and hurried to Dinah. He had known Dinah all his life, but while he was at Oxford and later, when he did a course with a volunteer air-reserve unit, he had seen little of her. When he returned to Pen Cuckoo, Dinah had finished her dramatic course, and had managed to get into the tail end of a small repertory company where she remained for six weeks. The small repertory company then fell to pieces and Dinah returned home, an actress. Three weeks ago he had met her unexpectedly on the hills above Cloudyfold, and with that encounter came love. He had felt as if he saw her for the first time. The bewildering rapture of discovery was still upon him. To meet her gaze, to speak to her, to stand near her, launched him upon a flood of bliss. His sleep was tinged with the colour of his love and when he woke he found her already waiting in his thoughts. "She is my whole desire," he said to himself. And, because he was not quite certain that she loved him in return, he had been afraid to declare himself until yesterday, in the shabby, charming old drawing-room at the rectory, when Dinah had looked so transparently into his eyes that he began to speak of love. And then, through the open door, he had seen Eleanor, a still figure, in the dark hall beyond. Dinah saw Eleanor a moment later and, without a word to Henry, went out and welcomed her. Henry himself had rushed out of the rectory and driven home to Pen Cuckoo in a white rage. He had not spoken to Dinah since then, and now he looked anxiously at her. Her wide eyes smiled at him.

" Dinah?"

" Henry?"

" When can I see you?"

" You see me now," said Dinah.

" Alone. Please?"

" I don't know. Is anything wrong?"

" Eleanor."

" Oh, Lord!" said Dinah.

" I must talk to you. Above Cloudyfold where we met that morning? To-morrow, before breakfast. Dinah, will you?"

" All right," said Dinah. " If I can."

Idris Campanula's conversation flowed in upon their consciousness. Henry was suddenly aware that she had asked him some sort of question.

"I'm so sorry," he began. "I'm afraid I——"

"Now, Henry," she interrupted, "where are we to go? You're forgetting your duties, gossiping there with Dinah." And she laughed her loud rocketing bray.

"The study, please," said Henry. "Will you lead the way?"

She marched into the study, shook hands with Jocelyn and exchanged pecks with Eleanor Prentice.

"Where's Dr. Templett?" she asked.

"He hasn't arrived yet," answered Miss Prentice. "We must always make allowances for our medical men, mustn't we?"

"He's up beyond Cloudyfold," said the rector. "Old Mrs. Thrinne is much worse. The third Cain boy has managed to run a nail through his big toe. I met Templett in the village and he told me. He said I was to ask you not to wait."

"Beyond Cloudyfold?" asked Miss Prentice sweetly. Henry saw her exchange a glance with Miss Campanula.

"Mrs. Ross doesn't have tea till five," said Miss Campanula, "which *I* consider a silly ostentation. We certainly will *not* wait for Dr. Templett. Ha!"

"Templett didn't say anything about going to Mrs. Ross's," said the rector, innocently, "though to be sure it is on his way."

"My dear good man," said Miss Campanula, "if you weren't a saint—however! I only hope he doesn't try and get her into our play."

"Idris dear," said Miss Prentice. "May I?"

She collected their attention and then said very quietly:

"I think we are all agreed, aren't we, that this little experiment is to be just among ourselves? I have got several little plays here for five and six people and I fancy Dinah has found some too."

"Six," said Miss Campanula very firmly. "Five characters won't do, Eleanor. We've three ladies and three men. And if the rector——"

"No," said the rector, "I shall not appear. If there's any help I can give behind the scenes, I shall be only too delighted, but I really don't want to appear."

"Three ladies and three men, then," said Miss Campanula. "Six."

"Certainly no more," said Miss Prentice.

"Well," said the squire, "if Mrs. Ross is very good at
18

acting, and I must say she's an uncommonly attractive little thing——"

"No, Jocelyn," said Miss Prentice.

"She is very attractive," said Henry.

"She's got a good figure," said Dinah. "Has she had any experience?"

"My dear child," said Miss Campanula loudly, "she's as common as dirt and we certainly don't want her. I may say that I myself have seen Eleanor's plays and I fully approve of *Simple Susan*. There are six characters: three men and three ladies. There is no change of scene, and the theme is suitable."

"It's rather old," said Dinah dubiously.

"My dear child," repeated Miss Campanula, "if you think we're going to do one of your modern questionable problem-plays you're very greatly mistaken."

"I think some of the modern pieces are really *not* quite suitable," agreed Miss Prentice gently.

Henry and Dinah smiled.

"And as for Mrs. Selia Ross," said Miss Campanula, "I believe in calling a spade a spade and I have no hesitation in saying I think we'll be doing a Christian service to poor Mrs. Templett, who we all know is too much an invalid to look after herself, if we give Dr. Templett something to think about besides——"

"Come," said the rector desperately, "aren't we jumping our fences before we meet them? We haven't appointed a chairman yet and so far nobody has suggested that Mrs. Ross be asked to take part."

"They'd better not," said Miss Campanula.

The door was thrown open by Taylor, who announced:

"Mrs. Ross and Dr. Templett, sir."

"What!" exclaimed the squire involuntarily.

An extremely well-dressed woman and a short rubicund man walked into the room.

"Hullo! Hullo!" shouted Dr. Templett. "I've brought Mrs. Ross along by sheer force. She's a perfectly magnificent actress and I tell her she's got to come off her high horse and show us all how to set about it. I know you'll be delighted."

CHAPTER TWO

Six Parts and Seven Actors

IT WAS HENRY who rescued the situation when it was on the verge of becoming a scene. Neither Miss Campanula nor Miss Prentice made the slightest attempt at cordiality. The squire uttered incoherent noises, shouted "What!" and broke out into uncomfortable social laughter. Dinah greeted Mrs. Ross with nervous civility. The rector blinked and followed his daughter's example. But on Henry the presence of Dinah acted like a particularly strong stimulant and filled him with a vague desire to be nice to the entire population of the world. He shook Mrs. Ross warmly by the hand, complimented Dr. Templett on his idea, and suggested, with a beaming smile, that they should at once elect a chairman and decide on a play.

The squire, Dinah, and the rector confusedly supported Henry. Miss Campanula gave a ringing sniff. Miss Prentice, smiling a little more widely than usual, said:

"I'm afraid we are short of one chair. We expected to be only seven. Henry, dear, you will have to get one from the dining-room. I'm so sorry to bother you."

"I'll share Dinah's chair," said Henry happily.

"Please don't get one for me," said Mrs. Ross. "Billy can perch on my arm."

She settled herself composedly in a chair on the rector's left and Dr. Templett at once sat on the arm. Miss Prentice had already made sure of her place on the rector's right hand and Miss Campanula, defeated, uttered a short laugh and marched to the far end of the table.

"I don't know whether this is where I am bidden, Eleanor," she said, "but the meeting seems to be delightfully informal, so this is where I shall sit. Ha!"

Henry, his father, and Dinah took the remaining chairs.

From the old chandelier a strong light was cast down on the eight faces round the table; on the squire, pink with embarrassment; on Miss Prentice, smiling; on Miss Campanula, like an angry mare, breathing hard through her nostrils; on Henry's dark Jernigham features; on Dinah's crisp and vivid beauty; on the rector's coin-sharp priestliness and on Dr. Templett's hearty undistinguished normality.

20

It shone on Selia Ross. She was a straw-coloured woman of perhaps thirty-eight. She was not beautiful but she was exquisitely neat. Her hair curved back from her forehead in pale waves. The thick white skin of her face was beautifully made-up and her clothes were admirable. There was a kind of sharpness about her so that she nearly looked haggard. Her eyes were pale and you would have guessed that the lashes were white when left to themselves. Almost every human being bears some sort of resemblance to an animal and Mrs. Ross was a little like a ferret. But for all that she had a quality that arrested the attention of many women and most men. She had a trick of widening her eyes, and looking slant ways. Though she gave the impression of fineness she was in reality so determined that any sensibilities she possessed were held in the vice of her will. She was a coarse-grained woman but she seemed fragile. Her manner was gay and good-natured, but though she went out of her way to do kindnesses, her tongue was quietly malicious. It was clear to all women who met her that her chief interest was men. Dinah watched her now and could not help admiring the cool assurance with which she met her frigid reception. It was impossible to guess whether Mrs. Ross was determined not to show her hurts or was merely so insensitive that she felt none. "She *has* got a cheek," thought Dinah. She looked at Henry and saw her own thoughts reflected in his face. Henry's rather startlingly fierce eyes were fixed on Mrs. Ross and in them Dinah read both awareness and appraisal. He turned his head, met Dinah's glance, and at once his expression changed into one of such vivid tenderness that her heart turned over. She was drowned in a wave of emotion and was brought back to the world by the sound of Miss Prentice's voice.

"——to elect a chairman for our little meeting. I should like to propose the rector."

"Second that," said Miss Campanula, in her deepest voice.

"There you are, Copeland," said the squire, "everybody says 'Aye' and away we go." He laughed loudly and cast a terrified glance at his cousin.

The rector looked amiably round the table. With the exception of Henry, of all the company he seemed the least embarrassed by the arrival of Mrs. Ross. If Mr. Copeland had been given a round gentle face with unremarkable features and kind shortsighted eyes it would have been a perfect expression of his temperament. But ironical nature had made him magnificently with a head so beautiful that to most

21

observers it seemed that his character must also be on a grand scale. With that head he might have gone far and become an important dignitary of the church, but he was unambitious and sincere, and he loved Pen Cuckoo. He was quite content to live at the rectory as his forebears had lived, to deal with parish affairs, to give what spiritual and bodily comfort he could to his people, and to fend off the advances of Idris Campanula and Eleanor Prentice. He knew very well that both these ladies bitterly resented the presence of Mrs. Ross, and that he was in for one of those hideously boring situations when he felt exactly as if he was holding down with his thumb the cork of a bottle filled with seething ginger-pop.

He said, "Thank you very much. I don't feel that my duties as chairman will be very heavy as we have only met to settle the date and nature of this entertainment, and when that is decided all I shall have to do is to hand everything over to the kind people who take part. Perhaps I should explain a little about the object we have in mind. The Young People's Friendly Circle, which has done such splendid work in Pen Cuckoo and the neigbouring parishes, is badly in need of funds. Miss Prentice as president and Miss Campanula as secretary, will tell you all about that. What we want more than anything else is a new piano. The present instrument was given by your father, wasn't it, squire?"

"Yes," said Jocelyn. "I remember quite well. It was when I was about twelve. It wasn't new then. I can imagine it's pretty well a dead horse."

"We had a tuner up from Great Chipping," said Miss Campanula, "and he says he can't do anything more with it. I blame the scouts. Ever since the eldest Cain boy was made scout-master they have gone from bad to worse. He's got no idea of discipline, that young man. On Saturday I found Georgie Biggins tramping up and down the keyboard in his boots and whanging the wires inside with the end of his pole. 'If I were your scout-master,' I said, 'I'd give you a beating that you'd not forget in a twelvemonth.' His reply was grossly impertinent. I told the eldest Cain that if he couldn't control his boys himself he'd better hand them over to someone who could."

"Dear me, yes," said the rector hurriedly. "Young barbarians they are sometimes. Well now, the piano is of course not the sole property of the Y.P.F.C. It was a gift to the parish. But I have suggested that, as they use it a great deal, perhaps it would be well to devote whatever

22

funds result from this entertainment to a piano fund, rather than to a general Y.P.F.C. fund. I don't know what you all think about this."

"How much would a new piano cost?" asked Dr. Templett.

"There's a very good instrument at Preece's in Great Chipping," said the rector. "The price is £50."

"We can't hope to make that at our show, can we?" asked Dinah.

"I tell you what," said the squire. "I'll make up the difference. The piano seems to be a Pen Cuckoo affair."

There was a general gratified murmur.

"Damned good of you, squire," said Dr. Templett. "Very generous."

"Very good indeed," agreed the rector.

Miss Prentice, without moving, seemed to preen herself. Henry saw Miss Campanula look at her friend and was startled by the singularly venomous glint in her eye. He thought, " She's jealous of Eleanor taking reflected glory from Father's offer." And suddenly he was appalled by the thought of these two ageing women united in so profound a dissonance.

"Perhaps," said the rector, "we had better have a formal motion."

They had a formal motion. The rector hurried them on. A date was fixed three weeks ahead for the performance in the parish hall. Miss Prentice who seemed to have become a secretary by virtue of her seat on the rector's right hand, made quantities of notes. And all the time each of these eight people knew very well that they merely moved in a circle round the true matter of their meeting. What Miss Prentice called " the nature of our little entertainment " had yet to be determined. Every now and then someone would steal a covert glance at the small pile of modern plays in front of Dinah and the larger pile of elderly French's acting editions in front of Miss Prentice. And while they discussed prices of admission, and dates, through each of their minds raced their secret thoughts.

II

The rector thought, " I cannot believe it of Templett. A medical man with an invalid wife! Besides, there's his professional position. But what persuaded him to bring her here? He must have known how they would talk. I wish Miss Campanula wouldn't look at me like that. She wants

23

to see me alone again. I wish I'd never said confession was recognised by the Church, but how could I not? I wish she wouldn't confess. I wish that I didn't get the impression that she and Miss Prentice merely use the confessional as a means of informing against each other. Six parts and seven people. Oh, dear!"

The squire thought, " Eleanor's quite right, I was good in *Ici on Parle Française.* Funny how some people take to the stage naturally. Now, if Dinah and Henry try to suggest one of those modern things, as likely as not there will be nothing that suits me. What I'd like is one of those charming not-so-young men in a Marie Tempest comedy. Mrs. Ross could play the Marie Tempest part. Eleanor and old Idris wouldn't have that at any price. I wonder if it's true that they don't really kiss on the stage because of the grease paint. Still, at rehearsals . . . I wonder if it's true about Templett and Mrs. Ross. I'm as young as ever I was. What the devil am I going to do about Henry and Dinah Copeland? Dinah's a prétty girl. Hard, though. Modern. If only the Copelands were a bit better off it wouldn't matter. I suppose they'll talk about me, both of them. Henry will say something clever. Blast and damn Eleanor! Why the devil couldn't she hold her tongue, and then I shouldn't have had to deal with it. Six parts and seven people. Why shouldn't she be in it, after all? I suppose Templett would want the charming not-so-young part and they'd turn me into some bloody comic old dodderer."

Eleanor Prentice thought, " If I take care and manage this well it will look as if it's Idris who is making all the trouble and he will think her uncharitable. Six parts and seven people. Idris is determined to stop that Ross woman at all costs. I can see one of Idris's tantrums coming. That's all to the good. I shall be forty-nine next month. Idris is more than forty-nine. Dinah should work in the parish. I wonder what goes on among actors and actresses. Dressing and undressing behind the scenes and travelling about together. If I could find out that Dinah had—— If I married, Jocelyn would make me an allowance. To see that woman look at Templett like that and he at her! Dinah and Henry! I can't bear it. I can't endure it. Never show you're hurt. I want to look at him, but I mustn't. Henry might be watching. Henry knows. A parish priest should be married. His head is like an angel's head. No. Not an angel's. A Greek god. Prostrate before Thy throne to lie and gaze and gaze on Thee. Oh, God, let him love me!"

Henry thought, "To-morrow morning if it's fine I shall meet Dinah above Cloudyfold and tell her that I love her. Why shouldn't Templett have his Selia Ross in the play? Six parts and seven people to the devil! Let's find a new play. I'm in love for the first time. I've crossed the border into a strange country and never again will there be a moment quite like this. To-morrow morning, if it's fine, Dinah and I will be up on Cloudyfold."

Dinah thought, "To-morrow morning, if it's fine, Henry will be waiting for me above Cloudyfold and I think he will tell me he loves me. There will be nobody in the whole wide world but Henry and me."

Templett thought, "I'll have to be careful. I suppose I was a fool to suggest her coming, but after she said she was so keen on acting it seemed the only thing to do. If those two starved spinsters get their teeth into us it'll be all up with the practice. I wish to God I was made differently. I wish to God my wife wasn't what she is. Perhaps it'd be all the same if she wasn't. Selia's got me. It's like an infection. I'm eaten up with it."

Selia Ross thought, "So far so good. I've got here. I can manage the squire easily enough, but he's got his eye on me already. The boy's in love with the girl, but he's a man and I think he'll be generous. He's no fool, though, and I rather fancy he's summed me up. Attractive, with those light grey eyes and black lashes. It might be amusing to take him from her. I doubt if I could. He's past the age when they fall for women a good deal older than themselves. I feel equal to the whole lot of them. It was fun coming in with Billy and seeing those two frost-bitten old virgins with their eyes popping out of their heads. They know I'm too much for them with my good common streak of hard sense and determination. They're both trying to see if Billy's arm is touching my shoulders. The Campanula is staring quite openly and the Poor Relation's looking out of the corner of her eyes. I'll lean back a little. There! Now have a good look. It's a bore about Billy's professional reputation and having to be so careful. I want like hell to show them all he's mine. I've never felt like this about any other man, never. It's as if we'd engulfed each other. I suppose it's love. I won't have him in their bogus school-room play without me. He might have a love scene with the girl. I couldn't stand that. Seven people and six parts. Now, then!"

And Idris Campanula thought, "If I could in decency
25

lay my hands on that straw-coloured wanton I'd shake the very life out of her. The infamous brazen effrontery! To force her way into Pen Cuckoo, without an invitation, under the protection of that man! I always suspected Dr. Templett of that sort of thing. If Eleanor had the gumption of a rabbit she'd have forbidden them the house. Sitting on the arm of her chair! A fine excuse! He's practically got his arm round her. I'll look straight at them and let her see what I think of her. There! She's smiling. She knows, and she doesn't care. It amounts to lying in open sin with him. The rector *can't* let it pass. It's an open insult to me, making me sit at the same table with them. Every hand against me. I've no friends. They only want my money. Eleanor's as bad as the rest. She's tried to poison the rector's mind against me. She's jealous of me. The play was *my* idea and now she's talking as if it was hers. The rector must be warned. I'll ask him to hear my confession on Friday. I'll confess the unkind thoughts I've had of Eleanor Prentice and before he can stop me I'll tell him what they were and then perhaps he'll begin to see through Eleanor. Then I'll say I've been un-charitable about Mrs. Ross and Dr. Templett. I'll say I'm an outspoken woman and believe in looking facts in the face. He *must* prefer me to Eleanor. I ought to have married. With my ability and my money and my brains I'd make a success of it. I'd do the Rectory up and get rid of that impertinent old maid. Dinah could go back to the stage as soon as she liked, or if Eleanor's gossip is true, she could marry Henry Jernigham. Eleanor wouldn't care much for that. She'll fight tooth and nail before she sees another chatelaine at Pen Cuckoo. I'll back Eleanor up as far as Dr. Templett and his common little light-of-love are con-cerned, but if she tries to come between me and Walter Copeland she'll regret it. Now then, I'll speak."

And bringing her large, ugly hand down sharply on the table she said:

" May I have a word?"

" Please do," said Mr. Copeland nervously.

" As secretary," began Miss Campanula loudly, " I have discussed this matter with the Y.P.F.C. members individually. They plan an entertainment of their own later on in the year and they are *most* anxious that this little affair should be arranged *entirely* by ourselves. Just five or six, they said, of the people who are really interested in the Circle. They mentioned you, of course, rector, and the squire, as patron, and you, Eleanor, naturally, as president. They said they hoped Dinah would not feel that our humble efforts were beneath her dignity and that she would grace our little performance. And you, Henry, they particularly mentioned you."

"Thank you," said Henry solemnly. Miss Campanula darted a suspicious glance at him and went on:

"They seem to think they'd like to see me making an exhibition of myself with all the rest of you. Of course, I don't pretend to histrionic talent——"

"*Of course* you must have a part, Idris," said Miss Prentice. "We depend upon you."

"Thank you, Eleanor," said Miss Campanula; and between the two ladies there flashed the signal of an alliance.

"That makes five, doesn't it?" asked Miss Prentice sweetly.

"Five," said Miss Campanula.

"Six, with Dr. Templett," said Henry.

"We should be very glad to have Dr. Templett," rejoined Miss Prentice, with so cunningly balanced an inflection that her rejection of Mrs. Ross was implicit in every syllable.

"Well, a G.P.'s an awkward sort of fellow when it comes to rehearsals," said Dr. Templett. "Never know when an urgent case may crop up. Still, if you don't mind risking it I'd like to take a part."

"We'll certainly risk it," said the rector. There was a murmur of assent followed by a deadly little silence. The rector drew in his breath, looked at his daughter who gave him a heartening nod, and said:

"Now, before we go any further with the number of performers, I think we should decide on the form of the entertainment. If it is going to be a play, so much will depend upon the piece chosen. Has anybody any suggestion?"

"I move," said Miss Campanula, "that we do a play, and I suggest *Simple Susan* as a suitable piece."

"I should like to second that," said Miss Prentice.

"What sort of play is it?" asked Dr. Templett. "I haven't heard of it. Is it new?"

"It's a contemporary of *East Lynne* and *The Silver King* I should think," said Dinah.

Henry and Dr. Templett laughed. Miss Campanula thrust out her bosom, turned scarlet in the face, and said:

"In my humble opinion, Dinah, it is none the worse for that."

"It's so amusing," said Miss Prentice. "You remember it, Jocelyn, don't you? There's that little bit where Lord Sylvester pretends to be his own tailor and proposes to

Lady Maude, thinking she's her own lady's maid. Such an original notion and so ludicrous."

"It has thrown generations of audiences into convulsions," agreed Henry.

"Henry," said the squire.

"Sorry, Father. But honestly, as a dramatic device——"

"*Simple Susan,*" said Miss Campanula hotly, "may be old-fashioned in the sense that it contains no disgusting innuendos. It does not depend on vulgarity for its fun, and that's more than can be said for most of your modern comedies."

"How far does Lord Sylvester go——" began Dinah.

"Dinah!" said the rector quietly.

"All right, Daddy. Sorry. I only——"

"How old is Lord Sylvester?" interrupted the squire suddenly.

"Oh, about forty-five or fifty," murmured Miss Prentice.

"Why not do *The Private Secretary*?" inquired Henry.

"I never thought *The Private Secretary* a very nice play," said Miss Prentice. "I expect I'm prejudiced." And she gave the rector a reverent smile.

"I agree," said Miss Campanula. "I always thought it in the worst of taste. I may be old-fashioned but I don't like jokes about the cloth."

"I don't think *The Private Secretary* ever did us much harm," said the rector mildly. "But aren't we wandering from the point? Miss Campanula has moved that we do a play called *Simple Susan*. Miss Prentice has seconded her. Has anybody else a suggestion to make?"

"Yes," said Selia Ross, "I have."

CHAPTER THREE

They Choose a Play

IF MRS. ROSS had taken a ticking bomb from her handbag and placed it on the table, the effect could have been scarcely more devastating. What she did produce was a small green book. Seven pairs of eyes followed the movements of her thin scarlet-tipped hands. Seven pairs of eyes fastened, as if mesmerised, on the black letters of the book cover. Mrs. Ross folded her hands over the book and addressed the meeting.

"I do hope you'll all forgive me for making my suggestion," she said, "but it's the result of a rather odd coincidence. I'd no idea of your meeting until Dr. Templett called in this afternoon, but I happened to be reading this play and when he appeared the first thing I said was, 'Some time or other we simply *must* do this thing.' Didn't I, Billy? I mean, it's absolutely marvellous. All the time I was reading it I kept thinking how perfect it would be for some of you to do it in aid of one of the local charities. There are two parts in it that would be simply ideal for Miss Prentice and Miss Campanula. The Duchess and her sister. The scene they have with General Talbot is one of the best in the play. It simply couldn't be funnier and you'd be magnificent as the General, Mr. Jernigham."

She paused composedly and looked sideways at the squire. Nobody spoke, though Miss Campanula wetted her lips. Selia Ross waited for a moment, smiling frankly, and then she said:

"Of course I didn't realise you had already chosen a play. Naturally I wouldn't have dreamt of coming if I had known. It's all this man's fault." She gave Dr. Templett a sort of comradely jog with her elbow. "He bullied me into it. I ought to have apologised and crept away at once, but I just couldn't resist telling you about my discovery." She opened her eyes a little wider and turned them on the rector. "Perhaps if I left it with you, Mr. Copeland, the committee might just like to glance at it before they quite decide. *Please* don't think I want a part in it or anything frightful like that. It's just that it *is* so good and I'd be delighted to lend it."

"That's very kind of you," said the rector.

"It's not a bit kind. I'm being thoroughly selfish. I just long to see you all doing it and I'm secretly hoping you won't be able to resist it. It's so difficult to find modern plays that aren't offensive," continued Mrs. Ross, with an air of great frankness, " but this really is charming."

" But what is the play?" asked Henry, who had been craning his neck in a useless attempt to read the title.

" *Shop Windows*, by Jacob Hunt."

" Good Lord!" ejaculated Dinah. "Of course! I never thought of it. It's the very thing."

" Have you read it?" asked Mrs. Ross, with a friendly glance at her.

" I saw the London production," said Dinah. " You're quite right, it would be grand. But what about the royalties?

Hunt charges the earth for amateur rights, and anyway he'd probably refuse them to us."

"I was coming to that," said Mrs. Ross. "If you should decide to do it I'd like to stand the royalties if you'd let me."

There was another silence, broken by the rector.

"Now, that's very generous indeed," he said.

"No, honestly it's not. I've told you I'm longing to see it done."

"How many characters are there?" asked the squire suddenly.

"Let me see, I think there are six." She opened the play and counted prettily on her fingers.

"Five, six—no, there seem to be seven! Stupid of me."

"Ha!" said Miss Campanula.

"But I'm sure you could find a seventh. What about the Moorton people?"

"What about you?" asked Dr. Templett.

"No, no!" said Mrs. Ross quickly. "I don't come into the picture. Don't be silly."

"It's a damn' good play," said Henry. "I saw the London show too, Dinah. D'you think we could do it?"

"I don't see why not. The situations would carry it through. The three character parts are really the stars."

"Which are they?" demanded the squire.

"The General and the Duchess and her sister," said Mrs. Ross.

"They don't come on till the second act," continued Dinah, "but from then on they carry the show."

"May I have a look at it?" asked the squire.

Mrs. Ross opened the book and passed it across to him.

"Do read the opening of the act," she said, "and then go on to page forty-eight."

"May I speak?" demanded Miss Campanula loudly.

"Please!" said the rector hurriedly. "Please do. Ah—order!"

II

Miss Campanula gripped the edge of the table with her large hands and spoke at some length. She said that she didn't know how everybody else was feeling but that she herself was somewhat bewildered. She was surprised to learn that such eminent authorities as Dinah and Henry and Mrs. Ross considered poor Pen Cuckoo capable of producing a modern play that met with their approval. She thought that perhaps this clever play might be a little too clever for poor Pen Cuckoo and the Young People's Friendly Circle. She asked the meeting if it did not think it would make a great mistake if it was over-ambitious. "I must confess," she said, with an angry laugh, "that I had a much simpler plan in mind. I did not propose to fly as high as West End successes and I don't mind saying I think we would be in a fair way to making fools of ourselves. And that's that."

"But, Miss Campanula," objected Dinah, "it's such a mistake to think that because the cast is not very experienced it will be better in a bad play than in a good one."

"I'm sorry you think *Simple Susan* a bad play, Dinah," said Miss Prentice sweetly.

"Well I think it's very dated and I'm afraid I think it's rather silly," said Dinah doggedly.

Miss Prentice gave a silvery laugh in which Miss Campanula joined.

"I agree with Dinah," said Henry quickly.

"Suppose we all read both plays," suggested the rector.

"I have read *Shop Windows*," said Dr. Templett. "I must say I don't see how we could do better."

"We seem to be at a disadvantage, Eleanor," said Miss Campanula unpleasantly, and Miss Prentice laughed again. So, astonishingly, did the squire. He broke out in a loud choking snort. They all turned to look at him. Tears coursed each other down his cheeks and he dabbed at them absent-mindedly with the back of his hand. His shoulders quivered, his brows were raised in an ecstasy of merriment, and his cheeks were purple. He was lost in the second act of Mrs. Ross's play.

"Oh! Lord! he said, "this is funny."

"Jocelyn!" cried Miss Prentice.

"Eh?" said the squire, and he turned a page, read half-a-dozen lines, laid the book on the table and gave himself up to paroxysms of unbridled laughter.

"Jocelyn!" repeated Miss Prentice. "Really!"

"What?" gasped the squire. "Eh? All right, I'm quite willing. Damn' good! When do we begin?"

"Hi!" said Henry. "Steady, Father! The meeting hasn't decided on the play."

"Well, we'd better decide on this," said the squire, and he leant towards Selia Ross. "When he starts telling her he's got the garter," he said, "and she thinks he's talking

31

about the other affair! And then when she says she won't take no for an answer. Oh, Lord!"

"It's heavenly, isn't it?" agreed Mrs. Ross, and she and Henry and Dinah suddenly burst out laughing at the recollection of this scene, and for a minute or two they all reminded each other of the exquisite facetiæ in the second act of *Shop Windows*. The rector listened with a nervous smile; Miss Prentice and Miss Campanula with tightly-set lips. At last the squire looked round the table with brimming eyes and asked what they were all waiting for.

"I'll move we do *Shop Windows*," he said. "That in order?"

"I'll second it," said Dr. Templett.

"No doubt I am in error," said Miss Campanula, "but I was under the impression that my poor suggestion was before the meeting, seconded by Miss Prentice."

The rector was obliged to put this motion to the meeting.

"It is moved by Miss Campanula," he said unhappily, "and seconded by Miss Prentice, that *Simple Susan* be the play chosen for production. Those in favour——"

"Aye," said Miss Campanula and Miss Prentice.

"And the contrary?"

"No," said the rest of the meeting with perfect good humour.

"Thank you," said Miss Campanula. "*Thank you.* Now we know where we are."

"You wait till you start learning your parts in this thing," said Jocelyn cheerfully, "and you won't know whether you're on your heads or your heels. There's an awful lot of us three, isn't there?" he continued, turning the pages. "I suppose Eleanor will do the Duchess and Miss Campanula will be the other one—Mrs. Thing or whoever she is! Gertrude! That the idea?"

"That was my idea," said Mrs. Ross.

"If I may be allowed to speak," said Miss Campanula, "I should like to say that it is just within the bounds of possibility that it may not be ours."

"Perhaps, Jernigham," said the rector, "you had better put your motion."

But of course the squire's motion was carried. Miss Campanula and Miss Prentice did not open their lips. Their thoughts were alike in confusion and intensity. Both seethed under the insult done to *Simple Susan*, each longed to rise and, with a few well-chosen words, withdraw from the meeting. Each was checked by a sensible reluctance to cut off her nose to spite her face. It was obvious that *Shop Windows* would be performed whether they stayed in or flounced out. Unless all the others were barefaced liars, it seemed that there were two outstandingly good parts ready for them to snap up. They hung off and on, ruffled their plumage, and secretly examined each other's face.

III

Meanwhile with the enthusiasm that all Jernighams brought to a new project Jocelyn and his son began to cast the play. Almost a century ago there had been what Eleanor, when cornered, called an " incident " in the family history. The Mrs. Jernigham of that time was a plain silly woman and barren into the bargain. Her Jocelyn, the fourth of that name, had lived openly with a very beautiful and accomplished actress and had succeeded in getting the world to pretend that his son by her was his lawful scion, and had jockeyed his wife into bringing the boy up as her own. By this piece of effrontery he brought to Pen Cuckoo a dram of mummery, and ever since those days most of the Jernighams had had a passion for theatricals. It was as if the lovely actress had touched up the family portraits with a stick of rouge. Jocelyn and Henry had both played in the O.U.D.S. They both had the trick of moving about a stage as if they grew out of the boards, and they both instinctively bridged that colossal gap between the stage and the front row of the stalls. Jocelyn thought himself a better actor than he was, but Henry did not realise how good he might be. Even Miss Prentice, a Jernigham, as the squire had pointed out, on her mother's side, had not escaped that dram of player's blood. Although she knew nothing about theatre, mistrusted and disliked the very notion of the stage as a career for gentle people, and had no sort of judgment for the merit of a play, yet in amateur theatricals she was surprisingly composed and perfectly audible, and she loved acting. She knew now that Idris Campanula expected her to refuse to take part in *Shop Windows,* and more than half her inclination was so to refuse. " What," she thought. " To have my own play put aside for something chosen by that woman! To have to look on while they parcel out the parts!" But even as she pondered on the words with which she would offer her resignation, she pictured Lady Appleby of Moorton Grange accepting the part that Jocelyn said was so good. And what

33

was more, the rector would think Eleanor herself uncharitable. That decided her. She waited for a pause in the chatter round Jocelyn, and then she turned to the rector.

"May I say just one little word?" she asked.

"Yes, yes, of course," said Mr. Copeland. "Please, everybody. Order!"

"It's only this," said Miss Prentice, avoiding the eye of Miss Campanula. "I do hope nobody will think I am going to be disappointed or hurt about my little play. I expect it *is* rather out-of-date, and I am only too pleased to think that you have found one that is more suitable. If there is anything that I can do to help, I shall be only too glad. Of course."

She received, and revelled in, the rector's beaming smile, and met Idris Campanula's glare with a smile of her own. Then she saw Selia Ross watching her out of the corners of her eyes and suddenly she knew that Selia Ross understood her.

"That's perfectly splendid," exclaimed Mr. Copeland. "I think it is no more than we expected of Miss Prentice's generosity, but we are none the less grateful." And he added confusedly, "A very graceful gesture."

Miss Prentice preened and Miss Campanula glowered. The others, vaguely aware that something was expected of them, made small appreciative noises.

"Now, how about casting the play?" said Dr. Templett.

IV

There was no doubt that the play had been well chosen. With the exception of one character, it practically cast itself. The squire was to play the General; Miss Prentice, the Duchess; Miss Campanula, of whom everybody felt extremely frightened, was cast for Mrs. Arbuthnott, a good character part. Miss Campanula, when offered this part, replied ambiguously:

"Who knows?" she looked darkly. "Obviously, it is not for me to say."

"But you will do it, Idris?" murmured Miss Prentice.

"I have but one comment," rejoined Miss Campanula. "Wait and see." She laughed shortly, and the rector, in a hurry, wrote her name down opposite the part. Dinah and Henry were given the two young lovers, and Dr. Templett said he would undertake the French Ambassador.

He began to read some of the lines in violently broken English. There remained the part of Hélène, a mysterious lady who had lost her memory, and who turned up in the middle of the first act at a country house-party.

"Obviously, Selia," said Dr. Templett, " you must be Hélène."

"No, no," said Mrs. Ross, "that isn't a bit what I meant. Now do be quiet, Billy, or they'll think I came here with an ulterior motive."

With the possible exception of the squire, that was precisely what they all did think, but not even Miss Campanula had the courage to say so. Having accepted Mrs. Ross's play they could do nothing but offer her the part, which, as far as lines went, was not a long one. Perhaps only Dinah realised quite how good Hélène was. Mrs. Ross protested and demurred.

"If you are quite sure you want me," she said, and looked sideways at the squire. Jocelyn, who had glanced through the play and found that the General had a love-scene with Hélène, said heartily that they wanted her very much indeed. Henry and Dinah, conscious of their own love-scenes, agreed, and the rector formally asked Mrs. Ross if she would take the part. She accepted with the prettiest air in the world. Miss Prentice managed to maintain her gentle smile and Miss Campanula's behaviour merely became a degree more darkly ominous. The rector put on his glasses and read his notes.

"To sum up," he said loudly. "We propose to do this play in the Parish Hall on Saturday 27th, three weeks from to-night. The proceeds are to be devoted to the piano-fund and the balance of the sum needed will be made up most generously by Mr. Jocelyn Jernigham. The committee and members of the Y.P.F.C. will organise the sale of tickets and will make themselves responsible for the—what is the correct expression, Dinah?"

"The front of the house, Daddy."

"For the front of the house, yes. Do you think we can leave these affairs to your young folk, Miss Campanula? I know you can answer for them."

"My dear man," said Miss Campanula, "I can't answer for the behaviour of thirty village louts and maidens, but they usually do what I tell them to. Ha!"

Everybody laughed sycophantly.

"My *friend*," added Miss Campanula, with a ghastly smile, " my *friend* Miss Prentice is president. No doubt, if they pay no attention to me, they will do anything in the world for her."

"Dear Idris!" murmured Miss Prentice.

"Who's going to produce the play?" asked Henry. "I think Dinah ought. She's a professional."

"Hear, hear!" said Dr. Templett, Selia Ross and the squire. Miss Prentice added rather a tepid little, "Of course, yes." Miss Campanula said nothing. Dinah grinned shyly and looked into her lap. She was elected producer. Dinah had not passed the early stages of theatrical experience when the tyro lards his conversation with professional phrases. She accepted her honours with an air of great seriousness and called her first rehearsal for Tuesday night, November 9th.

"I'll get all your sides typed by then," she explained. "I'm sure Gladys Wright will do them, because she's learning and wants experience. I'll give her a proper part so that she gets the cues right. We'll have a reading and if there's time I'll set positions for the first act."

"Dear me," said Miss Prentice, "this sounds very alarming. I'm afraid, Dinah dear, that you will find us all very amateurish."

"Oh, no!" cried Dinah gaily. "I know it's going to be marvellous." She looked uncertainly at her father and added, "I should like to say, thank you all very much for asking me to produce. I do hope I'll manage it all right."

"Well, you know a dashed sight more about it than any of us," said Selia Ross bluntly.

But somehow Dinah didn't quite want Mrs. Ross so frankly on her side. She was aware in herself of a strong antagonism to Mrs. Ross and this discovery surprised and confused her, because she believed herself to be a rebel. As a rebel, she should have applauded Selia Ross. To Dinah, Miss Prentice and Miss Campanula were the hated symbols of all that was mean, stupid, and antediluvian. Selia Ross had deliberately given battle to these two ladies and had won the first round. Why, then, could Dinah not welcome her as an ally after her own heart? She supposed it was because, in her own heart, she mistrusted and disliked Mrs. Ross. This feeling was entirely instinctive and it upset and bewildered her. It was as if some dictator in her blood refused an allegiance that she should have welcomed. She could not reply with the correct comradely smile. She felt her face turning pink with embarrassment and she said hurriedly:

36

"What about music? We'll want an overture and an entr'acte."

And with those words Dinah unconsciously rang up the curtain on a theme that was to engulf Pen Cuckoo and turn *Shop Windows* from polite comedy into outlandish, shameless melodrama.

CHAPTER FOUR

Cue for Music

AS SOON AS Dinah had spoken those fatal words everybody round the table in the study at Pen Cuckoo thought of "Rachmaninoff's Prelude in C. sharp Minor," and with the exception of Miss Campanula, everybody's heart sank into his or her boots. For the Prelude was Miss Campanula's speciality. In Pen Cuckoo she had the sole rights in this composition. She played it at all church concerts, she played it on her own piano after her own dinner parties, and, unless her hostess was particularly courageous, she played it after other people's dinner parties, too. Whenever there was any question of music sounding at Pen Cuckoo, Miss Campanula offered her services, and the three pretentious chords would boom out once again: " Pom, *Pom*, POM." And then down would go Miss Campanula's foot on the left pedal and the next passage would follow in a series of woolly but determined jerks. She even played it as a voluntary when Mr. Withers, the organist, went on his holidays and Miss Campanula took his place. She had had her photograph taken, seated at the instrument, with the Prelude .on the rack. Each of her friends had received a copy at Christmas. The rector's was framed, and he had not known quite what to do with it. Until three years ago when Eleanor Prentice had come to live at Pen Cuckoo, Idris Campanula and her Prelude had had it all their own way. But Miss Prentice. also belonged to a generation when girls learnt the pianoforte from their governesses, and she, too, liked to be expected to perform. Her *pièce de résistance* was Ethelbert Nevin's " Venetian Suite," which she rendered with muffled insecurity, the chords of the accompaniment never quite synchronising with the saccharine notes of the melody. Between the two ladies the battle had raged at parish entertainments, Sunday

School services, and private parties. They only united in deploring the radio and in falsely pretending that music was a bond between them.

So that when Dinah in her flurry asked, "What about music?" Miss Campanula and Miss Prentice both became alert.

Miss Prentice said, "Yes, of course. Now, couldn't we manage that amongst ourselves somehow? It's *so* much pleasanter, isn't it, if we keep to our own small circle?"

"I am afraid my poor wits are rather confused," began Miss Campanula. "Everything seems to have been decided out of hand. You must correct me if I'm wrong, but it appears that several of the characters in this delightful comedy—by the way, is it a comedy?"

"Yes," said Henry.

"Thank you. It appears that some of the characters do not appear until somewhere in the second act. I don't know which of the characters, naturally, as I have not yet looked between the covers."

With hasty mumbled apologies they handed the play to Miss Campanula. She said:

"Oh, thank you. Don't let me be selfish. I'm a patient body."

When Idris Campanula alluded to herself jocularly as a "body" it usually meant that she was in a temper. They all said, "No, no! Please have it." She drew her pince-nez out from her bosom by a patent extension and slung them across her nose. She opened the play and amidst dead silence she began to inspect it. First she read the cast of characters. She checked each one with a large bony forefinger, and paused to look round the table until she found the person who had been cast for it. Her expression, which was forbidding, did not change. She then applied herself to the first page of the dialogue. Still everybody waited. The silence was broken only by the sound of Miss Campanula turning a page. Henry began to feel desperate. It seemed almost as if they would continue to sit dumbly round the table until Miss Campanula reached the end of the play. He gave Dinah a cigarette and lit one himself. Miss Campanula raised her eyes and watched them until the match was blown out, and then returned to her reading. She had reached the fourth page of the first act. Mrs. Ross looked up at Dr. Templett who bent his head and whispered. Again Miss Campanula raised her eyes and stared at the offenders. The squire cleared his throat and said:

"Read the middle bit of Act II. Page forty-eight, it begins. Funniest thing I've come across for ages. It'll make you laugh like anything."

Miss Campanula did not reply, but she turned to Act II. Dinah, Henry, Dr. Templett, and Jocelyn waited with anxious smiles for her to give some evidence of amusement, but her lips remained firmly pursed, her brows raised, and her eyes fishy. Presently she looked up.

"I've reached the end of the scene," she said. "Was that the funny one?"

"Don't you think it's funny?" asked the squire.

"My object was to find out if there was anybody free to play the entr'acte," said Miss Campanula coldly. "I gather that there is. I *gather* that the Arbuthnot individual does not make her first appearance until half-way through the second act."

"Didn't somebody say that Miss Arbuthnot and the Duchess appeared together?" asked Miss Prentice to the accompaniment, every one felt, of the "Venetian Suite."

"Possibly," said Miss Campanula. "Do I understand that I am expected to take this Mrs. Arbuthnot upon myself?"

"If you will," rejoined the rector. "And we hope very much indeed that you will."

"I wanted to be quite clear. I dare say I'm making a great to-do about nothing but I'm a person that likes to know where she is. Now I *gather*, and you must correct me if I'm wrong, that if I do this part there is no just cause or impediment," and here Miss Campanula threw a jocular glance at the rector, "why I should not take a little more upon myself and seat myself at the instrument. You *may* have other plans. You *may* wish to hire Mr. Joe Hopkins and his friends from Great Chipping, though on a Saturday night I gather they are rather more undependable and tipsy than usual. *If* you have other plans then no more need be said. If not, I place myself at the committee's disposal."

"Well, that seems a most excellent offer," the poor rector began. "If Miss Campanula——"

"May I?" interrupted Miss Prentice sweetly. "May I say that I think it very kind indeed of dear Idris to offer herself, but may I add that I do also think we are a little too inclined to take advantage of her generosity. She will have all the young folk to manage and she has a large part to learn. I do feel that we should be a little selfish if we also expected her to play for us on that dreadful old piano. Now, as the new instrument is to be in part, as my

39

cousin says, a Pen Cuckoo affair, I think the very least I can do is to offer to relieve poor Idris of this unwelcome task. If you think my little efforts will pass muster I shall be very pleased to play the overture and entr'acte."

"Very thoughtful of you, Eleanor, but I am quite capable——"

"Of course you are, Idris, but at the same time——"

They both stopped short. The antagonism that had sprung up between them was so obvious and so disproportionate that the others were aghast. The rector abruptly brought his palm down on the table and then, as if ashamed of a gesture that betrayed his thoughts, clasped his hands together and looked straight before him.

He said, "I think this matter can be decided later."

The two women glanced quickly at him and were silent.

"That is all, I believe," said Mr. Copeland. "Thank you, everybody."

II

The meeting broke up. Henry went to Dinah who had moved over to the fire.

"Ructions!" he said under his breath.

"Awful!" agreed Dinah. "You'd hardly believe it possible, would you?"

They smiled secretly and when the others crowded about Dinah, asking if they could have their parts before Monday, what sort of clothes would be needed, and whether she thought they would be all right, neither she nor Henry minded very much. It did not matter to them that they were unable to speak to each other, for their thoughts went forward to the morning, and their hearts trembled with happiness. They were isolated by their youth, two scatheless figures. It would have seemed impossible to them that their love for each other could hold reflection, however faint, of the emotions that drew Dr. Templett to Selia Ross, or those two ageing women to the rector. They would not have believed that there was a reverse side to love, or that the twin-opposites of love lay dormant in their own hearts. Nor were they to guess that never again, as long as they lived, would they know the rapturous expectancy that now possessed them.

Miss Prentice and Miss Campanula carefully avoided each other. Miss Prentice had seized her opportunity and had cornered Mr. Copeland. She could be heard offering flowers from the Pen Cuckoo greenhouses for a special service next Sunday. Miss Campanula had tackled Jocelyn about some enormity committed on her property by the local fox-hounds. Dr. Templett, a keen follower of hounds, was lugged into the controversy. Mrs. Ross was therefore left alone. She stood a little to one side, completely relaxed, her head slanted, a half-smile on her lips. The squire looked over Idris Campanula's shoulder, and caught that half-smile.

"Can't have that sort of thing," he said vaguely. "I'll have a word with Appleby. Will you forgive me? I just want——"

He escaped thankfully and joined Mrs. Ross. She welcomed him with an air that flattered him. Her eyes brightened and her smile was intimate. It was years since any woman had smiled in that way at Jocelyn, and he responded with Edwardian gallantry. His hand went to his moustache and his eyes brightened.

"You know, you're a very alarming person," said Jocelyn.

"Now what precisely do you mean by that?" asked Mrs. Ross.

He was delighted. This was the way a conversation with a pretty woman ought to start. Forgotten phrases returned to his lips, waggishly nonsensical phrases that one uttered with just the right air of significance. One laughed a good deal and let her know one noticed how damned well-turned-out she was.

"I see that we have a most important scene together," said Jocelyn, "and I shall insist on a private rehearsal."

"I don't know that I shall agree to that," said Selia Ross.

"Oh, come now, it's perfectly safe."

"Why?"

"Because you are to be the very charming lady who has lost her memory. Ha, ha, ha! Damn' convenient, what!" shouted Jocelyn, wondering if this remark was as daring as it sounded. Mrs. Ross laughed very heartily and the squire glanced in a gratified manner round the room, and encountered the astonished gaze of his son.

"This'll show Henry," thought Jocelyn. "These modern pups don't know how to flirt with an attractive woman." But there was an unmistakably sardonic glint in Henry's eye, and the squire, slightly shaken, turned back to Mrs. Ross. She still looked roguishly expectant and he thought, "Anyway, if Henry's noticed *her*, he'll know I'm doing pretty well." And then Dr. Templett managed to escape Miss Campanula and joined them.

41

"Well, Selia," he said, "if you're ready I think I'd better take you home."

"Doesn't like me talking to her!" thought the squire in triumph. "The little man's jealous."

When Mrs. Ross silently gave him her hand, he deliberately squeezed it.

"*Au revoir,*" he said. "This is your first visit to Pen Cuckoo, isn't it? Don't let it be the last."

"I shouldn't be here at all," she answered. "There have been no official calls, you know."

Jocelyn made a slightly silly gesture and bowed.

"We'll waive all that sort of nonsense," he said. "Ha, ha, ha!"

Mrs. Ross turned to say good-bye to Eleanor Prentice.

"I have just told your cousin," she said, "that I've no business here. We haven't exchanged calls, have we?"

If Miss Prentice was at all taken aback, she did not show it. She gave her musical laugh and said, "I'm afraid I am very remiss about these things."

"Miss Campanula hasn't called on me either," said Mrs. Ross. "You must come together. Good-bye."

"Good-bye, everybody," said Mrs. Ross.

"I'll see you to your car," said the squire. "Henry!"

Henry hastened to the door. Jocelyn escorted Mrs. Ross out of the room and, as Dr. Templett followed them, the rector shouted after them:

"Just a minute, Templett. About the youngest Cain."

"Oh, yes. Silly little fool! Look here, rector——"

"I'll come out with you," said the rector.

Henry followed and shut the door behind them.

"Well!" said Miss Campanula. "Well!"

"*Isn't it?*" said Miss Prentice. "*Isn't it?*"

III

Dinah, left alone with them, knew that the battle of the music was postponed in order that the two ladies might unite in abuse of Mrs. Ross. That it was postponed and not abandoned was evident in their manner, which reminded Dinah of stewed fruit on the turn. Its sweetness was impregnated by acidity.

"Of course, Eleanor," said Miss Campanula, "I can't for the life of me see why you didn't show her the door. I should have refused to receive her. I should!"

" I was simply dumfounded," said Miss Prentice. " When Taylor announced them, I really couldn't believe my senses. I am deeply disappointed in Dr. Templett."

" Disappointed! The greatest piece of brazen effrontery I have ever encountered. He shan't have my lumbago! I can promise him that."

" I really should have thought he'd have known better," continued Miss Prentice. " It isn't as if we don't know who he is. He should be a gentleman. I always thought he took up medicine as a *vocation*. After all, there have been Templetts at Chippingwood for——"

" For as long as there have been Jernighams at Pen Cuckoo," said Miss Campanula. " But, of course, you wouldn't know that."

This was an oblique hit. It reminded Miss Prentice that she was a new-comer and not, strictly speaking, a Jernigham of Pen Cuckoo. Miss Campanula followed it up by saying, " I suppose in your position you could do nothing but receive her ; but I must say I was astonished that you leapt at her play as you did."

" I did not leap, Idris," said Miss Prentice. " I hope I took the dignified course. It was obvious that everybody but you and me was in favour of her play."

" Well, it's a jolly good play," said Dinah.

" So we have been told," said Miss Campanula. " Repeatedly."

" I was helpless," continued Miss Prentice. " What could I do? One can do nothing against sheer common persistence. Of course she has triumphed."

" She's gone off now, taking every man in the room with her," said Miss Campanula. " Ha!"

" Ah, well," added Miss Prentice, " I suppose it's always the case when one deals with people who are *not quite*. Did you hear what she said about our not calling?"

" I was within an ace of telling her that I understood she received men only."

" But, Miss Campanula," said Dinah, " we don't know there's anything more than friendship between them, do we? And even if there is, it's their business."

" Dinah, *dear*!" said Miss Prentice.

" As a priest's daughter, Dinah——" began Miss Campanula.

" As a priest's daughter," said Dinah, " I've got a sort of idea charity is supposed to be a virtue. And, anyway, I think

43

when you talk about a person's family it's better not to call
him a priest. It sounds so scandalous, somehow."

There was dead silence. At last Miss Campanula rose
to her feet.

"I fancy my car is waiting for me, Eleanor," she said.
"So I shall make my adieux. I am afraid we are neither
of us intelligent enough to appreciate modern humour. Good-
night."

"Aren't we driving you home?" asked Dinah.

"Thank you, Dinah, no. I ordered my car for six, and
it is already half-past. Good-night."

CHAPTER FIVE

Above Cloudyfold

THE NEXT MORNING was fine. Henry woke up at six and
looked out of his window at a clear, cold sky with paling
stars. In another hour it would begin to get light. Henry,
wide awake, his mind sharp with anticipation, leapt back
into bed and sat with the blankets caught between his chin
and his knees, hugging himself. A fine winter's dawn with
a light frost and then the thin, pale sunlight. Down in
the stables they would soon be moving about with lanthorns
to the sound of clanking pails, shrill whistling, and boots on
cobblestones. Hounds met up at Moorton Park to-day, and
Jocelyn's two mounts would be taken over by his groom
to wait for his arrival by car. Henry spared a moment to regret
his own decision to give up hunting. He had loved it so much:
the sound, the smell, the sight of the hunt. It had all seemed
so perfectly splendid until one day, quite suddenly as if a
new pair of eyes had been put into his head, he had seen
a mob of well-fed expensive people, with red faces, astraddle
shiny quadrupeds, all whooping ceremoniously after a very
small creature which later on was torn to pieces while the
lucky ones sat on their horses and looked on, well satisfied.
To his violent annoyance, he had found that he could not
rid himself of this unlovely picture and, as it made him feel
slightly sick, he had given up everything but drag-hunting.
Jocelyn had been greatly upset and had instantly accused
Henry of pacifism. Henry had just left off being a pacifist,
however, and assured his father that if England was invaded
he would strike a shrewd blow before he would see Cousin

Eleanor raped by a foreign mercenary. Hugging his knees, he chuckled at the memory of Jocelyn's face. Then he gave himself four minutes to revise the conversation he had planned to have with Dinah. He found that the thought of Dinah sent his heart pounding, just as it used to pound in the old days before he took his first fence. "I suppose I'm hunting again," he thought, and this primitive idea gave him a curiously exalted sensation. He jumped out of bed, bathed, shaved and dressed by lamplight, then he stole downstairs out into the dawn.

It's a fine thing to be abroad on Dorset hills on a clear winter's dawn. Henry went round the west wing of Pen Cuckoo. The gravel crunched under his shoes and the dim box-borders smelt friendly in a garden that was oddly remote. Familiar things seemed mysterious as if the experience of the night had made strangers of them. The field was rimmed with silver, the spinney on the far side was a company of naked trees locked in a deep sleep from which the sound of footsteps among the dead leaves and twigs could not awaken them. The hillside smelt of cold earth and frosty stones. As Henry climbed steeply upwards, it was as if he left the night behind him down in Pen Cuckoo. On Cloudyfold, the dim shapes took on some resolute form and became rocks, bushes and posts, expectant of the day. The clamour of far-away cock-crows rose vaguely from the valley like the overlapping echoes of dreams, and with this sound came the human smell of woodsmoke.

Henry reached the top of Cloudyfold and looked down the vale of Pen Cuckoo. His breath a small cold mist in front of his face, his fingers were cold and his eyes watered, but he felt like a god as he surveyed his own little world. Half-way down, and almost sheer beneath him, was the house he had left. He looked down into the chimney-tops, already wreathed in thin drifts of blue. The servants were up and about. Farther down, and still drenched in shadow, were the roofs of Winton. Henry wondered if they really leaked badly and if he and Dinah could ever afford to repair them. Beyond Winton his father's land spread out into low hills and came to an end at Selwood Brook. Here, half-screened by trees, he could see the stone façade of Chippingwood which Dr. Templett had inherited from his elder brother who had died in the Great War. And separated from Chippingwood by the hamlet of Chipping was Miss Campanula's Georgian mansion, on the skirts of the village but not of it. Farther away, and only just visible over the downlands that separated it from the Vale, was Great Chipping, the largest town in that part of Dorset. Half-way up the slope, below Winton and Pen Cuckoo, was the church, Winton St. Giles, with the rectory hidden behind it. Dinah would strike straight through their home copse and come up the ridge of Cloudyfold. If she came! Please God, make it happen, said Henry's thoughts as they used to do when he was a little boy. He crossed the brow of the hill. Below him, on the far side, was Moorton Park Road and Cloudyfold Village, and there, tucked into a bend in the road, Duck Cottage, with its scarlet door and window frames, newly done up by Mrs. Ross. Henry wondered why Selia Ross had decided to live in a place like Cloudyfold. She seemed to him so thoroughly urban. For a minute or two he thought of her, still snugly asleep in her renovated cottage, dreaming perhaps of Dr. Templett. Farther away over the brow of the hill was the Cains' farm, where Dr. Templett must drive to minister to the youngest Cain's big toe.

"They're all down there," thought Henry, "tucked up in their warm houses, fast asleep; and none of them knows I'm up here in the cold dawn waiting for Dinah Copeland."

He felt a faint warmth on the back of his neck. The stivered grass was washed with colour, and before him his attenuated shadow appeared. He turned to the east and saw the sun. Quite near at hand he heard his name called, and there, coming over the brow of Cloudyfold, was Dinah, dressed in blue with a scarlet handkerchief round her neck.

Henry could make no answering call. His voice stuck in his throat. He raised his arm, and the shadow before him sent a long blue pointer over the grass. Dinah made an answering gesture. Because he could not stand dumbly and smile until she came up with him, he lit a cigarette, making a long business of it, his hands cupped over his face. He could hear her footsteps on the frozen hill, and his own heart thumped with them. When he looked up she was beside him.

"Good-morning," said Henry.

"I've no breath left," said Dinah; "but good-morning to you, Henry. Your cigarette smells like heaven."

He gave her one.

"It's grand up here," said Dinah. "I'm glad I came. You wouldn't believe you could be hot, would you? But I am. My hands and face are icy and the rest of me's like a hot-cross bun."

"I'm glad you came, too," said Henry. There was a short silence. Henry set the Jernigham jaw, fixed his gaze on Miss Campanula's chimneys, and said, "Do you feel at all shy?"

"Yes," said Dinah. "If I start talking I shall go on and on talking, rather badly. That's a sure sign I'm shy."

"It takes me differently. I can hardly speak. I expect I'm turning purple, and my top lip seems to be twitching."

"It'll go off in a minute," said Dinah. "Henry, what would you do if you suddenly knew you had dominion over all you survey? That sounds Biblical. I mean, suppose you could alter the minds—and that means the destinies—of all the people living down there—what would you do?"

"Put it into Cousin Eleanor's heart to be a missionary in Polynesia."

"Or into Miss Campanula's to start a nudist circle in Chipping."

"Or my father might go surrealist."

"No, but honestly, what would you do?" Dinah insisted.

"I don't know. I suppose I would try and simplify them. People seem to me to be much too busy and complicated."

"Make them kinder?"

"Well, that might do it, certainly."

"It would do it. If Miss Campanula and your Cousin Eleanor left off being jealous of each other, and if Dr. Templett was sorrier for his wife, and if Mrs. Ross minded more about upsetting other people's apple-carts, we wouldn't have any more scenes like the one last night."

'Perhaps not,' Henry agreed. "But you wouldn't stop them falling in love, if you can call whatever they feel for each other, falling in love. I'm in love with you, as I suppose you know. It makes me feel all noble minded and generous and kind; but, just the same, if I had a harem of invalid wives, they wouldn't stop me telling you I loved you, Dinah. Dinah, I love you so desperately."

"Do you, Henry?"

"You'd never believe how desperately This is all wrong. I'd thought out the way I'd tell you. First we were to have a nice conversation and then, when we'd got to the right place, I was going to tell you."

"All elegant like?"

"Yes. But it's too much for me."

"It's too much for me, too," said Dinah.

They faced each other, two solitary figures. All their

47

lives they were to remember this moment, and yet they did not see each other's face very clearly, for their sight was blurred by the agitation in their hearts.

"Oh, Dinah," said Henry. "Darling, darling Dinah, I do love you so much."

He reached out his hand blindly and touched her arm. It was a curious tentative gesture. Dinah cried out: "Henry, my dear."

She raised his hand to her cold cheek

"Oh, God!" said Henry, and pulled her into his arms.

Jocelyn's groom, hacking quietly along the road to Cloudyfold, looked up and saw two figures locked together against the wintry sky.

II

"We must come back to earth," said Dinah. "There's the church clock. It must be eight."

"I'll kiss you eight times to wind up the spell," said Henry. He kissed her eyes, her cheeks, the tips of her ears, and he kissed her twice on the mouth.

"There!" he muttered. "The spell's wound up."

"Don't!" cried Dinah.

"What, my darling?"

"Don't quote from Macbeth. It couldn't be more unlucky!"

"Who says so?"

"In the theatre everybody says so."

"I cock a snook at them! We're not in the theatre: we're on top of the world."

"All the same, I'm crossing my thumbs."

"When shall we be married?"

"Married?" Dinah caught her breath, and Henry's pure happiness was threaded with a sort of wonder when he saw that she was no longer lost in bliss.

"What is it?" he said. "What has happened? Does it frighten you to think of our marriage?"

"It's only that we *have* come back to earth," Dinah said sombrely. "I don't know when we'll be married. You see, something pretty difficult has happened."

"Good Lord, darling, what are you going to falter in my ear? Not a family curse, or dozens of blood relations stark ravers in lunatic asylums?"

"Not quite. It's your Cousin Eleanor."

"Eleanor!" cried Henry. "She scarcely exists."

"Wait till you hear. I've got to tell you now. I'll tell you as we go down."

"Say first that you're as happy as I am."

"I couldn't be happier."

"I love you, Dinah."

"I love you, Henry."

"The world is ours," said Henry. "Let us go down and take it."

III

They followed the shoulder of the hill by a path that led down to the rectory garden. Dinah went in front, and their conversation led to repeated halts.

"I'm afraid," Dinah began, "that I don't much care for your Cousin Eleanor."

"You astonish me, darling," said Henry. "For myself, I regard her as a prize bitch."

"That's all right, then. I couldn't mention this before you'd declared yourself, because it's all about us."

"You mean the day before yesterday when she lurked outside your drawing-room door? Dinah, if she hadn't been there, what would you have done?"

This led to a prolonged halt.

"The thing is," said Dinah presently, "she must have told your father."

"So she did."

"He's spoken to you?"

"He has."

"Oh, Henry!"

"That sounds as if you were settling a quotation. Yes, we had a grand interview. 'What is this I hear, sir, of your attentions to Miss Dinah Copeland?' 'Forgive me, sir, but I refuse to answer you.' 'Do you defy me, Henry?' 'With all respect, sir, I do!' That sort of thing."

"He doesn't want it?"

"Eleanor has told him he doesn't, blast her goggling eyes!"

"Why? Becuse I'm the poor parson's daughter, or because I'm on the stage, or just because he hates the sight of me?"

"I don't think he hates the sight of you."

"I suppose he wants you to marry a proud heiress."

"I suppose he does. It doesn't matter a tuppeny button, my sweet Dinah, what he wants."

"But it does. You haven't heard. Miss Prentice came to see Daddy last night."

Henry stopped dead and stared at her.

"She said—she said——"

"Go on."

"She told him we were meeting, and that you were keeping it from your father, but he'd found out and was terribly upset and felt we'd both been very underhand and—oh, she must have been absolutely foul! She must have sort of hinted that we were——" Dinah boggled at this and fell silent.

"That we were living in roaring sin?" Henry suggested.

"Yes."

"My God, the minds of these women! Surely the rector didn't pay any attention."

"She's so loathsomely plausible. Do you remember the autumn day, weeks ago, soon after I came back, when you drove me to Moorton Bridge and we picnicked and didn't come back till the evening?"

"Every second of it."

"She'd found out about that. There was no reason why the whole world shouldn't know, but I hadn't told Daddy about it. It had been such a glowing, marvellous day that I didn't want to talk about it."

"Me, too."

"Well, now, you see, it looks all fishy and dubious, and Daddy feels I have been behaving in an underhand manner. When Miss Prentice had gone he took me into his study. He was wearing his beretta, a sure sign that he's feeling his responsibilities. He spoke more in sorrow than in anger, which is always rather toxic, and the worst of it is, he really was upset. He got more and more feudal and said we'd always been—I forget what—almost fiefs or vassals of this-man's-man of the Jernighams, and had never done anything disloyal, and here was I behaving like a housemaid having clandestine assignations with you. On and on and on; and Henry, my dear darling, ridiculous though it sounds, I began to feel shabby and common."

"He didn't believe——?"

"No, of course he didn't believe that. But, all the same, you know he's frightfully muddled about sex."

"They all are," said Henry, with youthful gloom. "And

with Eleanor and Idris hurling their inhibitions in his teeth——"

"I know. Well, anyway, the upshot was, he forbade me to see you alone. I said I wouldn't promise. It was the first really deadly row we've ever had. I fancy he prayed about it for hours after I'd gone to bed. It's very vexing to lie in bed knowing that somebody in the room below is praying away like mad about you. And, you see, I adore the man. At one moment I thought I would say my own prayers, but the only thing I could think of was the old Commination Service. You know: 'Cursed is he that smiteth his neighbour secretly. Amen.'"

"One for Eleanor," said Henry appreciatively.

"That's what I thought, but I didn't say it. But what I've been trying to come to is this: I can't bear to upset Daddy permanently, and I'm afraid that's just what would happen. No, please wait, Henry. You see, I'm only nineteen, and he can forbid the banns—and, what's more, he'd do it."

"But why?" said Henry. "Why? Why? Why?"

"Because he thinks that we shouldn't oppose your father and because, secretly, he's got a social inferiority complex. He's a snob, poor sweet. He thinks if he smiled on us it would look as if he was all agog to make a grand match for me, and was going behind the squire's back to do it."

"Absolutely drivelling bilge!"

"I know, but that's how it goes. It's just one of those things. And it's all due to Miss Prentice. Honestly, Henry, I think she's positively evil. *Why* should she mind about us?"

"Jealousy," said Henry. "She's starved and twisted and a bit dotty. I dare say it's physiological as well as psychological. I imagine she thinks you'll sort of dethrone her when you're my wife. And, as likely, as not, she's jealous of your father's affection for you."

They shook their heads wisely.

"Daddy's terrified of her," said Dinah. "*and* of Miss Campanula. They *will* ask him to hear their confessions, and when they go away he's a perfect wreck."

"I'm not surprised, if they tell the truth. I expect what they really do is to try to inform against the rest of the district. Listen to me, Dinah. I refuse to have our love for each other messed up by Eleanor. You're mine. I'll tell your father I've asked you to marry me, and I'll tell mine. I'll *make* them see reason; and if Eleanor comes creeping in— my God, I'll, I'll, I'll——"

51

"Henry," said Dinah, "how magnificent!"

Henry grinned.

"It'd be more magnificent," he said, "if she wasn't just an unhappy, warped, middle-aged spinster."

"It must be awful to be like that," agreed Dinah. "I hope it never happens to me."

"You!"

There was another halt.

"Henry," said Dinah suddenly. "Let's ask them to call an armistice until after the play."

"But we must see each other like this. Alone."

"I shall die if we can't; but all the same I feel, somehow, if we said we'd wait until then, that Daddy might sort of begin to understand. We'll meet at rehearsals, and we won't pretend we're not in love, but I'll promise him I won't meet you alone. It'll be—it'll be kind of dignified. Henry, *do* you see?"

"I suppose so," said Henry unwillingly.

"It'd stop those hateful old women talking."

"My dear, nothing would stop them talking."

"Please, darling Henry."

"Oh, Dinah."

"Please."

"All right. It's insufferable, though, that Eleanor should be able to spoil a really miraculous thing like Us."

"Insufferable."

"She's so completely insignificant."

Dinah shook her head.

"All the same," she said, "she's a bad enemy. She creeps and creeps, and she's simply brimful of poison. She'll drop some of it into our cup of happiness if she can."

"Not if I know it," said Henry.

CHAPTER SIX

Rehearsal

THE REHEARSALS WERE not going any too well. For all Dinah's efforts, she hadn't been able to get very much concerted work out of her company. For one thing, with the exception of Selia Ross and Henry, they would *not* learn their lines. Dr. Templett even took a sort of pride in it.

52

He was forever talking about his experiences in amateur productions when he was a medical student.

"I never knew what I was going to say," he said cheerfully. "I'm capable of saying almost anything. It was always all right on the night. A bit of cheek goes a long way. One can bluff it out with a gag or two. The great thing is not to be nervous."

He himself was not at all nervous. He uttered such lines of the French Ambassador's as he remembered, in a high-pitched voice, made a great many grimaces, waved his hands in a foreign manner, and was never still for an instant.

"I leave it to the spur of the moment," he told them. "It's wonderful what a difference it makes when you're all made-up, with funny clothes on. I never know where I ought to be. You can't do it in cold blood."

"But, Dr. Templett, you've got to," Dinah lamented. "How can we get the timing right or the positions, if at one rehearsal you're on the prompt and at the next on the o.p.?"

"Don't you worry," said Dr. Templett. "We'll be all right. Eet vill be—'ow you say?—so, so charmante."

Off-stage he continually spoke his lamentable broken English, and when he dried up, as he did incessantly, he interpolated his: "'ow you say?"

"If I forget," he said to the rector, who was prompting, "I'll just walk over your side and say, ''ow you say?' like that, and then you'll know."

Selia Ross and he had an irritating trick of turning up late for rehearsals. Apparently the youngest Cain's big toe still needed Dr. Templett's attention, and he explained that he picked up Mrs. Ross and brought her to rehearsal on his way back from Cloudyfold. They would walk in with singularly complacent smiles, half an hour late, while Dinah was reading both their parts and trying to play her own. Sometimes she got her father to read their bits, but the rector intoned them so carefully and slowly that everybody else was thrown into a state of deadly confusion.

Miss Campanula, in a different way, was equally troublesome. She refused to give up her typewritten part. She carried it about with her and read each of her speeches in an under-tone during the preceding dialogue, so that whenever she was on the stage the others spoke through a distressing mutter. When her cue came she seldom failed to say, "Oh. Now it's me," before she began. She would often rattle off her lines without any inflexion, and apparently without the slightest regard for their meaning. She was forever telling Dinah that she was open to correction, but she received all suggestions in huffy grandeur, and they made not the smallest difference to her performance. Worse than all these peculiarities were Miss Campanula's attempts at characterization. She made all sorts of clumsy and ineffective movements over which she herself seemed to have little control. She continually shifted her weight from one large foot to the other, rather in the manner of a penguin. She wandered about the stage and she made embarrassing grimaces. In addition to all this she had developed a frightful cold in her nose, and rehearsals were made hideous by her catarrhal difficulties.

Jocelyn was the type of amateur performer who learns his lines from the prompter. Unlike Miss Campanula, he did not hold his part in his hand. Indeed, he had lost it irrevocably immediately after the first rehearsal. He said that it did not matter, as he had already memorized his lines. This was a lie. He merely had a vague idea of their sense. His performance reminded Dinah of divine service, as he was obliged to repeat all his lines, like responses, after the rector. However, in spite of this defect, the squire had an instinctive sense of theatre. He did not fidget or gesticulate. With Dr. Templett tearing about the stage like a wasp, this was particularly refreshing.

Miss Prentice did not know her part either, but she was a cunning bluffer. She had a long scene in which she held a newspaper open in her hands. Dinah discovered that Miss Prentice had pinned several of her sides to *The Times*. Others were left in handy places about the stage. When, in spite of these manœuvres, she dried up, Miss Prentice stared in a gently reproachful manner at the person who spoke after her, so that everybody thought it was her *vis-à-vis* who was at fault.

Mrs. Ross had learnt her part. Her clear, hard voice had plenty of edge. Once there, she worked, tried to follow Dinah's suggestions, and was very good-humoured and obliging. If ever anything was wanted, Mrs. Ross would get it. She brought down to the Parish Hall her cushions, her cocktail glasses and her bridge table. Dinah found herself depending more and more on Mrs. Ross for " hand props " and odds and ends of furniture. But, for all that, she did not like Mrs. Ross, whose peals of laughter at all Dr. Templett's regrettable antics were extremely irritating. The determined rudeness with which Miss Prentice and Miss Campanula met all Mrs. Ross's advances forced Dinah into making friendly gestures

54

which she continually regretted. She saw, with something like horror, that her father had innocently succumbed to Mrs. Ross's charm, and to her sudden interest in his church. This, more than anything else she did, inflamed Miss Campanula and Eleanor Prentice against Selia Ross. Dinah felt that her rehearsals were shot through and through with a mass of ugly suppressions. To complete her discomfort, the squire's attitude towards Mrs. Ross, being ripe with Edwardian naughtiness, obviously irritated Henry and the two ladies almost to breaking point.

Henry had learnt his part and shaped well. He and Dinah were the only members of the cast who gave any evidence of team work. The others scarcely even so much as looked at each other, and treated their speeches as if they were a string of interrupted recitations.

II

The battle of the music had raged for three weeks. Miss Prentice and Miss Campanula, together and alternately, had pretended to altruistic motives, and accused each other of selfishness, sulked, denied all desire to perform on the piano, given up their parts, relented, and offered their services anew. In the end Dinah, with her father's moral support behind her, seized upon a moment when Miss Campanula had said she'd no wish to play on an instrument with five dumb notes in the treble and six in the bass.

"All right, Miss Campanula," said Dinah, "we'll have it like that. Miss Prentice has kindly volunteered, and I shall appoint her as pianist. As you've got the additional responsibility of the Y.P.F.C. girls in the front of the house, it really does seem the best idea."

After that Miss Campanula was barely civil to anybody but the rector and the squire.

Five days before the performance, Eleanor Prentice developed a condition which Miss Campanula called "a Place" on the index finger of the left hand. Everybody noticed it. Miss Campanula did not fail to point out that it would probably be much worse on the night of the performance.

"You'd better take care of that Place on your finger, Eleanor," she said. "It's gathering, and to me it looks very nasty. Your blood must be out of order."

Miss Prentice denied this with an air of martyrdom, but there was no doubt that the Place grew increasingly ugly.

55

Three days before the performance it was hidden by an obviously professional bandage, and everybody knew that she had consulted Dr. Templett. A rumour sprang up that Miss Campanula had begun to practise her Prelude every morning after breakfast.

Dinah had a private conversation with Dr. Templett.

"What about Miss Prentice's finger? Will she be able to play the piano?"

"I've told her she'd better give up all idea of it," he said. "There's a good deal of inflammation, and it's very painful. It'll hurt like the devil if she attempts to use it, and it's not at all advisable that she should."

"What did she say?"

Dr. Templett grinned.

"She said she wouldn't disappoint her audience, and that she could rearrange the fingering of her piece. It's the 'Venetian Suite,' as usual, of course?"

"It is," said Dinah grimly. " 'Dawn' and 'On the Canal' for the overture, and the 'Nocturne' for the entr'acte. She'll never give way."

"Selia says she wouldn't mind betting old Idris has put poison in her girl friend's gloves like the Borgias," said Dr. Templett, and added: "Good Lord, I oughtn't to have repeated that! It's the sort of thing that's quoted against you in a place like this."

"I won't repeat it," said Dinah.

She asked Miss Prentice if she would rather not appear at the piano.

"How thoughtful of you, Dinah, my dear," rejoined Miss Prentice, with her holiest smile. "But I shall do my little best. You may depend upon me."

"But, Miss Prentice, your finger!"

"Ever so much better," said Eleanor in a voice that somehow suggested that there was something slightly improper in mentioning her finger.

"They are waiting to print the programmes. Your name——"

"Please don't worry, dear. My name may appear in safety. Shall we just not say any more about it, but consider it settled?"

"Very well," said Dinah uneasily. "It's very heroic of you."

"Silly child!" said Eleanor playfully.

And now, on Thursday, November the 25th, two nights before the performance, Dinah stood beside the paraffin heater in the aisle of the parish hall, and with dismay in her heart prepared to watch the opening scenes in which she herself did not appear. There was to be no music at the dress rehearsal.

"Just to give my silly old finger time to get *quite* well," said Miss Prentice.

But Henry had told Dinah that both he and his father had seen Eleanor turn so white after knocking her finger against a chair that they thought she was going to faint.

"You won't stop her," said Henry. "If she has to play the bass with her feet, she'll do it."

Dinah gloomily agreed.

She had made them up for the dress rehearsal and had attempted to create a professional atmosphere in a building that reeked of parochial endeavour. Even now her father's unmistakably clerical voice could be heard beyond the green serge curtain, crying obediently:

"Beginners, please."

In front of Dinah, six privileged Friendly Young Girls, who were to sell programmes and act as ushers at the performance, sat in a giggling row to watch the dress rehearsal. Dr. Templett and Henry were their chief interest. Dr. Templett was aware of this and repeatedly looked round the curtain. He had insisted on making himself up, and looked as if he had pressed his face against a gridiron and then garnished his chin with the hearth-brush. Just as Dinah was about to ring up the curtain, his head again bobbed round the corner.

"Vy do you, 'ow you say, gargle so mooch?" he asked the helpers. A renewed paroxysm broke out.

"Dr. Templett!" shouted Dinah. "Clear stage, *please*."

"Ten thousand pardons, Mademoiselle," said Dr. Templett. "I vaneesh." He made a comic face and disappeared.

"All ready behind, Daddy?" shouted Dinah.

"I think so," said the rector's voice doubtfully.

"Positions, everybody. House lights, please." Dinah was obliged to execute this last order herself, as the house lights switch was in the auditorium. She turned it off and the six onlookers yelped maddeningly.

" Ssh, please! Curtain!"

" Just a minute," said the rector dimly.

The curtain rose in a series of uneven jerks, and the squire, who should have been at the telephone, was discovered gesticulating violently to someone in the wings. He started, glared into the house, and finally took up his position.

" Where's that telephone bell?" demanded Dinah.

" Oh, dear!" said the rector's voice dismally. He could be heard scuffling about in the prompt-corner and presently an unmistakable bicycle bell pealed. But Jocelyn had already lifted the receiver and, although the bell, which was supposed to summon him to the telephone, continued to ring off-stage, he embarked firmly on his opening lines:

" Hallo! Hallo! Well, who is it?"

The dress rehearsal had begun.

Actors say that a good dress rehearsal means a bad performance. Dinah hoped desperately that the reverse would prove true. Everything seemed to go wrong. She suspected that there were terrific rows in the dressing-rooms, but as she herself had no change to make, she stayed in front whenever she was not actually on the stage. Before the entrance of the two ladies in the second act, Henry came down and joined her.

" Frightful, isn't it?" he asked.

" It's the end," said Dinah.

" My poor darling, it's pretty bad luck for you. Perhaps it'll pull through to-morrow."

" I don't see how—— Dr. Templett!" roared Dinah. " What are you doing? You ought to be up by the fireplace. Go back, please."

Miss Prentice suddenly walked straight across the stage, in front of Jocelyn, Selia Ross and Dr. Templett, and out at the opposite door.

" *Miss Prentice!*"

But she had gone, and could be heard in angry conversation with Georgie Biggins, the call-boy, and Miss Campanula.

" You're a very naughty little boy, and I shall ask the rector to forbid you to attend the performance."

" You deserve a sound whipping," said Miss Campanula's voice. " And if I had my way——"

The squire and Dr. Templett stopped short and stared into the wings.

" What is it?" Dinah demanded.

58

Georgie Biggins was thrust on the stage. He had painted his nose carmine, and Miss Prentice's hat for the third act was on his head. He had a water pistol in his hand. The girls in the front row screamed delightedly.

"Georgie," said Dinah with more than a suspicion of tears in her voice, "take that hat off and go home."

"I never——" began Georgie.

"Do what I tell you."

"Yaas, Miss."

Miss Prentice's arm shot through the door. The hat was removed. Dr. Templett took Georgie Biggins by the slack of his pants and dropped him over the footlights.

"Gatcha!" said Georgie and bolted to the back of the hall.

"Go on, please," said poor Dinah.

Somehow or another they got through. Dinah took them back over the scenes that had been outstandingly bad. This annoyed and bored them all very much, but she was adamant.

"It'll be all right on the night," said Dr. Templett.

"Saturday's the night," said Dinah, "and it won't."

At midnight she sat down in the third bench and said she supposed they had better stop. They all assembled in one of the Sunday School rooms behind the stage and gathered round a heater, while Mrs. Ross gave them a very good supper. She had insisted on making this gesture and had provided beer, whisky, coffee and sandwiches. Miss Campanula and Miss Prentice had both offered to make themselves responsible for this supper, and were furious that Mrs. Ross had got in first.

Dinah was astounded to learn from their conversation that they thought they had done quite well. The squire was delighted with himself; Dr. Templett still retained his character as a Frenchman; and Selia Ross said repeatedly that she thought both of them had been marvellous. The other two ladies spoke only to Mr. Copeland, and each waited until she could speak alone. Dinah saw that her father was bewildered and troubled.

"Oh, Lord!" thought Dinah. "What's brewing now?" She wished that her father was a stronger character, that he would bully or frighten those two venomous women into holding their tongues. And suddenly, with a cold pang, she thought: "If he should lose his head and marry one of them!"

Henry brought her a cup of black coffee.

"I've put some whisky in it," he said. "You're as pale as a star, and look frightened. What is it?"

"Nothing. I'm just tired."

Henry bent his dark head and whispered:

"Dinah?"

"Yes."

"I'll talk to Father on Saturday night when he's flushed with his dubious triumphs. Did you get my letter?"

Dinah's hand floated to her breast.

"Darling," whispered Henry. "Yours, too. We can't wait any longer. After to-morrow?"

"After to-morrow," murmured Dinah.

CHAPTER SEVEN

Vignettes

"I HAVE SINNED," said Miss Prentice, "in thought, word and deed by my fault, by my own fault, by my most grievous fault. Especially I accuse myself that since that last confession, which was a month ago, I have sinned against my neighbour. I have harboured evil suspicions of those with whom I have come in contact, accusing them in my heart of adultery, unfaithfulness and disobedience to their parents. I have judged my sister-woman in my heart and condemned her. I have listened many times to evil reports of a woman, and because I could not in truth say that I did not believe them——"

"Do not seek to excuse rather than to condemn yourself," said the rector from behind the Norman confessional that his bishop allowed him to use. "Condemn only your own erring heart. You have encouraged and connived at scandal. Go on."

There was a brief silence.

"I accuse myself that I have committed sins of omission, not performing what I believed to be my bounden Christian duty to the sick, not warning one whom I believe to be in danger of great unhappiness."

The rector heard Miss Prentice turn a page of the note-book where she wrote her confessions. "I know what she's getting at," he thought miserably. But because he was a sincere and humble man, he prayed: "Oh, God, give me the strength of mind to tackle this woman. Amen."

Miss Prentice cleared her throat in a subdued manner and began again. " I have consorted with a woman whom I believe to be of evil nature, knowing that by doing so I may have seemed to connive in sin."

" Our Lord consorted with sinners and was sinless. Judge not that you be not judged. The sin of another should excite only compassion in your heart. Go on."

" I have had angry and bitter thoughts of two young people who have injured someone who is——"

" Stop! " said the rector. " Do not accuse others. Accuse only yourself. Examine your conscience. Be sure that you have come here with a contrite and humble heart. If it holds any uncharitable thoughts, repent and confess them. Do not try to justify your anger by relating the cause. God will judge how greatly you have been tempted."

He waited. There was no response at all from his penitent. The church, beyond the confessional, seemed to listen with him for the next whisper.

" My daughter, I am waiting," said the rector, and was horrified when he was answered by a harsh, angry sobbing.

II

In spite of her cold, Miss Campanula was happy. She was about to make her confession, and she felt at peace with the world and quite youthful and exalted. The terrible black mood that had come upon her when she woke up that morning had vanished completely. She even felt fairly good-humoured when she thought of Eleanor playing her " Venetian Suite " at the performance to-morrow evening. With that Place on her finger, Eleanor was likely enough to make a hash of the music, and then everybody would think it was a pity that she, Idris Campanula, had not been chosen. That thought gave her a happy, warm feeling. Nowadays she was never sure what her mood would be. It changed in the most curious fashion from something like ecstasy to a dreadful irritation that came upon her with such violence and with so little provocation that it quite frightened her. It was as if, like the people in the New Testament, she had a devil in her, a beast that could send her thoughts black and make her tremble with anger. She had confessed these fits of rage to Father Copeland (she and Eleanor called him that when they spoke of him together), and he had been kind and had prayed for her. He had also, rather to her surprise, suggested that she should see a doctor. But there was nothing wrong with her health, she reflected, except lumbago and the natural processes attached to getting a little bit older. She pushed that thought away quickly, as it was inclined to make her depressed, and when she was depressed the beast took advantage of her.

Her chauffeur drove her to church, but she was a few minutes early, so she decided that she would look in at the parish hall and see if the committee of the Y.P.F.C. had begun to get it ready for to-morrow night. The decorating, of course, would all be done in the morning under her supervision; but there were floors to be swept, forms shifted and tables moved. Perhaps Eleanor would be there—or even Father Copeland on his way to church. Another wave of ecstasy swept over her. She knew why she was so happy. He would perhaps be at Pen Cuckoo for this ridiculous " run through for words " at five o'clock; but, better than that, it was Reading Circle night in the rectory dining-room, and her turn to preside. After it was over she would look in at the study, and Father Copeland would be there alone and would talk to her for a little.

Telling her chauffeur to wait, she marched up the gravelled path to the hall.

It was locked. This was irritating. She supposed those young people imagined they had done enough for one day. You might depend upon it, they had made off, leaving half the work for to-morrow. She was just going away again when dimly, from within, she heard the sound of strumming. Someone was playing " Chop-sticks " very badly, with the loud pedal on. Miss Campanula felt a sudden desire to know who had remained inside the hall to strum. She rattled the doors. The maddening noise stopped immediately.

" Who's in there? " shouted Miss Campanula, in a cold-infected voice, and rattled again.

There was no answer.

" The back door! " she thought. " It may be open." And she marched round the building. But the back door was shut, and although she pounded angrily on it, splitting her black kid gloves, nobody came to open it. Her face burned with exertion and rising fury. She started off again and completed the circuit of the hall. The frosted windows were all above the level of her eyes. The last one she came to was open at the bottom. Miss Campanula returned to the lane and saw that her chauffeur had followed her in the car from the church.

"Gibson!" she shouted. "Gibson, come here!"

He got out of the car and came towards her. He was a wooden-faced man with a fine physique; very smart in his dark maroon livery and shiny gaiters. He followed his mistress round the front of the hall to the far side.

"I want you to look inside that window," said Miss Campanula. "There's somebody in there who's behaving suspiciously."

"Very good, miss," said Gibson.

He gripped the window sill. The muscles under his smart tunic swelled as he raised himself until his eyes were above the sill.

Miss Campanula sneezed violently, blew her nose on her enormous handkerchief drenched in eucalyptus, and said, "Cad you see anddythingk?"

"No, miss. There's nobody there."

"But there *bust* be," insisted Miss Campanula.

"I can't see any one, miss. The place is all tidied up, like, for to-morrow."

"Where's the piano?"

"Down on the floor, miss, in front of the stage."

Gibson lowered himself.

"They *bust* have gone into one of the back rooms," muttered Miss Campanula.

"Could whoever it was have come out at the front door, miss, while you were round at the back?"

"Did you see addybody?"

"Can't say I did, miss. Not round the hall. But I was turning the car. They would have gone round the bend in the lane before I would notice."

"I consider it bost peculiar and suspicious."

"Yes, miss. There's Miss Prentice just coming out of church, miss."

"Is she?" Miss Campanula peered short-sightedly down the lane. She could see the south porch of St. Giles and a figure in the doorway.

"I mustn't be late," she thought. "Eleanor has got in first as usual." And she ordered Gibson to wait for her outside the church. She crossed the lane and strode down to the lych-gate. Eleanor was still in the porch. One did not stop to gossip when going to confession, but she gave

63

Eleanor her usual nod and was astonished to see that she looked ghastly.

"There's something wrong with her," thought Miss Campanula, and somewhere, in the shifting hinterland between her conscious and unconscious thoughts, lay the warm hope that the rector had been displeased with Eleanor at confession.

Miss Campanula entered the church with joy in her heart.

III

At the precise moment when Miss Prentice and Miss Campanula passed each other in the south porch, Henry, up at Pen Cuckoo, decided that he could remain indoors no longer. He was restless and impatient. He and Dinah had kept their pact, and since their morning on Cloudyfold had not met alone. Henry had announced their intention to his father at breakfast while Eleanor Prentice was in the room.

"It's Dinah's idea," he had said. "She calls it an armistice. As our affairs seem to be so much in the public eye, and as her father has been upset by the conversation you had with him last night, Cousin Eleanor, Dinah thinks it would be a good thing if we promised him we would postpone what you have described as our clandestine meetings for three weeks. After that I shall speak to the rector myself." He had looked directly at Miss Prentice and added: "I shall be very grateful if you would not discuss the matter with him in the meantime. After all, it is primarily our affair."

"I shall do what I believe to be my duty, Henry," Miss Prentice had said; and Henry had answered, "I'm afraid you will," and walked out of the room.

He and Dinah had written to each other. Henry had found Miss Prentice eyeing Dinah's first letter as it lay beside his plate at breakfast. He had put it in the breast pocket of his coat, rather shocked at the look he had surprised in her face. After that morning he had come down early to breakfast.

During the three weeks' truce, Jocelyn never spoke to his son of Dinah, but Henry knew very well that Miss Prentice nagged at the squire whenever a chance presented itself. Several times Henry had walked into the study to find Eleanor closeted with Jocelyn. The silence that invariably followed his entrance, his father's uncomfortable attempts to break it, and Miss Prentice's tight smile as she glided away, left Henry in no doubt as to the subject of their conversation.

This afternoon, Jocelyn was hunting. Miss Prentice would come back from church before three, and Henry could not face the prospect of tea alone with his cousin. She had refused a car, and would return tired and martyred. Although Jocelyn had taught her to drive, it was her infuriating custom to refuse a car. She would walk to church after dark, on pouring wet nights, and give herself maddening colds in the head. To-day, however, was fine with glints of watery sunlight. He took a stick and went out.

Henry walked through the trees into a lane that came out near the church. Perhaps there would be a job of work to be done at the hall. If Dinah was there she would be surrounded by helpers, so that would be all right.

But about half-way down he walked round a sharp bend in the lane and found himself face to face and alone with Dinah.

For a moment they stood and stared at each other. Then Henry said, "I thought I might be able to help in the hall."

"We finished for to-day at two o'clock."

"Where are you going?"

"Just for a walk. I didn't know you'd—I thought you'd be——"

"I didn't know either. It was bound to happen sooner or later."

"Yes, I suppose so."

"Your face is white," said Henry, and his voice shook. "Are you all right?"

"Yes. It's only the shock. Yours is white, too."

"Dinah!"

"No, no. Not till to-morrow. We promised."

As if moved by some compulsion outside themselves, they moved like automatons into each other's arms.

When Miss Prentice, dry-eyed but still raging, came round the bend in the lane Henry was kissing Dinah's throat.

IV

"I can't see," said Selia Ross, "that it matters what a couple of shocking, nasty old church-hens choose to say."

"But it does," answered Dr. Templett. He kicked a log on the fire. "Mine is one of the few jobs where your private life affects your practice. Why it should be so, the Lord alone knows. And I can't afford to lose my practice, Selia. My brother went through most of what was left when my father died. I don't want to sell Chipping-wood, but it takes me all my time to keep it up. It's a beastly situation, I know. Other things being equal, I still couldn't ask Freda to divorce me. Lying there from one year's end to another! Spinal paralysis isn't much fun and —she's still fond of me."

"My poor darling," said Mrs. Ross softly. Templett's back was towards her. She looked at him speculatively. Perhaps she wondered if she should go to him. If so, she decided against it and remained, exquisitely neat and expensive, in a high-backed chair.

"Only just now," muttered Templett, "old Mrs. Cain said something about seeing my car outside. I've noticed things. They're beginning to talk, damn their eyes. And with this new fellow over at Penmoor I can't afford to take chances. It's all due to those two women. Nobody would have thought anything about it if they hadn't got their claws into me. The other day, when I fixed up old Prentice's finger she asked after Freda, and in almost the same breath she began to talk about you. My God, I wish she'd get gangrene! And now this!"

"I'm sorry I told you."

"No, it was much better you should. I'd better see the damn' thing."

Mrs. Ross went to her writing-desk and unlocked a drawer. She took out a sheet of note-paper and gave it to him. He stared at six lines of black capitals.

"You are given notice to leave the district. If you disregard this warning, your lover will suffer."

"When did it come?"

"This morning. The postmark was Chipping."

"What makes you think it's her?"

"Smell it."

"Eucalyptus, my God!"

"She's drenched in it."

"She's probably carried it in her bag?"

"That's it. You'd better burn it, Billy."

Dr. Templett dropped the paper on the smouldering log and then snatched it up again.

"No," he said. "I've got a note from her at home. I'll compare the paper."

"Surely hers has a printed address."

"This might be a plain sheet for the following on. It's good paper."

"She'd never be such a fool."

"The woman's pathological, my dear. She might do anything. Anyway. I'll see."

He put the paper in his pocket.

"In my opinion," said Selia Ross, "she's green with jealousy because I've rather got off with the parson and the squire."

"So am I."

"Darling," said Mrs. Ross, "you can't think how pure I am with them."

Templett suddenly burst out laughing.

CHAPTER EIGHT

Catastrophe

AT TEN MINUTES to eight on the night of Saturday, November 27th, the parish hall at Winton St. Giles smelt of evergreens, wet mackintoshes, and humanity. Members of the Young People's Friendly Circle, harried and dragooned by Miss Campanula, had sold all the tickets in advance, so in spite of the appalling weather, every seat was occupied. Even the Moorton Park people had come over with their house-party, and sat in the front row of less uncomfortable chairs at two shillings a head. Behind them were ranged the church workers including Mr. Prosser, chemist of Chipping, and Mr. Blandish, the police superintendent, both churchwardens. The Women's Institute was there with its husband and children. Farther back, in a gaggling phalanx, were those girls of the Friendly Circle who were not acting as ushers, and behind them, on the back benches, the young men of the farms and villages, smelling of hair-grease and animal warmth. In the entrance, Miss Campanula had posted Sergeant Roper, of the Chipping Constabulary, and sidesman of St. Giles. His duties were to collect tickets and subdue the backbenchers, who were inclined to guffaw and throw paper pellets at their girls. At the end of the fourth row from the front, on the left side of the centre aisle, sat Georgie Biggins with his parents. He seemed strangely untroubled by his dethronement from the position of call-boy. His hair was plastered down with water on his bullet-shaped head, his face shone rosily, and there was an unholy light in his black boot-button eyes, which were fixed on the piano.

The piano, soon to achieve a world-wide notoriety, stood beneath the stage and facing the centre aisle. One of the innumerable photographs that appeared in the newspapers on Monday, November 29th, shows a museum piece, a cottage pianoforte of the nineties, with a tucked silk panel, badly torn, in front. It has a hard-bitten look. It would not be too fanciful to compare it to a spinster, dressed in dilapidated moth-eaten finery, still retaining an air of shabby gentility, but given over to some very dubious employment. This air is enhanced by the presence of five aspidistras, placed in a row on the top of the bunting, which has been stretched across the top over the opening and the turned-back lid, tightly fixed to the edges with drawing pins, and allowed to fall in artistic festoons down the sides and in a sort of valance-like effect across the front. At ten to eight on the night of the concert, there on the fretwork rack under the valance of bunting was Miss Prentice's " Venetian Suite," rather the worse for wear, but ready for her attention.

There was a notice in the programmes about the object of the performance, a short history of the old piano, a word of thanks to Jocelyn Jernigham, Esq., of Pen Cuckoo, for his generous offer to make up the sum of money needed for a new instrument. The old piano came in for a lot of attention that evening.

At eight o'clock Dinah turned on the stage lights. Sergeant Roper, observing this signal, leant across the row of boys on the back bench and switched off the house lights. The audience made noises of pleasurable anticipation.

Improvised footlights shone upwards on the faded green curtain. After a moment's pause, during which many people in the audience said, " Ssh!" an invisible hand drew the curtain aside and the rector walked through. There was a great burst of applause in the second row, and the reporter from the *Chipping Courier* took out his pad and pencil.

Mr. Copeland's best cassock was green about the seams, the toes of his boots turned up because he always neglected to put trees in them. He was actually a good-looking, rather shabbily-dressed parish priest. But, lit dramatically from beneath, he looked magnificent. It was the head of a medi-æval saint, austere and beautiful, sharp as a cameo against its own black shadow.

" He ought to be a bishop," said old Mrs. Cain to her daughter.

Behind the curtain, Dinah took a final look at the set. The squire, satisfactory in plus-fours and a good clean make-up, was in his right position up-stage, with a telegram in his hand. Henry stood off-stage at the prompt entrance, very nervous. Dinah moved into the wings with the bicycle bell in her hands.

" Don't answer the telephone till it's rung twice," she hissed at Jocelyn.

" All right, all right, all right."

" Clear, please," said Dinah severely. " Stand by."

She went into the prompt box, seized the curtain lines and listened to her father.

"—So you see," the rector was saying, " the present piano is almost a historical piece, and I'm sure you will be glad to hear that this old friend will be given an honourable place in the small recreation room at the back of the stage."

Sentimental applause.

" I have one other announcement. You will see on your programmes that Miss Prentice of Pen Cuckoo, in addition to taking a part, was to play the overture and entr'acte this evening. I am sorry to say that Miss Prentice has—ah—has —ah—an injured finger which has given—and I am sorry to say is still giving her—a great deal of pain. Miss Prentice, with her customary pluck and unselfishness "—Mr. Copeland paused hopefully and was awarded a tentative outbreak of clapping—" was anxious not to disappoint us and was prepared, up to a minute or two ago, to play the piano. However, as she has an important rôle to fill later on in the evening, and as her hand is really not fit, she—ah—Dr. Templett has —ah—has taken matters in hand and ordered her not to—to play."

The rector paused again while the audience wondered if it should applaud Dr. Templett's efficiency, but decided that, on the whole, it had better not.

" Now, although you will be disappointed and will sympathize, I am sure, with Miss Prentice, we all know we mustn't disobey doctor's orders. I am happy to say that we shall still have our music—and very good music, too. Miss Idris Campanula, at literally a moment's notice, has consented to play for us. Now, I think this is particularly generous and sporting of Miss Campanula, and I'll ask you all to show your appreciation in a really——"

Deafening applause.

"Miss Campanula," ended Mr. Copeland, "will play Rach-maninoff's 'Prelude in C Sharp Minor,' Miss Campanula."

He led her from the wings, handed her down the steps to the piano, and returned to the stage through the side curtains.

It was wonderful to see Idris Campanula acknowledge the applause with an austere bend, smile more intimately at the rector, descend the steps carefully and, with her back to the aisle, seat herself at the instrument. It was wonderful to see her remove the "Venetian Suite," and place her famous Prelude on the music rack, open it with a masterly flip, deal it a jocular slap, and then draw out her pince-nez from the tucked silk bosom that so closely resembled the tucked silk bosom of the instrument. Miss Campanula and the old piano seemed to face each other with an air of understanding and affinity. Miss Campanula's back hollowed as she drew up her bosom until it perched on the top of her stays. She leant forward until her nose was within three inches of the music, and she held her left hand poised over the bass. Down it came.

Pom. *Pom.* POM.

The three familiar pretentious chords.

Miss Campanula paused, lifted her big left foot and planked it down on the soft pedal.

II

The air was blown into splinters of atrocious clamour. For a second nothing existed but noise—hard racketing noise. The hall, suddenly thick with dust, was also thick with a cloud of intolerable sound. And, as the dust fell, so the pandemonium abated and separated into recognisable sources. Women were screaming. Chair legs scraped the floor, branches of ever-greens fell from the walls, the piano hummed like a gigantic top.

Miss Campanula fell forward. Her face slid down the sheet of music which stuck to it. Very slowly and stealthily she slipped sideways to the keys of the piano, striking a final discord in the bass. She remained there, quite still, in a posture that seemed to parody the antics of an affected virtuoso. She was dead.

Lady Appleby in her chair by the piano turned to her husband as if to ask him a question and fainted.

Georgie Biggins screamed like a whistle.

The rector came through the curtain and ran down the steps to the piano. He looked at that figure leaning on the keys, wrung his hands and faced the audience. His lips moved, but he could not be heard.

Dinah came out of the prompt corner and stood transfixed. Her head was bent as if in profound meditation. Then she turned, stumbled past the curtain, calling, "Henry! Henry!" and disappeared.

Dr. Templett, in his appalling make-up, came through from the opposite side of the curtain. He went up to the rector, touched his arm and then descended to the piano. He bent down with his back to the audience, stayed so for a moment and then straightened up. He shook his head slightly at the rector.

Mr. Blandish, in the third row, pushed his way to the aisle and walked up to the stage.

He said, "What's all this?" in a loud, constabulary tone, and was heard. The hall went suddenly quiet. The voice of Mr. Prosser, the Chipping organist, said all by itself: "It was a gun. That's what it was. It was a gun."

Mr. Blandish was not in uniform, but he was dressed in authority. He examined the piano and spoke to Dr. Templett. There was a screen masking the corner on the prompt side between the stage and the wall. The two men fetched it and put it round the piano.

The rector mounted the steps to the stage and faced his parishioners.

"My dear people," he said in a trembling voice, "there has been a terrible accident. I beg of you all to go away quietly to your homes. Roper, will you open the door?"

"Just a minute," said Mr. Blandish. "Just a minute, if *you please*, sir. This is an affair for the police. Charlie Roper, you stay by that door. Have you got your note-book on you?"

"Yes sir," said Sergeant Roper.

"All right." Mr. Blandish raised his voice. "As you pass out," he roared, "I'll ask you to leave your names and addresses with the sergeant on duty at the door. Anybody who has had anything to do with this entertainment," continued

Mr. Blandish with no trace of irony in his voice, "either in the way of taking part or decorating the hall or so forth, will kindly remain behind. Now move along quietly, please, there's no need to rush. The back benches first. Keep your seats till your turn comes."

To the rector he said, "I'd be much obliged if you'd go to the back door, sir, and see nobody leaves that way. If it can be locked and you've got the key, lock it. We'll have this curtain up, if you please. I'm going to the telephone. It's in the back room, isn't it? Much obliged."

He went through the back of the stage, passing Dinah and Henry, who stood side by side in the wings.

"Good-evening, Mr. Jernigham," said the superintendent. "Do you mind raising the curtain?"

"Certainly," said Henry.

The curtain rose in a series of uneven jerks, revealing to the people still left in the hall a group of four persons: Jocelyn Jernigham, Selia Ross, Eleanor Prentice and the rector, who had returned from the back door with the key in his hand.

"I can't believe it," said the rector. "I simply cannot believe that it has happened."

"Is it murder?" asked Mrs. Ross sharply. Her voice pitched a note too high, sounded shockingly loud.

"I—I can't believe——" repeated Mr. Copeland.

"But see here, Copeland," interrupted the squire, "I don't know what the devil everybody's driving at. Shot through the head! What d'you mean? Somebody must have seen something. You can't shoot people through the head in a crowded hall without being spotted."

"The shot seems to have come from—from——"

"From where, for heaven's sake?"

"From inside the piano," said the rector unhappily. "We mustn't touch anything; but it seems to come from inside the piano. You can see through the torn silk."

"Good God!" said Jocelyn. He looked irritably at Miss Prentice, who rocked to and fro like a middle-aged marionette and moaned repeatedly.

"Do be quiet, Eleanor," said the squire. "Here! Templett!"

Dr. Templett had again gone behind the screen, but he came out and said, "What?" in an irascible voice.

"Has she been shot through the head?"

"Yes."

"How?"

"From inside the piano."

"I never heard of such a thing," said Jocelyn. "I'm coming to look."

"Yes. But, I say," objected Dr. Templett, "I don't think you ought to, you know. It's a matter for the police."

"Well, you've just been in there."

"I'm police surgeon for the district."

"Well, by God," said the squire, suddenly remembering it, "I'm Acting Chief Constable for the county."

"Sorry," said Dr. Templett. "I'd forgotten."

But the squire was prevented from looking behind the screen by the return of Mr. Blandish.

"That's all right," said the superintendent peaceably. He turned to the squire. "I've just rung up the station and asked for two chaps to come along, sir."

"Oh, yes. Yes. Very sensible," said Jocelyn.

"Just a minute, Blandish," said Dr. Templett. "Come down here, would you?"

They disappeared behind the screen. The others waited in silence. Miss Prentice buried her face in her hands. The squire walked to the edge of the stage, looked over the top of the piano, turned aside, and suddenly mopped his face with his handkerchief.

Blandish and Templett came out and joined the party on the stage.

"Lucky, in a way, your being here on the spot, sir," Blandish said to Jocelyn. "Your first case of this sort since your appointment, I believe."

"Yes."

"Very nasty affair."

"It is."

"Yes, sir. Well now, with your approval, Mr. Jernigham, I'd just like to get a few notes down. I fancy Mr. Henry Jernigham and Miss Copeland are with us."

He peered into the shadows beyond the stage.

"We're here," said Henry.

He and Dinah came on the stage.

"Ah, yes. Good-evening, Miss Copeland."

"Good-evening," said Dinah faintly.

"Now," said Blandish, looking round the stage, "this is the whole company of performers, I take it. *With* the exception of the deceased, of course."

"Yes," said Jocelyn.

"I'll just make a note of the names."

They sat round the stage while Blandish wrote in his

note-book. A group of ushers and two youths were huddled on a bench at the far end of the hall under the eyes of Sergeant Roper. Dinah fixed her gaze on this group, on Blandish, on the floor, anywhere but on the top of the piano jutting above the footlights and topped with pots of aspidistra. For down through the aspidistras, heavily shadowed by the screen, and not quite covered by the green and yellow bunting they had thrown over it, was Miss Campanula's body, face down on the keys of the piano. Dinah found herself wondering who was responsible for the aspidistras. She had meant to have them removed. They must mask quite a lot of the stage from the front rows.

"*Don't look at them*," said her mind. She turned quickly to Henry. He took her hands and pulled her round with her back to the footlights.

"It's all right, Dinah," he whispered, "it's all right, darling."

"I'm not panicked or anything," said Dinah.

"Yes," said Blandish, "that all the names. Now, sir—— Well, what is it?"

A uniformed constable had come in from the front door and stood waiting in the hall.

"Excuse me," said Blandish, and went down to him. There was a short rumbling conversation. Blandish turned and called to the squire.

"Can you spare a moment, sir?"

"Certainly," said Jocelyn, and joined them.

"Can you beat this, sir?" said Blandish, in an infuriated whisper. "We've had nothing better than a few old drunks and speed merchants in this place for the last six months or more, and now, to-night, there's got to be a breaking and entering job at Moorton Park with five thousand pounds' worth of her ladyship's jewellery gone and Lord knows what else besides. Their butler rang up the station five minutes ago, and this chap's come along on his motor bike and he says the whole place is upside down. Sir George and her ladyship and the party haven't got back yet. It looks like the work of the gang that cleaned up a couple of jobs in Somerset a fortnight back. It'll be a big thing to tackle. Now what am I to do, sir?"

Jocelyn and Blandish stared at each other.

"Well," said Jocelyn at last, "you can't be in two places at once."

"That's right, sir," said Blandish. "It goes against the grain when we've scarcely got started, but it looks as if it'll have to be the Yard."

74

CHAPTER NINE

C.I.D.

FIVE HOURS AFTER Miss Campanula struck the third chord of the Prelude, put her foot on the soft pedal, and died, a police car arrived at the parish hall of Winton St. Giles. It had come from Scotland Yard. It contained Chief Detective-Inspector Alleyn, Detective-Inspector Fox, Detective-Sergeant Bailey, and Detective-Sergeant Thompson.

Alleyn, looking up from his road map, saw a church spire against a frosty, moonlit hill, trees against stars, and nearer at hand the lighted windows of a stone building.

"This looks like the hidden treasure," he said to Thompson who was driving. "What's the time?"

"One o'clock, sir."

As if in confirmation a clock, outside in the night, chimed for an hour and tolled one.

"Out we get," said Alleyn.

The upland air was cold after the stuffiness of the car. It smelt of dead leaves and frost. They walked up a gravelled path to the front door of the building. Fox flashed a torch on a brass plate.

"Winton St. Giles Parish Hall. The Gift of Jocelyn Jernigham Esquire of Pen Cuckoo, 1805. To the Glory of God. In memory of his wife Prudence Jernigham who passed away on May 7th, 1801."

"This is the place, sir," said Fox.

"Sure enough," said Alleyn, and rapped smartly on the door.

It was opened by Sergeant Roper, bleary-eyed after a five hours' vigil.

"Yard," said Alleyn.

"Thank Gawd," said Sergeant Roper.

They walked in.

"The super asked me to say, sir," said Sergeant Roper, "that he was very sorry not to be here when you arrived, but seeing as how there's been a first-class breaking and entering up to Moorton Park——"

"That's all right," said Alleyn. "What's it all about?"

"Murder," said Roper. "Will I show you?"

"Do."

They walked up the centre aisle between rows of empty

benches and chairs. The floor was littered with programmes.

"I'll just turn on the other lights, sir," said Roper. "Deceased's behind the screen."

He trudged up the steps to the stage. A switch clicked and Dinah's improvised foot- and proscenium-lights flooded the stage. Bailey and Thompson pulled the screen to one side.

There was Miss Campanula with her face on the keyboard of the piano, waiting for the expert, the camera, and the pathologist.

"Good Lord!" said Alleyn.

Rachmaninoff's (and Miss Campanula's) Prelude was crushed between her face and the keys. A dark crimson patch had seeped out towards the margin of the music, but the title showed clearly. A hole had been blown through the centre. Without touching the music, Alleyn could see several pencilled reminders. After the last of the opening chords was an emphatic "S.P." The left hand had been pinned down by the face but the right had fallen, and hung inconsequently at the end of a long purple arm. The face itself was hidden. They stared down at the back of the head. Its pitiful knot of grey hair, broken and loosened, hung over a dark hole. Weepers of stained hair stuck to the thin neck.

"Through the back of the skull," said Fox.

"That's the wound of exit," said Alleyn. "We shall have to find the bullet."

Bailey turned away and began to search along the aisle.

Alleyn shone his torch on the tucked silk front of the piano. There was a rent exactly in the centre, extending above and below the central hole made by the bullet. Inside the hole, but quite close to the surface, the light picked up a shining circle. Alleyn leaned forward, peering, and uttered a soft exclamation.

"That's the gun that did the job, sir," said Roper. "Inside the piano."

"Has it been touched?"

"No, sir, no. The super was in the audience and he took over immediately, did super. Except for doctor, not a soul's been near."

"The doctor. Where is he?"

"He's gone home, sir. Dr. Templett it is, up to Chippingwood. He's police surgeon. He was here when it happened. He said would I ring him up when you came and if you wanted him he'd be over. It's only a couple of miles off."

76

"I think he'd better come. Ring him up now, will you?"
When Roper had gone, Alleyn said, "This is a rum go, Fox."

"Very peculiar, Mr. Alleyn. How's it been worked?"

"We'll take a look-see when we've got some pictures. Take every angle, Thompson."

Thompson had already begun to set up his paraphernalia. Soon the flashlight threw Miss Campanula into startling relief. For the second and last time she was photographed, seated at the instrument.

Roper came back from the telephone and watched the experts with avid interest.

"Funniest go you ever did see," he said to Bailey, who had moved to the end of the aisle. "I was on the spot. The old lady sits down at the piano in her bold way and wades into it. Biff, biff, plonk, and before you know where you are the whole works go off like a packet of crackers and she's lying there a corpse."

"Cuh!" said Bailey and stooped swiftly to the floor. "Here we are, sir," he said. "Here's the bullet."

"Got it? I'll look at it in a minute."

Alleyn marked the position of the head and arm and squatted on the floor to run a chalk line round the feet.

"Size eight," he murmured. "The left foot looks as if it's slipped on the soft pedal. Now, I wonder. Well, we'll soon find out. Got gloves on, all of you? Good. Go carefully, I should, and keep away from the front. Will you, sergeant—what is your name, by the way?"

"Roper, sir."

"Right. Will you clear the stuff off the top?"

Roper shifted the aspidistra and began to unpin the bunting. Alleyn went up to the stage and squatted over the footlights like a sort of presiding deity.

"Gently does it, the thing's tottering. Look at that!"

He pointed at the inside of the top lid, which was turned back.

"Wood-rot. No wonder they wanted a new one. Good Lord!"

"What, sir?"

"Come and look at this, Fox."

Allelyn shone his torch in at the top. The light glinted on a steel barrel. He slipped in his gloved fingers. There was a sharp click.

"I've just snicked over the safety-catch on a perfectly good automatic. Now, then."

Roper pulled away the bunting.

"Well, I'll be damned!" said Fox.

<h2 style="text-align:center">II</h2>

"Very fancy, isn't it?" said Alleyn.

"A bit too fancy for me, sir. How does it work?"

"It's a Colt. The butt's jammed between the pegs, where the wires are made fast, and the front of the piano. The nozzle fits into a hole in this fretwork horror in front of the silk bib. The bib's rotten with age and bulging. It could be tweaked in front of the nozzle. Anyway, the music would hide it. Of course the top was smothered in bunting and vegetables."

"But what pulled the trigger?"

"Half a second. There's a loop of string round the butt and over the trigger. The string goes on to an absurd little pulley in the back of the inner case. Then forward to another pulley on a front strut. Then it goes down." He moved his torch. "Yes, now you can see. The other end of the string is fixed to the batten that's part of the soft pedal action. When you use the pedal the batten goes backwards. Moves about two inches, I fancy. Quite enough to give a sharp jerk to the string. We'll have some shots of this, Thompson. It's a bit tricky. Can you manage?"

"I think so, Mr. Alleyn."

"It looks like a practical joke," said Fox.

Alleyn looked up quickly.

"Funny you should say that," he said. "You spoke my thoughts. A small boy's practical joke. The Heath Robinson touch with the string and pulleys is quite in character. I believe I even recognise those little pulleys, Fox. Notice how very firmly they've been anchored. My godson's got their doubles in one of those building sets, an infernal dithering affair that's supposed to improve the mind, and nearly sent me out of mine. 'Twiddletoy,' it's called. Yes, and by George, Brer Fox, that's the sort of cord they provide: thin green twine, very tough, like fishing line, and fits nicely into the groove of the pulley."

"D'you reckon some kid's gone wild and rigged this for the old girl?" asked Fox.

"A child with a Colt .32?"

"Hardly. Still, he might have got hold of one."

Alleyn swore softly.

"What's up, sir?" asked Fox.

"It's the whole damn' lay-out of the thing! It's exactly like a contraption they give in the book of the words of these toys. 'Fig. 1. Signal.' It's no more like a signal than your nose. Less, if anything. But you build it on this principle. I made the thing for my godson. The cord goes up in three steps to pulleys that are fixed to a couple of uprights. At the bottom it's tied to a little arm and at the top to a bigger one. When you push down the lower arm, the upper one waggles. I'll swear it inspired this job. You see how there's just room for the pulley in the waist of the Colt at the back? They're fiddling little brutes, these pulleys, as I know to my cost. Not much bigger than the end of a cigarette. Hole through the middle. Once you've threaded the twine it can't slip out. It's guarded by the curved lips of the groove. You see, the top one's anchored to the wires above that strip of steel. The bottom one's tied to a strut in the fretwork. All right, Thompson, your witness."

Thompson manœuvred his camera.

A car drew up outside the hall. A door slammed.

"That'll be the doctor, sir," said Roper.

"Ah, yes. Let him in, will you?"

Dr. Templett came in. He had removed his make-up and his beard and had changed the striped trousers and morning coat proper to a French Ambassador, for a tweed suit and sweater.

"Hullo," he said. "Sorry if I kept you waiting. Car wouldn't start."

"Dr. Templett?"

"Yes, and you're from Scotland Yard, aren't you? Didn't lose much time. This is a nasty business."

"Beastly," said Alleyn. "I think we might move her now."

They brought a long table from the back of the hall and on it they laid Miss Campanula. She had been shot between the eyes.

"Smell of eucalyptus," said Alleyn.

"She had a cold."

Dr. Templett examined the wounds while the others looked on. At last he straightened up, took a bottle of ether from his pocket, and used a little to clean his hands.

"There's a sheet in one of the dressing-rooms, Roper," he said. Roper went off to get it.

"What've you got there?" Templett asked Alleyn.

79

Alleyn had found Miss Prentice's Venetian Suite behind the piano. He turned it over in his hands. Like the Prelude, it was a very jaded affair. The red back of the cover had a discoloured circular patch in the centre. Alleyn touched it. It was damp. Roper returned with the sheet.

"Can't make her look very presentable, I'm afraid," said Dr. Templett. "Rigor's fairly well advanced in the jaw and neck. Rather quick after five hours. She fell at an odd angle. I didn't do more than look at her. The exit wound showed clearly enough what had happened. Of course, I assured myself she was dead."

"Did you realise at once that it was a wound of exit?"

"What? Yes. Well, after a second or two I did. Thought at first she'd been shot through the back of the head and then I noticed characteristics of an exit wound, direction of the matted hair and so on. I bent down and tried to see the face. I could just see the blood. Then I noticed the hole in the music. The frilling round the edge of the hole showed clearly enough which way the bullet had come."

"Very sound observation," said Alleyn. "You knew, then, what had happened?"

"I was damn' puzzled and still am. When we'd rigged up the screen I had another look and spotted the nozzle of the revolver or whatever it is, behind the silk trimmings. I told Blandish, the local superintendent, and he had a look too. How the devil was it done?"

"A mechanical device that she worked herself."

"Not suicide?"

"No, murder. You'll see when we open the piano."

"Extraordinary business."

"Very," agreed Alleyn. "Bailey, you might get along with your department now. When Thompson's finished, you can go over the whole thing for prints and then dismantle it. In the meantime, I'd better produce my note-book and get a few hard facts."

They carried the table into a corner and put the screen round it. Roper came down with a sheet and covered the body.

"Let's sit down somewhere," suggested Dr. Templett. "I want a pipe. It's given me a shock, this business."

They sat in the front row of stalls. Alleyn raised an eyebrow at Fox who came and joined them. Roper stood in the offing. Dr. Templett filled his pipe. Alleyn and Fox opened their note-books.

"To begin with," said Alleyn, " who was this lady?"

"Idris Campanula," said Templett. " Spinster of this parish."

" Address?"

" The Red House, Chipping. You passed it on your way up."

" Have the right people been told about this?"

" Yes. The rector did that. Only the three maids. I don't know about the next-of-kin. Somebody said it was a second cousin in Kenya. We'll have to find that out. Look here, shall I tell you the story in my own words?"

" I wish you would."

" I thought I'd find myself in the double rôle of police surgeon and eye-witness, so I tried to sort it out while I waited for your telephone call. Here goes. Idris Campanula was about fifty years of age. She came to the Red House as a child of twelve to live with her uncle, General Campanula, who adopted her on the death of her parents. He was an old bachelor and the girl was brought up by his acidulated sister, whom my father used to call one of the nastiest women he'd ever met. When Idris was about thirty, the general died, and his sister only survived him a couple of years. The house and money, a lot of money by the way, were left to Idris, who by that time was shaping pretty much like her aunt. Nil nisi and all that, but it's a fact. She never had a chance. Starved and repressed and hung about with a mass of shibboleths and Victorian conversation. Well, here she's stayed for the last twenty years, living on rich food, good works and local scandal. Upon my word, it's incredible that she's gone. Look here, I'm being too diffuse, aren't I?"

" Not a bit. You're giving us a picture in the round which is what we like."

" Well, there she was until to-night. I don't know if you've heard from Roper about the play."

" We haven't had time," said Alleyn, " but I hope to get volumes from him before dawn."

Roper looked gratified and drew nearer.

" The play was got up by a group of local people."

" Of whom you were one," said Alleyn.

" Hullo!" Dr. Templett took his pipe out of his mouth and stared at Alleyn. " Now, did any one tell you that, or is this the real stuff?"

" I'm afraid it's not even up to Form 1 at Hendon. There's a trace of grease paint in your hair. I wish I could

81

add that I have written a short monograph on grease paint."

Dr. Templett grinned.

"I'd lay you ten to one," he said, "that you can't deduce what sort of part I had."

Alleyn glanced sideways at him.

"We are not allowed to show off," he said, "but with Inspector Fox's austere eye on me, I venture to have a pot-shot. A character part, possibly a Frenchman, wearing a rimless eyeglass. Any good?"

"Did we bet in shillings?"

"It was no bet," said Alleyn apologetically.

"Well, let's have the explanation," said Templett. "I enjoy feeling a fool."

"I'm afraid I'll feel rather a fool making it," said Alleyn. "It's very small beer indeed. In the words of all detective heroes, you only need to consider. You removed your make-up in a hurry. Spirit gum, on which I have not written a monograph, leaves its mark unless removed with care and alcohol. Your chin and upper lips show signs of having been plucked and there's a very remote trace of black crêpe hairiness. Only on the tip of your chin and not on your cheeks. Ha! A black imperial. The foreign ambassadorial touch. A sticky reddish dint by the left eye suggests a rimless glass, fixed with more spirit gum. The remains of the heated line across the brow suggests a top-hat. And, when you mentioned your part, you moved your shoulders very slightly. You were thinking subconsciously of your performance. Broken English. ''Ow you say?' with a shrug. That sort of thing. For heaven's sake say I'm right."

"By gum!" said Sergeant Roper devoutly.

"Amen," said Dr. Templett. "In the words of Mr. Holmes——'

"——of whom nobody shall make mock in my presence. Pray continue your most interesting narrative," said Alleyn.

CHAPTER TEN

According to Templett

"——AND SO YOU SEE," concluded Templett, "there is absolutely nothing about any of us that is at all out of the ordinary. You might find the same group of people in almost any of the more isolated bits of English country-side. The parson, the squire, the parson's daughter, the squire's son, the two church hens and the local medico."

"And the lady from outside," added Alleyn, looking at his notes. "You have forgotten Mrs. Ross."

"So I have. Well, she's simply a rather charming new-comer. That's all. I'm blessed if I can see who, by the wildest flight of imagination, could have wanted to kill this very dull middle-aged frumpish spinster. I shouldn't have thought she had an enemy in the world."

"I wouldn't say that," said Sergeant Roper, unexpectedly, Alleyn looked up at him.

"No?"

"No, sir, I wouldn't say that. To speak frankly, she was a very sharp-tongued lady. Mischievous like. Well, over-bearing. Very curious, too. Proper nosey-parker. My missus always says you couldn't change your mind without it being overheard at the Red House. My missus is friendly with the cook up to Red House, but she never says anything she doesn't want everybody in the village to hear about. Miss Campanula used to order the meals and then wait for the news, as you might say. They call her the Receiving Set in Chipping."

"Do they, indeed," murmured Alleyn.

"You don't murder people for being curious," said Templett.

"You do sometimes, I reckon, doctor," said Roper.

"I can't imagine it with Miss Campanula."

"I don't reckon anybody *did* want to murder Miss Campanula," said Roper, stolidly.

"Hullo!" Alleyn ejaculated. "What's all this?"

"I reckon they wanted to murder Miss Prentice."

"Good God!" said Templett. "I never thought of that!"

"Never thought of what?" said Alleyn.

"I forgot to tell you. Good Lord, what a fool! Why didn't you remind me, Roper? Good Lord!"

"May we hear now?" asked Alleyn patiently.

"Yes, of course."

In considerable confusion, Templett explained about Miss Prentice's finger and the change of pianists.

"This is altogether another kettle of fish," said Alleyn. "Let's get a clear picture. You say that up to twenty minutes to eight Miss Prentice insisted that she was going to do the overture and entr'acte?"

"Yes. I told her three days ago she'd better give it
83

up. There was this whitlow on her middle finger and she mucked about with it and got some sort of infection. It was very painful. D'you think she'd give in? Not a bit of it. Said she'd alter the fingering of her piece. Wouldn't hear of giving it up. I asked her to-night if she'd let me look at it. Oh, no! It was 'much easier'! She'd got a surgical stall over it. At about twenty to eight I passed the ladies dressing-room. The door was half-open and I heard a sound like somebody crying. I could see her in there alone, rocking backwards and forwards holding this damned finger. I went in and insisted on looking at it. All puffed up and as fiery as hell! She was in floods of tears but she still said she'd manage. I put my foot down. Dinah Copeland came in, saw what was up, and fetched her father who's got more authority over these women than anybody else. He made her give in. Old Idris, poor old girl, had turned up by then and was all agog to play the famous Prelude. She's played it in and out of season for the last twenty years, if it's been written as long as that. Somebody was sent off to the Red House for the music and a dress; she was dressed up for her part, you see. The rector said he'd make an announcement about it. By that time Miss Prentice had settled down to being a martyr and—but, look here, I'm being most amazingly indiscreet. Now, don't go and write all this down in that note-book and quote me as having said it."

Dr. Templett looked anxiously at Fox whose note-book was flattened out on his enormous knee.

"That's all right, sir," said Fox blandly. "We only want the essentials."

"And I'm giving you all the inessentials. Sorry."

"I didn't say that, now, doctor."

"We can take it," Alleyn said, "that, in your opinion, up to twenty to eight everybody, including Miss Campanula and Miss Prentice, believed the music would be provided by Miss Prentice."

"Certainly."

"And this 'Venetian Suite' was Miss Prentice's music?"

"Yes."

"Nobody could have rigged this apparatus inside the piano after seven-forty?"

"Lord, no! The audience began to arrive at about half-past seven, didn't it, Roper? You were on the door."

"The Cains turned up at seven-twenty," said Roper, "and Mr. and Mrs. Biggins and that young limit Georgie, were

84

soon after them. I was on duty at seven. Must have been done before then, sir."

"Yes. What about the afternoon and morning? Anybody here?"

"We were all in and out during the morning," said Dr. Templett. "The Y.P.F.C. girls did the decorating and fixed up the supper arrangements and so on, and we got our stuff ready behind the scenes. Masses of people."

"You'd been rehearsing here, I suppose?"

"Latterly. We did most of the rehearsing up in the study at Pen Cuckoo. It was too cold here until they got extra heaters in. We had our dress rehearsal here on Thursday night. Yesterday afternoon at five, Friday I mean, we went up to Pen Cuckoo and had what Dinah calls a run-through for words."

"What about this afternoon before the performance?"

"It was shut up during the afternoon. I called in at about three o'clock to drop some of my gear. The place was closed then and the key hung up between the wall of the outside place and the main building. We'd arranged that with Dinah."

"Did you notice the piano?"

"Now, did I? Yes. Yes, I did. It was where it is now, with bunting all over the top and a row of pot plants. They'd fixed it up like that in the morning."

"Did anybody else look in at three o'clock while you were here?"

"Let me think. Yes, Mrs. Ross was there with some foodstuff. She left it in the supper-room at the back of the stage."

"How long were you both in the place?"

"Oh, not long. We—talked for a minute or two and then came away."

"Together?"

"No. I left Mrs. Ross arranging sandwiches on plates. By the way, if you want anything to eat, do help yourselves. And there's some beer under the table. I provided it, so don't hesitate."

"Very kind of you," said Alleyn.

"Not a bit. Be delighted. Where were we? Oh, yes. I had a case over near Moorton and I wanted to look in at the cottage hospital. I wasn't here long."

"Nobody else came in?"

"Not then."

"Who was the first to arrive in the evening?"

85

" I don't know. I was the last. Had an emergency case at six. When I got home I found my wife not so well again. We didn't get here till half-past seven. Dinah Copeland thought I wasn't going to turn up and had worked herself into a frightful stew. She'd be able to tell you all about times of arrival. I bet she got here long before the rest of the cast. Dinah Copeland. That's the parson's daughter. She produced the play."

" Yes. Thank you."

" Well, I suppose you don't want me any longer. Good Lord, it's nearly two o'clock!"

" Awful, isn't it? We shall be here all night, I expect. No, we won't bother you any more, Dr. Templett."

" What about moving the body? Shall I fix up for the mortuary van to come along as early as possible?"

" I wish you would."

" I'll have to do the P.M., I suppose?"

" Yes. Yes, of course."

" Pretty plain sailing, it'll be, poor old girl. Well, good-night or good-morning, er—I don't know your name, do I?"

" Alleyn."

" What, Roderick Alleyn?"

" Yes."

" By George, I've read your book of criminal investigation. Damned good. Fascinating subject, isn't it?"

" Enthralling."

" For the layman, what? Not such fun for the expert."

" Not quite such fun."

Dr. Templett shook hands, turned to go, and then paused.

" I tell you what," he said. " I'd like to see how this booby-trap worked."

" Yes, of course. Come and have a look."

Bailey was at the piano with an insufflator and a strong lamp.

Thompson stood by with his cameras.

" How's it going, Bailey?" asked Alleyn.

" Finished the case, sir. Not much doing. Somebody must have dusted the whole show. We may get some latent prints but I don't think there's a chance, myself. Same with the Colt. We're ready to take it down."

" All right. Go warily, we don't want to lose any prints if they're there. I'll move the front of the piano off and you hold the gun."

Bailey reached a gloved hand inside the top.

" I'll take off the pulley on the front panel, sir."

86

"Yes. That'll give us a better picture than if you dismantled the twine altogether."

Fox undid the side catches and Alleyn lifted away the front of the piano and put it on one side.

"Hullo," he said, "this silk panelling seems as though it's had water spilt on it. It's still dampish. Round the central hole."

"Blood?" suggested Dr. Templett.

"No. There's a little blood. This was water. A circular patch of it. Now, I wonder. Well, let's have a look at the works."

The Colt, supported at the end of the barrel by Bailey's thumb and forefinger, was revealed with its green twine attachments. The butt was still jammed against the pegs at the back. Alleyn picked up the detached pulley and held it in position.

"Good God!" said Dr. Templett.

"Ingenious, isn't it?" Alleyn said. "I think we'll have a shot of it like this, Thompson. It'll look nice and clear for the twelve good men and true."

"Is the safety catch on?" demanded Dr. Templett, suddenly stepping aside.

"It is. You've dealt with the soft pedal, haven't you, Bailey?" He stooped and pressed the left pedal down with his hand. The batten with its row of hammers moved towards the string. The green twine tightened in the minute pulleys. "That's how it worked. You can see where the pressure comes on the trigger."

"A very neat-fingered person, wouldn't you say, Mr. Alleyn?" said Fox.

"Yes," said Alleyn. "Neat and sure fingers."

"Oh, I don't know," said Templett. "It's amazingly simple really. The only tricky bit would be passing the twine through the trigger guard, round the butt, and through the top pulley. That could be done before the gun was jammed in position. No, it's simpler than it looks."

"It's like one of these affairs in books," said Bailey disgustedly. "Someone trying to think up a new way to murder. Silly, I call it."

"What do you say, Roper?" said Alleyn.

"To my way of thinking, sir," said Sergeant Roper, "these thrillers are ruining our criminal classes."

Dr. Templett gave a shout of laughter. Roper turned scarlet and stared doggedly at the wall.

"What d'you mean by that, my lad?" asked Fox, who was on his knees, staring into the piano.

Thompson, grinning to himself, touched off his flashlight.

"What I mean to say, Mr. Fox," said Roper. "It puts ideas in their foolish heads. And the talkies, too. Especially the young chaps. They get round the place talking down their noses and making believe they're gangsters. Look at this affair! I bet the chap that did this got the idea of it out of print."

"That's right, Roper, stick to it," said Dr. Templett. Roper disregarded him. Templett repeated his good-nights and went away.

"Go on, Roper. It's an idea," said Alleyn when the door had slammed. "What sort of print do you imagine would inspire this thing?"

"One of those funny drawings with bits of string and cogs and umbrellas and so forth?" suggested Thompson.

"Heath Robinson? Yes."

"Or more likely, sir," said Roper, "one of they four-penny boys' yarns in paper covers like you buy at the store in Chipping. I used to buy them myself as a youngster. There's always a fat lad and a comic lad and the comical chap plays off the fat one. Puts lighted crackers in his pants and all that. I recollect trying the cracker dodge under the rector's seat at Bible class, and he gave me a proper tanning for it, too, did rector."

"The practical joke idea again, you see, Fox," said Alleyn.

"Well," said Fox, stolidly. "Do we start off reading the back numbers of a boys' paper, or what?"

"You never know, Brer Fox. Have you noticed the back of the piano where the bunting's pinned down? There are four holes in the centre drawing-pin and three to each of the others. Will you take the Colt out now, and all the rest of the paraphernalia? I'm going to take a look round the premises. We'll have to start seeing these people in the morning. Who the devil's that?"

There was a loud knock at the front entrance.

"Will I see?" asked Sergeant Roper.

"Do."

Roper tramped off down the centre aisle and threw open the doors.

"Good-morning," said a man's voice outside. "I wonder if I can come in for a moment. It's raining like Noah's half-holiday and I'd like to have a word with——"

"Afraid not, sir," said Roper.

"But I assure you I want to see the representative from Scotland Yard. I've come all the way from London," continued the voice plaintively. "I have, indeed. I represent the *Evening Mirror*. He'll be delighted to see me. Is it by any chance——"

"Yes, it is," said Alleyn loudly and ungraciously. "You can let him in, Roper."

A figure in a dripping mackintosh and streaming hat made a quick rush past Roper, gave a loud exclamation expressive of delight, and hurried forward with outstretched hand.

"I am *not* pleased to see you," said Alleyn.

"Good-morning, Mr. Bathgate," said Fox. "Fancy it being you."

"Yes, just fancy!" agreed Nigel Bathgate. "Well, well, well! I never expected to find the old gang. Bailey, too, and Thompson. It's like the chiming of old bellses to see you all happily employed together."

"How the blue hell did you get wind of this?" inquired Alleyn.

"The gentleman who does market and social notes for the *Chipping Courier* was in the audience to-night and like a bright young pressman he rang up the Central News. I was in the office when it came through and you couldn't see my rudder for foam. Down here in four hours with one puncture. God bless my soul, now, what's it all about?"

"Sergeant Roper will perhaps spare a moment to throw you a bone or two. I'm busy. How are you?"

"Grand. Angela would send her love if she knew I was here, and your godson wants you to put him down for Hendon. He's three on Monday. Is it too late?"

"I'll inquire. Roper, you will allow Mr. Bathgate to sit quietly in a corner somewhere. I'll be back in a few minutes. Coming, Fox?"

Alleyn and Fox went up on the stage, looked round the box-set, and explored the wings.

"We'll have to go over this with a tooth-comb," Alleyn said, "looking for Lord knows what, as usual. Miss Dinah Copeland seems to have gone to a lot of trouble. The scenery's been patched up. Improvised footlights, you see, and I should think the two big overheads are introduced."

He went into the prompt corner.

"Here's the play. *Shop Window*, by Hunt. Rather a good comedy. Very professional, with all the calls marked and so on. A bicycle bell. Probably an adjunct of the telephone on the stage. Let's have a look behind."

A short flight of steps on each side of the back wall led down into a narrow room that ran the length of the stage.

"Mrs. Ross's supper arrangements all laid out on the table. Lord, Fox, those sandwiches look good."

"There's a lot more in this basket," said Fox. "Dr. Templett did say——"

"And beer under the table," murmured Alleyn. "Brer Fox?"

"A keg of it," said Fox, who was exploring. "Dorset draught beer. Very good, Dorset draught."

"You're right," said Alleyn after an interval. "It's excellent. Hullo!"

He stooped and picked something out of a box on the floor.

"Half a Spanish onion. Any onion in your sandwiches?"

"No."

"Nor in mine. It's got flour or something on it." He put the onion on the table and began to examine the plates of sandwiches. "Two kinds only, Fox. Ham and lettuce on the one hand, cucumber on the other. Hullo, here's a tray all set out for a stage tea. Nobody eats anything. Wait a bit."

He lifted the lid of the empty teapot and sniffed at the inside.

"The onion appears to have lived in the teapot. Quaint conceit, isn't it? Very rum, indeed. Come on."

They explored the dressing-rooms. There were two on each side of the supper-room.

"Gents to the right, ladies to the left," said Alleyn. He led the way into the first room on the left. He and Fox began a methodical search through the suitcases and pockets.

"Not quite according to Cocker, perhaps," Alleyn remarked, peering at Miss Prentice's black marocain on the wall. "But I think we'll ask afterwards. Anyway I'm provided with a blank search-warrant so we're all right. Damn this onion, my hand stinks of it. This must be the two spinsters' room, judging by the garments."

"Judging by the pictures," said Fox, "it's a Bible class-room in the ordinary way."

"Yes. The Infant Samuel. What about next door? Ah, rather more skittish dresses. This will be Dinah Copeland and Mrs. Ross. Dr. Templett seemed rather self-conscious about Mrs. Ross, I thought. Miss Copeland's grease paints are in a cardboard box with her name on it. They've been used a lot. Mrs. Ross's, in a brand new japanned tin affair and brand new themselves, from which, inspired by Dorset draught, I deduce that Miss Copeland may be a professional, but Mrs. Ross undoubtedly is not. Here's a card in the new tin box. 'Best luck for to-night, B.' A present, by gum! Who's B., I wonder. Now for the men's rooms."

They found nothing of interest in the men's rooms until Alleyn came to a Donegal tweed suit.

"This is the doctor's professional suit," he said. "It reeks of surgery. Evidently the black jacket is not done in a country practice. I suppose, in the hubbub, he didn't change but went home looking like a comic-opera Frenchman. He must have——"

Alleyn stopped short. Fox looked up to see him staring at a piece of paper.

"Found something, sir?"

"Look."

It was a thin piece of plain blue paper. Fox read the lines of capitals:

YOU ARE GIVEN NOTICE TO LEAVE THIS DISTRICT. IF YOU DISREGARD THIS WARNING YOUR LOVER SHALL SUFFER.

"Where did you find this, Mr. Alleyn?"

"In a wallet. Inside breast pocket of the police surgeon's suit," said Alleyn. He dropped it on the dressing-table and then bent down and sniffed at it.

"It smells of eucalyptus," he said.

CHAPTER ELEVEN

According to Roper

"THAT'S AWKWARD," grunted Fox, after a pause.

"Couldn't be more awkward."

"'Your *lover* shall suffer,'" quoted Fox. "That looks as if it was written to a woman, doesn't it?"

"It's not common usage nowadays the other way round, but it's English. Common enough in the mixed plural."

"He's a married man," Fox remembered.

91

"Yes, it sounded as if his wife's an invalid, didn't it? This may have been written to his mistress or possibly to him, or it may have been shown to him by a third person who is threatened and wants advice."

"Or he may have done it himself."

"Yes, it's possible, of course. Or it may be the relic of a parlour game. Telegrams, for instance. You make a sentence from a string of letters. He'd hardly carry that about next to his heart, though, would he? Damn! I'm afraid we're in for a nasty run, Brer Fox."

"How did the doctor strike you, Mr. Alleyn?"

"What? Rather jumpy. Bit too anxious to please. Couldn't stop talking."

"That's right," agreed Fox.

"We'll have to flourish the search-warrant a bit if we work on this," said Alleyn. "It'll be interesting to see if he misses it before we tackle him about it."

"He's doing the P.M."

"I know. We shall be present. Anyway, the lady was shot through the head. We've got the weapon and we've got the projectile. The post-mortem is not likely to be very illuminating. Hullo, Bailey, what is it?"

Bailey had come down the steps from the stage.

"I thought you'd better know, sir. This chap Roper's recognised the automatic. Mr. Bathgate ran him down to the station and they've checked up the number."

"Where is he?"

"Out in the hall." A reluctant grin appeared on Bailey's face. "I reckon he still thinks it's great to be a policeman. He wants to tell you himself."

"Very touching. All right, Bailey, I want you to test this paper for prints. Do it at once, will you, and put it between glass when you've finished. And, Bailey, have a shot at the teapot there. Inside and out."

"Teapot, sir?"

"Yes. Also the powdered onion on the table. I dare say it's quite immaterial, but it's queer, so we'd better tackle it."

They returned to the hall where they found Roper standing over the automatic with something of the air of a clever retriever.

"Well, Roper," said Alleyn, "I hear you've done a bit of investigation for us."

"Yes, sir, I have so. I've recognised the lethal weapon, sir."

"Well, whose is it?"

"I says to myself when I see it," said Roper, "I know you, my friend, I've had you in my hands, I said. And then I remembered it. It was when we checked up on fire-arms licences six months ago. Now, I suppose a hundred weapons must have passed under my notice that time, this being a sporting part of the world, so I reckon it's not surprising I didn't pick this affair as soon as I clapped eyes on her. I reckon that's not surprising, and yet she looked familiar, you understand?"

"Yes, Roper, I quite understand. Who is the owner?"

"This weapon, sir, is a Colt .32 automatic, the property of Jocelyn Jernigham, Esquire, of Pen Cuckoo."

"Is it, indeed?" murmured Alleyn.

"This gentleman, Mr. Bathgate, ran me down to the station, sir, and it didn't take me over and above five minutes to lay my finger on the files. You can take a look at the files, sir, and——"

"I shall do so. Now, Roper, see if you can give me some model answers. Short, crisp, and to the point. When did you see the automatic? Can you give me the date?"

"In the files!" shouted Sergeant Roper, triumphantly. "May 31st of the current year."

"Where was it?"

"In the study at Pen Cuckoo, sir, that being the room at the extreme end of the west wing facing the Vale."

"Who showed it to you?"

"Squire, himself, showed it to me. We'd checked up all the weapons in the gun-room, of which there was a number, and squire takes me into his study and says, 'There's one more,' he says, and he lays his hand on a wooden box on the table and opens the lid. There was this lethal masterpiece laying on her side, with a notice written clear in block letters. 'Loaded.' 'It's all right,' says Mr. Jernigham, seeing me step aside as he takes her out. 'The safety catch is on,' he says. And he showed me. And he says, 'It went all through the war with me,' he says, 'and there's half a clip left in it. I'd fired two shots when I got my Blighty one,' he says, 'and I've kept it like this ever since. I let it be known there's a loaded automatic waiting at Pen Cuckoo for anybody that feels like coming in uninvited.' We'd had some thieving in the district at that time, same as we've got it now. He told me this weapon had lain in that box for twenty years, did squire."

"Was the box locked?"

"No, sir. But he said all the maids was warned about it."

"Anybody else in the room?"

"Yes, sir. Mr. Henry was there and Miss Prentice, sitting quietly by the fire and smiling, pussy-like, same as she always does."

"Don't you like Miss Prentice?"

"I think she's all right, but my missus says she's proper sly. My missus is a great one for the institute and Miss Prentice is president of same."

"I see. Any local gossip about Miss Prentice?"

Roper expanded. He placed his hands in his belt with the classic heaving movement of all policemen. He then appeared to remember he was in the presence of authority and rearranged himself in an attitude of attention.

"Aye," he said, "they talk all right, sir. You see, Miss Prentice, she came along, new to the Vale, on three years back when Mrs. Jernigham died. I reckon the late Mrs. Jernigham was nigh-on the best liked lady in this part of Dorset. A Grey of Stourminster-Weston she was, Dorset born and bred, and a proper lady. Now, this Miss Prentice, for all she's half a Jernigham, is a foreigner as you might say, and she doesn't know our ways here. Mrs. Jernigham was welcome everywhere, cottage and big houses alike, and wherever she went she was the same. Never asking questions or if she did, out of real niceness and not nosey-parkishness. Now, folk about here say Miss Prentice is the other way round. Sly. Makes trouble between cottages and rectory, or would if she could. Cor!" said Roper, passing his ham of a hand over his face. "The way that old maiden got after rector! My missus says—well, my missus is an outspoken woman and come off a farm."

Alleyn did not press for a repetition of Mrs. Roper's agricultural similes.

"There was only one worse than her," continued Roper, "and that was the deceased. She was a dragon after rector. And before Miss Prentice came, Miss Campanula had it all her own way, but I reckon Miss Campanula kind of lost driving power when t'other lady got going with her insinuating antics."

"How did they get on together?"

"Fast as glue," said Roper. "Thick as thieves. My missus says they knew too much about each other to be anything else. Cook up to Red House, she says Miss Campanula was jealous fair-to-bust of Miss Prentice, but she was no match for her, however, being the type of woman that lets her anger be seen and rages out in the open, whereas Miss Prentice, with her foxy ways, goes quiet to work. Cook told my missus that deceased was losing ground daily and well-nigh desperate over it."

"How do you mean, losing ground?"

"With rector."

"Dear me," murmured Alleyn. "How alarming for the rector."

"Reckon he picks his way like that chap in Bible," said Roper. "He's a simple sort of chap is rector but he's a Vale man and he suits us. His father and grandfather were rectors here before him and he knows our ways."

"Quite so, Roper," said Alleyn, and lit a cigarette.

"No. But the rector met his match in those two ladies, sir, and it's a marvel one of them hasn't snapped him up by this time. Likely he holds them off with holy conversation, but I've seen the hunted look in the man's eyes more than once."

"I see," said Alleyn. "Do you think it generally known that Mr. Jernigham kept this loaded automatic in the study?"

"I should say it was, sir. If I make so bold, sir, I'd say it was never squire that did this job. He's peppery, is Mr. Jernigham, but I'd bet my last penny he's not a murderer. Flares up and forgets all about it the next minute. Very outspoken. Mr. Henry, now, he's deeper. A nice young fellow but quiet-like. You never know what he's thinking. Still, he's got no call to kill anybody, and wouldn't if he had."

"Who is Mrs. Ross of Duck Cottage, Cloudyfold?"

"Stranger to these parts. She only came here last April." Roper's blue eyes became hard and bright.

"Young?" asked Alleyn.

"Not what you'd say so very young. Thin. Pale hair, done very neat, and very neat in her dressing. Her clothes look different to most ladies. More like the females in the talkies only kind of simpler. Dainty. She's dressed very quiet, always, but you notice her." Roper paused, six-foot-two of dim masculine appreciation. "I reckon she's got It," he said at last. "It's not my place to say so, but I suppose a chap always knows her sort. By instinct."

There was an odd little silence during which the other five men stared at Sergeant Roper.

"Dr. Templett does, anyway," he said at last.

"Oh," said Alleyn. "More local gossip?"

"The women-folk. You know what they are, sir. Given it a proper thrashing, they have. Well, there's a good deal of feeling on account of Mrs. Templett being an invalid."

"Yes, I suppose so. Let me see, that's all the cast of the play, isn't it? Except Miss Copeland."

"Miss Dinah? She'll be in a taking-on, I make no doubt. After all the work she's given to this performance for it to go up, as you might say, in a cloud of dust. Still, she's courting, that'll be a kind of comfort to the maid. Mr. Henry was watching over her after the tragedy, holding her hand for all to see. They're well-matched and we're hoping to hear it's a settled matter any time now. My missus says it'll be one in the eye for Miss Prentice."

"Why on earth?"

"She won't be fancying another lady at Pen Cuckoo. I saw her looking blue murder at them even while deceased was lying, you might say, a corpse at their feet. She's lucky it wasn't her. Should be thanking her Creator she's still here to make trouble."

"Miss Prentice," said Nigel, "seems to be a very unpleasant cup of tea. Perhaps her sore finger was all a bluff and she rigged the tackle for the girl-friend."

"Dr. Templett said it was no bluff, Mr. Bathgate," said Fox. "He said she held out till the last moment that she was going to play."

"That's right enough, sir," said Roper. "I went round to the back to see Miss Dinah just after it had happened and there was Miss Prentice crying her eyes out with her finger looking that unwholesome it'd turn your stomach, and Miss Dinah telling her she was ruining the paint on her face and the doctor saying, 'I absolutely forbid it. Your finger's in a very nasty state and if you weren't playing this part to-night,' he said, 'I'd open it up.' Yes he threatened her with the knife, did doctor. Mr. Henry says, 'You'll make a mess of Mr. Nevin's ecstasies.' Her piece was composed by a chap of that sort name as you'll see in the programme. 'You'll never stay the course, Cousin Eleanor,' says Mr. Henry. 'I know it's hurting you like stink,' says Mr. Henry, 'because you're crying,' he says. But no, she wouldn't give in till Miss Dinah fetched her father. 'Come,' he says, 'we all know how you feel about it, but there are times when generosity is better than heroism.' She looked up at rector, then, and she said, 'If you say so, Father,' and with that Miss Campanula says, 'Now, who'll go and get my music?'

Where's Gibson?' Which is the name of her chauffeur. So she give in, but very reluctant."

"A vivid enough picture of the rival performances, isn't it?" said Alleyn. "Well, there's the history of the case. It's getting on for three o'clock. I think, on second thoughts, Fox, we won't wait for the light of day. We'll make a night of it. This place must be overhauled some-time and it looks as though we'll have a busy day to-morrow. You can turn in if you like, Roper. Some one can relieve us at seven."

"Are you going to search the premises, sir?"

"Yes."

"Reckon I'd like to give a hand if it's agreeable to you."

"Certainly. Fox, you and Thompson make sure we've missed nothing in the dressing-rooms and supper-room. Bailey, you can take Roper with you on the stage. Go over every inch of it. I'll tackle the hall and join you if I finish first."

"Are you looking for anything in particular?" asked Nigel.

"The usual unconsidered trifles. Spare bits of Twiddle-toy, for instance. Even a water pistol."

"Not forgetting any kid's annuals that happen to be lying round," added Fox.

"Poor things!" said Nigel. "Back to childhood's day, I see. Is there a telephone here?"

"In a dressing-room," said Alleyn. "But it's only an extension."

"I'll ring up the office from a pub, then. In the mean-time, I may as well write up a pretty story."

He took out his pad and settled himself at a table on the stage.

Police investigation is for the most part a dull business. Nothing could be more tedious than searching for things. Half a detective's life is spent in turning over dreary objects, finding nothing, and replacing them. Alleyn started in the entrance porch of the parish hall and began a meticulous crawl over dusty surfaces. He moved like a snail, across and across, between the rows of benches. He felt cold and dirty and he smelt nothing but dust. He could not allow his thoughts to dwell pleasantly on his own affairs, his coming marriage and the happiness that kept him company nowadays; because it is when his thoughts are abstracted from the business in hand that the detective misses the one small sign events have set in his path. Sometimes the men on the stage heard a thin whistling down in the hall. Sergeant Roper's voice droned interminably. At intervals the church clock sweetly recorded the journey of the hours. Miss Campanula lay stealthily stiffening behind a red baize screen, and Nigel Bathgate recorded her departure in efficient journalese.

Alleyn had passed the benches and chairs and was grovelling about in the corner with an electric torch. Presently he uttered a soft exclamation. Nigel looked up from his writing and Bailey, who had the loose seat of a chair in his hands, shaded his eyes and peered down into the corner.

Alleyn stood by the stage, on the audience's left. He held a small shining object between finger and thumb. His hand was gloved. One of his eyebrows was raised and his lips were pursed in a soundless whistle.

" Struck a patch, sir? " asked Bailey.

" Yes, I rather think so, Bailey."

He walked over to the piano.

" Look."

Bailey and Nigel came to the footlights.

The shining object Alleyn held in his hands was a boy's water-pistol.

II

" As you said yourself, Bathgate, back to childhood days."

" What's the idea, sir? " asked Bailey.

" It seems to be a recurrent idea," said Alleyn. " I found this thing stuffed away in a sort of locker under the stage over there. It was poked in a dark corner, but there's little or no dust on it. The rest of the stuff in the locker's smothered in dirt. Look at the butt, Bailey. Do you see that shiny scratch? It's rather a super sort of water pistol, isn't it? None of your rubber bulbs that you squeeze— but a proper trigger action. Fox!"

Fox and Thompson appeared from the direction of the supper-room.

Alleyn went to the small table where Bailey had placed the rest of the exhibits, lifted the covering cloth and laid his find beside the Colt automatic.

" The length is the same to within a fraction of an inch," he said; " and there's a mark on the butt of the Colt very much like the mark on the butt of the water-pistol. That, I believe, is where it was rammed in the piano, between the steel pegs where the strings are fastened."

"But what the devil," asked Nigel, "is the explanation?"

Alleyn pulled off his gloves and fished in his pockets for his cigarette-case.

"Where's Roper?"

"Out at the back, sir," said Bailey. "He'll be back shortly with a new set of reminiscences. His super ought to issue a gag for that chap."

"This is a rum go," said Fox profoundly.

"'Jones Minor' all over it," said Alleyn. "You were right, Bailey, I believe, when you suggested the death-trap in the piano was too elaborate to be true. It *is* only in books that murder is quite as fancy as all this. The whole thing carries the hall-mark of the booby-trap and the signature of the practical joker. It is somehow difficult to believe that a man or woman would, as Bailey has said, think up murder on these lines. But what if a man with murder in his heart came upon this booby-trap, this water-pistol aimed through a hole in the torn silk bib? What if this potential murderer thought of substituting a Colt for the water-pistol? It becomes less far-fetched, then, doesn't it? What's more, there are certain advantages. The murderer can separate himself from his victim and from the *corpus delicti*. The spadework has been done. All the murderer has to do is remove the water-pistol, jam in the Colt and tie the loose end of twine round the butt. It's not his idea, it's Jones Minor's."

"He'd want to be sure the Colt was the same length," said Fox.

"He could measure the water-pistol."

"And then go home and check up his Colt?"

"Or somebody else's Colt," said Bailey.

"One of the first points we have to clear up," Alleyn said, "is the accessibility of Jernigham's war souvenir. Roper says he thinks everybody knew about it, and apparently it was there in the study for the picking up. They've all been rehearsing in the study. They were there last night—Friday night, I mean. It's Sunday now, heaven help us."

"If Dr. Templett recognised the Colt," observed Fox, "he didn't let on."

"No more he did."

The back door banged and boots resounded in the supper-room.

"Here's Roper," said Fox.

"Roper!" shouted Alleyn.

" Yes, sir?"

" Come here."

Sergeant Roper stumbled up the steps and appeared on the stage.

" Come and have a look at this."

" Certainly, sir."

Roper placed his palm on the edge of the stage and vaulted deafeningly to the floor. He approached the table with an air of efficiency and contemplated the water-pistol.

" Know it?" asked Alleyn.

Roper reached out his hand.

"Don't touch it!" said Alleyn sharply.

" 'T, 't, 't!" said Fox and Bailey.

" Beg pardon, sir," said Roper. " Seeing that trifling toy, and recognising it in a flash, I had a natural impulse, as you might say——"

" Your natural impulses must be mortified if you want to grow up into a detective," said Alleyn. " Whose water-pistol is this?"

" Mind," said Roper warningly, " there may be two of this class in the district, sir. Or more. I'm not taking my oath there aren't. But barring that eventuality, I reckon I can put an owner on it. And seeing he had the boldness to take a shot at me outside the Jernigham Arms, me being in uniform——"

" Roper," said Alleyn, " it is only about three hours to the dawn. Don't let the sun rise on your parentheses. Whose water-pistol is this?"

" George Biggins," said Roper.

CHAPTER TWELVE

Further Vignettes

AT TWELVE O'CLOCK the Yard car dropped Alleyn and Fox at the Jernigham Arms.

The rain had stopped, but it was a dank, dreary morning, and so cloudy that only a mean thinning of the night, a grudging disclosure of vague, wet masses, gave evidence that somewhere beyond the Vale there was dawnlight.

Bailey and Thompson drove off for London. Alleyn stared after the tail-light of the car while Fox belaboured the front door of the Jernigham Arms.

"There's *somebody* moving about in there," he grumbled. "Here they come."

It was the pot-boy, very tousled and peepy, and accompanied by a gust of stale beer. Alleyn thought that he looked like all pot-boys at dawn throughout time and space.

"Good-morning," Alleyn said. "Can you give us rooms for a day or two, and breakfast in an hour? There's a third man on his way here."

"I'll aask Missus," said the pot-boy. He gaped at them, blinked, and went off down a passage. They could hear him calling with the cracked uncertainty of adolescence:

"Missus! 'Be detec-er-tives from Lunnon, along of Miss Campanula's murder, likely. Mrs. Pe-e-each! Missus!"

"The whole place buzzing with it," said Alleyn.

II

At seven o'clock Henry found himself suddenly awake. He lay still, wondering for a moment why this day would be different from any other day. Then he remembered. He saw with precision a purple heap, the top of a head, the nape of a neck laced with dark, shining streaks. He saw a sheet of music, crumpled, pinned to the keys of a piano by the head. The picture was framed in aspidistras like a nightmarish valentine and across the lower margin was the top of a piano.

"I have looked down at a murdered woman." And for a time his thoughts would not move beyond this sharp memory, so that he found himself anxiously re-tracing the pattern of the head, the neck, the white sheet of music, and the fatuous green leaves. Then the memory of Dinah's cold fingers crept into his hands. He closed his hands on the memory, clenching them as he lay in bed, and the whole idea of Dinah came into his mind.

"If it had been Eleanor, there would have been an end to our troubles."

He pushed this thought away from him, telling himself it was horrible, but it returned repeatedly, and at last he said, "It is stupid to pretend otherwise. I do wish it had been Eleanor." He began to think of all that happened after Idris Campanula died; of how his father went aside with Superintendent Blandish, and of the solemn, ridiculous look on his father's face. He remembered Dr. Templett's explanations and Miss Prentice's moans which had irritated them all very

101

much. He remembered that when he looked at Mr. Copeland he saw that his lips were moving, and realised, with embarrassment, that the rector was at prayer. He remembered Mrs. Ross's almost complete silence and the way she and Templett had not spoken to each other. And again his thoughts returned to Dinah. He had walked to the rectory with Dinah and her father, and on the threshold he had kissed her openly, the rector seeming scarcely aware of it. On the way home to Pen Cuckoo, the squire had not forgotten that, in the absence of Sir George Dillington, he was Chief Constable, and had discoursed solemnly on the crime, saying again and again that Henry was to treat everything he heard as confidential, and relating how, with Blandish, he had come to a decision to call in Scotland Yard. When they were indoors at last, Eleanor Prentice had fainted, and the squire had forced brandy down her throat with such an uncertain hand that he had half-asphyxiated her. They helped her to her room and Jocelyn, nervously assiduous, had knocked the bandaged finger so that she screamed with pain. Henry and his father had a solemn drink together in the dining-room, Jocelyn still discoursing on his responsibilities.

Henry went cold all over, his heart dropped like a plummet, and he faced the worst memory of all, the one that he had been pushing away ever since he woke.

It was when Jocelyn told him how, strong in his position of Acting Chief Constable, he had peered through the hole in the tucked silk front, and had seen the glimmer of a firearm.

" A revolver," Jocelyn had said, " or else an automatic."

At that moment the picture of the box in the study had risen in Henry's imagination. He had hurried his father to bed, but when he was alone had been afraid to go into the study and lift the lid of the box. Now he knew that he must do it. Quickly, before the servants were up. He leapt out of bed, threw on his dressing-gown, and crept downstairs through the dark house. There was an electric torch in the hall. He found it and made his way to the study.

The box was empty. The notice "LOADED" in block capitals lay at the bottom.

Henry turned away with panic in his heart, and a minute later he was knocking at his father's door.

Selia Ross had been awake for a very long time. She was wondering when she could telephone to Dr. Templett or whether it would be altogether too unsafe to get into touch with him. She knew the telephone rang at his bedside until eight o'clock in the morning, and that he slept far enough away from his wife's room for it not to disturb her. Mrs. Ross wanted to ask him what he had done with the anonymous letter. She knew that he had put it in his wallet, and that he kept his wallet in his breast pocket. She remembered that after the catastrophe he had not changed back into his ordinary suit, and she was hideously afraid that the letter might still be in his coat at the hall. He was very forgetful and careless about such things, and had once left one of her letters, open, on his dressing-table, only remembering it later on in the day.

She had no knowledge of what the police would do. She had a sort of idea she had read in a criminal novel that they were not allowed to search through private houses without a permit of some kind. But did that apply to a public hall? And surely if the body of a murdered person was there, in the hall, they would hunt everywhere. What would they think if they found that letter? She wanted to warn Dr. Templett to be ready with an answer.

But he himself was an official.

But he had almost certainly remembered the letter.

Would it be better to say he knew the author to be someone else—his wife, even? Anyone but one of those two women.

Her thoughts, needle-sharp, darted in and out of the fabric of her terror.

Perhaps if he went down early . . .

Perhaps she should have telephoned an hour ago.

She switched on her bedside lamp and looked at her clock. It was five minutes to eight.

Perhaps she was too late.

In a panic she reached for the telephone and dialled his number.

Miss Prentice's finger had kept her awake, but it is doubtful if she would have slept even if it had not throbbed all night. Her thoughts were too hurried and busy, weaving backwards and forwards between the rector, herself and Idris Campanula, who was murdered. She thought of all sorts of things: of how when she first came to Pen Cuckoo she and Idris had been such friends, confiding the secrets of their bosoms to each other like schoolgirls. She remembered all the delicious talks they had had together, talks full of exciting conjectures about the behaviour of other people in the village and the county. There would be nobody now who would speak her language and discuss things and people in that way. They had been so intimate until Idris grew jealous. That was the form Miss Prentice gave to their differences: Idris grew jealous of her friend's rising influence in the village and in church affairs.

She would not think yet of Mr. Copeland. The memory of the things he had said to her at confession must be thrust down into oblivion, and that other memory, that other frightful revelation of Idris's perfidy.

No. Better to remember the old friendly days and to think of Idris's will. It had been a very simple will. A lot for Mr. Copeland, a little for the distant nephew, and seven thousand for Eleanor herself. Idris had said she'd never had a real friend until Eleanor came, and that if she died first she would be happy in the thought that she had been able to do this. Eleanor even then rather resented her friend's air of patronage.

But it was true that if she had this money she would no longer be so dependent on Jocelyn.

Mr. Copeland would be very well off indeed, for Idris was an extremely rich woman.

Dinah would be an heiress.

She had not thought of that before. There would be no worldly reason now why Dinah and Henry should not marry.

If she were to withdraw her opposition quickly, before the will was known—would not that seem generous and kind? If she could only stifle the recollection of that scene on Friday afternoon. Dinah limp in Henry's arms, lost in rapture. It had nearly driven Eleanor mad. How could she unsay all that she had said before she turned away and stumbled up the lane, escaping from so much agony? But with Dinah married to Henry, then her father would be lonely. A rich lonely man, fifty years old, and too dignified to look for a young wife. Surely then!

Then! Then!

The first bell, calling the people to eight o'clock service, roused her from her golden plans. She rose, dressed and went out into the dark morning.

V

The rector was astir at seven. It was Sunday, and he would be in church in an hour. He dressed hurriedly, unable to lie thinking any longer of the events of the night that was past. All sorts of recollections flocked into his thoughts, and in all of them the murdered woman was present, turning them into nightmares. He felt as if he was dyed in guilt, as if he would never rid himself of his dreadful memories. His thoughts were chaotic and quite uncontrollable.

Long before the warning bell sounded for early celebration, he stole out of the house and walked, as he had done every Sunday for twenty years, down the drive, through the nut walk and over the stile into the churchyard.

When he was alone inside the dark church he fell on his knees and tried to pray.

VI

Somewhere, a long way off, somebody was knocking at a door. Bang, bang, *bang*. Must be old Idris pounding away at that damned lugubrious tune. Blandish needn't have locked Eleanor up inside the piano. As Deputy Chief Constable, I object to that sort of thing; it isn't cricket. Let her out! If she knocks much louder she'll blow the place up, and then we'll have to get in the Yard. Bang, bang——

The squire woke with a sickening leap of his nerves.

"Wha-a-a?"

"Father, it's me! Henry! I want to speak to you."

VII

When Dinah heard her father go downstairs long before his usual hour, she knew that he hadn't slept, that he was miserable, and that he would go into church and pray. She hoped that he had remembered to wear a woollen cardigan under his cassock, because he seemed to catch cold more easily in church than anywhere else. She knew last night that she was in for a difficult time with him. For some extraordinary reason, he had already begun to blame himself for the tragedy, saying that he had been weak and vacillating, not zealous enough in his duties as a parish priest.

Dinah was unable to follow her father's reasoning, and with a sinking heart she had asked him if he suspected any one as the murderer of Idris Campanula. That was when they got home last night and she was fortified by Henry's kiss.

"Daddy, do you think you know?"

"No, darling, no. But I haven't helped them as I should. And then when I did try, it was too late."

"But what do you mean?"

"You mustn't ask me, darling."

And then she had realised that she was thinking of the confessional. What on earth had Idris Campanula told him on Friday? What had Eleanor Prentice told him? Something had upset him very much, Dinah was sure. Well, one of them was gone and wouldn't make mischief any more. It was no good trying to be sorry. She wasn't sorry, she was only frightened and filled with horror whenever she thought of the dead body. It was the first dead body Dinah had ever seen.

Of course it was obvious to everybody that the trap had been set for Eleanor Prentice. Her father must realise that. Who, then, had a motive to kill Eleanor Prentice?

Dinah sat up in bed, cold with terror. She remembered the meeting in the lane on Friday afternoon, the things Eleanor Prentice had said in a breathless whisper, and the answer Henry had made.

"If she tells them what he said," thought Dinah, "they'll say Henry had a motive."

And with her whole soul she tried to send out a warning message to Henry.

But Henry, at that moment, was pounding his father's bedroom door, and into his startled mind there came no warning message from Dinah. There was no need for one, for already he was afraid.

VIII

Dr. Templett was dreamlessly and peacefully asleep when

the telephone rang at his bedside. At once, and with the accuracy born of long practice, he reached out in the half-light for the receiver.

"Dr. Templett here," he said, as he always did when the telephone rang at an ungodly hour. He remembered that young Mrs. Cartwright might now be in labour.

But it was Selia Ross.

"Billy? Billy, have you got that letter?"

"What!"

He lay there quite still, holding the receiver to his ear and listening to his own thumping heart.

"Billy! Are you there?"

"Yes," he said, "yes. It's all right. There's nothing to worry about. I'll look in some time to-day."

"Do, for God's sake."

"All right. Good-bye."

He hung up the receiver and lay staring at the ceiling. What had he done with that letter?

CHAPTER THIRTEEN

Sunday Morning

ALLEYN AND FOX were at breakfast and Nigel was still asleep when Superintendent Blandish walked in. He was blue about the chin and his eyes and nose were watery.

"You must wonder if there is anybody except that jabbering chap Roper in the Great Chipping Constabulary," he said as he shook hands. "I'm sorry to have neglected you like this; but we're in for a picnic, and no mistake, with this case up at Moorton Park."

"Damn' bad luck, the two cases cropping up at the same time," said Alleyn. "Of course, you'd have liked to handle our business yourself. Have you had breakfast?"

"Haven't taken a look at food since six o'clock yesterday."

Alleyn went to the hatch and shouted:

"Mrs. Peach! Another lot of eggs and bacon, if you can manage it."

"Well, I won't say no," said Blandish, and sat down. "And I won't say I wouldn't have liked to try my hand at this business. But there you are: never rains but it pours, does it?"

"That's right," agreed Fox. "We get the same thing

at the Yard. Though lately it's been quietish—hasn't it, Mr. Alleyn?"

Blandish chuckled. "Maybe that's why we've been honoured with the top-notchers," he said. "Well, Mr. Alleyn, it will be quite an experience for us to see you working. Needless to say, we'll give you all the help we can."

"Thank you," said Alleyn. "We'll need it. This is a remarkably rum business. You were in the audience, weren't you?"

"I was, and I can give you my word I got a fright. Thought the whole place had exploded. The old piano went on buzzing for Lord knows how long. By gum, it took all my self-control not to have a peep inside the lid before I went off to Moorton. But, 'No,' I thought, 'You're handing over, and you'd better not meddle.'"

"Extraordinarily considerate. We breathed our fervent thanks, didn't we, Fox? I suppose that conversation piece you've got for a sergeant has told you all about it?"

Blandish pulled an expressive grimace.

"I shut him up after the second recital," he said. "He wants sitting on, does Roper, but he's got his wits about him. I'd like to hear your account."

While he devoured his eggs and bacon, Alleyn gave him the history of the night. When he came to the discovery of the message in Dr. Templett's coat, Blandish laid down his knife and fork and stared at him.

"Glory!" he said.

"I know."

"This is hell," said Blandish. "I mean to say, it's awkward."

"Yes."

"Not to put too fine a point on it, Mr. Alleyn, it's bloody awkward."

"It is."

"By gum, I'm not so sure I do regret being out of it. It may not be anything, of course, but it can't be overlooked. And I've been associated with the doctor I don't know how many years."

"Like him?" asked Alleyn.

"Do I like him? Well, now, yes. I suppose I do. We've always got on very pleasantly, you know. Yes, I—well, I'm accustomed to him."

"You'll know the questions we're going to ask. In this sort of affair we have to batten on local gossip."

Alleyn went to the corner of the dining-room, got his

case and took from it the anonymous letter. It was flattened between two sheets of glass joined, at the edges, with adhesive tape. The corner, back and sides of the paper bore darkened impressions of fingers.

"There it is. We brought up three sets of latent prints. One of them corresponds with a print taken from a powder box in the dressing-room used by the victim and Miss Prentice. It has been identified as the victim's. A second has its counterpart on a new japanned make-up box, thought to be the property of Mrs. Ross. The third is repeated on other papers in the wallet, and is obviously Dr. Templett's."

"Written by the deceased, sent to Mrs. Ross and handed by her to the doctor?"

"It seems indicated. Especially as two of Mrs. Ross's prints, if they are hers, appear to be superimposed on the deceased's prints, and one of Dr. Templett's lies across two of the others. We'll get more definite results when Bailey develops his photographs."

"This is an ugly business. You mentioned local gossip, Mr. Alleyn. There's been a certain amount in this direction, no denying it, and the two ladies in question were mainly responsible, I fancy."

"But is it a motive for murder?" asked Fox of nobody in particular.

"Well, Brer Fox, it might be. A doctor, in a country district especially, doesn't thrive on scandal. Is Templett a wealthy man, do you know, Blandish?"

"No, I wouldn't say he was," said Blandish. "They're an old Vale family, and the doctor's a younger son. His elder brother was a bit of a rip. Smart regiment before the war, and expensive tastes. It's always been understood the doctor came in for a white elephant when he got Chippingwood. I'd say he needs every penny he earns. He's a hunting man, too, and that costs money."

"What about Mrs. Ross?"

"Well, there you are! If you're to believe everything you hear, they are pretty thick. But gossip's not evidence, is it?"

"No, but it's occasionally based on some sort of foundation, more's the pity. Ah, well! It indicates a line and we'll follow the pointer. Now, about the automatic. It's Mr. Jernigham's all right."

"I've heard all about that, Mr. Alleyn, and that's not too nice either, though I wouldn't believe, if I saw the weapon smoking in his hand, that the squire would shoot a woman, let alone plan to murder his own flesh and blood. Unlikely enough people have turned out to be murderers, as we all know, and I suppose that it is not beyond the possibilities that Mr. Jernigham might kill his man in hot blood; but I've known him all my life, and I'd stake my reputation he's not the sort to do an underhand fantastic sort of job like this. The man's not got it in him. That's not evidence, either——"

"It's expert opinion, though," said Alleyn, "and to be respected as such."

"The squire's acting Chief Constable while Sir George Dillington's away."

"We seem to be on official preserves wherever we turn," said Alleyn. "I'll call at Pen Cuckoo later in the morning. The mortuary van came before it was light. Dr. Templett's doing the post-mortem this afternoon. Either Fox or I will be there. I think our first job now is to call on Mr. Georgie Biggins."

"Young limb of Satan! You'll find him in the last cottage on the left, going out of Chipping. The station's in Great Chipping, you know—only five miles from here. Roper and a P-c enjoy their midday snooze at a sub-station in this village. Both are at your service."

"Is there a car of sorts I could hire for the time being? You'll need the official bus for your own work, of course."

"As a matter of fact, I'm afraid we shall. It's a tidy stretch over to Moorton Park, and we'll be going backwards and forwards. No doubt about our men being Posh Jimmy & Co. Typical job. Funny how they stick to their ways, isn't it? About a car. As a matter of fact, the Biggins have got an old Ford they hire."

"Splendid. An admirable method of approaching Mr. Georgie. How old is he?"

"In years," said Blandish, "He's about thirteen. In sin he's a hundred. A limb, if ever there was one. Nerve of a rhinoceros."

"We'll see if we can shake it," said Alleyn.

The superintendent departed, lamenting the amount of work that lay before him.

II

Alleyn and Fox lit their pipes and walked through Chipping. By daylight it turned out to be a small hamlet with a row of stone cottages on each side of the road, a general store, a post office, and the Jernigham Arms. Even the slope of Cloudyfold, rising steeply above it from the top of Pen Cuckoo Vale, did not rob Chipping of its upland character. It felt high in the world, and the cold wind blew strongly down the Vale road.

The Bigginses' cottage stood a little apart from the rest of the village, and had a truculent air. It was one of those bare-faced Dorset cottages, less picturesque than its neighbours, and more forbidding.

As Alleyn and Fox approached the front door, they heard a woman's voice:

"Whatever be the matter with you, then, mumbudgeting so close to my apron strings? Be off with you!"

Silence.

"To be sure," continued the voice, "if you wasn't so strong as a young foal, Georgie Biggins, I'd think something ailed you. Stick out your tongue."

Silence.

"As clean as a whistle. Stick it in again, then. Standing there like you was simple Dick with your tongue lolling! I never see! What ails you?"

"Nuthun," said a small voice.

"Nuthun killed nobody."

Alleyn tapped on the door.

Another silence was broken by a sharp whispering and an unmistakable scuffle.

"Do what I tell you!" ordered the voice. "Me in my working apron, and Sunday morning! Go *on* with you."

There was a sound of rapid retreat and then the door opened three inches to disclose a pair of boot-button eyes and part of a very white face.

"Hullo," said Alleyn. "I've come to see if I can hire a car. This is Mr. Biggins's house, isn't it?"

"Uh."

"Have you got a car for hire?"

"Uh."

"Well, how about opening the door a bit wider and we can talk about it?"

The door opened very slowly to another five inches. Georgie Biggins stood revealed in his Sunday suit. His moon-face was colourless and he had the look of a boy who may bolt without warning.

Alleyn said, "Now, what about this car? Is your father at home?"

"Along to pub corner," said Georgie in a stifled voice. "Mum's comeun."

The cinema has made all little boys familiar with the look of a detective. Alleyn kept a change of clothes in the Yard in readiness for sudden departures. His shepherd's plaid coat, flannel trousers and soft hat may have reassured George Biggins, but when the boot-button eyes ranged farther afield and lit on Inspector Fox, in his dark suit, mackintosh and bowler, their owner uttered a yelp of pure terror, turned tail and charged into his mother, who had at that moment walked out of the bedroom. She was a large woman, and she caught her son with a practised hand.

"Now!" she said. "That's enough and more, for sure. What's the meanings of these goings-on? You wait till your Dad comes home. I never see!"

She advanced to the door, bringing her son with her by the scruff of the neck.

"I'm sure I'm sorry to keep you waiting," she said.

Alleyn asked about the car and was told he could have it. Mrs. Biggins examined both of them with frank curiosity and led the way round the house to a dilapidated shed where they found a Ford car, six years old, but, as Alleyn cheerfully remarked, none the worse for that. He paid a week's rental in advance. Mrs. Biggins kept a firm but absent-minded grip on her son's shirt-collar.

"I'll get you a receipt," she said. "Likely you're here on account of this terrible affair."

"That's it," said Alleyn.

"Are you from Scotland Yard, then?"

"Yes, Mrs. Biggins, that's us." Alleyn looked good naturedly at Master Biggins. "Is this Georgie?" he asked. The next second, Master Biggins had left the best part of his Sunday collar in his mother's hand and had bolted like a rabbit, only to find himself held as if in a vice by the terrible man in the mackintosh and bowler.

"Now, now, now," said Fox. "What's all this?"

The very words he had so often heard on the screen.

"Georgie!" screamed Mrs. Biggins in a maternal fury. Then she looked at her son's face and at the hands that held him.

"Here, you!" she stormed at Fox. "What are you at, laying your hands on my boy?"

"There's nothing to worry about, Mrs. Biggins," said Alleyn. "Georgie may be able to help us, that's all. Now look here, wouldn't it be better if we went indoors out of sight and sound of your neighbours?"

The shot went home.

"Mighty me!" said Mrs. Biggins, still almost as white as her child, but rallying. "Mighty me, it's true enough they spend most of the Lord's Day minding other folks' business and clacking their tongues. Georgie Biggins, if you don't hold your noise I'll have the skin off you. Do us go in, then."

III

In a cold but stuffy parlour, Alleyn did his best with mother and son. Georgie was now howling steadily. Mrs. Biggins's work-reddened hands pleated and re-pleated the folds of her dress. But she listened in silence.

"It's just this," said Alleyn. "Georgie is in no danger, but we believe he is in a position to give us extremely important information."

Georgie checked a lamentable roar and listened.

Alleyn took the water-pistol from his pocket and handed it to Mrs. Biggins.

"Do you recognise it?"

"For sure," she said slowly. "It's his'en."

Georgie burst out again.

"Young Biggins," said Alleyn, "is this your idea of being a detective? Come here."

Georgie came.

"See here, now. How would you like to help the police bring a murderer to justice? How would you like to work with us? We're from Scotland Yard, you know. It's not often you'll get the chance to work with the Yard, is it?"

The black eyes fastened on Alleyn's and brightened.

"What are the other chaps going to think if you, if you "—Alleyn hunted for the right phrase—" if you solve the problem that has baffled the greatest sleuths of all time?" He glanced at his colleague. Fox, looking remarkably bland, closed one eye.

"If you come in with us," Alleyn continued, "you'll be doing a man's job. How about it?"

A faintly hard-boiled expression crept over Georgie Biggins's undistinguished face.

"Okay," he said in a treble voice still fuddled with tears.

"Good enough." Alleyn took the water-pistol from Mrs. Biggins. "This is your gun, isn't it?"

"Yaas," said Georgie; and, remembering James Cagney the week before last at Great Chipping Plaza, he added with a strong Dorset accent: "Sure it's my gat."

"You fixed that water-pistol in the piano at the hall, didn't you?"

"So what?" said Georgie.

This was a little too much for Alleyn. He contemplated the child for a moment and then said:

"Look here, Georgie, never you mind about the pictures. This is real. There's somebody about who ought to be locked up. You're an Englishman, a man of Dorset, and you want to see right done, don't you? You thought it would be rather fun if Miss Prentice got a squirt of water in the eye when she put her foot on the soft pedal. I'm afraid I agree. It would have been funny."

Georgie grinned.

"But how about the music? You'd forgotten about that, hadn't you?"

"Nah, I had not. My pistol's proper strong pistol. 'Twould have bowled over the music, for certain, sure."

"You may be right," said Alleyn. "Did you try it after you had fixed it up?"

"Nah."

"Why not?"

"'Cause something happened."

"What happened?"

"Nuthin! Somebody made a noise. I went away."

"Where did you get the idea?" said Alleyn after a pause. "Come on, now."

"I'll be bound I know, the bad boy," interrupted his mother. "If our Georgie's been up to such-like capers, it's out of one of the clap-trappey tales he's always at. Ay, only last week he tied an alarm clock under Father's chair and set 'un for seven o'clock when he takes his nap, and there was the picture in this rubbish to give him away."

"Was it out of a book, Georgie?"

"Yaas. Kind of."

"I see. And partly out of your Twiddletoy model wasn't it?"

Georgie nodded.

"When did you do it?"

"Froiday."

"What time?"

114

" Aafternoon. Two o'clock, about."

" How did you get into the hall?"

" Was there with them girls and I stayed behind."

" Tell me about it. You must have been pretty smart for them not to see what you were up to."

Georgie it seemed, had slipped into a dark corner as the Friendly Young People left at about a quarter-past two. His idea had been to shoot at them with his water-pistol as they passed; but at the last moment a more amusing notion occurred to him. He remembered the diverting tale of a piano booby-trap which he had read with the greatest enjoyment in the last number of *Bingo Bink's Weekly*. He had some odds and ends of Twiddletoy in his pockets, and as soon as the front door slammed he got to work. First he silently examined the piano and made himself familiar with the action of the pedals. At this juncture his mother told Alleyn that Georgie was of a markedly mechanical turn of mind and had made many astonishing models from Twiddletoy all of which could be made to revolve or even propel. Georgie had gone solidly to work. Stimulated by Alleyn's ardent attention, he described his handiwork. When it was finished he played a triumphant stanza or two of " Chopsticks," taking care to use the loud pedal only.

" And nobody came?"

The devilish child turned white again.

" Nobody saw," he muttered. " They never saw nuthun. Only banged at door and shouted."

" And you didn't answer? I see. Know who it was?"

" I never saw 'em."

" All right. How did you leave?"

" By front door. I shut 'un behind me."

There was a brief silence. Georgie's face suddenly twisted into a painful grimace, his upper lip trembled again, and he looked piteously at Alleyn.

" I never meant no harm," he said. " I never meant it to kill her."

" That's all right," said Alleyn. He reached out a hand and took the child by the shoulder.

" It's nothing to do with you, young Biggins," said Alleyn.

But over the boy's head he saw the mother's stricken face and knew he could not help her so easily.

CHAPTER FOURTEEN

According to the Jernighams

ALLEYN WENT ALONE to Pen Cuckoo. He left Fox to
visit Miss Campanula's servants, find out the name of her
lawyers, and pick up any grain of information that might
be the fruit of his well-known way with female domestics.

The Bigginses' car chugged doggedly up the Vale Road
in second gear. It was a stiff grade. The Vale rises steeply
above Chipping, mounting past Winton to Pen Cuckoo Manor
and turning into Cloudyfold Rise at the head of the valley.
It is not an obviously picturesque valley, but it has a
charm that transcends mere prettiness. The lower slopes
of Cloudyfold make an agreeable pattern, the groups of
trees are beautifully disposed about the flanks of the hills,
and the scattered houses, being simple, seem to have
grown out of the country, as indeed they have, since they
are built of Dorset stone. It is not a tame landscape, either.
The four winds meet on Cloudyfold, and in winter the
small lake in Pen Cuckoo grounds holds its mask of ice for
days together.

Alleyn noticed that several lanes came down into the
Vale Road. He could see that at least one of them led
crookedly up to the Manor, and one seemed to be a sort
of bridle path from the Manor down to the church. He
drove on through the double gates, up the climbing avenue
and out on the wide sweep before Pen Cuckoo house.

A flood of thin sunshine had escaped the heavy clouds,
and Pen Cuckoo looked its wintry best, an ancient and
gracious house, not very big, not at all forbidding, but
tranquil. "A happy house," thought Alleyn, "with a certain
dignity."

He gave his card to Taylor.

"I should like to see Mr. Jernigham, if I may."

"If you will come this way, sir."

As he followed Taylor through the west wing, he thought:
"With any luck, it'll be the study."

It was, and the study was empty.

As soon as the door had shut behind Taylor, Alleyn
looked for the box described by Sergeant Roper. He found
it on a table underneath one of the windows. He lifted
the lid and saw that the box was empty. He looked closely

at the notice "LOADED," which was painted in block capitals. Alleyn gently let fall the lid and walked over to the french window. It was not locked. It looked across the end of the gravelled sweep and over the tops of the park trees right down Pen Cuckoo Vale to Chipping and beyond.

Alleyn was still tracing the course of the Vale Road as it wound through the valley when the squire walked in.

Jocelyn looked fresh and composed. Perhaps his eyes were a little more prominent than usual and his face a little less red, but he had the look of a man who has come to a decision, and there was a certain dignity and resolution in his manner.

"I'm glad to see you," he said as he shook hands. "Sit down, won't you? This is a terrible affair."

"Yes," said Alleyn. "It's both terrible and bewildering."

"Good God, I should think it was bewildering! It's the most damned complicated, incomprehensible business I ever want to come up against. I suppose Blandish has told you that in Dillington's absence I've got his job?"

"As Chief Constable? Yes, sir, he told me. That's partly my reason for calling on you."

The squire stared solemnly into the fire and said, "Quite."

"Blandish says you were present when the thing happened."

"Good God, yes. I don't know why it happened, though, or exactly how. As soon as we decided to call you in, Blandish was all for leaving things severely alone. Be damn' glad if you'd explain."

Alleyn explained. Jocelyn listened with his eyes very wide open and his mouth not quite closed.

"Beastly, underhand, ingenious sort of thing," he said. "Sounds more like a woman's work to me. I don't mean to say I think women are particularly underhand, you know; but when they do turn nasty, in my opinion they are inclined to turn crooked-nasty."

He laughed unexpectedly and uncomfortably.

"Yes," agreed Alleyn.

"Sort of inverse ratio or something, what?" added the squire dimly.

"That's it, sir. Now, the first thing we've got to tackle is the ownership of the Colt. I don't know——"

"Wait a bit," said Jocelyn. He stood up, drove his hands into his breeches pockets and walked over to the french windows.

"It's mine," he said.

Alleyn did not answer. The squire turned and looked at him. Seeing nothing but polite attention in Alleyn's face, he made a slight inarticulate noise, strode to the table under the window and opened the box.

"See for yourself," he said. "It's been in that box for the last twenty years. It was there last week. Now it's gone."

Alleyn joined him.

"Hellish unpleasant," said Jocelyn, "isn't it? I only found out this morning. My son was thinking about the business, it seems, and suddenly remembered that the Colt is always lying there, loaded. He came downstairs and looked, and then he came to my room and told me. I'm wondering if I ought not to resign my position as C.C."

"I shouldn't do that, sir," said Alleyn. "With any luck, we ought to be able to clear up the disappearance of the automatic."

"I feel pretty shaken up about it, I don't mind telling you."

"Of course you do. As a matter of fact, I've brought the Colt up here to show you. May I just fetch it? I can slip out to the car this way."

He went straight through the french windows and returned with his case, from which he took the automatic wrapped in a silk handkerchief.

"There's really no need for all these precautions," said Alleyn as he unwrapped it. "We've been all over it for prints and found none. My fingerprint man travels with half a laboratory in his kit. This thing's been dusted, peered at and photographed. It was evidently very thoroughly cleaned after it was put in position."

He laid the automatic in the box. It exactly fitted the indentation in the green baize lining.

"Seems a true bill," said Alleyn.

"How many rounds gone?" asked Jocelyn.

"Three," answered Alleyn.

"I fired the first two in 1917," said Jocelyn; "but I swear before God I'd nothing to do with the third."

"I hope you'll at least have the satisfaction of knowing who had," said Alleyn. "Did you write this notice, 'Loaded,' sir?"

"Yes," said Jocelyn. "What of it?"

Alleyn paused for a fraction of a second before he said, "Only routine, sir. I was going to ask if it always lay on top of the Colt."

"Certainly."

"Do you mind, sir, if I take this box away with me? There may be prints; but I'm afraid your housemaids are too well trained."

"I hope to God you find something. Do take it. I tell you, I'm nearly worried to death by the whole thing. It's a damned outrage that this blasted murderer——"

The door opened and Henry came into the room.

"This is my son," said Jocelyn.

II

From an upstairs window Henry had watched the arrival of Alleyn's car. Ever since his visit to the study at dawn and his subsequent interview with the abruptly awakened Jocelyn, Henry had been unable to think coherently, to stay still, or do anything definite. It struck him that he was in very much the same condition as he had been last night while waiting in the wings for the curtain to go up. He had telephoned to Dinah and arranged to see her at the rectory. He had prowled miserably about the house. At intervals he had tried to reassure his father, who had taken the news well, but was obviously very shaken. He had wondered what they would do with Eleanor when she chose to appear. She had gone straight to her room on her return from church, and was reported to be suffering from a headache.

When Jocelyn went downstairs to meet Alleyn, Henry's condition became several degrees more uncomfortable. He imagined his father making a bad job of the automatic story, getting himself further and further involved, and finally losing his temper. The Yard man would probably be maddeningly professional and heavy handed. Henry pictured him seated on the edge of one of the study chairs, staring at his father with sharp, inhuman eyes set in a massive policeman's face. "He will carry his bowler in with him and his boots will be intolerable," thought Henry. "A mammoth of officialdom!"

At last his own idleness became insupportable, and he ran downstairs and made for the study.

He could hear his father's voice raised, as it seemed, in protest. He opened the door and walked in.

"This is my son," said Jocelyn.

Henry's first thought was that this was some stranger, or perhaps a friend of Jocelyn's arrived with hideous inconvenience to visit them. He saw an extremely tall man, thin, and wearing good clothes, with an air of vague distinction.

"This is Mr. Alleyn," said Jocelyn, "from Scotland Yard."

"Oh," said Henry.

He shook hands, felt suddenly rather young, and sat down. His next impression was that he had seen Mr. Alleyn before. He found himself looking at Alleyn in terms of a pencil drawing. A drawing that might have been done by Durer with a sharp, hard pencil and then washed delicately with blue-blacks and ochres. "A grandee turned monk," thought Henry, "but retaining some amusing memories." And he sought to find a reason for this impression which seemed more like a recollection. The accents of the brows, the winged corners to the mouth and eyes, the sharp insistence of the skull—he had seen them all before.

"Henry!" said his father sharply.

Henry realised that Alleyn had been speaking.

"I'm so sorry," he said. "I'm afraid I didn't—— I'm very sorry."

"I was only asking," said Alleyn, "if you could help us with this business of the Colt. Your father says it was in its box last week. Can you get any nearer to it than that?"

"It was there on Friday afternoon at five," said Henry.

"How d'you know?" demanded the squire.

"You'll scarcely credit it," said Henry slowly, "but I've only just remembered. It was before you came down. I was here with Cousin Eleanor waiting for the others to come in for Dinah's run-through for words. They all arrived together, or within two or three minutes of each other. Somebody, Dr. Templett, I think, said something about the burglaries in Somerset last week. Posh Jimmy and his Boys, and all that. We wondered if they'd come this way. Miss Campanula talked about burglar alarms and what she'd do if she heard stealthy footsteps in the small hours. I told them about your war relic, Father, and we all looked at it. Mrs. Ross said she didn't think it was safe to have a loaded firearm lying about. I showed her the safety catch was on. Then we talked about something else. You came in and we started the rehearsal."

"That's a help," said Alleyn. "It narrows the time down to twenty-seven hours. That was Friday evening. Now, did either of you go to the hall on Friday afternoon?"

"I was hunting," said Jocelyn. "I didn't get back till five, in time for this run-through."

Alleyn looked at Henry.

"I went for a walk," said Henry. "I left at about half-past two. I remember now. It was half-past two."

"Did you go far?"

Henry looked straight before him.

"No. About half-way down to the church."

"How long were you away?"

"About two hours."

"You stopped somewhere, then?"

"Yes."

"Did you speak to anybody?"

"I met Dinah Copeland." Henry looked at his father. "*Not* by appointment. We talked. For some time. Then my cousin, Eleanor Prentice, came up. She had been to church. If it's of any interest, I remember hearing the church clock strike three when she came up. After that Dinah went back to the rectory and I struck up a path to Cloudyfold. I came home by the hill path."

"At what time did you get home?"

"Tea-time. About half-past four."

"Thank you. Now for Friday at five, when the company met here and you showed them the automatic. Did they all leave together?"

"Yes," said Henry.

"At what time?"

"Soon after six."

"Nobody was alone in here at any time before they left?"

"No. We rehearsed in here. They all went out by the french window. It saves trailing through the house."

"Yes. Is it always unlocked?"

"During the day it is."

"I lock it before we go to bed," said Jocelyn, "and fasten the shutters. Lock up the whole place."

"You did this on Friday night, sir?"

"Yes. I was in here reading, all Friday evening."

"Alone?"

"I was here part of the time," Henry said. "Something had gone wrong with one of Dinah's light plugs in the hall and I'd brought it up here to mend. I started in here, and then went to my own room where I had a screwdriver. I tried to ring Dinah up, but our telephone was out of order. A branch had fallen across it in Top Lane."

"I see. Now, how about yesterday? Any visitors?"

"Templett came up in the morning to borrow an old four-in-hand tie of mine," said Jocelyn. "He seemed to think he'd like to wear it in the play. He offered to look at my cousin's finger, but she wouldn't come down."

"She was afraid he'd tell her she couldn't play her filthy 'Venetian Suite,'" said Henry. "Do you admire the works of Ethelbert Nevin, Mr. Alleyn?"

"No," said Alleyn.

"They're gall and wormwood to me," said Henry gloomily. "And I suppose we'll have them here for the rest of our lives. Not that I like the bloody Prelude much better. Do you know what that Prelude is supposed to illustrate?"

"Yes, I think I do. Isn't it——"

"Burial," said Henry. "It's supposed to be a man buried alive. Bump, bump, bump on the coffin lid. Well, I suppose it's not so frightfully inappropriate."

"Not so frightfully," agreed Alleyn rather grimly. "Now, about yesterday's visitors."

But Henry and his father were rather vague about yesterday's visitors. The squire had driven into Great Chipping in the morning.

"And Miss Prentice?" asked Alleyn.

"Same thing. She went with us. She was in the hall all the morning. They were all there."

"All?"

"Well, not Templett," said Henry. "He called in here as we've described, at about ten o'clock, and my father gave him the tie. And a pretty ghastly affair it is, I may add."

"They were damn' smart at one time," said the squire hotly. "I remember I wore that tie——"

"Well, anyway," said Henry, "he got the tie. I didn't see him. I was hunting up my own clothes. We all went out soon after he'd gone. You saw him off, didn't you, Father?"

"Yes," said the squire. "Funny sort of fellow, Templett. First I knew about him was that Taylor told me he was in here and wanted the four-in-hand. I told Taylor to hunt it up and came down and found Templett. We talked for quite a long time and I'm blessed if, when I walked out with him to the car, poor little Mrs. Ross wasn't sitting there. Damn' funny thing to do," said Jocelyn, brushing up his moustache. "'Pon my word, I think the fellow wanted to keep her to himself."

Alleyn looked thoughtfully at him.

"How was Dr. Templett dressed?" he asked.

"What? I don't know. Yes, I think I do. Donegal tweed."

"An overcoat?"

"No."

"Bulging pockets?" asked Henry, with a grin at Alleyn.

"I don't think so. Why? Good Lord, you don't suppose he took my Colt, do you?"

"We've got to explore the possibilities, sir," said Alleyn.

"My God," said Jocelyn, "I suppose they're all under suspicion! What?"

"Including us," said Henry. "You know," he added, "theoretically one wouldn't put it past Templett. Eleanor's been poisonous about his alleged—notice how I protect myself, Mr. Alleyn—his alleged affair with Selia Ross."

"Good God!" shouted Jocelyn angrily, "haven't you got more sense than to talk like that, Henry? This is a damn' serious business, let me tell you, and you go blackening Mr. —Mr. Alleyn's mind against a man who——"

"I spoke theoretically, remember," said Henry. "I don't really suppose Templett is a murderer, and as for Mr. Alleyn's mind——"

"It doesn't blacken very readily," said Alleyn.

"And after all," Henry continued, "you might make out just as bad a case against me. If I thought I could murder Cousin Eleanor in safety I dare say I should undertake it. And I should think Mr. Copeland would feel sorely tempted after the way she's——"

"*Henry!*"

"But, my dear Father, Mr. Alleyn is going to hear all the local gossip if he hasn't done so already. Of course, Mr. Alleyn will suspect each of us in turn. Even dear Cousin Eleanor herself is not above suspicion. She may have infected her finger in the approved manner with a not too deadly toxin. Or made it up to look septic. Why not? There were the grease paints. True, she overdid it a bit, but that may have been pure artistry."

"Damn' dangerous twaddle," shouted Jocelyn. "It was hurting her like hell. I've known Eleanor since we were children, and I've never seen her cry before. She's a Jernigham."

"A good deal of it was straight-out annoyance at not being able to perform the 'Venetian Suite,' if you ask me. Tears of anger, they were, and the only sort you'll ever wring from Eleanor's eyes. Did she cry when they yawked out her gall-bladder? No. She's a Jernigham."

"Be quiet, sir," stormed Jocelyn.

123

" As far as I can see, the only one of us who could *not* have set the trap is poor old Idris Campanula. Oh, God!"

Alleyn, watching Henry, saw him turn very white before he moved away to the window.

"All right," Henry said to the landscape. "One's got to do something about it. Can't go on all day thinking of an old maid with her brains blown out. Might as well be funny in our hard, decadent modern way."

"I remember getting the same reaction in the war," said Alleyn vaguely. "As they say in vaudeville, 'I had to laugh.' It's not an uncommon rebound from shock."

"I don't suppose I was being anything but excessively commonplace," said Henry tartly.

III

"Then you don't know if anybody came while you were out yesterday morning?" asked Alleyn, after some considerable time spent in collecting the attention of the two Jernighams.

"I'll ask the servants," said Jocelyn importantly, and rang for Taylor.

As Alleyn expected, the evidence of the servants was completely inconclusive. Nobody had actually rung the door bells, but on the other hand anybody might have walked into the study and done anything. They corroborated Jocelyn and Henry's statements about their own movements and Taylor remembered seeing Miss Prentice come in at four on Friday afternoon. When the last maid had gone Alleyn asked if they had all been at Pen Cuckoo for some time.

"Lord, yes," said the squire. "Out of the question they should have anything to do with this affair. No motive, no opportunity."

"And not nearly enough sense," added Henry.

"In addition to which," said Alleyn, "they have provided each other with alibis for the whole day until they all went down in a solid body to the church hall at seven-thirty."

"I understand the entertainment provided," said Henry, "caused cook to vomit three times on the way home, and this morning, Father, I am told, the boot-boy heaved everything he had into the tops of your hunting boots."

"Well, that's a nice thing!" began Jocelyn crossly.

Alleyn said, "You told me it is out of the question that

124

the automatic could have been substituted for the water-
pistol during yesterday morning."

"Unless it was done under the noses of a bevy of Friendly
Young People and most of the company," said Henry.

"How about the afternoon?"

"It was locked up then and the key, instead of being
at the rectory as usual, was hidden, fancifully enough, behind
the outside lavatory," said Henry. "Dinah invented the place
of concealment, and announced it at rehearsal. Cousin
Eleanor was too put-out to object. Nobody but the members
of the cast knew about it. As far as I know, only Templett and
Mrs. Ross called in during the afternoon."

"What did you do?" asked Alleyn.

"I went for a walk on Cloudyfold. I met nobody," said
Henry, "and I can't prove I was there."

"Thank you," said Alleyn mildly. "What about you, sir?"

"I went round the stables with Rumbold, my agent,"
said Jocelyn, "and then I came in and went to sleep in the
library. I was waked by my cousin at five. We had a
sort of high tea at half-past six and went down to the hall
at a quarter to seven."

"All three of you?"

"Yes."

"And now, if you please," said Alleyn, "I should like
to see Miss Prentice."

CHAPTER FIFTEEN

Alleyn goes to Church

MISS PRENTICE came in looking, as Henry afterwards
told Dinah, as much like an early Christian martyr as her
clothes permitted. Alleyn, who had never been able to
conquer his proclivity for first impressions, took an instant dis-
like to her.

The squire's manner became nervously proprietary.

"Well, Eleanor," he said, "here you are. We're sorry
to bring you down. May I introduce Mr. Alleyn? He's looking into this business for us."

Miss Prentice gave Alleyn a forbearing smile and a hand
like a fish. She sat on the only uncomfortable chair in the
room.

125

"I shall try not to bother you too long," Alleyn began.

"It's only," said Miss Prentice, in a voice that suggested the presence of Miss Campanula's body in the room, "it's only that I hope to go to church at eleven."

"It's a few minutes after ten. I think you'll have plenty of time."

"I'll drive you down," said Henry.

"Thank you dear, I think I should like to walk."

"I'm going, anyway," said Jocelyn.

Miss Prentice smiled at him. It was an approving, understanding sort of smile, and Alleyn thought it would have kept him away from church for the rest of his life.

"Well, Miss Prentice," he said, "we are trying to see daylight through a mass of strange circumstances. There is no reason why you shouldn't be told that Miss Campanula was shot by the automatic that is kept in a box in this room."

"Oh, Jocelyn!" said Miss Prentice, "how terrible! You know, dear, we *have* said it wasn't really quite advisable, haven't we?"

"You needn't go rubbing it in, Eleanor."

"Why wasn't it advisable," asked Henry. "Had you foreseen, Cousin Eleanor, that somebody might pinch the Colt and rig it up in a piano as a lethal booby-trap?"

"Henry dear, please! We just said sometimes that perhaps it wasn't very wise."

"Are you employing the editorial or the regal 'we'?"

Alleyn said, "One minute, please. Before we go any further I think, as a matter of pure police routine, I would like to see your finger, Miss Prentice."

"Oh, dear! It's very painful. I'm afraid——"

"If you would rather Dr. Templett unwrapped it——"

"Oh, no. No."

"If you will allow me, I think I can do a fairly presentable bandage."

Miss Prentice raised her eyes to Alleyn's and a very peculiar expression visited her face, a mixture of archness and submission. She advanced her swathed hand with an air of timidity. He undid the bandage very quickly and lightly and exposed the finger with a somewhat battered stall drawn over a closer bandage. He peeled off the stall and completely unwrapped the finger. It was inflamed, discoloured and swollen.

"A nasty casualty," said Alleyn. "You should have it dressed again. Dr. Templett——"

"I do not wish Dr. Templett to touch it."

126

" But he could give you fresh bandages and a stall that has not been torn."

" I have a first-aid box. Henry, would you mind, dear?"

Henry was despatched for the first-aid box. Alleyn redressed the finger deftly. Miss Prentice watched him with a sort of eager concentration, never lowering her gaze from his face.

" How beautifully you manage," she said.

" I hope it will serve. You should have a sling, I fancy. Do you want the old stall?"

She shook her head. He dropped it in his pocket and was startled when she uttered a little coy murmur of protestation, for all the world as if he had taken her finger-stall from some motive of gallantry.

" You deserve a greater reward," she said.

" Lummy!" thought Alleyn in considerable embarrassment. He said, " Miss Prentice, I am trying to get a sort of timetable of everybody's movements from Friday afternoon until the time of the tragedy. Do you mind telling me where you were on Friday afternoon?"

" I was in church."

" All the afternoon?"

" Oh, no," said Eleanor softly.

" Between what hours were you there, please?"

" I arrived at two."

" Do you know when the service was over?"

" It was not a service," said Miss Prentice with pale forbearance.

" You were there alone?"

" It was confession," said Henry impatiently.

" Oh, I see." Alleyn paused. " Was anybody else there besides yourself and—and your confessor?"

" No. I passed poor Idris on my way out."

" When was that?"

" I think I remember the clock struck half-past two."

" Good. And then?"

" I went home."

" Directly?"

" I took the top lane."

" The lane that comes out by the church?"

" Yes."

" Did you pass the parish hall?"

" Yes."

" You didn't go in?"

" No."

"Was any one there, do you think?"

"The doors were shut," said Miss Prentice. "I think the girls only went in for an hour."

"Were the keys in their place of concealment on Friday?" asked Alleyn.

Miss Prentice instantly looked grieved and shocked. Henry grinned broadly and said, "There's only one key. I don't know if it was there on Friday. I think it was. Dinah would know about that. Some of the committee worked there on Friday, as Cousin Eleanor says, but none of us. They may have returned the key to the rectory. I only went half-way down."

"At what part of the top lane on Friday afternoon did you meet Henry Jernigham and Miss Copeland, Miss Prentice?"

Alleyn heard her draw in her breath and saw her turn white. She looked reproachfully at Henry and said:

"I'm afraid I don't remember."

"I do," said Henry. "It was at the sharp bend above the foot-bridge. You came round the corner from below."

She bent her head. Henry looked as if he dared her to speak.

"There's something damned unpleasant about this," thought Alleyn.

He said, "How long did you spend in conversation with the others before you went on to Pen Cuckoo?"

An unlovely red stained her cheeks.

"Not long."

"About five minutes, I should think," said Henry.

"And you arrived home, when?"

"I should think about half-past three. I really don't know."

"Did you go out again on Friday, Miss Prentice?"

"No," said Miss Prentice.

"You were about the house? I'm sorry to worry you like this, but you see I really do want to know exactly what everybody did on Friday."

"I was in my room," she said. "There are two little offices that Father Copeland has given us for use after confession."

"Oh, I see," said Alleyn, in some embarrassment.

II

Alleyn waded on. Miss Prentice's air of patient martyrdom increased with every question, but he managed to get a

128

good deal of information from her. On Saturday, the day of the performance, she had spent the morning in the parish hall with all the other workers. She left when the others left, and, with Jocelyn and Henry, returned to Pen Cuckoo for lunch. She had not gone out again until the evening but had spent the afternoon in her sitting-room. She remembered waking the squire at tea-time. After tea she returned to her room.

"During yesterday morning you were all at the hall?" said Alleyn. "Who got there first?"

"Dinah Copeland, I should think," said Jocelyn promptly. "She was there when we arrived. She was always the first."

Alleyn made a note of it and went on, "Did any of you notice the position and appearance of the piano?"

They all looked very solemn at the mention of the piano.

"I think I did," said Miss Prentice in a low voice. "It was as it was for the performance. The girls had evidently arranged the drapery and pot-plants on Friday. I looked at it rather particularly as I was—I was to play it."

"Good Lord!" ejaculated the squire, "you were strumming on the damned thing. I remember now."

"Jocelyn, dear, please! I did just touch the keys, I believe, with my right hand. Not my left," said Miss Prentice with her most patient smile.

"This was yesterday morning, wasn't it?" said Alleyn, "Now, please, Miss Prentice, try to remember. Did you use the soft pedal at all when you tried the piano?"

"Oh, dear, now I wonder. Let me see. I did sit down for a moment. I expect I did use the soft pedal. I always think soft playing is so much nicer. Yes, I should think almost without doubt I used the soft pedal."

"Was anybody by the piano at the time?" asked Alleyn.

Miss Prentice turned a reproachful gaze on him.

"Idris," she whispered. "Miss Campanula."

"Here, wait a bit," shouted Jocelyn. "I've remembered the whole thing. Eleanor, you sat down and strummed about with your hand and she came up and asked you why you didn't try with your left to see how it worked."

"So she did," said Henry softly. "And so, of course, she would."

"And you got up and went away," said the squire. "Old Camp—well, Idris Campanula—gave a sort of laugh and dumped herself down and——"

"And away went the Prelude!" cried Henry. "You're quite right, Father. Pom. *Pom!* POM!! And then down with the soft pedal. That's it, sir," he added, turning to Alleyn. "I watched her. I'll swear it."

"Right," said Alleyn. "We're getting on. This was yesterday morning. At what time?"

"Just before we packed up," said Henry. "About midday."

"And—I know we've been over this before, but it's important—you all left together?"

"Yes," said Henry. "We three drove off in the car. I remember that I heard Dinah slam the back door just as we started. They were all out by then."

"And none of you returned until the evening? I see. When you arrived at a quarter to seven you found Miss Copeland there."

"Yes," said Jocelyn.

"Where was she?"

"On the stage with her father, putting flowers in vases."

"Was the curtain drawn?"

"Yes."

"What did you all do?"

"I went to my dressing-room," said the squire.

"I stayed in the supper-room and talked to Dinah," said Henry. "Her father was on the stage. After a minute or two I went to my dressing-room."

"Here!" ejaculated Jocelyn, and glared at Miss Prentice. "What, dear?"

"Those girls were giggling about in front of the hall. I wonder if any of them got up to any hanky panky with the piano."

"Oh, my dear Father!" said Henry.

"They were strictly forbidden to touch the instrument," said Miss Prentice. "Ever since Cissie Drury did such damage."

"How long was it before the others arrived? Dr. Templett and Mrs. Ross?" asked Alleyn.

"They didn't get down until half-past seven," said Henry. "Dinah was in a frightful stew and so were we all. She rang up Mrs. Ross's cottage in the end. It took ages to get through. The hall telephone's an extension from the rectory and we rang for a long time before anybody at the rectory answered and at last, when it was connected with Mrs. Ross's house, there was no reply, so we knew she'd left."

"She came with Dr. Templett?"

"Oh, yes," murmured Miss Prentice.

"The telephone is in your dressing-room, isn't it, Mr. Jernigham?"

"Mine and Henry's. We shared. We were all there round the telephone."

"Yes," said Alleyn. He looked from one face to another. Into the quiet room there dropped the Sunday morning sound of chiming bells. Miss Prentice rose.

"Thank you so much," said Alleyn. "I think I've got a general idea of the two days now. On Friday afternoon Miss Prentice went to church, Mr. Jernigham hunted, Mr. Henry Jernigham went for a walk. On her return from church, Miss Prentice met Mr. Henry Jernigham and Miss Copeland, who had themselves met by chance in the top lane. That was at about three. Mr. Henry Jernigham returned home by a circuitous route, Miss Prentice by the top lane. Miss Prentice went to her room. At five you had your reheasal for words in this room, and everybody saw the automatic. You all three dined at home and remained at home. It was also on Friday afternoon that some helpers worked for about an hour at the hall, but apparently they had finished at two-thirty when Miss Prentice passed that way. On Saturday (yesterday) morning Dr. Templett and Mrs. Ross called here for the tie. You all went down to the hall and you, sir, drove to Great Chipping. You all returned for lunch. By this time the piano was in position with the drapery and aspidistras on top. In the afternoon Mr. Henry Jernigham walked up Cloudyfold and back. As far as we know, only Dr. Templett and Mrs. Ross visited the hall yesterday afternoon. At a quarter to seven you all arrived there for the performance."

"Masterly, sir," said Henry.

"Oh, I've written it all down," said Alleyn. "My memory's hopeless."

"What about your music, Miss Prentice? When did you put it on the piano?"

"Oh, on Saturday morning, of course."

"I see. You had it here until then?"

"Oh, no," said Miss Prentice. "Not *here*, you know."

"Then, where?"

"In the hall, naturally."

"It lives in the hall?"

"Oh, no," she said opening her own eyes very wide, "why should it?"

"I'm sure I don't know. When did you take it to the hall?"

131

"On Thursday night for the dress-rehearsal. Of course."

"I see. You played for the dress-rehearsal?"

"Oh, no."

"For the love of heaven!" ejaculated Jocelyn. "Why the dickens can't you come to the point, Eleanor. She wanted to play on Thursday night but her finger was like a bad sausage," he explained to Alleyn.

Miss Prentice gave Alleyn her martyred smile, shook her head slightly at the bandaged finger, and looked restlessly at the clock.

"H'm," she said unhappily.

"Well," said Alleyn. "The music was in the hall from Thursday onwards and you put it in the rack yesterday morning. And none of you went into the hall before the show last night. Good."

Miss Prentice said, "Well—I think I shall just—Jocelyn, dear, that's the first bell, isn't it?"

"I'm sorry," said Alleyn, "but I should like, if I may, to have a word with you, Miss Prentice. Perhaps you will let me drive you down. Or if not——"

"Oh," said Miss Prentice, looking very flurried, "thank you. I think I should prefer—I'm afraid I really can't——"

"Cousin Eleanor," said Henry. "I will drive you down, Father will drive you down, or Mr. Alleyn will drive you down. You might even drive yourself down. It is only twenty-five to eleven now and it doesn't take more than ten minutes to *walk* down, so you can easily spare Mr. Alleyn a quarter of an hour."

"I'm afraid I do fuss rather, don't I, but you see I like to have a few quiet moments before——"

"Now, look here, Eleanor," said the squire warmly, "this is an investigation into murder. Good Lord, it's your best friend that's been killed, my dear girl, and when we're right in the thick of it, damme, you want to go scuttling off to church."

"*Jocelyn!*"

"Come on, Father," said Henry. "We'll leave Mr. Alleyn a fair field."

III

"——you see," said Alleyn, "I don't think you quite realise your own position. Hadn't it occurred to you that you were the intended victim?"

"It is such a dreadful thought," said Miss Prentice.

132

"I know it is, but you've got to face it. There's a murderer abroad in your land and as far as one can see his first coup hasn't come off. It's been a fantastic and horrible failure. For your own, if not for the public's good, you must realise this. Surely you want to help us."

"I believe," said Miss Prentice, "that our greatest succour lies in prayer."

"Yes," Alleyn said slowly, "I can appreciate that. But my job is to ask questions, and I do ask you, most earnestly, if you believe that you have a bitter enemy among this small group of people."

"I cannot believe it of any one."

Alleyn looked at her with something very like despair. She had refused to sit down after they were alone, but fidgeted about in the centre of the room, looked repeatedly down the Vale, and was thrown into a fever of impatience by the call of the church bells.

A towering determined figure, he stood between Eleanor and the window, and concentrated his will on her. He thought of his mind as a pin-pointed weapon and he drove it into hers.

"Miss Prentice. Please look at me."

Her glance wavered. Her pale eyes travelled reluctantly to his. Deliberately silent until he felt he had got her whole attention, he held her gaze with his own. Then he spoke. "I may not try to force information from you. You are a free agent. But think for a moment of the position. You have escaped death by an accident. If you had persisted in playing last night you would have been shot dead. I am going to repeat a list of names to you. If there is anything between any one of these persons and yourself which, if I knew of it, might help me to see light, ask yourself if you should not tell me of it. These are the names:

"Mr. Jocelyn Jernigham?

"His son, Henry Jernigham?

"The rector, Mr. Copeland?"

"No!" she cried, "no! Never! Never!"

"His daughter, Dinah Copeland?

"Mrs. Ross?"

He saw the pale eyes narrow a little.

"Dr. Templett?"

She stared at him like a mesmerised rabbit.

"Well, Miss Prentice, what of Mrs. Ross and Dr. Templett?"

"I can accuse nobody. Please let me go."

"Have you ever had a difference with Mrs. Ross?"

"I hardly speak to Mrs. Ross."

"Or with Dr. Templett?"

"I prefer not to discuss Dr. Templett," she said breathlessly.

"At least," said Alleyn, "he saved your life. He dissuaded you from playing."

"I believe God saw fit to use him as an unworthy instrument."

Alleyn opened his mouth to speak and thought better of it. At last he said, "In your own interest, tell me this. Has Mrs. Ross cause to regard you as her enemy?"

She wetted her lips and answered him with astounding vigour:

"I have thought only as every decent creature who sees her must think. Before she could silence the voice of reproach she would have to murder a dozen Christian souls."

"Of whom Miss Campanula was one?"

She stared at him vacantly and then he saw she had understood him.

"That's why he wouldn't let me play," she whispered.

On his way back, Alleyn turned off the Vale Road and drove up past the church to the hall. Seven cars were drawn up outside St. Giles and he noticed a stream of villagers turning in at the lych-gate.

"Full house, this morning," thought Alleyn grimly. And suddenly he pulled up by the hall, got out, and walked back to the church.

"The devil takes a holiday," he thought, and joined in with the stream.

He managed to elude the solicitations of a sidesman and slip into a seat facing the aisle in the back row where he sat with his long hands clasped round his knee. His head looked remotely austere in the cold light from the open doors.

Winton St. Giles is a beautiful church and Alleyn, overcoming that first depression inseparable from the ecclesiastical smell, and the sight of so many people with decorous faces, found pleasure in the tranquil solidity of stone shaped into the expression of devotion. The single bell stopped. The organ rumbled vaguely for three minutes, the congregation stood, and Mr. Copeland followed his choir into church.

Like everybody else who saw him for the first time, Alleyn was startled by the rector's looks. The service was a choral Eucharist and he wore a cope, a magnificent vestment that shone like a blazon in the candle light. His silver hair, the incredible perfection of his features, his extreme pallor, and great height, made Alleyn think of an actor admirably suited for the performance of priestly parts. But when the time came for the short sermon, he found evidence of a simple and unaffected mind with no great originality. It was an unpretentious sermon touched with sincerity. The rector spoke of prayers for the dead and told his listeners that there was nothing in the teaching of their church that forbade such prayers. He invited them to petition God for the peace of all souls departed in haste or by violence, and he commended meditation and a searching of their own hearts lest they should harbour anger or resentment.

As the service went on, Alleyn looking down the aisle, saw a dark girl with so strong a resemblance to the rector that he knew she must be Dinah Copeland. Her eyes were fixed on her father and in them Alleyn read anxiety and affection.

Miss Prentice was easily found, for she sat next the aisle in the front row. She rose and fell like a ping-pong ball on a water jet, sinking in solitary genuflexions and crossing herself like a sort of minor soloist. The squire sat beside her. The back of his neck wore an expression of indignation and discomfort, being both scarlet and rigid. Much nearer to Alleyn, and also next the aisle, sat a woman whom he recognised as probably the most fashionable figure in the congregation. Detectives are trained to know about clothes and Alleyn knew hers were impeccable. She wore them like a Frenchwoman. He could only see the thin curve of her cheek and an immaculate wing of straw-coloured hair, but presently, as if aware of his gaze, she turned her head and he saw her face. It was thinnish and alert, beautifully made-up, hard, but with a look of amused composure. The pale eyes looked into his and widened. She paused with unmistakable deliberation for a split second, and then turned away. Her luxuriously gloved hand went to her hair.

"That was once known as the glad eye," thought Alleyn. Under cover of a hymn he slipped out of church.

He crossed the lane to the hall. Sergeant Roper was on duty at the gate and came smartly to attention.

"Well, Roper, how long have you been here?"

"I relieved Constable Fife an hour ago, sir. The super sent him along soon after you left. About seven-thirty, sir."

"Anybody been about?"

"Boys," said Roper, "hanging round like wasps and as bold as brass with that young Biggins talking that uppish you'd have thought he was as good as the murderer, letting on as he was as full of inside knowledge as the Lord Himself, not meaning it in the way of blasphemy. I subdued him, however, and his mother bore him off to church. Mr. Bathgate took a photograph of the building, and asked me to say, sir, that he'd look back in a minute or two in case you were here."

"I dare say," grunted Alleyn.

"And the doctor came along, too, in a proper taking on. Seems he left one of his knives for slashing open the body in the hall last night, and he wanted to fetch her out for to lay bare the youngest Cain's toe. I went in with the doctor but she was nowhere to be found, no not even in the pockets of his suit which seemed a strange casual spot for a naked blade, no doubt so deadly sharp as 'twould penetrate the very guts of a man in a flash. Doctor was proper put about by the loss and made off without another word."

"I see. Any one else?"

"Not a living soul," said Roper. "I reckon rector will have brought this matter up in his sermon, sir. The man couldn't well avoid it, seeing it's his job to put a holy construction on the face of disaster."

"He did just touch on it," Alleyn admitted.

"A ticklish affair and you may be sure one that he didn't greatly relish, being a timid sort of chap."

"I think I'll have a look round the outside of the hall, Roper."

"Very good, sir."

Alleyn wandered round the hall on the lane side, his eyes on the gravelled path. Roper looked after him wistfully until he disappeared at the back. He came to the rear door, saw nothing of interest, and turned to the outhouses. Here, in a narrow gap between two walls, he found a nail where he supposed the key had hung yesterday. He continued his search round the far side of the building and came at last to a window, where he stopped.

He remembered that they had shut this window last night before they left the hall. It was evidently the only one that was ever opened. The others were firmly sealed in accumulated grime. Alleyn looked at the wall underneath it. The surface of the weathered stone was grazed in many places, and on the ground he discovered freshly detached chips. Between the gravelled path and the side of the building was a narrow strip of grass. This bore a rectangular impress that the night's heavy rain had softened but not obliterated. Within the margin of the impress he found traces of several large footprints and two smaller ones. Alleyn returned to a sort of lumber-shed at the back and fetched an old box. The edges at the open end bore traces of damp earth. He took it to the impression and found that it fitted exactly. It also covered the lower grazes on the wall. He examined the box minutely, peering into the joints and cracks in the rough wood. Presently he began to whistle. He took a pair of tweezers from his pocket, and along the edge, from a crack where the wood had split, he pulled out a minute red scrap of some springy substance. He found two more shreds caught in the rough surface of the wood, and on a projecting nail. He put them in an envelope and sealed it. Then he replaced the box. He measured the height from the box to the window-sill.

"Good-morning," said a voice behind him. "You must be a detective."

Alleyn glanced up and saw Nigel Bathgate leaning over the stone fence that separated the parish hall grounds from a path on the far side.

"What a fascinating life yours must be," continued Nigel.

Alleyn did not reply. Inadvertently he released the catch on the steel tape. It flew back into the container.

"Pop goes the weasel," said Nigel.

"Hold your tongue," said Alleyn, mildly, "and come here."

Nigel vaulted over the wall.

"Take this tape for me. Don't touch the box if you can help it."

"It would be pleasant to know why."

"Five-foot-three from the box to the sill," said Alleyn. "Too far for Georgie, and in any case we know he didn't. That's funny."

" Screamingly."

" Go to the next window, Bathgate, and raise yourself by the sill. If you can."

" Only if you tell me why."

" I will in a minute. Please be quick. I want to get this over before the hosts of the godly are upon us. Can you do it?"

" Listen, Chief. This is your lucky day. Look at these biceps. Three months ago I was puny like you. By taking my self-raising course——"

Nigel reached up to the window sill, gave a prodigious heave, and cracked the crown of his head smartly on the sill.

" Great strength rings the bell," said Alleyn. " Now try and get foothold."

" Blast and damn you!" said Nigel, scraping at the wall with his shoes.

" That will do. I'm going into the hall. When I call out, I want you to repeat this performance. You needn't crack your head again."

Alleyn went into the hall, forced open the second window two inches, and went over to the piano.

" Now!"

The shape of Nigel's head and shoulders rose up behind the clouded glass. His collar and tie appeared in the gap. Alleyn had a fleeting impression of his face.

" All right."

Nigel disappeared and Alleyn rejoined him.

" Are you playing Peep Bo or what?" asked Nigel sourly.

" Something of the sort. I saw you all right. Yes," continued Alleyn, examining the wall. " The lady used the box. We will preserve the box. Dear me."

" At least you might say I can come down."

" I'm so sorry. Of course. And your head?"

" Bloody."

" But unbowed, I feel sure. Now I'll explain."

CHAPTER SIXTEEN

The Top Lane Incident

ALLEYN GAVE Nigel his explanation as they walked up Top Lane by the route Dinah had taken on Friday afternoon. They walked briskly, their heads bent, and a look of solemn absorption on their faces. In a few minutes they crossed a rough bridge and reached a sharp turn in the lane.

"It was here," said Alleyn, "that Henry Jernigham met Dinah Copeland on Friday afternoon. It was here that Eleanor Prentice found them on her return from the confessional. I admit that I am curious about their encounters, Bathgate. Miss Prentice came upon them at three, yet she left the church at half-past two. Young Jernigham says he was away two hours. He left home at two-thirty. It can take little more than five minutes to come down here from Pen Cuckoo. They must have been together almost half an hour before Miss Prentice arrived."

"Perhaps they are in love."

"Perhaps they are. But there is something that neither Miss Prentice nor Master Henry cares to remember when one speaks of this meeting. They turn pale. Henry becomes sardonic and Miss Prentice sends out waves of sanctimonious disapproval in the manner of a polecat."

"What can you mean?"

"It doesn't matter. She left the church at three. She only spent five minutes here with the others and yet she did not reach Pen Cuckoo till after four. There seems to be a lot of time to spare. Henry struck up this path to the hill-top. Miss Copeland returned by the way we have come, Miss Prentice went on to Pen Cuckoo. I have a picture of three specks of humanity running together, exploding, and flying apart."

"There are a hundred explanations."

"For their manner of meeting and parting? Yes, I dare say there are, but not so many explanations for their agitation when the meeting is discussed. Say that she surprised them in an embrace, Master Henry might feel foolish at the recollection, but why should Miss Prentice go white and trembly?"

"She's an old maid, isn't she? Perhaps it shocked her."

"It may have given her a shock."

Alleyn was searching the wet lane.

"The rain last night was the devil. This great bough must have been blown down quite recently. Master Henry told me that their telephone was dumb on Friday night. He said it was broken by a falling bough in Top Lane. There are the wires and it almost follows as the night the day that this is the bough. It's protected the ground. Wait, I believe we've struck a little luck."

139

They moved the still unwithered bough.

"Yes. See here, Bathgate, here is where they stood. How much more dramatic footprints can be than the prints of hands. Look, here are Dinah Copeland's, if indeed they are hers, coming round the bend into the protection of the bank. The ground was soft but not too wet. Coming downhill we pick *his* prints up, as they march out of the sodden lane into the lee of the bank and overlapping trees. Surface water has seeped into them but there they are. And here, where the bough afterwards fell, they met."

"And what a meeting!" ejaculated Nigel, looking at the heavy impressions of overlapping prints.

"A long meeting. Yes, and a lover's meeting. She looks a nice girl. I hope Master Henry——"

He broke off.

"Here we are, by George. Don't come too far. Eleanor Prentice must have rounded the corner, taken two steps or so, and stopped dead. There are her feet planted side by side. She stood for some time in this one place, facing the others and then—what happened? Ordinary conversation? No, I don't think so. I'll have to try and get it from the young ones. *She* won't tell me. Yes, there are her shoes, no doubt of it. Black-calf with pointed toes and low heels. Church hen's shoes. She was wearing them this morning."

Alleyn squatted by the two solitary prints, reached out a long finger and touched the damp earth. Then he looked up at Nigel.

"Well, it's proved one thing," he said.

"What?"

"If these are Eleanor Prentice's prints, and I think they are, it wasn't Eleanor Prentice who tried to see in at the window of the parish hall. Wait here, will you, Bathgate? I'm going down to the car for my stuff. We'll have a cast of these prints."

II

At half-past twelve Alleyn and Nigel arrived at the Red House, Chipping. An elderly parlourmaid told them that Mr. Fox was still there, and showed them into a Victorian drawing-room which, in the language of brassware and modernish silk Japanese panels, spoke unhappily of the late General Campanula's service in the East. It was an ugly room, over-furnished and unfriendly. Fox was seated at a writing desk in the window and before him were many neat stacks of papers. He rose and looked placidly at them over the tops of his glasses.

"Hullo, Brer Fox," said Alleyn. "How the hell are you getting on?"

"Fairly comfortably, thank you, sir. Good-morning, Mr. Bathgate."

"Good-morning, Inspector."

"What have you got there?" asked Alleyn.

"A number of letters, sir, none of them very helpful."

"What about that ominous wad of foolscap, you old devil? Come on, now; it's the will, isn't it?"

"Well, it is," said Fox.

He handed it to Alleyn and waited placidly while he read it.

"This was a wealthy woman," said Alleyn.

"How wealthy?" demanded Nigel, "and what has she done with it?"

"Nothing that's for publication."

"All right, all right."

"She's left fifty thousand. Thirty of them go to the Reverend Walter Copeland of Winton St. Giles in recognition of his work as a parish priest and in deep gratitude for his spiritual guidance and unfailing wisdom. Lummy! He is to use this money as he thinks best but she hopes that he will not give it all away to other people. Fifteen thousand to her dear friend, Eleanor Jernigham Prentice, four thousand to Eric Campanula, son of William Campanula, and second cousin to the testatrix. Last heard of in Nairobi, Kenya. A stipulation that the said four thousand be invested by Miss Campanula's lawyers, Messrs. Waterworth, Waterworth and Biggs, and the beneficiary to receive the interest at their hands. The testatrix adds the hope that the beneficiary will not spend the said interest on alcoholic beverages or women, and will think of her and mend his ways. One thousand to be divided among the servants. Dated May 21st, 1938."

"There was a note enclosed dated May 21st of this year," said Fox. "Here it is, sir."

Alleyn read aloud with one eyebrow raised:

"To all whom it may concern. This is my last Will and Testament so there's no need for anybody to go poking about my other papers for another. I should like to say that the views expressed in reference to the principal beneficiary are the views I hold at the moment. If I could add anything to this appreciation of his character to make it more emphatic, I would do so. There have been disappointments, and friends who have failed me, but I am a lonely woman and see no reason to alter my Will. Idris Campanula."

"She seems to have been a very outspoken lady, doesn't she?" asked Fox.

"She does. That's a nasty jab in the eye for her dear friend, Eleanor Prentice," said Alleyn.

"Well, now," said Nigel briskly, "do you think either of these two have murdered her? You always say, Alleyn, that money is the prime motive."

"I don't say so in this instance," Alleyn said. "It may be, but I don't think it is. Well, there we are, Fox. We must get hold of the Waterworths and Mr. Biggs, before they read about it in the papers."

"I've rung them up, Mr. Alleyn. The parlourmaid knew Mr. Waterworth senior's private address."

"Excellent, Fox. Anything else?"

"There's the chauffeur, Gibson. I think you might like to talk to him."

"All right. Produce Gibson."

Fox went out and returned with Miss Campanula's chauffeur. He wore his plum-coloured breeches and shining gaiters and had the air of having just crammed himself into his tunic.

"This is Gibson, sir," said Fox. "I think the Chief Inspector would like to hear about this little incident on Friday afternoon, Mr. Gibson."

"Good-morning," said Alleyn. "What's the incident?"

"It concerns deceased's visit to church at two-thirty, sir," Fox explained. "It seems that she called at the hall on her way down."

"Really?" said Alleyn.

"Not to say called, sir," said Gibson. "Not in a manner of speaking, seeing she didn't go in."

"Let's hear about it?"

"She used to go regular, you see, sir, to the confessing affair. About every three weeks. Well, Friday, she orders the car and we go down, getting there a bit early. She says, drive on to the hall, so I did and she got out and went to the front door. She'd been in a good mood all the morning. Pleased at going down to church and all, but soon as I saw her rattling the front door I knew one of her tantrums was coming on. As I was explaining to Mr. Fox, sir, she was a lady that was given to tantrums."

" Yes."

" I watched her. Rattle, rattle, rattle! And then I heard her shouting. 'Who's in there! Let me in!' I thought I could hear the piano, too. Off she goes round to the back. I turned the car. When I looked out again she had come round the other side, the one away from the lane. Her face was red, and, Gawd help us, I thought, here we go, and sure enough she starts yelling out for me to come. 'There's someone in there behaving very suspicious,' she says. 'Take a look through that open window.' I hauled myself up and there wasn't a blooming thing to be seen. 'Where's the piano?' Well, I told her. The piano was there right enough down on the floor by the stage. I knew she was going to tell me to go to the rectory for the key, when I see Miss Prentice coming out of the church. So I drew her attention to Miss Prentice and she was off like a scalded cat, across the lane and down to the church. I followed along slow, it's only a couple of chain or so, and pulled up outside the church."

" What about the box?"

" Pardon, sir?"

" Didn't you get a box out of the shed at the back of the hall for Miss Campanula to stand on in order to look through the window?"

" No, sir. No."

Nigel grinned and whistled softly.

" All right," said Alleyn. " It's no matter. Anything else?"

" No, sir. Miss Prentice come out looking very upset, passed me, and went up the lane. I reckon she was going home by Top Lane."

" Miss Prentice looked upset?"

" She did so, sir. It's my belief Mr. Copeland had sent her off with a flea in her ear, if you'll excuse the liberty."

" Did you watch her go? Look after her, I mean?"

" No, sir, I didn't like, seeing she was looking so queer."

" D'you mean she was crying?"

" She wasn't actually that way, sir. Not shedding tears or anything, but she looked queer. Upset, very down in the mouth."

" You don't know if she went to the hall?"

" No, sir, I can't say. I did have a look in the driving mirror and I saw her cross the road as soon as she'd gone a few steps, but she'd do that, anyway, sir, very likely."

" Gibson, can you remember exactly how the piano looked? Describe it for me as accurately as you possibly can."

Gibson scraped his jaw with his mechanic's hand.

"Down on the floor where it was in the evening, sir. Stool in front of it. No music on it. Er—let's see now. It wasn't quite the same. No, that's right. It *was* kind of different."

Alleyn waited.

"I got it," said Gibson loudly. "Yes, by gum, I got it." "Yes?"

"Those pot plants was on the edge of the stage and the top of the piano was open."

"Ah," said Alleyn, "I hoped so."

III

"What's the inner significance of all that?" demanded Nigel when Gibson had gone. "What about this box? Is it the one you had under the window?"

"It is." Alleyn spoke to Fox. "At some time since Gibson hauled himself up to look in at the window, somebody has put an open box there and stood on it. It's left a deep rectangular scar overlapping one of Gibson's prints. I found the box in the outhouse. It wasn't young Georgie. He used the door, and anyway the window would have been above his eye-level. The only footprints are Miss C.'s and some big ones, no doubt Gibson's. They trod on the turf. The box expert must have come later, perhaps on Saturday and only stood on the gravel. We'll try the box for prints, but I don't think we'll do any good. When I heard Gibson's story I expected we would find that Miss Campanula had used it. Evidently not. It's a tedious business but we'll have to clear it up. Have you said much to the maids?"

"It looks as if deceased was a proper tartar," said Fox. "I've heard enough to come to the conclusion. Mary, the parlourmaid, you saw just now, sir, seems to have acted as a kind of lady's-maid as well. Miss Campanula had a very open way with Mary when she was in the mood. Surprising some of the things she used to tell her."

"For instance, Brer Fox?"

"Well, Mr. Alleyn, to Mary's way of thinking, Miss C. was a bit queer on the subject of Mr. Copeland. Potty on him is the way Mary puts it. She says that about the time the rector walks through the village of a morning, deceased used to go and hang about under one pretext or another until she could meet him."

144

"Oh, Lord!" said Alleyn distastefully.

"Yes, it's kind of pitiful, sir, isn't it? Mary says she'd dress herself up, very particularly, walk up to Chipping, and go into the little shop. She'd keep the woman there talking, while she bought some trifle or another, and all the time she'd be looking through the glass door. If the rector showed up, Miss Campanula would be off like lightning. She was a very uncertain tempered lady, and when things went wrong she used to scare the servants by the wild way she talked, saying she'd do something violent, and so on."

"This is getting positively Russian," said Alleyn, "and remarkably depressing. Go on."

"It wasn't so bad till Miss Prentice came. She had it her own way in the parish till then. But Miss Prentice seems to have put her in the shade, as you might say. Miss Prentice beat her to all the top places. She's president of this Y.P.F.C. affair and Miss C. was only secretary. Same sort of thing with the Girl Guides."

"She's never a Girl Guide!" Alleyn ejaculated.

"Seems like it, and she beats Miss C. hands down, teaching the kids knots and camp cookery. Got herself decorated with badges and so on. Started at the bottom and swotted it all up. The local girls didn't fancy it much, but she kind of got round them; and when Lady Appleby gave up the Commissioner's job Miss Prentice got it. Same sort of thing at the Women's Circle and all the other local affairs. Miss P. was too smart for Miss C. They were as thick as thieves; but Mary says sometimes Miss C. would come back from a Friendly meeting or something of the sort, and the things she'd say about Miss Prentice were surprising."

"Oh, Lord!"

"She'd threaten suicide and all the rest of it. Mary knew all about the will. Deceased often talked about it, and as short time back as last Thursday, when they had their dress rehearsal, she said it'd serve Miss Prentice right if she cut her out, but she was too charitable to do that, only she hoped if she did go first the money would be like scalding water on Miss Prentice's conscience. On Friday, Mary says, she had one of her good days. Went off to confession and came back very pleased. Same thing after the five o'clock affair at Pen Cuckoo, and in the evening she went to some Reading Circle or other at the rectory. She was in high feather when she left, but she didn't get back until eleven—very much later than usual. Gibson says she didn't speak on the way back, and Mary says when she came in she had a scarf pulled round her face and her coat collar turned up and——"

"It wasn't her," said Nigel. "Miss Prentice had disguised herself in Miss C.'s clothes in order to have a look at the will."

"Will you be quiet, Bathgate. Go on, Fox."

"Mary followed her to her room; but she said she didn't want her, and Mary swears she was crying. She heard her go to bed. Mary took in her tea first thing yesterday morning, and she says Miss Campanula looked shocking. Like an Aunt Sally that had been left out in the rain, was the way Mary put it."

"Graphic! Well?"

"Well, she spent yesterday morning at the hall with the others, but when she came back she wrote a note to the lawyers and gave it to Gibson to post; but she stayed in all yesterday afternoon."

"I knew you had something else up your sleeve," said Alleyn. "Where's the blotting paper?"

Fox smiled blandly.

"It's all right, as it turns out, sir. Here it is."

He took a sheet of blotting paper from the writing-table and handed it to Alleyn. It was a clean sheet with only four lines of writing. Alleyn held it up to an atrocious mirror and read:

"De   S
             K   dly   nd   our   presentative to   ee
me at   our earliest   on enience
                          ours faithfully
                          RIS C MP NULA."

"Going to alter her will," said Nigel over Alleyn's shoulder.

"Incubus!" said Alleyn. "Miserable parasite! I wouldn't be surprised if you were right. Anything else, Fox?"

"Nothing else, sir. She seemed much as usual when she went down to the performance. She left here at seven. Not being wanted till the second act, she didn't need to be so early."

"And they know of nobody, beyond the lawyers, whom she should inform?"

"Nobody, Mr. Alleyn."

146

"We'll have some lunch and then visit the rectory. Come on."

When they returned to the Jernigham Arms they found that the representative of the *Chipping Courier* had been all too zealous. A crowd of young men wearing flannel trousers and tweed coats greeted Nigel with a sort of wary and suspicious cordiality, and edged round Alleyn. He gave them a concise account of the piano and its internal arrangements, said nothing at all about the water-pistol, told them the murder appeared to be motiveless, and besought them not to follow him about wherever he went.

"It embarrasses me and it's no use to you. I'll see that you get photographs of the piano."

"Who's the owner of the Colt, Chief Inspector?" asked a pert young man wearing enormous glasses.

"It's a local weapon, thought to have been stolen," said Alleyn. "If there's anything more from the police, gentlemen, you shall hear of it. You've got enough in the setting of the thing to do your screaming worst. Off you go and do it. Be little Pooh Bahs. No corroborative details required. The narrative is adequately unconvincing, and I understand artistic verisimilitude is not your cup of tea."

"Try us," suggested the young man.

"*Pas si bête,*" said Alleyn. "I want my lunch."

"When are you going to be married, Mr. Alleyn?"

"Whenever I get a chance. Good-morning to you."

He left them to badger Nigel.

Alleyn and Fox finished their lunch in ten minutes, left the inn by the back door, and were off in Biggins's car before Nigel had exhausted his flow of profanity. Alleyn left Fox in the village. He was to seek our Friendly Young People, garner more local gossip, and attend the post-mortem. Alleyn turned up the Vale Road, and in five minutes arrived at the rectory.

IV

Like most clerical households on Sunday, the rectory had a semi-public look about it. The front door was wide open. On a hall table Alleyn saw a neat stack of children's hymn-books. A beretta lay beside them. In a room some way down the hall they heard a female voice.

"Very well, Mr. Copeland. Now the day is over."

"I think so," said the rector's voice.

"Through the night of doubt and sorrow," added the lady brightly.

"Do they like that?"

"Aw, they love it, Mr. Copeland."

"Very well," said the rector wearily. "Thank you, Miss Wright."

A large village maiden came out into the hall. She gathered the hymn-books into a straw bag and bustled out, not neglecting to look pretty sharply at Alleyn.

Alleyn rang the bell again, and presently an elderly maid appeared.

"May I see Mr. Copeland?"

"I'll just see, sir. What name, please?"

"Alleyn. I'm from Scotland Yard."

"Oh! Oh, yes, sir. Will you come this way, please?"

He followed her through the hall. She opened a door and said:

"Please, sir, the police."

He walked in.

Mr. Copeland looked as if he had sprung to his feet. At his side was the girl whom Alleyn had recognised as his daughter. They were indeed very much alike, and at this moment their faces spoke of the same mood: they looked startled and alarmed.

Mr. Copeland, in his long cassock, moved forward and shook hands.

"I'm so sorry to worry you like this, sir," said Alleyn. "It's the worst possible day to badger the clergy, I know; but, unfortunately, we can't delay things."

"No, no," said the rector, "we are only too anxious. This is my daughter. I'm afraid I don't——"

"Alleyn, sir."

"Oh, yes. Yes. Do sit down. Dinah, dear?"

"Please don't go, Miss Copeland," said Alleyn. "I hope you may be able to help us."

Evidently they had been sitting with the village maiden in front of the open fireplace. The chairs, drawn up in a semi-circle, were comfortably shabby. The fire, freshly mended with enormous logs, crackled companionably and lent warmth to the faded apple-green walls, the worn beams, the rector's agreeable prints, and a pot of bronze chrysanthemums from the Pen Cuckoo glasshouses.

They sat down, Dinah primly in the centre chair, Alleyn and the rector on either side of her.

Something of Alleyn's appreciation of this room may have appeared in his face. His hand went to his jacket pocket and was hurriedly withdrawn.

"Do smoke your pipe," said Dinah quickly.

"That was very well observed," said Alleyn. "I'm sure you will be able to help us. May I, really?"

"Please."

"It's very irregular," said Alleyn; "but I think I might, you know."

And as he lit his pipe he was visited by a strange thought. It came into his mind that he stood on the threshold of a new relationship, that he would return to this old room and again sit before the fire. He thought of the woman he loved, and it seemed to him that she would be there, too, at this future time, and that she would be happy. "An odd notion!" he thought, and dismissed it.

The rector was speaking: "——Terribly distressed. It is appalling to think that among the people one knows so well there should have been one heart that nursed such dreadful anger against a fellow creature."

"Yes," said Alleyn. "The impulse to kill, I suppose, is dormant in most people; but when it finds expression we are so shockingly astonished. I have noticed that very often. The reaction after murder is nearly always one of profound astonishment."

"To me," said Dinah, "the most horrible thing about this business is the grotesque side of it. It's like an appalling joke."

"You've heard the way of it, then?"

"I don't suppose there's a soul within twenty miles who hasn't," said Dinah.

"Ah," said Alleyn. "The industrious Roper."

He lit his pipe and, looking over his thin hands at them, said, "Before I forget, did either of you put a box outside one of the hall windows late on Friday or some time on Saturday?"

"No."

"No."

"I see. It's no matter."

The rector said, "Perhaps I shouldn't ask, but have you any idea at all of who——?"

"None," said Alleyn. "At the moment, none. There are so many things to be cleared up before the case can begin to make a pattern. One of them concerns the key of the hall. Where was it on Friday?"

" On a nail between an outhouse and the main building,"
said Dinah.

" I thought that was only on Saturday."

" No. I left it there on Friday for the Friendly Circle
members who worked in the lunch hour. They moved the
furniture and swept up, and things. When they left at two
o'clock they hung the key on the nail."

" But Miss Campanula tried to get in at about half-
past two and couldn't."

" I don't think Miss Campanula knew about the key.
I told the girls, and I think I said something about it at
the dress rehearsal in case the others wanted to get in,
but I'm pretty sure Miss Campanula had gone by then.
We've never hung it there before."

" Did you go to the hall on Friday?"

" Yes," said Dinah. " I went in the lunch hour to super-
vise the work. I came away before they had quite finished,
and returned here."

" And then you walked up Top Lane towards Pen Cuckoo?"

" Yes," said Dinah, in surprise, and into her eyes came
the same guarded look he had seen in Henry's.

" Was Georgie Biggins in the hall when you left at about
two o'clock?"

" Yes. Making life hideous with his beastly water-pistol.
He *is* a naughty boy, Daddy," said Dinah. " I really think
you ought to exorcise Georgie. I'm sure he's possessed of
a devil."

" Then you haven't heard about Georgie?" murmured
Alleyn. " Roper has his points."

" What about Georgie?"

Alleyn told them.

" I want," he said, " to make as little as possible of
the obvious implication. There seems to be little doubt that
Georgie, plus Twiddletoy, and his water-pistol made the
bullets that the murderer subsequently fired. It's an unpleasant responsibility to lay on a small boy's shoulders,
however bad he may be. I'm afraid it must come out
in evidence, but as far as possible I think we ought to
try and avoid village gossip."

" Certainly," said the rector. " At the same time, he knew
he was doing something wrong. The terrible conse-
quences——"

" Are disproportionately terrible, don't you think."

" I do. I agree with you," said Dinah.

Alleyn, seeing priest's logic in the rector's eye, hurried on.

"You will see," he said, "that the substitution of the Colt for the water-pistol must have taken place after two o'clock on Friday when George was flourishing his pistol. I know he stayed behind on Friday and rigged it up. He has admitted this. Miss Campanula's chauffeur, at her request, looked through the open window at two-thirty and saw the piano with the top open. His story leads us to believe that at that time Georgie was hiding somewhere in the building. Georgie did not tell me that at all willingly, and I confess I am afraid the memory of Miss Campanula, banging at the doors and demanding admittance, is likely to become a childish nightmare. I don't pretend to understand child psychology."

"The law," said Dinah, "in the person of her officer, seems to be surprisingly merciful."

Alleyn disregarded this.

"So that gives us two-thirty on Friday as a starting-off point. You, Miss Copeland, walked up Top Lane and by chance encountered Mr. Henry Jernigham."

"What!" the rector ejaculated. "Dinah!"

"It's all right," said Dinah in a high voice. "It *was* by accident, Daddy. I did meet Henry and we did behave as you would have expected. Our promise was almost up. It's my fault. I couldn't help it."

"Miss Prentice arrived some time later, I believe," said Alleyn.

"*Has she told you that?*"

"Mr. Henry Jernigham told me and Miss Prentice agreed. Do you mind, Miss Copeland, describing what happened at this triple encounter?"

"If they haven't told you," said Dinah, "I won't."

CHAPTER SEVENTEEN

Confession from a Priest

"WON'T YOU?" said Alleyn mildly. "That's a pity. We shall have to do the Peer Gynt business."

"What's that?"

"Go roundabout. Ask servants about the relationship between Miss Prentice and her young cousin. Tap the fabulous springs of village gossip—all that."

"I thought," flashed Dinah, "that nowadays the C.I.D. was almost a gentleman's job."

"Oh, no, I" said Alleyn. "You couldn't be more mistaken."

Her face was scarlet. "That was a pretty squalid remark of mine," said Dinah.

"It was inexcusable, my dear," said her father. "I am ashamed that you have been capable of it."

"I find no offence in it at all," Alleyn said cheerfully. "It was entirely apposite."

But Mr. Copeland's face was pink with embarrassment, and Dinah's still crimson with mortification. The rector addressed her as if she was a children's service. His voice became markedly more clerical, and in the movement of his head Alleyn recognised one of his pulpit mannerisms. He said, "You have broken a solemn promise, Dinah, and to this fault you add a deliberate evasion and an ill-bred and entirely unjustifiable impertinence. You force me to make Mr. Alleyn some sort of explanation." He turned to Alleyn. "My daughter and Henry Jernigham," he said, "have formed an attachment of which his father and I do not approve. Dinah suggested that they should give their word not to meet alone for three weeks. Friday was the final day of the three weeks. Miss Prentice was also of our mind in this matter. If she came upon them at a moment when, as Dinah has admitted, they had completely forgotten or ignored this promise, I am sure she was extremely disappointed and distressed."

"She wasn't I" exclaimed Dinah, rallying a little. "She wasn't a bit like that. She was absolutely livid with rage and beastliness."

"Dinah!"

"Oh, Daddy, *why* do you shut your eyes? You must know what she's like—you of all people!"

"Dinah, I must insist——"

"No!" cried Dinah. "No! First you say I've been underhand; and then, when I go all upperhand and open, you don't like it any better. I'm sorry in a way that Henry and I didn't stay the course; but we nearly did, and I *won't* think there was anything very awful about Friday afternoon. I won't have Henry and me made seem grubby. I'm sorry I was rude to Mr. Alleyn and I—well, I mean it's quite obvious it wasn't only rude, but silly. I mean, it's obvious from the way he's taken it—I mean—oh, hell! Oh, Daddy, I'm sorry."

Alleyn choked down a laugh.

The rector said, "Dinah! Dinah!"

"Yes, well I *am* sorry. And now Mr. Alleyn will think heaven knows what about Friday afternoon. I may as well tell you, Mr. Alleyn, that in Henry's and my opinion Miss Prentice is practically ravers. It's a well-known phenomenon with old maids. She's tried to sublimate her natural appetites and—and—work them off in religion. I can't help it, Daddy, she *has*. And it's been a failure. She's only repressed and repressed, and when she sees two natural, healthy people making love to each other she goes off pop."

"It is I," said the rector, looking hopelessly at his child, "who have been a failure."

"*Don't*. You haven't. It's just that you don't understand these women. You're an angel, but you're not a modern angel."

"I should be interested to know," said Alleyn, "how an angel brings himself up to date. Stream-lined wings, I suppose."

Dinah grinned.

"Well, you know what I mean," she said. "And I'm right about these two. If you had heard Miss Prentice! It was simply too shaming and hideous. She actually shook all over and sort of gasped. And she said the most ghastly things to us. She threatened at once to tell you, Daddy, and the squire. She suggested—oh, she was beyond belief. What's more, she dribbles and spits."

"Dinah, my dear!"

"Well, Daddy, she *does*. I noticed the front of her beastly dress, and it was *disgusting*. She either dribbles and spits, or else she spills her tea. Honestly! And, anyway, she was perfectly *septic*, the things she said."

"Didn't either of you try to stop her?" asked Alleyn.

"Yes," said Dinah. She turned rather white and added quickly: "In the end she just blundered past us and went on up the lane."

"What did you do?"

"I went home."

"And Mr. Jernigham?"

"He went up to Cloudyfold, I think."

"By the steep path? He didn't walk down with you?"

"No," said Dinah. "He didn't. There's nothing in that."

II

"I cannot see," said the rector, "that this unhappy story can have any bearing on the tragedy."

"I think I can promise," said Alleyn, "that any information found to be irrelevant will be completely blotted out. We are, quite literally, not interested in any facts that cannot be brought into the pattern."

"Well, that can't," Dinah declared. She threw up her chin and said loudly:

"If you think, because Miss Prentice made us feel uncomfortable and embarrassed, it's a motive for murder, you're quite wrong. We're not in the least afraid of Miss Prentice or anything she might say or do. It can't make any difference to Henry and me." Dinah's lower lip trembled and she added: "We simply look at her from a detached analytical angle and are vaguely sorry for her. That's all." She uttered a dry sob.

The rector said: "Oh, my darling child, what nonsense," and Dinah walked over to the window.

"Well," said Alleyn mildly, "let's go on being detached and analytical. What did you both do on Saturday afternoon? That's yesterday."

"We were both in here," said Dinah. "Daddy went to sleep. I went over my part."

"What time did you get to the hall last evening?"

"We left here at half-past six," answered Mr. Copeland, "and walked over by the path through our garden and wood."

"Was anybody there?"

"Yes. Yes, Gladys Wright was there, wasn't she, Dinah? She is one of our best workers and was in charge of the programmes. She was in the front of the hall. I think the other girls were either there, or came in soon after we did."

"Can you tell me exactly what you did up to the time of the catastrophe?"

"I can, certainly," rejoined the rector. "I saw that the copy of the play and the bicycle bell I had to ring were in their right places, and then I sat in an arm-chair on the stage to keep out of the way and see that nobody came in from the front of the hall. I was there until Dinah came for me to speak to Miss Prentice."

"Did you expect Miss Prentice would be unable to play?"

"No, indeed. On the contrary, she told me her finger was much better. That was soon after she arrived."

"Had you much difficulty in persuading Miss Prentice not to play?"

"Yes, indeed I had. She was most determined about it, but her finger was really very bad. It was quite impos-

154

sible, and I told her I should be very displeased if she persisted."

"And apart from that time you never left the stage?"

"Oh! Oh, yes, I *did* go to the telephone before that, when they were trying to get Mrs. Ross's house. That was at half-past seven. The telephone is an extension of ours and our maid, Mary, is deaf and takes a long time to answer."

"We were all frantic," said Dinah, from the window. "The squire and Henry and Father and I were all standing round the telephone, with Miss Campanula roaring instructions, poor old thing. The squire hadn't got any trousers on, only pink woollen underpants. Miss Prentice came along, and when she saw him she cackled like a hen and flew away, but no one else minded about the squire's pants, not even Miss C. We were all in a flat spin about the others being late, you see. Father was just coming over to ring from here, when we got through."

"I returned to the stage then," said the rector.

"I can't tell you exactly what I did," said Dinah. "I was all over the place." She peered through the window. "Here's Henry now."

"Why not go and meet him?" suggested Alleyn. "Tell him how I bullied you."

"You haven't, but I will," said Dinah.

She opened the window and stepped out over the low sill into the garden.

"I'm so sorry," said Alleyn, when the window had slammed.

"She's a good child, really," said the rector sadly.

"I'm sure she is. Mr. Copeland, you see what a strange position we are in, don't you? If Miss Prentice was the intended victim we must trace her movements, her conversation—yes, and if we could, even her thoughts during these last days. We are in the extraordinary position of having, apparently, a living victim in a case of homicide. There is even the possibility that the murderer may make a second attempt."

"No! No! That's too horrible."

"I am sure that, as your daughter says, you know a great deal about these two ladies—the actual and, as far as we know, the intended victim. Can you tell me anything, anything at all, that may throw a glint of light on this dark tangle of emotions?"

The rector clasped his hands and stared into the fire.

"I am very greatly troubled," he said. "I cannot see my way."

"Do you mean that you have got their confidence, and that under ordinary circumstances you would never speak of your knowledge?"

"Let me make myself clear. As no doubt you already know, I have heard the confessions of many of my parishioners. Under no condition will I break the seal of the confessional. That goes without saying. Moreover, it would serve no purpose if I did. I tell you this lest you should think I hold a key to the mystery."

"I recognise the position," said Alleyn, "and I shall respect it."

"I'm glad of that. There are many people, I know, who regard the sacrament of confession in the Anglo-Catholic Church as an amateurish substitute for the Roman use. It is no such thing. The Romans say, 'You must,' the Protestant Nonconformists say, 'You must not,' the Catholic Church of England says, 'You may!'"

But Alleyn was not there for doctrinal argument, and wouldn't have welcomed it under any circumstances.

He said, "I realise that a priest who hears confession, no matter what faith he professes, must regard the confessional as inviolate. That, I take, is not what troubles you. Do you perhaps wonder if you should tell me something that you have heard from one of your penitents outside the confessional?"

The rector gave him a startled glance. He clasped his hands more tightly and said:

"It is not that I believe it would be any help. It's only that I am burdened with the memory and with a terrible doubt. You say that this murderer may strike again. I don't believe that is possible. I am sure it is not possible."

"Why?" asked Alleyn in astonishment.

"Because I believe that the murderer is dead," said the rector.

III

Alleyn turned in his chair and regarded Mr. Copeland for some seconds before he answered.

At last he said: "You think she did it herself?"

"I am sure of it."

156

"Will you tell me why?"

"I suppose I must. Mr. Alleyn, I am not, unfortunately, a man of strong character. All my life I have avoided unpleasantness. I know this very well and try to conquer my weakness. I have vacillated when I should have insisted; temporised when I should have taken definite action. Because of these veritable sins of omission I believe I am morally responsible, or at any rate in part responsible, for this terrible crime."

He paused, still looking at the fire. Alleyn waited.

"On Friday night," said Mr. Copeland, "the Reading Circle met in the rectory dining-room. It usually meets in St. Giles Hall; but because of the preparations for the play they all came here instead. It was Miss Campanula's turn to preside. I went in for a short time. Dinah read a scene from *Twelfth Night* for them, and after that they went on with their book. It is G. K. Chesterton's *The Ball and the Cross*, and Miss Campanula had borrowed my copy. When they had finished she came in here to return it. I was alone. It was about a quarter past ten."

"Yes?"

"Mr. Alleyn, it is very difficult and disagreeable for me to tell you of this incident. Really, I—I don't know quite how to begin. You may not be familiar with parochial affairs, but I think many clergy find that there is an unfortunately rather common type of church worker who is always a problem to her parish priest. I don't know if you will understand me when I say that one finds this type among —dear me—among ladies who are not perhaps very young and who have no other interests."

The rector was now very pink.

"I think I understand," said Alleyn.

"Do you? Well, I am sorry to say poor Miss Campanula was really an advanced—er—specimen of this type. Poor soul, she was lonely and she had a difficult temperament which I am sure she did her best to discipline, but at times I could not help thinking that she needed a doctor as well as a priest to help her. I have even suggested as much."

"That was very wise advice, sir."

"She didn't take it," said the rector wistfully. "She stuck to me, you see, and I'm afraid I failed her."

"About Friday night?" Alleyn reminded him gently.

"Yes, I know. I'm coming to Friday night; but, really, it's *very* difficult. There was a terrible scene. She—I think

157

she had got it into her head that if Dinah married or went away again—Dinah is on the stage, you know—I should be as lonely as she was. She said as much. I was very much startled and alarmed and I was at a loss how to reply. I think she misunderstood my silence. I really can't quite remember the order of events. It was rather like a bad dream, and still is. She was trembling dreadfully and looking at me with such a desperate expression in her eyes that I—I—I——"

He shut his eyes tight and added in a great hurry: "I patted her hand."

"That was quite a natural thing to do, wasn't it?"

"You wouldn't have said so if you'd seen the result."

"No?"

"No, indeed. The next moment she was, to be frank, in my arms. It was without any exception the most awful thing that has ever happened to me. She was sobbing and laughing at the same time. I was in agony. I couldn't release myself. We never draw our blinds in this room, and there was I in this appalling and even ludicrous situation. I was obliged actually to—to support her. And I was so sorry for her, too. It was so painfully evident that she had made a frightful mistake. I believe she was hysterically delighted. It makes me feel ashamed and, as we used to say when I was young, caddish to repeat all this."

"It's beastly of you," said Alleyn; "but I'm sure you should tell me."

"I would have preferred, before doing so, to take the advice of one of my brother clergy, but there is no one who—— However, that is beside the point. You are being very patient."

"How did it end?"

"Very badly," said the rector, opening his eyes wide. "It couldn't have ended worse. When she had quietened down a little—and it was a long time before she did—I hastened to release myself, and I am afraid the first thing I did was to draw the curtains. You see, some members of the Reading Circle might still have been about. Their young men come up to meet them. Worse than that, Miss Prentice rang up in the morning and said she wanted to speak to me that evening. While Miss Campanula was still with me she telephoned to say she was not coming. That was about 10.15. Dinah took the message and afterwards said she sounded upset. I—I'm afraid I had been obliged to be rather severe with her—I mean as her priest—that afternoon. I had given her certain instructions which would keep her at

158

home, and in any case I think perhaps her finger was too painful. But at the time I expected her, and if she had seen, it would have been—well, really——"

The rector gulped and added quickly: " But that is beside the point. I drew the curtains, and in my flurry I said something to Miss Campanula about expecting Miss Prentice. It turned out that I couldn't have said anything worse, because when I tried to tell this unfortunate soul that she was mistaken, she connected my explanation with Miss Prentice's visit."

" Help! " said Alleyn.

" What did you say? Yes. Yes, indeed. She became quite frantic and I really can *not* repeat what she said, but she uttered the most dreadful abuse of Miss Prentice and, in a word, she suggested that Miss Prentice had supplanted her, not only in the affairs of the parish, but in my personal regard. I became angry—justly angry, as I thought at the time. As her priest I ordered her to stop. I rebuked her and reminded her of the deadly sin of envy. I told her that she must drive out this wickedness from her breast by prayer and fasting. She became much quieter, but as she left she said one sentence that I shall never forget. She turned in the doorway and said, ' If I killed myself she would suffer for it; but if, as I stand here in this room, I could strike Eleanor Prentice dead, I'd do it!' And before I could answer her she had gone out and shut the door "

IV

" Darling," said Henry, " I think I'd better tell him."

" But *why*?"

" Because I believe Eleanor will if I don't."

" How could she? It would be too shaming for her. She'd have to say how she behaved when she saw us."

" No, she wouldn't. She'd just twist it round somehow so that it looked as if she found us in a compromising position and that you were covered with scarlet shame and I was furious and threatened to scrag her."

" But, Henry, that would be a deliberate attempt to make him suspect you."

" I wouldn't put it past her."

" Well, I would. If you were tried for murder, it'd be a pretty good scandal, and she wouldn't care for that at all."

"No, that's true enough. Perhaps I may as well keep quiet."

"I should say you'd better."

"Dinah," said Henry, "who do you think——?"

"I *can't* think. It seems incredible that any of us should do it. It just isn't possible."

"Daddy thinks she did it herself. He won't say why."

"What, fixed it up for Eleanor and then at the last minute decided to take the count herself?"

"I suppose so. It must be something she said to him."

"What do you think of Alleyn?" asked Henry abruptly.

"I like him. Golly, I was rude to him," said Dinah, hurling another log of wood on the schoolroom fire.

"Were you, my sweet?"

"Yes. I implied he was no gent."

"Well, that was a lie," said Henry cheerfully.

"I know it was. He couldn't have been nicer about it. How I could! Daddy was livid."

"Naturally. Honestly, Dinah!"

"I know."

"I love you all the way to the Great Bear and round the Southern Cross and back again."

"Henry," said Dinah suddenly, "don't let's ever be jealous."

"All right. Why?"

"I keep thinking of those two. If they hadn't been jealous I don't believe this would have happened."

"Good heavens, Dinah, you don't think Eleanor——"

"No. But I sort of feel as if the whole thing was saturated in their jealousy. I mean, it was only jealousy that made them so beastly to each other and to us and to that shifty beast, Mrs. Ross."

"Why do you call her a shifty beast?"

"Because I know in my bones she is," said Dinah.

"I must say I wish my papa would restrain his middle-aged ardours when he encounters her. His antics are so damn' silly."

"Daddy's completely diddled by her conversion to his ways. She's put her name down for the retreat in Advent."

"That's not so bad as my parent's archness. I could wish she didn't respond in kind, I must say. Apart from that, I don't mind the lady."

"You're a man."

"Oh, nonsense," said Henry, answering the implication.

"I wouldn't trust her," said Dinah, "as far as I could toss a grand piano."

"Why bring pianos into it?"

"Well, I wouldn't. She's the sort that's always called a man's woman."

"It's rather a stupid sort of phrase," said Henry.

"It simply means," said Dinah, "that she's nice to men and would let a woman down as soon as look at her!"

"I should have thought it just meant that she was too attractive to be popular with her own sex."

"Darling, that's simply a masculine cliché," said Dinah.

"I don't think so."

"There are tons of devastating woman who are enormously popular with their own sex."

Henry smiled.

"Do you think she's attractive?" asked Dinah casually.

"Yes, very. I dare say she's rather a little bitch, but she is pleasing. For one thing, her clothes fit her."

"Yes, they do," said Dinah sombrely. "They must cost the earth."

Henry kissed her.

"I'm a low swine," he muttered. "I was being tiresome. You're my dear darling and I'm no more fit to love you than a sweep, but I do love you so much."

"We must never be jealous," whispered Dinah.

"Dinah!" called the rector in the hall below.

"Yes, Daddy?"

"Where are you?"

"In the schoolroom."

"May I go up, do you think?" asked a deep voice.

"That's Alleyn," said Henry.

"Come up here, Mr. Alleyn," called Dinah.

CHAPTER EIGHTEEN

Mysterious Lady

"SIT DOWN, Mr. Alleyn," said Dinah. "The chairs are all rather rickety in this room, I'm afraid. You know Henry, don't you?"

"Yes, rather," said Alleyn. "I'll have this, if I may." He squatted on a stuffed footstool in front of the fire.

"I told Henry how rude I'd been," said Dinah.

"I was horrified," said Henry. "She's very young, poor girl."

161

"You couldn't by any chance just settle down and spin us some yarns about crime?" suggested Dinah.

"I'm afraid not. It would be delightful to settle down, but you see we're not allowed to get familiar when we're on duty. It looks impertinent. I've got a monstrous lot of things to do before to-night."

"Do you just collect stray bits of evidence," asked Henry, "and hope they'll make sense?"

"More or less. You scavenge and then you arrange everything and try and see the pattern."

"Suppose there's no pattern?"

"There must be. It's a question of clearing away the rubbish."

"Any sign of it so far?" asked Dinah.

"Not a great many signs."

"Do you suspect either of us?"

"Not particularly."

"Well, we didn't do it," said Dinah.

"Good."

"Cases of homicide," said Henry, "must be different from any other kind. Especially cases that occur in these sorts of surroundings. You're not dealing with the ordinary criminal classes."

"True enough," said Alleyn. "I'm dealing with people like yourself who will be devastatingly frank up to a certain point—far franker than the practical criminal, who lies to the police from sheer force of habit—but who will probably bring a great deal more *savoir faire* to the business of with-holding essentials. For instance, I know jolly well there's something more to that meeting you both had with Miss Prentice on Friday afternoon; but it's no good saying to you, as I would to Posh Jimmy: 'Come on, now. It's not you I'm after. Tell me what I want to know and perhaps we'll forget all about that little job over at Moorton.' Unfortunately, I've nothing against you."

"That's exactly what I mean," said Henry. "Still, you can always go for my Cousin Eleanor."

"Yes. That's what I'll have to do," agreed Alleyn.

"Well, I hope you don't believe everything she tells you," said Dinah, "or you *will* get in a muddle. Where we're concerned she's as sour as a quince."

"And, anyway, she's practically certifiable," added Henry. "It's a question which was dottiest: Eleanor or Miss C."

"Lamentable," said Alleyn vaguely. "Mr. Jernigham,

162

did you put a box outside one of the hall windows after 2.30 on Friday?"

"No."

"What *is* this about a box?" asked Dinah.

"Nothing much. About the piano. When did those aspidistras make their appearance?"

"They were there on Saturday morning, anyway," said Dinah. "I meant to have them taken away. They must have masked the stage from the audience. I think the girls put them there after I left on Friday."

"In which case Georgie moved them off to rig his pistol."

"And the murderer," Henry pointed out, "must have moved them again."

"Yes."

"I wonder when," said Henry.

"So do we. Miss Copeland, did you see Miss Campanula on Friday night?"

"Friday night? Oh, I saw her at the Reading Circle meeting in the dining-room."

"Not afterwards?"

"No. As soon as I got out of the dining-room I came up here. She went into the study to see Daddy. I could just hear her voice scolding away as usual, I should think, poor thing."

"The study is beneath this room, isn't it?"

"Yes. I wanted to have a word with Daddy, but I waited until I heard her and the other person go."

Alleyn paused for a second before he said:

"The other person?"

"There was somebody else in the study with Miss C. I can't help calling her 'Miss C.' We all did."

"How do you know there was someone else there?"

"Well, because they left after Miss C.," said Dinah impatiently. "It wasn't Miss Prentice, because she rang up from Pen Cuckoo just about that time. Mary called me to the telephone, so I suppose it must have been Gladys Wright. She's leader of the Reading Circle. She lives up the lane. She must have gone out by the window in the study, because I heard the lane gate give a squeak. That's how I knew she'd been here."

Alleyn walked over to the window. It looked down on a gravelled path, a lawn, and a smaller earthen path that led to a rickety gate and evidently ran on beyond it through a small plantation to the lane.

"I suppose you always go that way to the hall?" asked Alleyn.

"Oh, yes. It's much shorter than going round the house from the front door."

"Yes," said Alleyn, "it would be."

He looked thoughtfully at Dinah and said, "Did you hear this other person's voice?"

"Hi!" said Dinah. "What *is* all this? No, I didn't. Ask Daddy. He'll tell you who it was."

"Stupid of me," said Alleyn. "Of course he will."

I I

He didn't ask the rector, but before he left he crunched boldly round the gravel path and walked across the lawn to the gate. It certainly creaked very loudly. It was one of those old-fashioned gates that has a post stile beside it. The path was evidently used very often. There was no hope of finding anything useful on its hard but greasy surface. There had been too much rain since Friday night. "Much too much rain," sighed Alleyn. But just inside the gate he found two softened but unmistakable depressions. Horseshoe-shaped holes about two inches in diameter that had held water. "Heels," he thought, "but not a hope of saying whose. Female. Stood there a long time facing the house." He could see the rector crouched over the study fire. "Oh, well," he said, and plunged into the little wood. "Nothing at all that's to the purpose. Nothing."

He saw that the hall was only a little way up on the other side from where this path came out on the lane. He returned, circled the rectory, perfectly aware that Dinah and Henry watched him from the schoolroom window. As he got into the car Henry opened the window and leaned out.

"I say," he shouted.

"Shut up," said Dinah's voice behind him. "*Don't*, Henry."

"What is it?" called Alleyn, squinting up through his driving-window.

"It's nothing," said Dinah. "He's gone ravers, that's all. Good-bye."

Henry's head shot out of sight and the window slammed.

"Now I wonder," thought Alleyn, "if Master Henry has got the same idea as I have."

He drove away.

At the Jernigham Arms he found Nigel, but no Fox.

"Where are you going?" Nigel demanded when Alleyn returned to the car.

"To call on a lady."

"Let me come."

"Why the devil?"

"I won't go in with you if you'd rather not."

"Naturally. All right. I can do with some comic relief."

"Oh, God, your only jig-maker," said Nigel and got in. "Now, who's the lady?" he said. "Speak up, dearie."

"Mrs. Ross."

"The mysterious stranger."

"Why do you call her that?"

"It's the part she played in their show. I've got a programme."

"So it is," said Alleyn.

He turned the car up the Vale Road and presently he began to talk. He went over the history of the case from midday on Friday. As far as he could, he traced the movements of the murdered woman and each of her seven companions. He correlated their movements and gave Nigel a time-table he had jotted down in his note-book.

"I hate these damn' things," Nigel grumbled. "They shatter my interest; they remind me of a Bradshaw, and they are therefore completely unintelligible."

"It's a pity about you," said Alleyn dryly. "Look at the list at the bottom."

Nigel looked and read:

"Piano. Drawing-pin holes. Automatic. Branch. Onion. Chopsticks. Key. Letter. Creaky gate. Window. Telephone."

"Thank you," said Nigel. "Now, of course, I see the whole thing in a blinding flash. It's as clear as the mud in your eye. The onion is particularly obvious, and as for the drawing-pins—— It's ludicrous that I didn't spot the exquisite reason of the drawing-pins."

He returned the paper to Alleyn.

"Go on," he continued acidly. "Say it. 'You have the facts, Bathgate. You know my methods, Bathgate. What of the little grey cells, Bathgate?' Sling in a quotation; add: 'Oh, my dear chap,' and vanish in a fog of composite fiction."

"This is Cloudyfold," said Alleyn. "Cold, isn't it? They had twelve degrees of frost on the pub thermometer last night."

"Oh, Mr. Mercury, how you did startle me!"

"That must be Mrs. Ross's cottage down there."

"Can't I come in as your stenographer?"

"Very well. I may send you out on an errand into the village."

Duck Cottage stands in a bend of the road before it actually reaches Cloudyfold Village. It is a typical Dorset cottage, plain fronted, well proportioned, cold-grey and weather-worn. Mrs. Ross had smartened it up. The window sashes and sills and the front door were painted vermilion, and a vermilion tub with a Noah's Ark tree stood on each side of the entrance which led straight off the road.

Alleyn gave a double rap on the shiny brass knocker. The door was opened by a maid, all cherry-red and muslin. Mrs. Ross was at home. The maid took Alleyn's card away with her and returned to usher them in.

Alleyn had to stoop his head under the low doorway, and the ceilings were not much higher. They walked through a tiny ante-room, down some uneven steps and into Mrs. Ross's parlour. She was not there. It was a charming parlour looking out on a small formal garden. There were old prints on the walls, one or two respectable pieces of furniture, a deep carpet, some very comfortable chairs, and a general air of chintz, sparkle and femininity. It was a delicate little room. Alleyn looked at a bookcase filled with modern novels. He noticed one or two works by authors whose sole distinction had been conferred by the censor, and at three popular collections of famous criminal cases. They all had startling wrappers and photographic illustrations. Within their covers one would find the cases of Brown and Kennedy, Bywaters, Seddon, and Stinie Morrison. Their style would be characterized by a certain arch taciturnity. Alleyn grinned to himself and took one of them from the shelf. He let it fall upon his hands and a discourse on dactylography faced him. The groove between the pages was filled with cigarette ash. A photograph of prints developed and enlarged from a letter illustrated the written matter. A woman's voice sounded. Alleyn returned the book to its place. The door opened and Mrs. Ross came in.

She was the lady Alleyn had noticed in church. This did not surprise him much, but it made him feel wary. She greeted him with a sensible good-humoured air, shook hands and then gave him a slanting smile.

"This is Mr. Bathgate," said Alleyn. He noticed that Nigel's fingers had flown to his tie.

She settled them by the fire with the prettiest air in the world, and he saw her glance at the little cupid clock on the mantelpiece.

"I do think all this is too ghastly," she said. "That poor wretched old creature! How anybody could!"

"It's a bad business," said Alleyn.

She offered them cigarettes. Alleyn refused and Nigel, rather unwillingly, followed suit. Mrs. Ross took one and leaned towards Alleyn for a light.

"*Chanel, Numéro Cinq,*" thought Alleyn.

"I've never been 'investigated' before," said Mrs. Ross. "Dear me, that sounds rather peculiar, doesn't it? I don't mean what you mean."

She chuckled. Nigel uttered rather a flirtatious laugh, caught Alleyn's eye and was silent.

Alleyn said, "I shan't bother you for long, I hope. We've got to try and find out where everybody was from about midday Friday up to the moment of the disaster."

"Heavens!" said Mrs. Ross. "I'll never be able to remember that; and if I do, it's sure to sound too incriminating for words."

"I hope not," said Alleyn sedately. "We've got a certain amount of it already. On Friday you went to a short five o'clock rehearsal at Pen Cuckoo, didn't you?"

"Yes. Apart from that, I was at home all day."

"And Friday evening?"

"Still at home. We aren't very gay in Cloudyfold, Mr. Alleyn. I think I've dined out twice since I came here. The county is simply rushing me, as you see."

"On Saturday evening I suppose you joined the others at the hall?"

"Yes. I carted down one or two things they wanted for the stage. We towed them in a trailer behind Dr. Templett's Morris."

"Did you go straight to the hall?"

"No. We called at Pen Cuckoo. I'd quite forgotten that. I didn't get out of the car."

167

"Dr. Templett went into the study?"

"He went into the house," she said lightly. "I don't know which room."

"He didn't return by the french window?"

"I don't remember." She paused and then added: "The squire, Mr. Jernigham, came and talked to me. I didn't notice Dr. Templett until he was actually at the car window."

"Ah, yes. You came back here for lunch?"

"Yes."

"And in the afternoon?"

"Saturday afternoon. That's only yesterday, isn't it? Heavens, it seems a lifetime! Oh, I took the supper down to the hall."

"At what time?"

"I think it was about half-past three when I got there."

"Was the hall empty?"

"Yes. No, it wasn't. Dr. Templett was there. He arrived just after I did. He'd brought down his clothes."

"How long did you stay there, Mrs. Ross?"

"I don't know. Not long. It might have been half an hour."

"And Dr. Templett?"

"He left before I did. I was putting out sandwiches."

"And cutting up onions?"

"*Onions!* Good Lord, why should I do that? No, thank you. I'm sick at the sight of one, and I have got some respect for my hands."

They were luxurious little hands. She held them to the fire.

"I'm sorry," said Alleyn. "There was an onion in the supper-room."

"I don't know how it got there. The supper-room was all scrubbed out on Friday."

"It's no matter. Did you look at the piano on Saturday afternoon?"

"No, I don't think so. The curtain was down, so I suppose if anything had been out of order I shouldn't have noticed. I didn't go to the front of the hall. The one key opens both doors."

"And only Dr. Templett came in?"

"Yes."

"Could anyone have come unnoticed into the front of the hall while you were in the supper-room?"

"I suppose they might have. No. No, of course they couldn't. We had the key and the front door was locked."

"Did Dr. Templett go into the auditorium at all?"

"Only to shut the window."

"Which window was open?"

"It's rather odd," she said quickly. "I'm sure I shut it in the morning."

III

"It's the window on the side away from the lane, nearest the front," continued Mrs. Ross after a pause. "I remember that, just as we were leaving, I pulled it down in case the rain blew in. That was at midday."

"Were you the last to leave at noon?"

"No. Well, we all left together; but I think Dr. Templett and I actually walked out first. The Copelands always leave by the back door."

"So presumably someone reopened the window?"

"Presumably."

"Were you on the stage when Dr. Templett shut the window?"

"Yes."

"What were you doing there?"

"We—I tidied it up and arranged one or two ornaments I'd brought."

"Dr. Templett helped you?"

"He—well, he looked on."

"And all this time the window was open?"

"Yes, I suppose so. Yes, of course it was."

"Did you tell him you thought you had shut it?"

"Yes."

"You don't think somebody pushed it open from outside?"

"No," she said positively. "We were certain they didn't. The curtain was up. We'd have seen."

"I thought you said the curtain was down."

"Oh, how stupid of me. It was up when we got there, but we let it down. It was supposed to be down. I wanted to try the effect of a lamp I'd taken."

"Did you lower the curtain before or after you noticed the window?"

"I don't remember. Oh. Yes, please, I think it was afterwards."

She leaned forward and looked at Nigel, who had been making notes.

169

"It's simply petrifying to see all this going down," she said to him. "Do I read it over and sign it?"

"It would have to go into long-hand first," said Nigel.

"Do let me see."

He gave her his notes.

"They look exactly like journalists' copy," said Mrs. Ross.

"That's our cunning," said Nigel boldly, but rather red in the face.

She laughed and gave them back to him.

"Mr. Alleyn thinks we're terribly flippant, I can see," she said. "Don't you, inspector?"

"No," said Alleyn. "I regard Bathgate as a zealous and serious-minded young officer."

Nigel tried to look zealous and serious minded. He was a little shaken.

"You mustn't forget that telegram, Bathgate," added Alleyn. "I think you'd better go into Cloudyfold and send it. You can pick me up on the way back. Mrs. Ross will excuse you."

"Very good, sir," said Nigel and left.

"What a very charming young man," said Mrs. Ross, with her air of casual intimacy. "Are all your officers as Eton and Oxford as that?"

"Not quite all," rejoined Alleyn.

What a curious trick she had of widening her eyes! The pupils actually seemed to dilate. It was as if she was aware of something, recognised it, and gave just that one brief signal. Alleyn read into it a kind of polite wantonness. "She proclaims herself," he thought, "by that trick. She is a woman with a strong, determined appetite." He knew very well that, for all her impersonal manner, she had made small practised signals to him, and he wondered if he should let her see he had recognised these signals.

He leaned forward in his chair and looked deliberately into her eyes.

"There are two more questions." he said.

"Two more? Well?"

"Do you know whose automatic it was that shot Miss Campanula between the eyes and through the brain?"

She sat quite still. The corners of her thin mouth drooped a little. Her short blackened lashes veiled her light eyes.

"It was Jocelyn Jernigham's, wasn't it?" she said.

"Yes. The same Colt that Mr. Henry Jernigham showed you on Friday evening."

"That's awful," she said and looked squarely at him. "Does it mean that you suspect one of us?"

"By itself, it doesn't amount to so much. But it was his automatic that killed her."

"*He'd* never do it," she said contemptuously.

"Did you put a box outside one of the hall windows at any time after 2.30 on Friday?" asked Alleyn.

"No. Why?"

"It's of no importance."

Alleyn put his hand in the breast pocket of his coat and took out his note-book.

"Heavens!" said Selia Ross. "What next?"

His long fingers drew out a folded paper. That trick with her eyes must after all be unconscious. She looked slantways at the paper and the lines of block capitals, painstakingly executed by Inspector Fox. She took it from Alleyn, raising her eyebrows, and handed it back.

"Can you tell me anything about this?" asked Alleyn.

"No."

"I think perhaps I should tell you we regard it as an important piece of evidence."

"I've never seen it before. Where did you find it?"

"It just cropped up," said Alleyn.

Somebody had come into the adjoining room. There came the sound of stumbling feet on the uneven steps. The door burst open. Alleyn thought, "Blast Bathgate!" and glanced up furiously.

It was Dr. Templett.

CHAPTER NINETEEN

Statement from Templett

"SELIA?" said Dr. Templett, and stopped short.

The paper dangled from Alleyn's fingers.

"Hullo, chief inspector," said Templett breathlessly. "I thought I might find you here. I've just done the P.M."

"Yes?" said Alleyn. "Anything unexpected?"

"Nothing."

Alleyn held out the paper.

"Isn't this your letter?"

Templett stood absolutely still. He then shook his head, but the gesture seemed to repudiate the implication rather than the statement.

171

"Were you not looking for it this morning in the breast pocket of your coat?"

"Is it yours, Billy?" she said. "Who's been writing comic letters to you?"

The skin of his face seemed to tighten. Two sharp little cords sprang up from his nostrils to the corners of his mouth. He turned to the fire and stooped as if to warm his hands. They trembled violently and he thrust them into his pockets. His face was quite without colour, but the firelight dyed it crimson.

Alleyn waited.

Mrs. Ross lit a cigarette.

"I think I'd like to speak to Mr. Alleyn alone," said Templett.

"Can you come back to Chipping with me?" asked Alleyn.

"What? Yes. Yes, I'll do that."

Alleyn turned to Mrs. Ross and bowed.

"Good-evening, Mrs. Ross."

"Is it so late? Good-bye. Billy, is anything wrong?"

Alleyn saw him look at her with a sort of wonder. He shook his head and walked out. Alleyn followed him.

Nigel was sitting in the Bigginses' car. Alleyn signalled quickly to him and followed Templett to his Morris.

"I'll come with you, if I may," said Alleyn.

Templett nodded. They got in. Templett turned the car and accelerated violently. Cloudyfold Rise leapt at them. They crossed the hill-top in two minutes. It was already dusk and the houses in the Vale were lit. A cold mist hung about the hills.

"God damn it," said Dr. Templett, "you needn't watch me like that! I'm not going to take cyanide."

"Of course not."

As they skidded round Pen Cuckoo corner, Templett said, "I didn't do it."

"All right."

At the church lane turning the car skated twenty yards on the greasy road, and fetched up sideways. Alleyn held his peace and trod on imaginary brakes. They started off again more reasonably, but entered Chipping at forty miles an hour.

"Will you stop outside the Jernigham Arms for a minute?" asked Alleyn.

Templett did not slow down until they were within two hundred yards of the inn. They shot across the road and stopped with screaming brakes. The pot-boy came running out.

"Is Mr. Fox there? Ask him to come out, will you?" called Alleyn cheerfully. "And when Mr. Bathgate arrives, send him on to the police station at Great Chipping. Ask him to bring my case with him."

Fox came out, bare-headed.

"Pop in at the back, Brer Fox," said Alleyn. "We're going into Great Chipping. Dr. Templett will take us."

"Good-evening, doctor," said Fox, and got in.

Dr. Templett put in his clutch and was off before the door shut. Alleyn's arm hung over the back of the seat. He twiddled his long fingers eloquently.

They reached the outskirts of Great Chipping in ten minutes, and here Templett seemed to come to his senses. He drove reasonably enough through the narrow provincial streets and pulled up at the police station.

Blandish was there. A constable showed them into his office and stood inside the door.

"Good-evening, gentlemen," said the superintendent, who seemed to be in superb form. "Some good news for me, I hope? Glad to say we're getting on quite nicely with our little job, Mr. Alleyn. I wouldn't surprised if we won't be able to give the City a bit of very sound information by to-morrow. The bird's flown to Bermondsey, and we ought to be able to pull him in. Very gratifying. Well, now, sit down, all of you. Smith! The chair by the door."

He bustled hospitably, caught sight of Templett's face and was abruptly silent.

"I'll make a statement," said Templett.

"I think perhaps I should warn you——" said Alleyn.

"I know all that. I'll make a statement."

Fox moved up to the table. Superintendent Blandish very startled and solemn, shoved across a pad of paper.

II

"On Friday afternoon," said Dr. Templett, "on my return from hunting, an anonymous letter came into my possession. I believe the police now have this letter. Inspector Alleyn has shown it to me. I attached very little importance to it. I do not know who wrote it. I put it in my pocket-book in the inside breast-pocket of my coat. I intended to destroy it. At five o'clock on Friday I attended a rehearsal at

Pen Cuckoo. On my return home I was immediately called
out on a difficult case. I did not get back until late night.
I forgot all about the letter. Yesterday, Saturday, wearing the
same suit, I left my house at about 8.30, having only just got
up. I collected some furniture from Duck Cottage, called
at Pen Cuckoo, went on to the hall, where I left the furniture. She was with me. The rest of Saturday was spent
on my rounds. I was unusually busy. They gave me some
lunch at the cottage hospital. In the afternoon I called at
the hall. I was only there for about half an hour. I did not
go near the piano and I didn't remember the letter. I was not
alone at the hall at any time. I arrived there for the evening
performance at half-past seven, or possibly later. I went
straight to my dressing-room and changed, hanging up my coat
on the wall. Henry Jernigham came in and helped me. After
the tragedy I did not change until I got home. At no
time did I remember the letter. The next time I saw it,
was this afternoon when Inspector Alleyn showed it to me.
That's all."

Fox looked up.

Blandish said, " Make a full transcript of Inspector Fox's
notes, Smith."

Smith went out with the notes.

Alleyn said, " Before we go any further, Dr. Templett,
I think I should tell you that the letter I showed you
was a copy of the original and made on identical paper.
The original is in our possession and it is in my bag. Fox,
do you mind seeing if Bathgate has arrived?"

Fox went out and in a minute returned with Alleyn's
case.

" Have you," Alleyn asked Templett, " as far as your
memory serves, given us the whole truth in the statement
you have just made?"

" I've given you everything that's relevant."

" I am going to put several questions to you. Would you
like to wait until your lawyer is present?"

" I don't want a lawyer. I'm innocent."

" Your answers will be taken down and——"

" And may be used in evidence. I know."

"—And may be used in evidence," Alleyn repeated.

" Well?" asked Templett.

" Have you shown the letter to any one else?"

" No."

" Did you receive it by post?"

" Yes."

174

Alleyn nodded to Fox, who opened the case and took out the original letter between its two glass cover sheets.

"Here it is," said Alleyn. "You see, we have developed the prints. There are three sets—yours, the deceased's, and another's. I must tell you that the unknown prints will be compared with any that we find on the copy which Mrs. Ross has held in her hands. You can see, if you look at the original, that one set of prints is superimposed on the other two. Those are your own. The deceased's prints are the undermost."

Templett did not speak.

"Dr. Templett, I am going to tell you what I believe to have happened. I believe that this letter was sent in the first instance to Mrs. Ross. The wording suggests that it was addressed to a woman rather than a man. I believe that Mrs. Ross showed it to you on Saturday, which was yesterday morning, and that you put it in your pocket-book. If this is so, you know as well as I do that you will be ill-advised to deny it. You have told us the letter came by post. Do you now feel it would be better to alter this statement?"

"It makes no difference."

"It makes all the difference between giving the police facts instead of fiction. If we find what we expect to find from the fingerprints, you will not help matters by adding your misstatement to the one that was made at Duck Cottage."

Alleyn paused and looked at the undistinguished, dogged face.

"You have had a great shock," he said, and added in a voice so low that Blandish put his hand to his ear like a deaf rustic: "It's no good trying to protect people who are ready at any sacrifice of loyalty to protect themselves."

Templett laughed.

"So it seems," he said. "All right. That's how it was. It's no good denying it."

"Mrs. Ross gave you the letter on Saturday?"

"I suppose so. Yes."

"Did you guess at the authorship?"

"I *guessed*."

"Did you notice the smell of eucalyptus?"

"Yes. But I'm innocent. My God, I tell you I had no opportunity. I can give you an account of every moment of the day."

"When you were at the hall with Mrs. Ross, did you not leave her to go down to the auditorium?"

"Why should I?"

"Mrs. Ross told me you shut one of the windows."

"Yes. I'd forgotten. Yes, I did."

"But if Mrs. Ross says she had shut this window herself in the morning?"

"I know. We couldn't make it out."

"You noticed the open window, shut it, returned to the stage, and lowered the curtain?"

"*Did she tell you that!*"

Templett suddenly collapsed into the chair behind him and buried his face in his hands. "My God," he said, "I've been a fool. *What* a fool!"

"They say it happens once to most of us," said Alleyn unexpectedly and not unkindly. "Did Mrs. Ross not mention at the time that she thought she had already shut the window."

"Yes, yes, yes. She said so. But the window was *open*. It was opened about three inches. How can I expect you to believe it? You think I lowered the curtain, went to the piano, and fixed this bloody trap. I tell you I didn't."

"Why did you lower the curtain?"

Templett looked at his hands.

"Oh, God," he said. "Have we got to go into all that?"

"I see," said Alleyn. "No, I don't think we need. There was a scene that would have compromised you both if anybody had witnessed it?"

"Yes."

"Did you at any time speak about the letter?"

"She asked me if I'd found out—I may as well tell you. I've got a note somewhere from Miss Campanula. I thought I'd compare the paper. I'd been so rushed during the day I hadn't had time. That's why I didn't destroy the thing."

"When you opened the window did you look out?"

"What? Yes. Yes. I think I did." There was a curious note of uncertainty in his voice.

"Have you remembered something?"

"What's the good! It sounds like something I've made up at the last moment."

"Let's have it anyway."

"Well, she caught sight of the window. She noticed it first; saw it over my shoulder, and got an impression that there was something that dodged down behind the sill. It was only a flash, she said. I thought it was probably one of those damned scouts. When I got to the window I looked out. There was nobody there."

"Were you upset by the discovery of an eavesdropper?"
Templett shrugged his shoulders.

"Oh, what's the good!" he said. "Yes, I suppose we were."

"Who was this individual?"

"I can't tell you."

"But didn't Mrs. Ross say who it was? She must have had some impression."

"Ask her if you must," he said violently. "I can't tell you."

"When you looked out they had gone," murmured Alleyn. "But you looked out."

He watched Dr. Templett, and Blandish and Fox watched him. Fox realised that they had reached a climax. He knew what Alleyn's next question would be, he saw Alleyn raise one eyebrow and screw his mouth sideways before he asked his question.

"Did you look down?" asked Alleyn.

"Yes."

"And you saw?"

"There was a box under the window."

"Ah!" It was the smallest sigh. Alleyn seemed to relax all over. He smiled to himself and pulled out his cigarette case.

"That seemed to suggest," said Templett, "that somebody had stood there, using the box. It wasn't there when I got to the hall because I went round that way to get the key."

Alleyn turned to Fox.

"Have you asked them about the box?"

"Yes, sir. Mr. Jernigham, Miss Prentice, every kid in the village, *and* all the helpers. Nobody knows anything about it."

"Good," said Alleyn, heartily.

For the first time since they got there, Dr. Templett showed some kind of interest.

"Is it important?" he asked.

"Yes," said Alleyn. "I think it's of the first importance."

III

"You knew about this box?" asked Templett after a pause.

"Yes, why don't you smoke, Dr. Templett?" Alleyn held out his case.

" Are you going to charge me?"

" No. Not on present information."

Templett took a cigarette and Alleyn lit it for him.

" I'm in a hell of a mess," said Templett. " I see that."

" Yes," agreed Alleyn. " One way and another you've landed yourself in rather a box." But there was something in his manner that drove the terror out of Templett's eyes.

Smith came in with the transcript.

" Sergeant Roper's outside, sir," he said. " He came down with Mr. Bathgate and wants to see you particularly."

" He can wait," said Blandish. " He's wanted to see me particular about ten times a day ever since we got busy."

" Yes, sir. Will I leave this transcript?"

" Leave it here," said Blandish, " and wait outside."

When Smith had gone Blandish spoke to Dr. Templett for the first time that evening.

" I'm very sorry about this, doctor."

" That's all right," said Templett.

" I think Mr. Alleyn will agree with me that if it's got no bearing on the case we'll do our best to bury it."

" Certainly," said Alleyn.

" I don't care much what happens," said Templett.

" Oh, come now, doctor," said Blandish uncomfortably, " you mustn't say that."

But Alleyn saw a gay little drawing-room with a delicate straw-coloured lady, whose good nature did not stretch beyond a very definite point, and he thought he understood Dr. Templett.

" I think," he said, " you had better give us a complete time-table of your movements from two-thirty on Friday up to eight o'clock last night. We shall check it, but we'll make the process an impersonal sort of business."

" But for those ten minutes in the hall, I'm all right," said Templett. " God, I was with her all the time, until I shut the window! Ask her how long it took! I wasn't away two minutes over the business. Surely to God she'll at least bear me out in that. She's nothing to lose by it."

" She shall be asked," said Alleyn.

Templett began to give the names of all the houses he had visited on his rounds. Fox took them down.

Alleyn suddenly asked Blandish to find out how long the Pen Cuckoo telephone had been disconnected by the falling branch. Blandish rang up the exchange.

" From eight-twenty until the next morning."

" Yes," said Alleyn. " Yes."

Dr. Templett's voice droned on with its flat recital of time and place.

"Yes, I hunted all day Friday. I got home in time to change and go to the five o'clock rehearsal. The servants can check that. When I got home again I found this urgent message. . . . I was out till after midnight. Mrs. Bains at Mill Farm. She was in labour twenty-four hours . . . yes. . . ."

"May I interrupt?" asked Alleyn. "Yesterday morning, at Pen Cuckoo, Mrs. Ross did not leave the car?"

"No."

"Were you shown into the study?"

"Yes."

"You were there alone?"

"Yes," said Templett, showing the whites of his eyes.

"Dr. Templett, did you touch the box with the automatic?"

"Before God, I didn't."

"One more question. Last night did you use all your powers of authority and persuasion to induce Miss Prentice to allow Miss Campanula to take her place?"

"Yes, but—she wouldn't listen to me."

"Will you describe again how you found her?"

"I told you last night. I came in late. I thought Dinah would be worried and after I'd changed, I went along to the women's dressing-room to show her I was there. I heard some one snivelling and moaning, and through the open door I saw Miss Prentice in floods of tears, rocking backwards and forwards and holding her hand. I went in and looked at it. No doctor in his senses would have let her thump the piano. She *couldn't* have done it. I told her so, but she kept on saying, 'I will do it. I will do it.' I got angry and spoke my mind. I couldn't get any further with her. It was damned near time we started and I wasn't even made-up."

"So you fetched Miss Copeland and her father, knowing the rector would possibly succeed where you had failed."

"Yes. But I tell you it was physically impossible for her to use the finger. I could have told her that——"

He stopped short.

"Yes? You could have told her that, how long ago?" said Alleyn.

"Three days ago."

Smith returned.

"It's Sergeant Roper, sir. He says it's very particular indeed and he knows Mr. Alleyn would want to hear it."

"Blast!" said Blandish. "All right, all right."

Smith left the door open. Alleyn saw Nigel crouched over an anthracite stove and Roper, sweating and expectant, in the middle of the room.

"Right oh, Roper," said Smith, audibly. Roper hurriedly removed his helmet, cleared his throat, and marched heavily into the room.

"Well, Roper?" said Blandish.

"Sir," said Roper, "I have a report." He took his official note-book from a pocket in his tunic and opened it, bringing it into line with his nose. He began to read very rapidly in a high voice.

"This afternoon, November 28th, at 4 p.m. being on duty at the time outside the parish hall of Winton St. Giles I was approached and accosted by a young female. She was well-known to me being by name Gladys Wright (Miss) of Top Lane, Winton. The following conversation eventuated. Miss Wright enquired of me if I was waiting for my girl or my promotion. Myself (P.S. Roper): I am on duty, Miss Wright, and would take it kindly if you would pass along the lane. Miss Wright: Look what our cat's brought in. P.S. Roper: And I don't want no lip or saucy boldness. Miss Wright: I could tell you something and I've come along to do it, but seeing you're on duty maybe I'll keep it for your betters. P.S. Roper: If you know anything, Gladys, you'd better speak up for the law comes down with majesty on them that aids and abets and withholds. Miss Wright: What will you give me? The succeeding remarks are not evidence and bear no connection with the matter in hand. They are therefore omitted."

"What the hell did she tell you?" asked Blandish. "Shut that damned book and come to the point."

"Sir, the girl told me in her silly way that she came down to the hall at six-thirty on yesterday evening being one of them selected to usher. She let herself in and finding herself first to arrive, living nearby and not wishing to return home, the night being heavy rain with squalls and her hair being artificially twisted up with curls which to my mind——"

"*What did she tell you?*"

"She told me that at six-thirty she sat down as bold as brass and played 'Nearer my Gawd to Thee' with the soft pedal on," said Roper.

CHAPTER TWENTY

According to Miss Wright

SERGEANT ROPER, sweating lightly, allowed an expression of extreme gratification to suffuse his enormous face. The effect of his statement on his superiors left nothing to be desired. Superintendent Blandish stared at his sergeant like a startled codfish, Detective-Inspector Fox pushed his glasses up his forehead and brought his hands down smartly on his knees. Dr. Templett uttered in a whisper a string of amazing blasphemies. Chief Inspector Alleyn pulled his own nose, made a peculiar grimace, and said:

"Roper, you shall be hung with garlands, led through the village, and offered up at the Harvest Festival."

"Thank you, sir," said Roper.

"Where," asked Alleyn, "is Gladys Wright?"

Roper flexed his knees and pointed with his thumb over his shoulder.

"Stuck to her like glue, I have. I telephoned Fife from the hall to relieve me, keeping the silly maiden under observation the while. I brought her here, sir, on the bar of my bike, all ten stone of her, and seven mile if it's an inch."

"Magnificent. Bring her in, Roper."

Roper went out.

"I didn't get there till half-past seven," whispered Dr. Templett, shaking his finger at Alleyn. "Not till half-past seven. You see! You see! The hall was full of people. Ask Dinah Copeland. She'll tell you I never went on the stage. Ask Copeland. He was sitting on the stage. I saw him through the door when I called him down. Ask any of them. My God!"

Alleyn reached out a long arm and gripped his wrist.

"Steady, now," he said. "Fox, there's the emergency flask in that case."

He got Templett to take the brandy before Roper returned.

"Miss Gladys Wright, sir," said Roper, flinging back the door and expanding his chest.

He shepherded his quarry into the room with watchful pride, handed her over, and retired behind the door to wipe his face down excitedly with the palm of his hand.

Miss Wright was the large young lady whom Alleyn had encountered in the rectory hall. Under a mackintosh she wore a plushy sort of dress with a hint of fur about it. Her head was indeed a mass of curls. Her face was crimson and her eyes black.

"Good-evening, Miss Wright," said Alleyn. "I'm afraid we've put you to a lot of trouble. Will you sit down?"

He gave her his own chair and sat on the edge of the desk.

Miss Wright backed up to the chair rather in the manner of a draught-horse, got half-way towards sitting on it, but thought better of this, and giggled.

"Sergeant Roper tells us you've got some information for us," continued Alleyn.

"Aw him!" said Miss Wright. She laughed and covered her mouth with her hand.

"Now I understand that you arrived at the parish hall at half-past six last night. Is that right?"

"That's right."

"Sure of the time?"

"Yass," said Miss Wright. "I heard the clock strike, see?"

"Good. How did you get in?"

"I got the key from outside and came in by the back door," said Miss Wright, and looked at the floor. "Miss Dinah was soon after me."

"Nobody else was in the hall. You switched on the light, I suppose?"

"Yass, that's right."

"What did you do next?"

"Well, I looked round, like."

"Yes. Have a good look round?"

"Aaw, yass. I suppose so."

"Back and front of the stage, what? Yes. And then?"

"I took off my mac, and put out my programmes, like, and counted up my change, see, for selling."

"Yes?"

"Aw deer," said Miss Wright, "it does give me such a turn when I think about it."

"I'm sure it does."

"You know! When you think! What I was saying to Charley Roper, you never know. And look, I never thought of it till this afternoon at the Children's Service. I was collecting up hymn-books and it come all over me, so when

182

I see Charley Roper hanging about outside the hall, I says, 'Pardon me, Mr. Roper,' I says, 'but I have a piece of information I feel it my duty to pass on.'"

"Very proper," said Alleyn with a glance at Roper.

"Yass, and I told him. I told him I might be laying where she is, seeing what I did!"

"What did you do?"

"I sat down and played a hymn on that rickety old affair. Aw, *well*!"

"Did you play loudly or softly?"

"Well, well, both, ackshully. I was seeing which pedal worked best on that shocking old affair, see?"

"Yes," said Alleyn. "I see. Did you put the pedal on suddenly and hard?"

"Aw no. Because one time the soft pedal went all queer because Cissie Dewry put her foot on it, so we always use it gentle-like. I didn't try it but the bare once. The loud one worked better," said Miss Wright.

"Yes," agreed Alleyn. "I expect it would."

"Well, it did," confessed Miss Wright, and giggled again.

"But you did actually press the soft pedal down?" insisted Alleyn.

"Yass. Firm like. Not sharp."

"Exactly. Was there a piece of music on the rack?"

"Oo yass, Miss Prentice's piece. I never touched it. Truely!"

"I'm sure you didn't. Miss Wright, suppose you were in a court of law, and someone put a Bible in your hand, and you were asked to swear solemnly in God's name that at about twenty to seven last night you put your foot firmly on the left pedal, would you swear it?"

Miss Wright giggled.

"It's very important," said Alleyn. "You see, there would be a prisoner in the court on trial for murder. Please think very carefully indeed. Would you make this statement on oath?"

"Oh *yass*," said Miss Wright.

"Thank you," said Alleyn. He looked at Templett. "I don't think we need keep you, Dr. Templett, if you are anxious to get home."

"I—I'll drive you back," said Templett.

"That's very nice of you—I shan't be long." He turned back to Gladys Wright. "Did any one come in while you were playing?"

"I stopped when I heard them coming. Cissie Dewry come first and then all the other girls."

"Did you notice any of the performers?"

"No. We was all talking round the door, like." She rolled her eyes at Roper. "That was when you come, Mr. Roper."

"Well, Roper?"

"They were in the entrance, sir, giggling and cackling in their female manner, sure enough."

"Oo you *are*," said Miss Wright.

"And had any of the company arrived at that time?"

"Yes, sir," said Roper. "Miss Copeland was there ahead of me, but she went to the back door same as all the performers, I don't doubt. And the Pen Cuckoo party was there, sir, but I didn't know that till I went round to back of stage when I found them bedizening their faces in the Sunday-school rooms."

"So that there was a moment when the ladies were at the front door, talking, and the Pen Cuckoo party and Miss Copeland were behind the scenes?"

"That's right, sir."

"They were ringing and ringing at the telephone," interjected Miss Wright, "all the time us girls was there."

"And you say, Miss Wright, that none of the performers came into the front of the hall."

"Not one. Truly."

"Sure?"

"Yass. Certain sure. We would have seen them. Soon after that the doors were open and people started to come in."

"Where did you stand?"

"Up top by the stage, ushering the two shillingses."

"So if anybody had come down to the piano from the stage you would have seen them?"

"Nobody came down. Not ever. I'd take another Bible oath on that," said Miss Wright, with considerable emphasis.

"Thank you," said Alleyn. "That's splendid. One other question. You were at the Reading Circle meeting at the rectory on Friday night. Did you go home by the gate into the wood. The gate that squeaks?"

"Oo no! None of us girls goes that way at night." Miss Wright giggled, extensively. "It's too spooky. Oo, I wouldn't go that way for anything. The others, they all went together, and my young gentleman, he took me home by lane."

"So you're sure nobody used the gate?"

"Yass, for sure. They'd all gone," said Miss Wright, turning scarlet, "before us. And we used lane."

"You passed the hall, then. Were there any lights in the hall?"

"Not in front."

"You couldn't see the back windows, of course. Thank you so much, Miss Wright. We'll get you to sign a transcript of everything you have told us. Read it through carefully, first. If you wouldn't mind waiting in the outer office I think I can arrange for you to be driven home."

"Oo well, thanks ever so," said Miss Wright, and went out.

II

Alleyn looked at Templett.

"I ought to apologise," he said, "I've given you a damned bad hour."

"I don't know why you didn't arrest me," said Templett with a shaky laugh. "Ever since I realised I'd left that bloody note in the dressing-room I've been trying to think how I could prove I hadn't rigged the automatic. There seemed to be no possible proof. Even now I don't see—— Oh, well, it doesn't matter. Nothing much matters. If you don't mind, I'll wait outside in the car. I'd like a breath of fresh air."

"Certainly."

Dr. Templett nodded to Blandish and went out.

"Will I shadow the man?" asked Roper, earnestly.

Blandish's reply was unprintable.

"You might ask Mr. Bathgate to drive your witness home, Roper," said Alleyn. "Let her sign her statement first. Tell Mr. Bathgate I'm returning with Dr. Templett. And Roper, as tactfully as you can, just see how Dr. Templett's getting on. He's had a shock."

"Yes, sir."

Roper went out.

"He's got about as much tact as a cow," said Blandish.

"I know, but at least he'll keep an eye on Templett."

"The lady let him down, did she?"

"With a thump that shook the crockery."

"S-s-s-s!" said Blandish appreciatively. "Is that a fact?"

"He's had two narrow escapes," said Fox, "and *that's*

a fact. The lady's let him down with a jerk and he's lucky the hangman won't follow suit."

"Fox," said Alleyn, "you have the wit of a Tyburn broadsheet, but there's matter in it."

"I don't know where I am," said Blandish. "Are we any nearer to an arrest?"

"A good step," said Alleyn. "The pattern emerges."

"What does that mean, Mr. Alleyn?"

"Well," said Alleyn, apologetically, "I mean all these mad little things like the box, and the broken telephone, and the creaking gate—I'm not sure of the onion——"

"The onion!" cried Fox, triumphantly. "I know all about the onion, Mr. Alleyn. Georgie Biggins is responsible for that, the young limb. I saw him this afternoon and asked him, as well as every other youngster in the village, about the box. He's going round as pleased as Punch, letting on he's working at the case with the Yard. Answers me as cool as you please, and when I'm going he says, 'Did you find an onion in the teapot, mister?' Well, it seems that they had a tea-party on the stage, with Miss Prentice and Miss Campanula quarrelling about which should pour out. If the young devil didn't go and put an onion in the pot. It seems they each had to take the lid off and look in the pot and this was another of Georgie's bright ideas. I suppose someone found it in time and threw it into the box on the floor, where you picked it up."

"Dear little Georgie," said Alleyn. "Dear little boy! We've had red herrings before now, Fox, but never a Spanish onion. Well, as I was saying, all these mad little things begin to bear some sort of relationship."

"That's nice, Mr. Alleyn," said Fox, woodenly. "You're going to tell us you know who did it, I suppose?"

"Oh, yes," said Alleyn looking at him in genuine surprise. "I do *now*, Brer Fox. Don't you?"

III

When a man learns that his mistress, faced with putting herself in a compromising position, will quite literally see him hanged first, he is not inclined for conversation. Templett drove slowly back towards Chipping and was completely silent until the first cottage came into view. Then he said, "I don't see how any one could have done it. The piano was safe at six-thirty. The girl used the soft pedal. It was safe."

"Yes," agreed Alleyn.

"I suppose, putting the pedal down softly, the pressure wasn't enough to pull the trigger?"

"It's a remarkably light pull," said Alleyn. "I've tried."

Templett brushed his hand across his eyes. "I suppose my brain won't work."

"Give the thing a rest."

"But how could anybody fix that contraption inside the piano after half-past six when those girls were sky-larking about in the front of the house? It's impossible."

"If you come down to the hall to-morrow night, I'll show you."

"All right. Here's your pub. What time's the inquest? I've forgotten. I'm all to pieces." He pulled up the car.

"Eleven o'clock to-morrow."

Alleyn and Fox got out. It was a cold windy evening. The fine weather had broken again and it had begun to rain. Alleyn stood with the door open and looked at Templett. He leaned on the wheel and stared with blank eyes at the windscreen.

"The process of convalescence," said Alleyn, "should follow the initial shock. Take heart of grace, you will recover."

"I'll go home," said Templett. "Good-night."

"Good-night."

He drove away.

They went upstairs to their rooms.

"Let's swap stories, Brer Fox," said Alleyn. "I'll lay my case, for what it's worth, on the dressing-table. I want a shave. You can open your little heart while I'm having it. I don't think we'll unburden ourselves to Bathgate just yet."

They brought each other up-to-date before they went downstairs again in search of a drink.

They found Nigel alone in the bar parlour.

"I'm not going to pay for so much as half a drink and I intend to drink a very great deal. I've had the dullest afternoon of my life and all for your benefit. Miss Wright smells. When I took her to her blasted cottage she made me go in to tea with her brother who turns out to be the village idiot. Yes, and on the way back from Duck Cottage, your lovely car sprang a puncture. Furthermore——"

"Joe!" shouted Alleyn. "Three whiskies-and-sodas."

"I should damn' well think so. What are you ordering for yourselves?"

Nigel calmed down presently and listened to Alleyn's account of the afternoon. Mrs. Peach, a large flowing woman, told them she had a proper juicy steak for their dinner and there was a fine fire in the back parlour. They moved in, taking their drinks with them. It was pleasant, when the curtains were drawn and the red-shaded oil lamp was lit, to hear the rain driving against the leaded windows and to listen to the sound of grilling steak beyond the kitchen slide.

"Not so many places left like this," said Fox. "Cosy, isn't it? I haven't seen one of those paraffin lamps for many a long day. Mrs. Peach says old Mr. Peach, her father-in-law, you know, won't have electricity in the house. He's given in as far as the tap-room's concerned but nowhere else. Listen to the rain! It'll be a wild night again."

"Yes," said Alleyn. "It's strange, isn't it, to think of the actors in this silly far-fetched crime, all sitting over their fires, as we are now, six of them wondering what the answer is, and the seventh nursing it secretly in what used to be known as a guilty heart."

"Oo-er," said Nigel.

Mrs. Peach's daughter brought in the steak.

"Are you going out again?" asked Nigel after an interval.

"I've got a report to write," answered Alleyn. "When that's done I think I might go up to the hall."

"Whatever for?"

"Practical demonstration of the booby-trap."

"I might come," said Nigel. "I can ring up the office from there."

"You'll have to square up with the Copelands if you do. The hall telephone is on an extension from the rectory. Great hopping fleas!" shouted Alleyn, "why the devil didn't I think of that before!"

"What!"

"The telephone."

"Excuse him," said Nigel to Fox.

IV

"We'll take half an hour's respite," said Alleyn, when the cloth had been drawn and a bottle of 'port, recommended by old Mr. Peach, had been set before them. "Let's go over the salient features."

"Why not?" agreed Nigel, comfortably.

Alleyn tried the port, raised an eyebrow, and lit a cigarette. "It's respectable," he said. "An honest wine and all that. Well, as I see it, the salient features are these. Georgie Biggins rigged his booby-trap between two and three on Friday afternoon. Miss Campanula rattled on the door just before two-thirty. Georgie was in the hall, but must have hidden, because when Gibson looked through the window, the top of the piano was open and Georgie nowhere to be seen. Miss Campanula didn't know that the key was hung up behind the outhouse. The rest of the company were told but they are vague about it. Now Georgie didn't test his booby-trap because, as he says, 'somebody came.' I think this refers to Miss Campanula's onslaught on the door. I'm afraid Miss Campanula is a nightmare to Georgie. He won't discuss her. I'll have to try again. Anyway, he didn't test his booby-trap. But *somebody* did, because the silk round the hole made by the bullet was still damp last night. That means something was on the rack, possibly Miss Prentice's ' Venetian Suite ' which seems to have been down in the hall for the last week. It has a stain on the back which suggests that the jet of water hit it and splayed out, wetting the silk. Now, Georgie left the hall soon after the interruption, because he finished up by playing "Chop-sticks" with the loud pedal on, and Miss Campanula overheard this final performance. The next eighteen hours or so are still wrapped in mystery but, as far as we know, any of the company may have gone into the hall. Miss Prentice passed it on her way home from confession, the Copelands live within two minutes of the place. Master Henry says that after his meeting with Dinah Copeland he roamed the hills most of that unpleasantly damp afternoon. He may have come down to the hall. Jernigham senior seems to have hunted all day and so does Templett, but either of them may have come down in the evening. Miss Prentice says she spent the evening praying in her room, Master Henry says he tinkered with a light plug in his room, the squire says he was alone in the study. It takes about eight minutes to walk down Top Lane to the hall and perhaps fifteen to return. On Friday night the rector had an agonising encounter in his own study. I'll tell you about it."

Alleyn told them about it.

"Now the remarkable thing about this is that I believe he spoke the truth, but his story is made so much nonsense if Dinah Copeland was right in thinking there was a third
189

person present. Miss C. would hardly make passionate advances and hang herself round the rector's neck, with a Friendly Helper to watch the fun. Dinah Copeland bases her theory on the fact that she heard the gate opposite the study window squeak, as if somebody had gone out that way. She tells us it couldn't have been Miss Prentice because Miss Prentice rang up a few minutes later to say she wasn't coming down. We know Miss Prentice was upset when she left confession that afternoon. The rector had ticked her off and given her a penance or something and he thinks that's why she didn't come. It wasn't any of the readers. Who the devil was it?"

" The rector himself," said Nigel promptly, " taking a short cut to the hall."

" He says that after Miss C. left him he remained a wreck by his fireside."

" That may not be true."

" It may be as false as hell," agreed Alleyn. " There are one or two points about this business. I'll describe the lay-out and repeat the rector's story."

When he had done this he looked at Fox.

" Yes," said Fox. " Yes, I think I get you there, Mr. Alleyn."

" Obviously, I'm right," said Nigel, flippantly. " It's the reverend."

" Mr. Copeland's refusing the money, Mr. Bathgate," said Fox. " I was telling the chief, just now. I got that bit of information this afternoon. Mr. Henry told the squire in front of the servants and it's all round the village."

" Well, to finish Friday," said Alleyn. " Dr. Templett spent the best part of the night on a case. That can be checked. Mrs. Ross says she was at home. To-morrow, Foxkin, I'll get you to use your glamour on Mrs. Ross's maid."

" Very good, sir."

" Now then. Some time before noon yesterday, the water-pistol disappeared, because at noon Miss P. strummed with her right hand and used the soft pedal. Nothing happened."

" Perhaps Georgie's plan didn't work," suggested Nigel.

" We are going to see presently if Georgie's plan works. Whether it works or not, the fact remains that somebody found the water-pistol, removed and hid it, and substituted the Colt."

" That must have been later still," said Nigel.

"I agree with you, but not, I imagine, for the same reason. Dr. Templett's story seems to prove that the box was placed outside the window while he and Mrs. Ross were in the hall. He got the impression that someone dodged down behind the sill. Now this eavesdropper was not Miss Campanula because the servants agree that she didn't go out yesterday afternoon. Miss Prentice, the squire, Dinah Copeland and her father were all in their respective houses, but any of them could have slipped out for an hour. Master Henry was again roving the countryside. None of them owns to the box outside the window. Fox has asked every soul in the place and not a soul professes to know anything about the box."

"That's right," said Fox. "I reckon the murderer was hanging about with the Colt and had a look in to see who was there. He'd see the cars in the lane but he'd want to find out if the occupants were in the hall or had gone that way into the vicarage. On the far side of the hall he'd have been out of sight, and he'd have plenty of time to dodge if they sounded as if they were coming round that way. But they never would, of course, seeing it's the far side. He'd be safe enough. Or she," added Fox with a bland glance at Nigel.

"That's how I read it," agreed Alleyn. "Now, look here."

He took an envelope from his breast pocket, opened it, and, using tweezers, took out four minute reddish-brown scraps, which he laid on a sheet of paper.

"Salvage from the box," he said.

Nigel prodded at them with the tweezers.

"Rubber," said Nigel.

"Convey anything?"

"Somebody wearing goloshes. Miss Prentice, by gosh. I bet she wears goloshes. Or Miss C. herself. Good Lord," said Nigel, "perhaps the rector's right. Perhaps it is a case of suicide."

"These bits of rubber were caught on a projecting nail and some rough bits of wood inside the box."

"Well, she might have trodden inside the box before she picked it up."

"You have your moments," said Alleyn. "I suppose she might."

"Goloshes!" said Fox and chuckled deeply.

"Here!" said Nigel, angrily. "Have you got a case?"

191

" The makings of one," said Alleyn. " We're not going to tell you just yet, because we don't want to lower our prestige."

" We like to watch your struggles, Mr. Bathgate," said Fox.

" We are, as it might be," said Alleyn, " two experts on a watch-tower in the middle of a maze. ' Look at the poor wretch,' we say as we nudge each other, ' there he goes into the same old blind alley. Jolly comical,' we say, and then we laugh like anything. Don't we, Fox?"

" So we do," agreed Fox. " But never you mind, Mr. Bathgate, you're doing very nicely."

" Well, to hell with you anyway," said Nigel. " And moreover what about Gladys Wright putting her splay foot on the soft pedal an hour and a half before the tragedy?"

" Perhaps she wore goloshes," said Fox, and for the first time in these records he broke into a loud laugh.

CHAPTER TWENTY-ONE

According to Mr. Saul Tranter

ALLEYN finished his report by nine o'clock. At a quarter-past nine they were back in the Biggins' Ford, driving through pelting rain to the hall.

" I'll have to go up to the Yard before this case is many hours older," said Alleyn. " I telephoned the A.C. this morning but I think I ought to see him and there are a lot of odd things to be cleared up. Perhaps to-morrow night. I'd like to get to the bottom of that meeting between Master Henry, Dinah Copeland and Miss Prentice. I rather think Master Henry wishes to unburden himself and Miss Dinah won't let him. Here we are."

Once more they crunched up the gravel path to the front door. The shutters had been closed and they and the windows were all locked. P.C. Fife was on duty. He let them in and being an incurious fellow retired thankfully when Alleyn said he would not be wanted for two hours.

" I'll ring up the Chipping station when we're leaving," said Alleyn.

The hall smelt of dying evergreens and varnish. It was extremely cold. The piano still stood in its old position against the stage. The hole in the faded silk gaped mournfully. The aspidistras drooped a little in their pots. A fine dust had settled over everything. The rain drove down steadily on the old building and the wind shook the shutters and howled desperately under the eaves.

"I'm going to light these heaters," said Nigel. "There's a can of paraffin in one of the back rooms. This place smells of mortality."

Alleyn opened his case and took out Georgie Biggins's water-pistol. Fox wedged the butt between steel pegs in the iron casing. The nozzle fitted a hole in the fretwork front. They had left the cord and pulleys in position.

"On Friday," said Alleyn, "there was only the long rent in the tucked silk. You see there are several of them. The material has rotted in the creases. No doubt Georgie arranged the silk tastefully behind the fretwork, so that the nozzle didn't catch the light. We'll have a practical demonstration from Mr. Bathgate, Fox. Now, if you fix the front pulley, I'll tie the cord round the butt of the pistol. Hurry up. I hear him clanking in the background."

They had just dropped a sheet of newspaper on the rack when Nigel reappeared with a large can.

"There's some fairly good beer in that room," said Nigel. He began to fill the tank of the heater from his can.

Alleyn sat down at the piano, struck two or three chords, and began to vamp "*Il était une Bergère.*"

"That's odd, Fox," he said.

"What's wrong, Mr. Alleyn?"

"I can't get the soft pedal to budge. You try. Don't force it."

Fox seated himself at the piano and picked out "Three Blind Mice," with a stubby forefinger.

"That's right," he said, "It makes no difference."

"What's all this?" demanded Nigel, and bustled forward.

"The soft pedal doesn't work."

"Good Lord!"

"It makes no difference to the sound," said Fox.

"You're not using it."

"Yes, I am, Mr. Bathgate," lied Fox.

"Here," said Nigel, "let me try."

Fox got up. Nigel took his place with an air of importance.

"Rachmaninoff's Prelude in C—Minor," he said. He squared his elbows, raised his left hand and leant forward. The voice of the wind mounted in a thin wail and seemed to encircle the building. Down came Nigel's left hand like a sledge-hammer.

"Pom. *Pom*. POM!"

Nigel paused. A violent gust shook the shutters so impatiently that, for a second, he raised his head and listened. Then he trod on the soft pedal.

The newspaper fell forward on his hands. The thin jet of water caught him between the eyes like a cold bullet. He jerked backwards, uttered a scandalous oath, and nearly lost his balance.

"It does work," said Alleyn.

But Nigel did not retaliate. Above all the uneasy clamour of the storm, and like an echo of the three pretentious chords, sounded a loud triple knock on the front door.

"Who the devil's that?" said Alleyn.

He started forward, but before he could reach the door it crashed open, and on the threshold stood Henry Jernigham with streaks of rain lacing his chalk-white face.

II

"What the hell's happening in here?" demanded Henry.

"Suppose you shut the door," said Alleyn.

But Henry stared at him as if he had not heard. Alleyn walked past him, slammed the door, and secured the catch. Then he returned to Henry, took him by the elbow, and marched him up the hall.

Fox waited stolidly. Nigel wiped his face with his handkerchief and stared at Henry.

"Now what is it?" demanded Alleyn.

"My God!" said Henry, "who played those three infernal chords?"

"Mr. Bathgate. This is Mr. Bathgate, Mr. Jernigham, and this is Detective-Inspector Fox." Henry looked dimly at the other two and sat down suddenly.

"Oh, Lord," he said.

"I say," said Nigel. "I'm most extraordinarily sorry if I gave you a shock, but I assure you I never thought——"

"I'd come into the lane," said Henry, breathlessly, "the rectory trees were making such a noise in the wind that you couldn't hear anything else."

"Yes?" said Alleyn.

"Don't you see? I'd come up the path and just as I

reached the door a great gust of wind and rain came screeching round the building like the souls of the damned. And then, when it dropped, those three chords on a cracked piano! My God, I tell you I nearly bolted."

Henry put his hand to his face and then looked at his fingers.

"I don't know whether it's sweat or rain," he said, " and that's a fact. Sorry! Not the behaviour of a pukka sahib. No, by Gad, sir. Blimp wouldn't think anything of it."

"I can imagine it was rather trying," said Alleyn. "What were you doing there, anyway?"

"Going home. I stayed on to supper at the rectory. Only just left. Mr. Copeland's in such a hoo that he's forgotten all about choking me off. When I occurred at cold supper he noticed me no more than the High Church blanc-mange. I say, sir, I am sorry I made such an ass of myself. Honestly! How I could!"

"That's all right," said Alleyn. "But why did you turn in here?"

"I thought if that splendid fellow Roper held the dog-watch, I might say, ' Stand ho! What hath this thing appeared?' and get a bit of gossip out of him."

"I see."

"Have a cigarette?" said Nigel.

"Oh, thank you. I'd better take myself off."

"Would you like to wait and see a slight experiment?" asked Alleyn.

"Very much indeed, sir, if I may."

"Before we begin, there's just one thing I'd like to say to you, as you are here. I shall call on Miss Prentice to-morrow and I shall use every means within the law to get her to tell me what took place on that encounter in Top Lane on Friday. I don't know whether you'd rather give me your version first."

"I've told you already, she's dotty," said Henry with nervous impatience. "It's my belief she is actually and literally out of her senses. She looks like death and she won't leave her room except for meals, and then she doesn't eat anything. She said at dinner to-night that she's in danger, and that in the end she'll be murdered. It's simply ghastly. God knows whom she suspects, but she suspects somebody, and she's half dead with fright. What sort of sense will you get out of a woman like that?"

"Why not give us a sane version first?"

"But it's nothing to do with the case," said Henry, " and

195

if you feel like saying 'tra-la,' I'd be grateful if you'd restrain yourselves."

"If it turns out to be irrelevant," said Alleyn, "it shall be treated as such. We don't use irrelevant statements."

"Then why ask for them?"

"We like to do the winnowing ourselves."

"Nothing happened in Top Lane."

"You mean Miss Prentice stood two feet away from you both, stared into your face until her heels sank an inch into the ground, and then walked away without uttering a word?"

"It was private business. It was altogether our affair."

"You know," said Alleyn, "that won't do. This morning at Pen Cuckoo, and this afternoon at the rectory, frankness was the keynote of your conversation. You have said that you wouldn't put it past Miss Prentice to do murder, and yet you boggle at repeating a single word that she uttered in Top Lane. It looks as though it's not Miss Prentice whom you wish to protect."

"What do you mean?"

"Hasn't Miss Copeland insisted on your taking this stand because she's nervous on your account? What were you going to call out to me this afternoon when she stopped you?"

"Well," said Henry unexpectedly, "you're quite right."

"See here," said Alleyn, "if you are innocent of murder, I promise you that you are not going the right way to make us think so. Remember that in a little place like this we are bound to hear of all the rifts and ructions and this thing only happened twenty-six hours ago. We've scarcely touched the fringe of local gossip, and already I know that Miss Prentice is opposed to your friendship with Miss Dinah Copeland. I know very well that to you police methods must seem odious and——"

"No, they don't," said Henry. "Of course, you've got to do it."

"Very well, then."

"I'll tell you this much, and I dare say it's no more than you've guessed ; My Cousin Eleanor was thrown into a dither by finding us there together, and our conversation consisted of a series of hysterical threats and embarrassing accusations on her part."

"And did you make no threats?"

"She'll probably tell you I did," said Henry ; "but, as I have said six or eight times already, she's mad. And I'm sorry, sir, but that's all I can tell you."

"All right," said Alleyn with a sigh. "Let's get to work, Fox."

They removed the water-pistol and set up the Colt in its place. Alleyn produced the "Prelude" from his case and put it on the rack. Henry saw the hole blown through the centre and the surrounding ugly stains. He turned away and then, as if he despised this involuntary revulsion, moved closer to the piano and watched Alleyn's hands as they moved inside the top.

"You see," said Alleyn, "all the murderer had to do was exactly what I'm doing now. The Colt fits into the same place, and the loose end of cord which was tied round the butt of the water-pistol is tied round the butt of the Colt. It passes across the trigger. It is remarkably strong cord, rather like fishing line. I've left the safety catch on. Now look."

He sat on the piano stool and pressed the soft pedal. The two pulleys stood out rigidly from their moorings, the cord tautened as the dampers moved towards the strings and checked.

"It's stood firm," said Alleyn. "Georgie made sure of his pulleys. Now."

"By gum!" ejaculated Nigel, "I never thought of——"

"I know you didn't."

Alleyn reached inside and released the safety catch. Again he trod lightly on the soft pedal. This time the soft pedal worked. The cord tightened in the pulleys and the trigger moved back. They all heard the sharp click of the striker.

"Well, there you are for what it's worth," said Alleyn lightly.

"Yes, but last night the top of the piano was smothered in bunting and six he-men aspidistras," objected Henry.

"So you think it was done last night," said Alleyn.

"I don't know when it was done, and I don't think it could have been done last night, unless it was before we all got to the hall."

Alleyn scowled at Nigel, who was obviously pregnant with a new theory.

"It's perfectly true," said Nigel defiantly. "Nobody could have moved those pots after 6.30."

"I so entirely agree with you," said Alleyn. A bell pealed distantly. Henry jumped.

"That's the telephone," he said and started forward.

"I'll answer it, I think," said Alleyn. "It's sure to be for me."

He crossed the stage, found a light switch and made his way to the first dressing-room on the left. The old-fashioned manual telephone pealed irregularly until he lifted the receiver.

"Hullo?"

"Mr. Alleyn? It's Dinah Copeland. Somebody wants to speak to you from Chipping."

"Thank you."

"Here you are," said Dinah. The telephone clicked and the voice of Sergeant Roper said, "Sir?"

"Hullo?"

"Roper, sir. I thought I should find you, seeing as how Fife is still asleep here. I have a small matter in the form of a recent arrest to bring before your notice, sir."

"In *what* form?"

"By name Saul Tranter, and by employment as sly a poacher as ever you see; but we've cotched him very pretty, sir, and the man's sitting here at my elbow with guilt written all over him in the form of two fine cock-pheasants."

"What the devil——?" began Alleyn, and checked himself. "Well, Roper, what about it?"

"This chap says he's got a piece of information that'll make the court think twice about giving him the month's hard he's been asking for these last two years. He won't tell me, sir, but in his bold way he asks to be faced with you. Now, we've got to get him down to the lock-up some time and——"

"I'll send Mr. Bathgate down, Roper. Thank you." Alleyn hung up the receiver and stared thoughtfully at the telephone.

"I'll have to see about you," he told it and returned to the front of the hall.

"Hullo," he said, "where's Master Henry?"

"Gone home," said Fox. "He's a funny sort of young gentleman, isn't he?"

"Rather a bumptious infant, I thought," said Nigel.

"He's about the same age as you were when I first met you," Alleyn pointed out, "and not half as bumptious. Bathgate, I'm afraid you'll have to go into Chipping and get a poacher."

"A poacher!"

"Yes. Treasure-trove of Roper's. Apparently the gentleman wishes to make a blunderbuss about his impending

198

sentence. He says he's got a story to unfold. Bring Fife with him. Stop at the pub on the way back and get your own car, and let Fife drive the Ford here and he can use it afterwards to deliver this gentleman to the lock-up. We'll clear up this place to-night."

" Am I representative of a leading London daily or your odd-boy?"

" You know the answer to that better than I do. Away you go."

Nigel went, not without further bitter complaint. Alleyn and Fox moved to the supper-room.

" All this food can be thrown away to-morrow," said Alleyn. " There's something else I want to see down here, though. Look, there's the tea-tray ready to be carried on in the play. Mrs. Ross's silver, I dare say. It looks like her. Modern, expensive and streamlined."

He lifted the lid of the teapot.

" It reeks of onion. Dear little Georgie."

" I suppose someone spotted it and threw it out. You found it lying on the floor here, didn't you, Mr. Alleyn?"

" In that box over there. Yes, Bailey has found Georgie's and Miss P.'s prints in the pot, so presumably Miss P. hawked out the onion."

He stooped down and looked under the table.

" You went all over here last night, didn't you, Fox? Last night! This morning! 'Little Fox, we've had a busy day.' "

" All over it, sir. You'll find the onion peel down there. Young Biggins must have skinned it and then put it in the teapot."

" Did you find any powder in here?"

" Powder? No. No, I didn't. Why?"

" Or flour?"

" No. Oh, you're thinking of the flour on the onion."

" I'll just get the onion."

Alleyn fetched the onion. He had put it in one of his wide-necked specimen bottles.

" We haven't had time to deal with this as yet," he said. " Look at it, Fox, it's pinkish. That's powder, not flour."

" Perhaps young Biggins fooled round with it in one of the dressing-rooms."

" Let's look at the dressing-rooms."

They found that on each dressing-table there was a large box of theatrical powder. They were all new, and it looked as if Dinah had provided them. The men's boxes contained

199

a yellowish powder, the women's a pinkish cream. Mrs. Ross, alone, had brought her own in an expensive-looking French box. In the dressing-room used by Miss Prentice and Miss Campanula, some of their powder had been spilled across the table. Alleyn stooped and sniffed at it.

"That's it," he said. "Reeks of onion." He opened the box. "But this doesn't. Fox, ring up Miss Copeland and ask her when the powder was brought into these rooms. It's an extension telephone. You just turn the handle."

Fox plodded away. Alleyn, in a sort of trance, stared at the top of the dressing-table, shook his head thoughtfully and returned to the stage. He heard a motor-horn, and in a minute the door opened. Roper and Fife came in shepherding between them a pigmy of a man who looked as if he had been plunged in a water-butt.

Mr. Saul Tranter was an old man with a very bad face. His eyes were no bigger than a pig's and they squinted, wickedly close together, on either side of his mean little nose. His mouth was loose and leered uncertainly, and his few teeth were objects of horror. He smelt very strongly indeed of dirty old man, dead birds and whisky. Roper thrust him forward as if he was some fabulous orchid, culled at great risk.

"Here he be, sir," said Roper. "This is Saul Tranter, sure enough, with all his wickedness hot in his body, having been taken in the act with two of squire's cock-pheasants and his gun smoking in his hands. Two years you've dodged us, haven't you, Tranter, you old fox? I thought I'd come along with Fife, sir, seeing I've got the hang of this case, having brought my mind to bear on it."

"Very good of you, Roper."

"Now then, Tranter," said Roper, "speak up to the chief inspector and let him have the truth—if so be it lies in you to tell it."

"Heh, my sonnies!" said the poacher in a piping voice. "Be that the instrument that done the murder?" And he pointed an unspeakably dirty hand at the piano.

"Never you mind that," ordered Roper. "That's not for your low attention."

"What have you got to tell us, Tranter?" asked Alleyn. "Good Lord, man, you're as wet at a water-rat!"

"Wuz up to Cloudyfold when they cotched me," admitted Mr. Tranter. He drew a little closer to the heater and began stealthily to steam.

"Ay, they cotched me," he said. "Reckon it do have

200

to happen so soon or so late. Squire'll sit on me at court and show what a mighty man he be, no doubt, seeing it's his woods I done trapped and shot these twenty year. 'Od rabbit the man, he'd change his silly, puffed-up ways if he knew what I had up my sleeve for 'un."

"That's no way to talk," said Roper severely, "you, with a month's hard hanging round your neck."

"Maybe. Maybe not, Charley Roper." He squinted up at Alleyn. "Being I has my story to tell which will fix the guilt of this spring-gun on him as set it. I reckon the hand of the law did ought to be light on my ancient shoulders."

"If your information is any use," said Alleyn, "we might put in a word for you. I can't promise. You never know. I'll have to hear it first."

"'Tain't good enough, mister. Promise first, story afterwards, is my motter."

"Then it's not ours," said Alleyn coolly. "It looks as though you've nothing to tell, Tranter."

"Is threats nothing? Is blasting words nothing? Is a young chap caught red-handed same as me, with as pretty a bird as ever flewed into a trap, nothing?"

"Well?"

Fox came down into the hall, joined the group round the heater and stared with a practised eye at Tranter. Nigel arrived and took off his streaming mackintosh. Tranter turned his head restlessly and looked sideways from one face to another. A trickle of brown saliva appeared at the corner of his mouth.

"Well?" Alleyn repeated.

"Sour, tight-fisted men be the Jernighams," said Tranter. "What's a bird or two to them! I'm up against all damned misers, and so be all my side. Tyrants they be, and narrow as the grave, father and son."

"You'd better take him back, Roper."

"Nay, then, I'll tell you. I'll tell you. And if you don't give me my dues, dang it, if I don't fling it in the faces of the J.P.s. Where be your pencils and papers, souls? This did oughter go down in writing."

CHAPTER TWENTY-TWO

Letter to Troy

"ON FRIDAY AFTERNOON," said Mr. Tranter, "I were up to Cloudyfold. Never mind why. I come down by my own ways, and proper foxy ways they be, so quiet as moonshine. I makes downhill to Top Lane. Never mind why."

"I don't in the least mind," said Alleyn. "Do go on."

Mr. Tranter shot a doubtful glance at him and sucked in his breath.

"A'most down to Top Lane, I wuz, when I heard voices. A feymell voice and a man's voice, and raised in anger. 'Ah,' thinks I. 'There's somebody down there kicking up Bob's-a-dying in the lane, and, that being the case, the lane's no place for me, with never-mind-what under my arm and never-mind-what in my pockets, neither.' So I worms my way closer, till at last I'm nigh on bank above lane. There's a great ancient beech tree a-growing theer, and I lays down and creeps forward, so cunning as a serpent, till I looks down atwixt the green stuff into the lane. Yass. And what do I see?"

"What *do* you see?"

"Ah! I sees young Henry Jernigham, as proud as death and with the devil himself in his face, and rector's wench in his arms."

"That's no way to talk," admonished Roper. "Choose your words."

"So I will, and mind your own business, Charley Roper. And who do I see standing down in lane a-facing of they two with her face so sickly as cheese and her eyes like raging fires and her limbs trimbling like a trapped rabbit. Who do I see?"

"Miss Eleanor Prentice," said Alleyn.

Mr. Tranter, who was now steaming like a geyser and smelling like a polecat, choked and blinked his eyes.

"She's never told 'ee?"

"No. Go on."

"Trimbling as if to take a fit, she was, and screeching feeble, but uncommon venomous. Threating 'em with rector, she was, and threating 'em with squire. She says she caught 'em red-handed in vice and she'd see every decent critter in parish heard of their goings-on. And more besides. You'd never believe that old maiden had the knowledge of sinful youth in her, like she do seem to have. Nobbut what she don't tipple."

"Really?" Alleyn ejaculated.

"Aye. One of them hasty secret drinkers, she is. She'd sloshed her tipple down her bosom, as I clearly saw. No doubt that's what'd inflamed the old wench and caused her to rage and storm at 'em. She give it 'em proper hot and sizzling, did Miss Prentice. And when she was at the full blast of her fury, what does t' young spark do but round on 'er. Aye t' young toad! Grabs her by shoulders and hisses in 'er face. If she don't let 'em be, 'e says, and if she tries to blacken young maid's name in eyes of the world, he says, he'll stop her wicked tongue for good an' all. He were in a proper rage, more furious than her. Terrible. And rector's maid, she says, 'Doan't, Henry, doan't!' But young Jernigham 'e take no heed of the wench, but hammer-and-tongs he goes to it, so white as a sheet and blazing like a furnace. Aye, they've all got murderous, wrathy, passionate tempers, they Jernighams, as is well known hereabouts; I've heard the manner of this bloody killing, and I reckon there's little doubt he set his spring-gun for t'one old hen and catched t'other. Now!"

II

"Damn!" said Alleyn, when Mr. Tranter had been removed. "What a *bloody* business this is."

"Is it what you expected?" asked Nigel.

"Oh, I half expected it, yes. It was obvious that something pretty dramatic had happened on Friday afternoon. Miss Prentice and Henry Jernigham showed the whites of their eyes whenever it was mentioned, and the rector told me that he and the squire and Miss Prentice had all been opposed to this match. Why, the Lord alone knows. She seems a perfectly agreeable girl, rather a nice girl, blast it. And look at the way Master Henry responded to inquiry! Fox, did you ever know such a case? One cranky spinster is enough, heaven knows; and here we have two, each a sort of Freudian prize packet, and one a corpse on our hands."

"The whole thing seems very unlikely sort of stuff to me, Mr. Alleyn, and yet there it is. She *was* murdered. If that kid had never read his comic paper, and if he hadn't had his Twiddletoy outfit, it wouldn't have happened."

"I believe you're right there, Brer Fox."

"I suppose, sir, that was what Miss Prentice wanted to see the rector about on Friday evening. The meeting in Top Lane, I mean."

"Yes, I dare say it was. Oh, hell, we'll have to tackle Miss Prentice in the morning. What did Dinah Copeland say about the face-powder?"

"She brought it down with her last night. Georgie Biggins wasn't behind the scenes at all last night. He made such a nuisance of himself that they gave him the sack. He was call-boy at the dress rehearsal, but the tables and dressing-rooms have all been scrubbed out since then. That powder must have been spilt after half-past six last evening. And another thing: Miss Dinah Copeland never heard about the onion—or says she didn't."

"That makes sense, anyway!"

"*Does it?*" said Nigel bitterly. "I don't mind owning that I fail to see the faintest significance in anything you've been saying. Why this chat about an onion?"

"Why, indeed," sighed Alleyn. "Come on. We'll pack up and go home. Even a policeman must sleep."

III

But before Alleyn went to sleep that night he wrote to his love:

The Jernigham Arms,
November 29

MY DARLING TROY,

What a chancey sort of lover you've got. A fly-by-night who speaks to you at nine o'clock on Saturday evening, and soon after midnight is down in Dorset looking at lethal pianos. Shall you mind this sort of thing when we are married? You say not, and I suppose and hope not. You'll turn that dark head of yours and find your husband gone from your side. "Off again, I see," you'll say, and fall to thinking of the picture you are to paint next day. My dear and my darling Troy, you shall disappear, too, when you choose, into the austerity of your work, and never, never, never shall I look sideways, or disagreeably, or in the manner of the martyred spouse. Not as easy a promise as you might think, but I make it.

This is a disagreeable and unlikely affair. You will see

the papers before my letter reaches you, but in case you'd like to know the official version, I enclose a very short account written in Yard language, and kept as colourless as possible. Fox and I have come to a conclusion, but are hanging off and on, hoping for a bit more evidence to turn up before we make an arrest. You told me once that your only method in detection would be based on character: and a very sound method, too, as long as you've got a flair for it. Now, here are our seven characters for you. What do you make of them?

First, the squire, Jocelyn Jernigham of Pen Cuckoo, and Acting Chief Constable to make things more difficult. He's a reddish, baldish man, with a look of perpetual surprise in his rather prominent light eyes. A bit pomposo. You would always know from the tone of his voice whether he spoke to a man or a woman. I think he would bore you and I think you would frighten him. The ladies, you see, should be gay and flirtatious and winsome. You are not at all winsome, darling, are you? They should make a man feel he's a bit of a dog. He's not altogether a fool, though, and, I should think, has a temper of his own. I think his cousin, Eleanor Prentice, frightens him, but he's full of family pride, and probably considers that even half a Jernigham can't be altogther wrong.

Miss Eleanor Prentice is half a Jernigham. She's about forty-nine or fifty, and I think rather a horrid woman. She's quite colourless and she's got buck teeth. She disseminates an odour of sanctity. She smiles a great deal, but with an air of forbearance as if hardly anything was really quite nice. I think she's a religious fanatic, heavily focused on the rector. This morning when I interviewed her she was thrown into a perfect fever by the sound of the church bells. She could scarcely listen to the simplest question, much less return a reasonable answer, so ardent and impatient was her longing to go to church. Now, in your true religious that's understandable enough. If you believe in the God Christ preached, you must be overwhelmed by your faith, and in time of trouble turn, with a heart of grace, to prayer. But I don't think Eleanor Prentice is that sort of religious. God knows I'm no psycho-analyst, but I imagine she'd be meat and drink to any one who was. Does one talk about a sex-fixation? Probably not. Anyway, she's gone the way modern psychlogy seems to consider axiomatic with women of her age and condition. This opinion is based partly on the statements of Henry Jernigham and Dinah

Copeland and partly on my own impression of the woman.

Henry Jernigham is a good-looking young man. He's dark, with a jaw, grey eyes and an impressive head. He adopts the conversational manner of the moment, ironic and amusing, and gives the impression that he says whatever comes . . . into his head. But I don't believe any one has ever done that. How deep are our layers of thought, Troy. So deep that the thought of thought is terrifying to most of us. After many years, or perhaps only a few years, you and I may sometimes guess at each other's thoughts before they are spoken ; and how strange that will seem to us. " A proof of our love! " we shall cry.

This young Jernigham is in love with Dinah Copeland. Why didn't we meet when I was his age and you were a solemn child? Should I have loved you when you were fourteen and I was twenty-three? In those days I seem to remember I had a passion for full-blown blondes. But, without doubt, I would have loved and you would have never noticed it. Well, Henry loves Dinah, who is a nice, intelligent child and vaguely on the stage, as almost all of them seem to be nowadays. I long to drivel on about the damage that magnificent chap Irving did to his profession when he made it respectable. No art should be fashionable, Troy, should it? But Dinah is evidently a serious young actress and probably quite a good one. She adores Master Henry.

Dr. Templett, as you will see, looks very dubious. He could have taken the automatic, he could have fixed it in position, he has a motive, and he used all his authority to bring about the change of pianists. But he didn't get down to the hall until the audience had arrived, and he was never alone from the time he arrived until the time of the murder. To meet, he's a commonplace enough fellow. Under ordinary circumstances. I think he'd be tiresomely facetious. There is no doubt that he was infected with a passion for Mrs. Selia Ross, and woe betide the man who loves a thin straw-coloured woman with an eye to the main chance. If she doesn't love him she'll let him down, and if she does love him she'll suck away his character like a leech. He'll develop anæmia of the personality. Mrs. Ross as you will have gathered, *is* a thin, straw-coloured woman, with the sort of sex appeal that changes men's faces when they speak of her. Their eyes turn bright and at the same time guarded, and the muscle from the nostril to the corner of the mouth becomes accentuated. Do you think that a very humourless observation? It's very true, my girl, and if you ever want to draw a sensualist, draw him like that. Trust a policeman: old Darwin found it out in spite of those whiskers. Mrs. Ross could have nipped out of the car and dodged through the french window into the squire's study while Templett was handing his hat and coat to the butler. Had you thought of that? But she came down to the hall with Templett for the evening performance.

The rector, Walter Copeland, B.A. Oxon: The first thing you think of is his head. He's an amazingly fine-looking fellow. Everything the photographer or the producer ordered for a magnificent cleric. Silver hair, dark eyebrows, saintly profile. It's like a head on a coin or a statue, and much too much like any magazine illustration of "A handsome Man." He seems to be less startling than his looks, and appears, in fact, to be a conscientious priest, rather disinclined for difficult jobs, but capable, suddenly, of digging in his toes. He is High Church, and I am sure very sincerely so. I should say that, if his belief came into question, he could be obstinate and even ruthless, but the general impression is of gentle vagueness.

The murdered woman seems to have been an arrogant, lonely, hysterical spinster. She and Miss Prentice might be taken as the positive and negative poles of parochial fanaticism with the rector as the needle. Not a true analogy. The general opinion is that she was a tartar.

It's midnight. I didn't get to bed last night, so I must leave you now. Troy, shall we have a holiday cottage in Dorset? A small house with a stern grey front, not too picturesque, but high up in the world so that you could paint the curves of the hills and the solemn changing cloud shadows that hurry over Dorset? Shall we have one? I'm going to marry you next April, and I love you with all my heart.

Good-night,
R.

IV

Alleyn laid down his pen and stretched his cramped fingers.

He was, he supposed, the only waking being in the inn, and the silence of a country dwelling at night flowed in upon his mind. The wind had dropped again, and he realised that for some time there had been no sound of rain. The fire had fallen into a glow. The timbers of the inn crackled abruptly and startled him. He was suddenly weary. His body was a stranger to his mind and he looked at it in wonder. He stood as if in a trance, alarmed at meeting himself as a stranger, yet aware of this experience which was not new to him. As always, some part of his mind tried to step across the threshold of the unknown, but was unable to give purpose to his whole thought. He returned to himself and, rousing, lit his candle, turned out the lamp, and climbed the stairs to his room.

His window looked up the Vale. High above him he could see a light. "They are late at bed at Pen Cuckoo," he thought, and opened the window. The sound of water dripping from the eaves came into the room and the smell of wet grass and earth. "Perhaps it will be fine to-morrow," he thought, and went happily to bed.

CHAPTER TWENTY-THREE

Frightened Lady

"—LET ME REMIND you, gentlemen," said the coroner, looking severely at Mr. Prosser, "that you are not concerned with theories. It is your duty to decide how this unfortunate lady met with her death. If you find you are able to do so, you must then make up your minds whether you are to return a verdict of accident, suicide or murder. If you are unable to arrive at this second decision, you must say so. Now, there is no difficulty in describing the manner of death. On Friday afternoon a small boy, after the manner of small boys, set an ingenious booby-trap. At some time before Saturday night, someone interfered with this comparatively harmless piece of mechanism. A Colt automatic was substituted for a water-pistol. You have heard that this automatic, the property of Mr. Jocelyn Jernigham, was in a room which is accessible from outside all day and every day. You have heard that it was common knowledge that the weapon was kept loaded in this room. You realise, I am sure, that on Saturday it would have been possible for anybody to enter the room through the french window and take the automatic. You have listened to a lucid description of the mechanism of this death-trap. You have examined the Colt automatic. You have been told that at 6.30 Miss Gladys Wright used the left-hand pedal of the piano, and that nothing untoward occurred. You have heard her say that from 6.30 until the moment of the catastrophe the front of the hall was occupied by herself, her fellow-helpers and, as they arrived, the audience. You have been shown photographs of the piano as it was at 6.30. The open top was covered in bunting which was secured to the sides by drawing-pins. On top of the piano and standing on the bunting, which stretched over the turned-back lid, were six pot plants. You realise that up to within fifteen minutes of the tragedy, every member of the company of performers, and every person in the audience, believed that it was Miss Prentice who was to play the overture. You may therefore have formed the opinion that Miss Prentice, and not Miss Campanula, was the intended victim. This need not affect your decision and, as a coroner's jury, does not actually concern you. If you agree that at eight o'clock Miss Campanula pressed the left-hand or soft pedal and was killed by a charge from the automatic and that somebody had put the automatic in the piano with felonious intent, in short with intent to murder, and if you consider there is no evidence to show who this person was—why, then, gentlemen, you may return a verdict to this effect."

"O upright beak!" said Alleyn as Mr. Prosser and the jury retired. "O admirable and economic coroner! Slap, bang, and away they go. Slap, bang, and here they are again."

They had indeed only gone into a huddle in the doorway, and returned looking rather as if they had all washed their faces in rectitude.

"Yes, Mr. Prosser?"

"We are all agreed, sir."

"Yes?"

"We return a verdict of murder," said Mr. Prosser, looking as if he feared he hadn't got it quite as it ought to be, "against person or persons unknown."

"Thank you. The only possible conclusion, gentlemen."

"I should like to add," said the smallest juryman, suddenly, "that I think them water-pistols ought to be put down by law."

II

Immediately after the inquest, Fox and Ford left for Duck Cottage. Alleyn's hand was on the door of Nigel's car, when he heard his name called. He turned and found himself face to face with Mrs. Ross.

"Mr. Alleyn—I'm so sorry to bother you, but may I come and see you? I've remembered something that I think you ought to know."

"Certainly," said Alleyn. "Now, if it suits you."

"You're staying at the Jernigham Arms, aren't you? May I come there in ten minutes?"

"Yes, of course. I shall drive straight there."

"Thank you so much."

Alleyn replaced his hat and climbed into the car.

"*Now*, what the devil?" he wondered. "It's fallen out rather well, as it happens. Fox will have a longer session with the pretty housemaid."

Nigel came out and drove him to the inn. Alleyn asked Mrs. Peach if he could use the back parlour as an office for an hour. Mrs. Peach was volubly agreeable.

Nigel was told to take himself off.

"Why should I? Who are you going to see?"

"Mrs. Ross."

"Why can't I be there?"

"Because I think she'll speak more freely if she sees me alone."

"Well, let me sit in the next room with the slide a crack open."

Alleyn looked thoughtfully at him.

"Very well," he said, "you may do that. Take notes. It can't be used in evidence, but it may be handy. Wait a second. You've got your camera?"

"Yes."

"See if you can get a shot of her as she comes in. Careful about it. Get there quickly. She'll arrive in a second."

Nigel was only just in time. In five minutes the pot-boy announced Mrs. Ross, who came in looking much more like the Ritz than the Jernigham Arms.

"It *is* nice of you to see me," she said. "Ever since I remembered it, I've been so worried about this thing. I felt very bold, accosting you outside the hall of justice or whatever it was. You must be rushed off your feet."

"It's my job to listen," said Alleyn.

"May I sit down?"

"Please. I think this is the most comfortable chair."

She sat down with a pretty air of intimacy. She drew off her gloves, rummaged in her bag for her cigarettes, and then accepted one of his. Alleyn remained standing.

"You know," said Mrs. Ross, "you're not a bit my idea of a detective."

"No?"

"Not a *bit*. That enormous man who drives about with you looks much more the thing done at the Yard."

"Perhaps you would rather see Inspector Fox?"

"No, I'd much rather see you. Don't snub me."

"I'm sorry if I seemed to do that. What is it you would like to tell me?"

She leant forward. Her manner lost its flippancy and took on an air of practical concern, but it also managed to suggest that she knew he would understand and sympathise with her motive in coming to him.

"You'll think I was such a fool not to remember it before," she said; "but the whole thing's been rather a shock. I suppose I simply had a blank moment or something. Not that I had any affection for the poor old thing; but, for all that, it was rather a shock."

"I'm sure it was."

"When you came to see me yesterday I had a ghastly headache and could hardly think. Did you ask me if I went out on Friday night?"

"Yes. You told me you were at home."

"I *thought* I did. Honestly, I don't know what I could have been thinking about. I *was* at home practically all the evening, but I went out for about half an hour. I drove from here to post a letter. I quite forgot."

"That's not very serious."

"I'm extremely relieved to hear you say so," she said, and laughed. "I was afraid you'd be *angry* with me."

She had a comical trick of over-emphasis, as if she parodied her own conversation. She drew out the word *angry*, making a grimace over it and opening her eyes very wide.

"Is that the whole story?" asked Alleyn.

"No, it's not," she said flatly. "The thing is, on my way down I came by Church Lane, past the hall. Church Lane goes on over the hills, you know, and comes out close to my cottage."

"Yes."

"Well, there was a light in one of the dressing-rooms."

"What time was this?"

"It was eleven when I got back. Say about twenty to eleven. No, a little earlier."

"Which dressing-room was it, do you know?"

211

"Yes. I've worked it out. It was too far away to be either of the women's rooms, and anyway they've got blinds. Miss Prentice, who is a very pure woman, thought it wasn't quite nice for us not to have blinds. The one Billy Templett uses has its window on the far side. It must have been the squire's. Mr. Jernigham's. But the funny thing about it was that it only flashed on for a few seconds and then went out again."

"Are you quite sure it wasn't the reflection of your headlights?"

"Absolutely positive. It was much too far to my right, and anyway it wasn't a bit like that. The glass is that thick stuff. No, a yellow square just popped up and popped out again."

"I see."

"It may not be anything at all, but it was on my conscience, so I thought I'd own up, and *come clean* and all that. I didn't think anything of it at the time. It might have been Dinah Copeland messing about over there, or any old thing; but as every moment after Friday seems important——"

"It's much better to let the police know of anything you remember that may have even the slightest significance," said Alleyn.

"I hoped you'd say that. Mr. Alleyn, I'm so terribly worried, and you're so human and unofficial, I wonder if I dare ask you something rather awkward."

Alleyn's manner could scarcely have been more formal as he replied: "I am here as a policeman, you know."

"Yes, I know. Well, when in doubt, ask a policeman." She grinned charmingly. "No, but honestly I'm in a horrid —awful muddle. It's about Billy Templett. I'm sure you've already heard all the local gossip, and you'll have found out for yourself that the charming people in this aristocratic part of the world have got minds like sinks and worse. No doubt they've told you all the local lies about Billy Templett and me. Well, we *are* great friends. He's the only soul in the entire district with an idea beyond hunting and other people's business, and we've got a lot in common. Of course, as a doctor, he's not supposed to look on women as anything but sets of insides and collections of complaints. I never dreamt it might actually do his practice no good if he saw rather more of me than old Mrs. Cain and the oldest inhabitant. Oh, dear, this *is* difficult. May I have another cigarette, please?"

Alleyn gave her another cigarette.

"I may as well choke it out before I lose my nerve altogether. Do you suspect Billy of this beastly crime?"

"As the case stands," said Alleyn, "it appears to be quite impossible that Dr. Templett should have had any hand in it."

"Is that true?" she asked, and her voice was as sharp as a knife.

"It is a very serious offence for a policeman to set traps or deliberately mislead his witnesses."

"I'm sorry. I know that. It was just the relief. You remember that letter you showed me yesterday? The anonymous letter?"

"Yes."

"It was written to me."

"Yes."

"I knew I hadn't taken you in. You are a clever beast, aren't you?" She laughed again. Alleyn wondered how many people had told her she laughed like a gamine and whether she ever forgot it.

"Do you want to amend your statement about the letter?" he asked.

"Yes, please. I want to explain. I showed the letter to Billy and we discussed it and decided to take no notice. When you showed it to me I supposed you'd picked it up somewhere in the hall, and as I knew it had nothing to do with this murder, and I wanted to protect poor old Billy. I said I didn't know anything about it. And then he came in and I thought he'd take his cue from me and—well, it went wrong."

"Yes," said Alleyn, "it went very wrong."

"Mr. Alleyn, what did he tell you last evening when he went away with you? Was he—was he angry with me? He didn't realise I'd tried to help him, did he?"

"I don't think so."

"He might have known! It's one of those hideous things that turn into a muddle."

"I'm afraid your explanation has gone equally astray."

"What do you mean?"

"I mean that you knew where Dr. Templett put the letter and that it is very unlikely we picked it up in the hall. I mean that yesterday you spoke instinctively and with the object of getting out of an awkward position. You have since remembered that there is a fingerprint system, so you come to me with a story of altruistic motives. When

213

I told you Dr. Templett is not, on the evidence we have, a likely suspect you regretted that you had shown your hand. I think I know a frightened woman when I see one, and yesterday you were very frightened, Mrs. Ross."

She had let her cigarette burn down to her fingers. Her hand jerked and she dropped the butt on the floor. He picked it up and threw it in the fire.

"You're wrong," she said. "I did it for *him*."

Alleyn made no answer.

She said, "I thought she'd written it. The murdered woman. And I thought old Prentice was going to play."

"Dr. Templett didn't tell you on Saturday morning that it would be a physical impossibility for Miss Prentice to play?"

"We didn't discuss it. Billy didn't do it and neither did I. We didn't get to the place till nearly eight o'clock."

"You arrived soon after 7.30," Alleyn corrected her.

"Well, anyway, it was too late to do anything to the piano. The hall was packed. We were never alone."

"Mrs. Ross, when I asked you yesterday about the episode of the window, why did you not tell me you saw someone dodge down behind the sill?"

She seemed startled but not particularly alarmed at this. She looked at him, as he thought, speculatingly, as though she deliberately weighed his question and pondered the answer. At last she said:

"I suppose Billy told you that. It was only an impression, through the thick glass. The window was only open about two inches."

"I suggest that you were alarmed at the idea of an eavesdropper. I suggest that you noticed this shadow at the window only after you had been for some little time on the stage with Dr. Templett, and that enough had taken place in that time for you to be seriously compromised. I suggest that you told Dr. Templett to shut the window and that you lowered the curtain to ensure privacy."

She tilted her head to one side and looked at him under her lashes.

"You really ought to join the Women's Circle. They'd adore that story at a tea-party."

"I shall work," said Alleyn, "on the theory that you said nothing more to Dr. Templett of this shadowy impression, as you did not wish to alarm him, but that it was not too shadowy or too fleeting for you to recognise the watcher at the window."

214

That shot did go home. Her whole face seemed to sharpen and she made a quick involuntary movement of her hands. She waited for a moment, and he knew that she was mustering her nerves. Then in one swift movement she was on her feet, close to him, her hand on his coat.

"You don't believe I'd do anything like that, do you? You're not such a fool. I don't even understand how it worked, and I've never been able to tie a knot in my life. Mr. Alleyn? Please?"

"If you are innocent you're in no danger."

"Do you promise that?"

"Certainly."

Before he could move she dropped her head against him and clung to his coat. She murmured broken phrases. Her hair was scented. He felt her uneven breathing.

"No, no," he said, "this won't do."

"I'm sorry—you've frightened me. Don't be nervous, I'm not trying to seduce you. I'm only rather shaken. I'll be all right in a moment."

"You're all right now," said Alleyn. He took her wrists and held her away from him. "That's better."

She stood before him with her head bent down. She achieved a look of helpless captivity. Her whole posture seemed to proclaim her subjection. When she raised her face it wore a gamine grin.

"You're either made of dough," she said, "or else you're afraid I'll compromise you. Poor Mr. Alleyn."

"You would have been wiser to call on Mr. Jernigham," said Alleyn. "He's Acting Chief Constable, you know."

III

When she had been gone some minutes, Nigel looked cautiously into the back parlour.

"Hell knows no fury," he said.

"An intensely embarrassing lady," said Alleyn. "Did you get a shot of her?"

"Yes. Ought to be all right. I got her as she came in."

"Let me have the film or plate, or whatever it is."

"Do explain all this, Alleyn."

"It's as plain as daylight. She's got a genius for self-preservation. When I showed her the anonymous letter she was hell-bent on keeping out of suspicion, and on the

215

spur of the moment denied all knowledge of it. She'd do her best for Templett up to a point, but a charge of homicide is definitely beyond that point. Yesterday she let him down with a thud. Now she's regretting it. I think she's probably as much in love with him as she could be with anybody. She's read a popular book on criminal investigation. She remembered that she'd handled the letter and realised we'd find her prints. So she hatched up this story. Now she knows we're not after Templett she'll try to get him back. But she's a sensible woman, and she wouldn't hang for him."

"I wonder if he'll believe her," said Nigel.

"Probably," said Alleyn. "If she gets a chance to see him alone."

Fox came in.

"I've seen Mrs. Ross's maid, sir. There's nothing much, except that Mrs. Ross did go out on Friday night. It was the maid's night off, but her boy had a cold and it was raining, so she stayed in. She only mentioned this to Mrs. Ross this morning."

"And Mrs. Ross mentioned it to me in case the maid got in first."

"Is that a fact, sir?"

"It is, Brer Fox. You shall hear of our interview."

Fox listened solemnly to the account of the interview.

"Well," he said, "she's come off worst in that bout, sir. What'll she do now?"

"I think she'd like to have a shot at old Jernigham. She's frightened and rattled. A shrewd woman, but not really clever."

"Does she think you suspect her, Mr. Alleyn?"

"She's afraid I might."

"*Do* you suspect her?" asked Nigel.

"Of all sorts of things," said Alleyn lightly. He sniffed at his coat. "Blast the woman. I stink of Chanel No. 5."

Nigel burst out laughing.

"Don't you think she's attractive?" he said. "I do."

"Fortunately I don't. I can see she might be; but she gives me housemaid's creeps. What do you think, Fox?"

"Well, sir, under more favourable conditions I dare say she'd be quite an experience in a way. There's something about her."

"You licentious old article."

"She's not very comfortable, if you know what I mean. More on the frisky side. I'd say she's one of these society ladies who, if they were born in a lower walk of life, would

216

set up for themselves in a rather exclusive way, but well within the meaning of the act."

"Yes, Fox."

"What do we do now, Mr. Alleyn?"

"We lunch. After lunch we have a word together. And to-night I think we play a forcing hand, Fox. We've got about as much information as we'll ever screw out of them by separate interviews. Let's see how we get on with a mixed bunch. There's a fast train from Great Chipping in an hour. I think I'll catch it. Will you see the telephone people? Have one more stab at the villagers for Saturday afternoon. The person who stood at the box and peeped through the window. Ask if any one saw anybody about the place. You won't get anything, but we've got to try. Arrange the meeting with Jernigham senior. I'd better see him myself beforehand. There are one or two things—— Go carefully with him, Fox. And telephone to me at the Yard before half-past five."

"I'll come up with you, if I may," said Nigel.

"Do. There's a good train that gets to Great Chipping at 8.15. I'll return by that, and send a car ahead with two people and clanking chains, in case we feel like arresting somebody. All right?"

"Very good, sir," said Fox.

"Then we'd better lunch."

CHAPTER TWENTY-FOUR

The Peculiarity of Miss P.

"IT'S NO GOOD taking it like this, Eleanor," said the squire, laying down his napkin and glaring at his cousin. "How do you suppose we feel? You won't help matters by starving yourself."

"I'm sorry, Jocelyn, but I cannot eat."

"You can't go on like this, my dear girl. You'll get ill."

"Would that matter very much?"

"Don't be an ass, Eleanor. Henry, give her some apple tart."

"No, thank you, Henry."

"What you want, Cousin Eleanor," said Henry from the side table, "is a good swinging whisky."

"Please, dear. I'm sorry if I'm irritating you both. It would be better if I didn't come down to lunch."

"Good Gad, woman," shouted the squire. "Don't talk such piffling drivel. We simply don't want you to kill yourself."

"It's a pity," said Miss Prentice stonily, "that I wasn't killed. I realise that. It would have been a blessed release. They say poor Idris didn't feel anything. It's the living who suffer."

"Cousin Eleanor," said Henry, returning with a loaded plate, "have you ever read *Our Mutual Friend*?"

"No, Henry."

"Because you're giving a perfectly brilliant impersonation of Mrs. R. W."

"Was she very irritating?"

"Very."

"That'll do, Henry," said the squire. He darted an uncomfortable glance at Miss Prentice, who sat upright in her chair with her head bowed. At intervals she drew in her breath sharply and closed her eyes.

"Is your finger hurting you?" demanded Jocelyn after a particularly noticeable hiss from the sufferer. She opened her eyes and smiled palely.

"A little."

"You'd better let Templett see it again."

"I'm not likely to do that, Jocelyn."

"Why not?" asked Henry. "Do you think he's the murderer?"

"Oh, Henry, Henry," said Miss Prentice. "Some day you'll be sorry you have grieved me so much."

"Upon my word," said Henry, "I can't for the life of me see why that should grieve you. One of us is a murderer. I only asked if you thought it might be Templett."

"You are fortunate to be able to speak so lightly of this terrible, terrible tragedy."

"We're as much worried as you are," protested Jocelyn with an appealing glance at his son. "Aren't we, boy?"

"Of course we are," said Henry cheerfully.

"As a matter of fact, I've asked Copeland to come up here and talk the whole thing over."

Miss Prentice clasped her hands and gave a little cry. A dull flush stained her cheeks and her eyes brightened.

"Is he coming? How wise of you, Jocelyn! He is so wonderful. He will help us all. It will all come out right. It will come out quite, quite all right."

She laughed hysterically and clapped her hands.

"When is he coming?"

Jocelyn looked at her with positive terror.

"This evening," he said. "Eleanor, you're not well."

"And is dear Dinah coming, too?" asked Miss Prentice shrilly.

"Hullo!" said Henry. "Here's a change." And he stared fixedly at his cousin.

"Henry," said Miss Prentice very rapidly. "Shall we forget our little differences? I have your happiness so much at heart, dear. If you had been more candid and straightforward with me——"

"Why should I?" asked Henry.

"—I think you would have found me quite understanding. Shall we let bygones be bygones? You see, dear, you have no mother to——"

"Will you excuse me, sir?" said Henry. "I feel slightly sick." And he walked out of the room.

"I thought," said Miss Prentice, "that I had been deeply enough injured already. So deeply, deeply injured. I am sorry I am rather excited, Jocelyn dear, but, you see, when someone is waiting down at St. Giles to shoot you—— *Jocelyn, is that somebody coming?*"

"What the devil's the matter, Eleanor?"

"It's that woman! It was her car! I saw it through the window. Jocelyn, I won't meet that woman. She'll do me an injury. She's wicked, wicked, wicked. A woman of Babylon. They're all the same. All bad, horrible creatures."

"Eleanor, be quiet."

"You're a man. You don't understand. *I will not meet her.*"

Taylor came in.

"Mrs. Ross to see you, sir."

"Damnation!" said the squire. "All right. Take her to the study."

II

The squire was worried about Eleanor. She was really very odd indeed, far odder than even these uncomfortable circumstances warranted. There was no knowing what she'd say next. If he didn't look out, she'd land him in a pretty tight corner with one of these extraordinary statements of hers. She'd got such a damned knowing look in her eye. When she thought he wasn't noticing her, she'd sit in a corner watching him, with an expression which could only be described as a leer. If she was going mad! Well, there was one thing: mad people couldn't give evidence. Perhaps the best thing would be to ask an alienist down for the week-end. He hoped to heaven she wouldn't take it into her head to come raging into the study and go for poor little Mrs. Ross. His thoughts raced through his head as he crossed the hall, passed through the library and entered his study. Anyway, it'd be a relief to talk to an attractive woman.

She did look very attractive. Pale-ish, but that was under-standable. She wore her clothes like a Frenchwoman. He'd always liked black. Damn' good figure and legs. He took the little hand in its delicate glove and held it tightly.

" Well," he said, " this *is* nice of you."

" I simply had to see you. You'll think me a most fright-ful bore, coming at this time."

" Now you knew that wasn't true before you said it." The little hand started in his.

" Have I hurt you?" asked the squire. " I am a clumsy brute."

" No. Not really. Only you are rather strong, aren't you? It's just my ring."

" I insist on investigating."

He peeled back the glove and drew it down.

" Look at that! A red mark on the inside of your finger. Now, what can be done about that?"

A subdued laugh. He separated the white fingers and kissed them.

" Ha-ha, my boy!" thought the squire, and led her to a chair.

" You've done me good already," he said. " Do you realise that, madam?"

" Have I?"

" Don't you think you're rather an attractive little thing?"

" What am I supposed to say to that?"

" You know it damned well, so you needn't say anything. Ha, ha, ha!"

" Well, I *have* heard something like it before."

" How often?" purred the squire.

" Never you mind."

" Why are you so attractive?"

" Just made that way."

" Little devil," he said and kissed the hand again. He felt quite excited. Everything was going like clockwork.

"Oh, dear," whispered Mrs. Ross. "You're going to be simply livid with me."

"Simply furious?" he asked tenderly.

"Yes. Honestly. I don't want to tell you; but I must!"

"Don't look at me like that or I shall have to kiss you."

"No, please. You must listen. Please."

"If I listen I expect to be rewarded."

"We'll see about that," she said.

"Promise?"

"Promise."

"I'm listening," said the squire, rather feverishly.

"It's about this awful business. I want to tell you first of all, very, very sincerely that you've nothing to fear from me."

"Nothing——?"

He still held her hand, but his fingers relaxed.

"No," she said, "nothing. If you will just trust me——"

Her voice went on and on. Jocelyn heard her to the end, but when it was over he did not remind her of her promise.

III

When Alleyn left the assistant commissioner and returned to his own office, he found Bailey there.

"Well, Bailey?"

"Well, sir, Thompson's developed Mr. Bathgate's film. He's got a couple of shots of the lady."

He laid the still wet prints on the desk.

There was Mrs. Ross in profile on the front step of the Jernigham Arms, and there she was again full face as she came up the path. Nigel must have taken his snapshots through the open window. Evidently she had not seen him. The pointed chin was set a little to one side, the under lip projected very slightly, and the thin mouth was drawn down at the corners. They were not flattering photographs.

"Any luck?" asked Alleyn.

With his normal air of mulish disapproval Bailey laid a card beside the prints. On it was mounted a double photograph. Sharp profile, thin mouth, pointed chin; and the front view showed the colourless hair drawn back in two immaculate shining wings, from the rather high forehead.

Alleyn muttered: "Sarah Rosen. Age 33. Height 5 ft.

5¼ ins. Eyes, light blue. Hair, pale blonde. Very well dressed, cultured speech, usually poses as widow. Detained with Claude Smith on blackmailing charge, 1931. Subsequently released—insufficient evidence. Claude got ten years, didn't he?"

"That's right, sir. They stayed at the Ritz as brother and sister."

"I remember. What about the prints?"

"They're good enough."

"Blackmail," said Alleyn thoughtfully.

"I've looked up the case. She was in the game all right, but they hadn't a thing on her. She seems to have talked her way out."

"She would. Thank you, Bailey. I wish I'd known this a little earlier. Oh, well, no matter, it fits in very prettily."

"Anything else, Mr. Alleyn?"

"I'm going to my flat for half an hour. If Fox rings up before I'm back, tell him I'm there. The car ought to leave now. I'll fix that up. We'd better take a wardress, I suppose. All right, Bailey. Thank you."

IV

Henry wondered what the devil Mrs. Ross had to say to his father. He had watched, with extreme distaste their growing intimacy. "How sharper than a serpent's tooth it is," he thought, "to have a prancing parent." When Jocelyn spoke to Mrs. Ross his habit of loud inexplicable laughter, his manner of leaning backwards, of making a series of mysterious little bows, the curious gesture he employed, the inclination his eyes exhibited towards protuberance, and the naked imbecility of his conversation, all vexed and embarrassed his son to an almost insupportable degree. If Jocelyn should marry her! Henry had no particular objection to Mrs. Ross, but the thought of her as a stepmother struck dismay to his heart. His affection for his father was not weakened by Jocelyn's absurdities. He loved him deeply, he realised, and now the thought that his father might be making a fool of himself in there with that woman was more than he could endure. Miss Prentice had, no doubt, gone to her room; Dinah was out; there was nothing to do.

He wandered restlessly into the library, half-hoping that the door into the study would be open. It was closed. He could hear the murmur of a woman's voice. On and on.

What the hell could she have to say? Then a baritone interjection in which he read urgency and vehemence. Then a long pause.

" My God!" thought Henry. " If he has proposed to her!"

He whistled raucously, took an encyclopædia from the shelves, banged the glass door and slammed the book down on the table.

He heard his father exclaim. A chair castor squeaked and the voices grew more distant. They had moved to the far end of the room.

Henry flung himself into an arm-chair, and once again the conundrum of the murder beset him. Who *did* the police believe had tried to murder Eleanor Prentice? Which would they say had the greatest reason for wishing Eleanor dead? With the thud of fear that came upon him whenever he thought of this, he supposed that he himself had the most reason for wishing Eleanor out of the way. Was it possible that Alleyn suspected him? Whom *did* Alleyn suspect? Not Dinah, surely, not the rector, not his own father. Templett, then? Or—yes—Mrs. Ross? But, Alleyn would surely reason, if Templett was the murderer, it was a successful murder, since it was Templett who insisted that Eleanor shouldn't play the piano. Alleyn would wonder if Templett had told Mrs. Ross he would not allow Eleanor to play. Did Dinah's tirade against Mrs. Ross mean that Dinah suspected her? Had the police any idea who could have gone to the piano after there were people in the hall, and yet not be seen? Already the story of Gladys Wright had reached Pen Cuckoo. And as a final conjecture, perhaps they would ask themselves if Eleanor Prentice in some way had faked her finger and set the trap for her bosom enemy. Or might they agree with the rector and call it a case of attempted murder and suicide?

He leapt to his feet. There was no longer a sound of voices in the study. They must have gone out by the french window.

Henry opened the door and walked in. No. They were still there. Mrs. Ross sat in the window with her back to the light. Jocelyn Jernigham faced the door. When Henry saw Jocelyn he cried out: " Father, what's the matter?"

Jocelyn said, " Nothing's the matter."

Mrs. Ross said, " Hullo! Good-afternoon."

" Good-afternoon," said Henry. " Father, are you ill?"

" No. Don't come bursting into the room asking people if they're ill. It's ridiculous."

"But your face! It's absolutely ashen."

"I've got indigestion."

"I don't believe it."

"I thought he looked pale," said Mrs. Ross solicitously.

"He's absolutely green."

"I'm nothing of the sort," said Jocelyn angrily. "Mrs. Ross and I are talking privately, Henry."

"I'm sorry," said Henry stubbornly, "but I know there's something wrong here. What is it?"

"There's nothing wrong, my dear boy," she said lightly. He stared at her.

"I'm afraid I still think there is."

"Well, I very much hope you won't still think there is when we tell you all about it. At the moment I'm afraid it's a secret." She looked up at Jocelyn. "Isn't it?"

"Yes. Of course. Go away, boy, you're making a fool of yourself."

"Are you sure," Henry asked slowly, "that nobody is making a fool of you?"

Taylor came in. He looked slightly disgruntled.

"Inspector Fox to see you, sir. I told him——"

"Good-afternoon, sir," said a rumbling voice, and the bulk of Inspector Fox filled the doorway.

V

Henry saw the squire look quickly from the open window to Mrs. Ross. Taylor stood aside and Fox walked in.

"I hope you'll excuse me coming straight in like this, sir," said Fox. "Chief Inspector Alleyn asked me to call. I took the liberty of following your butler. Perhaps I ought to have waited."

"No, no," said Jocelyn. "Sit down, er——"

"Fox, sir. Thank you very much, sir."

Fox placed his bowler on a near-by table. He turned to Henry.

"Good-afternoon, sir. We met last night, didn't we?"

"This is Inspector Fox, Mrs. Ross," said Henry.

"Good-afternoon, madam," said Fox tranquilly. Then he sat down. As Alleyn once remarked to Nigel, there was a certain dignity about Fox.

Mrs. Ross smiled charmingly.

"I must take myself off," she said, "and not interrupt Mr. Fox. Don't move, anybody, please."

"If it's not troubling you too much, Mrs. Ross," said Fox, "I'd be obliged if you'd wait for a moment. There are one or two little routine questions for general inquiry, and it will save me taking up your time later on."

"But I'm longing to stay, Mr. Fox."

"Thank you, madam."

Fox took out his spectacles and placed them on his nose. He then drew his note-book from an inside pocket, opened it and stared at it.

"Yes," he said. "Now, the first item's a small matter, really. Did anybody present find the onion in the teapot?"

"*What!*" Henry ejaculated.

Fox fixed his eyes on him.

"The onion in the teapot, sir."

"Which onion in what teapot?" demanded Jocelyn.

Fox turned to him.

"Young Biggins, sir, has admitted that he put a Spanish onion in the teapot used on the stage. We'd like to know who removed it."

Mrs. Ross burst out laughing.

"I'm so sorry," she said, "but it *is* rather funny."

"It sounds a rather ridiculous sort of thing, doesn't it, madam?" agreed Fox gravely. "Do you know anything about it?"

"I'm afraid not. I think Mr. Alleyn has already accused me of an onion."

"Did you happen to hear anything of it, sir?"

"Good Lord, no," said Jocelyn.

"And you, Mr. Henry?"

"Not I," said Henry.

"The next matter," said Fox, making a note, "is the window. I understand you found it open on Saturday afternoon, Mrs. Ross."

"Yes. We shut it."

"Yes. You'd already shut it once, hadn't you? At midday?"

"Yes, I had."

"Who opened it?" inquired Fox, and he looked first at Jocelyn and then at Henry. They both shook their heads.

"I should think it was probably Miss Prentice. My cousin," said Henry. "She has a deep-rooted mania——" He checked himself. "She's a fresh-air fiend of the worst variety, and continually complained that the hall was stuffy."

"I wonder if I might ask Miss Prentice?" said Fox. "Is she at home, sir?"

The squire looked extremely uncomfortable.

"I think she's—ah—she's—ah—in. Yes."

"Do you want me any longer, Mr. Fox?" asked Mrs. Ross.

"I think that will be all for the present, thank you, madam. The chief inspector would be much obliged if you could come down to the hall at about 9.15 this evening."

"Oh? Yes, very well."

"Thank you very much, madam."

"I'll see you out," said the squire hurriedly.

They went out by the french window.

Henry offered Fox a cigarette.

"No. Thank you very much, all the same, sir."

"Mr. Fox," said Henry. "What do you think of the rector's theory? I mean, the idea that Miss Campanula set the trap for my cousin, and that something happened to make her so miserable that when she was asked to play she thought: 'Oh, well, this settles it. Here goes!'"

"Would you have said the deceased lady seemed very unhappy, sir?"

"Well, you know, I didn't notice her very much. But I've been thinking it over, and—yes—she was rather odd. She was damned odd. For one thing, she'd evidently had a colossal row with my cousin. Or rather my cousin seemed friendly enough, but Miss C. wouldn't say a word to her. She was a cranky old cup of tea, you know, and we none of us took much notice. Know what I mean?"

"I understand, sir," said Fox, looking hard at Henry. "Perhaps if I could just have a word with Miss Prentice."

"Oh, Lord!" said Henry ruefully. "Look here, Mr. Fox, you'll find her pretty rum. You'll think we specialize in eccentric spinsters in this part of the world, but I promise you I think the shock of this business has pushed her off at the deep-end. She seems to think the murderer's made a mess of the first attempt, and sooner or later will have another go at her."

"That's not unnatural, is it, sir? Perhaps the lady would feel more comfortable with police protection."

"I pity the protector," said Henry. "Well, I suppose I'd better see if she'll come down."

"If you wouldn't mind, sir," said Fox comfortably.

In some trepidation, Henry mounted the stairs and tapped on Miss Prentice's door. There was no answer. He tapped again. The door opened suddenly and Miss Prentice was revealed with her fingers to her lips, like some mysterious buck-toothed sybil.

"What's happened!" she whispered.

"Nothing's happened, Cousin Eleanor. It's simply one of the men from Scotland Yard with a rather childish question to ask you."

"Is that woman there? I won't meet that woman."

"Mrs. Ross has gone."

"Henry, is that true?"

"Of course it's true."

"Now, I've made you angry again. You're very unkind to me, Henry."

"My dear cousin Eleanor!"

Her hand moved restlessly across the bosom of her dress. "Yes, you are. So unkind. And I'm so fond of you. It's only for your own good. You're young and strong and handsome. All the Jernighams are very strong and beautiful. Don't listen to women like that, Henry. Don't listen to any woman. They'll do you harm. Except dear Dinah."

"Will you come down and speak to Inspector Fox?"

"It's not a trap to make me meet that woman? Why is it a different man? Fox? Where's the other man? He was a gentleman. So tall! Taller than Father Copeland."

He saw with astonishment that the movement of her hand traced a definite pattern on her bosom. She was crossing herself.

"This man is perfectly harmless," said Henry. "Do come."

"Very well. My head's splitting. I suppose I must come."

"That's better," said Henry. He added awkwardly: "Cousin Eleanor, your dress is undone."

"Oh!" She blushed crimson and, to his horror, laughed shrilly and turned aside her head. Her fingers fumbled with the fastening of her dress. Then she shrank past him and, with a kind of coquettishness in her gait, hurried downstairs.

Henry followed with a sinking heart and escorted her to the study. His father had returned and stood before the fire. Jocelyn glared uncomfortably at Miss Prentice.

"Hullo, Eleanor, here you are. This is Inspector Fox."

Miss Prentice offered her hand and, as soon as Fox touched it, snatched it away. Her eyes were downcast, her hands pleated a fold in her dress. Fox looked calmly at her.

227

"I'm sorry to trouble you, Miss Prentice. I only wanted to ask if you opened one of the hall windows as you left at noon on Saturday."

"Oh, yes," she whispered. "Was that the unpardonable sin?"

"I beg your pardon, miss?"

"Did I let it in?"

"Let what in, Miss Prentice?"

"You know. But I only opened it the least little bit. A tiny crack. Of course it can make itself very small, can't it?"

Fox adjusted his spectacles and made a note.

"You did open the window?" he said.

"You shouldn't keep on asking. You know I did."

"Miss Prentice, did you find anything in the teapot you were to use on the stage?"

"Is that where it hid?"

"Where what hid?"

"The unpardonable sin. You know. The thing she did!"

"You're talking nonsense, Eleanor," said Jocelyn. He got behind her and made violent grimaces at Fox.

"I'm sorry if I irritate you, Jocelyn."

"You don't know anything about an onion that a small boy put in the teapot, Miss Prentice?"

She opened her eyes very wide and shaped her mouth like an O. Then she slowly shook her head. Once started, she seemed unable to leave off shaking her head, but went on and on until the movement lost all meaning.

"Well," said Fox, "I think that's all I need trouble you about, thank you, Miss Prentice."

"Henry," said Jocelyn. "See your cousin upstairs."

She went without another word. Henry hurried after her. Jocelyn turned to Fox.

"See how it is!" he said. "The shock sent her out of her mind. There are no ways about it. See for yourself. Have to get a specialist. Better not believe a word she says."

"She's never been like this before, sir?"

"Good God, no."

"That's very distressing, sir, isn't it? The chief inspector asked me to speak to you, sir, about this evening. He thinks it would be a good idea to see, at the same time, all the people who were in the play, and he wonders if you would be good enough to send your party down to the hall."

"I must say I don't quite see—— As a matter of fact,

228

I've asked the Copelands for dinner to talk things over."

"That will fit in very nicely, then, won't it, sir? You can come on to the hall."

"Yes, but I don't see what good it'll do."

"The chief inspector will explain when he comes, sir. He asked me to say he'd be very much obliged if you would give the lead in this little matter. In view of your position in the county, sir, he thought you would prefer to come before the others. You've two cars, haven't you, sir?"

"I suppose I'd better." Jocelyn stared very hard at a portrait of his actress-ancestress and said, "Have you got any idea who it is?"

"I couldn't say what the chief intends just at the moment, sir," answered Fox so blandly that the evasion sounded exactly like a direct answer. "No doubt he will report to you himself, sir. Would nine o'clock suit you at the hall, Mr. Jernigham?"

"What? Oh, yes. Yes, certainly."

"I'm much obliged, sir. I'll say good-afternoon."

"Good-afternoon," said Jocelyn restlessly.

VI

"This is Miss Bruce," said the supervisor. "She was on duty on Friday night, but I doubt if she'll be able to help you."

Fox looked placidly at Miss Bruce and noted that she seemed a bright young person.

He said, "Well, Miss Bruce, we'll be very pleased if you can put us right in this little matter. I understand you were on duty as an operator at ten o'clock on Friday evening."

"Yes, that's right."

"Yes. Now the call we're interested in came through somewhere round about 10.30. It was to the rectory, Winton St. Giles. It's a party line with the old manual telephones and a long extension. Not many of those left, are there?"

"They'll be gone by this time next year," said the supervisor.

"Is that a fact?" said Fox comfortably. "Well, well. Now, Miss Bruce, can you help us?"

"I don't remember any calls on the rectory phone on Friday night," said Miss Bruce. "Chipping 10, the number is. I'm in the Y.P.F.C., so I know. We always have to ring a long time there, because the old housemaid Mary's a bit deaf, and Miss Dinah's room's away upstairs, and the rector never answers until he's fetched. It's a line that's used a lot, of course."

"It would be."

"Yes. Friday was Reading Circle night, and they're usually over at the hall, so everybody knows not to ring up on Friday, see, because they won't be in. Actually, last Friday it was at the rectory because of the play; but people wouldn't know that, see. They'd think: 'Well, Friday. It's no use ringing on Friday.'"

"So you're sure nobody rang?"

"Yes. Yes, I'm sure of it. I'd swear to it if that's what's wanted."

"If the extension was used you wouldn't know, I suppose?"

"I wouldn't know a thing about that."

"No," agreed Fox. "Well, thank you very much, miss. I'm greatly obliged. Good-afternoon."

"Pleasure, I'm sure," said Miss Bruce. "Ta-ta."

CHAPTER TWENTY-FIVE

Final Vignettes

THE EXPRESS FROM London roared into Great Chipping station. Alleyn, who had been reading the future in the murky window pane, rose hurriedly and put on his overcoat.

Fox was on the platform.

"Well, Brer Fox?" said Alleyn when they reached the Bigginses' Ford.

"Well, sir, the Yard car's arrived. They're to drive up quietly after we've all assembled. Allison can come into the supper-room with his two men and I'll wait inside the front door."

"That'll be all right. I'd better give you all a cue to stand by, as Miss Copeland would say. Let's see. I'll ask Miss Prentice if she's feeling the draught. We'll sit on the stage round that table so there'll probably be a hell of a draught. How did you get on at Pen Cuckoo?"

"She was there."

"Not?"

"Ross or Rosen. You had a lucky strike there, Mr.

230

Alleyn. Fancy her being Claude Smith's girl. We were on the Quantock case at that time, weren't we?"

"We weren't at the Yard, anyway. I've never seen her before this."

"More've I. Well, she was there. Something up—between him and her—I should say."

"Between who and her, Mr. Fox?" asked Nigel. "You're very dark and cryptic this evening."

"Between Jernigham senior and Mrs. Ross, Mr. Bathgate. When I arrived he was looking peculiar, and Mr. Henry seemed as if he thought something was up. She was cool enough, but I'd say the other lady was a case for expert opinion."

"Miss Prentice?" murmured Alleyn.

"That's right, sir. Young Jernigham went and fetched her. She owned up to opening the window as sweet as you please, and then began to talk a lot of nonsense about letting in the unpardonable sin. I took it all down, but you'd be surprised how silly it was."

"The unpardonable sin? Which one's that, I wonder?"

"Nobody owned to the onion," said Fox gloomily.

"I think onions, in any form, the unpardonable sin," said Nigel.

"I reckon you're right about the onion, Mr. Alleyn."

"I think so, Fox. After all, on finding onions in teapots, why not exclaim on the circumstance? Why not say, 'Georgie Biggins for a certainty,' and raise hell?"

"That's right, sir. Well, from the way they shaped up to the question, you'd say none of them had ever smelt one. Mr. Jernigham's talking about getting a doctor in. Do you know what? I think he's sweet on her. On Rosen, I mean."

Fox changed into second gear for Chipping Rise and said, "The telephone's right. I told you that when I rang up, didn't I?"

"Yes."

"And I've seen the four girls who helped Gladys Wright. Three of them are ready to swear on oath that nobody came down into the hall from the stage, and the fourth is certain nobody did, but wouldn't swear, as she went into the porch for a minute. I've re-checked the movements of all the people behind the scenes. Mr. Copeland sat facing the floodlights from the time he got there until he went in to Mr. Jernigham's room, when they tried to telephone to Mrs. Ross. He went back to the stage and didn't leave it again until they all crowded round Miss Prentice."

231

"I think it's good enough, Fox."

"I think so, too. This Chief Constable business is awkward, isn't it, Mr. Alleyn?"

"It is, indeed. I know of no precedent. Oh, well, we'll see what the preliminary interview does. You arranged that?"

"Yes, sir, that's all right. Did you dine on the train?"

"Yes, Fox. The usual dead fish and so on. Mr. Bathgate wants to know who did the murder."

"I do know," said Nigel in the back seat; "but I won't let on."

"D'you want to stop at the pub, Mr. Alleyn?"

"No. Let's get it over, Brer Fox, let's get it over."

II

At Henry's suggestion, they had invited Dinah and the rector to dinner.

"You may as well take Dinah and me for granted, Father. We're not going to give each other up, you know."

"I still think—however!"

And Henry, watching his father, knew that the afternoon visit of Miss Campanula's lawyers to the rectory, was Vale property. Jocelyn boggled and uttered inarticulate noises; but already, Henry thought, his father was putting a new roof on Winton. It would be better not to speak, thought Henry, of his telephone conversation with Dinah after Fox had gone. For Dinah had told Henry that her father felt he could not accept the fortune left by Idris Campanula.

Henry said, "I don't suppose you suspect either the rector or Dinah, do you, even though they do get the money? They don't suspect us. Cousin Eleanor, who suspects God knows who, is in her room and won't appear until dinner."

"She ought not to be alone."

"One of the maids is with her. She's quietened down again and is quite normally long-suffering and martyred."

Jocelyn looked nervously at Henry.

"What do you think's the matter with her?"

"Gone ravers," said Henry cheerfully.

The Copelands accepted the invitation to dinner, sherry was served in the library, but Henry managed to get Dinah into the study, where he had made up a large fire and had secretly placed an enormous bowl of yellow chrysanthemums.

"Darling Dinah," said Henry, "there are at least fifty things of the most terrific importance to say to you, and

232

when I look at you I can't think of one of them. May I kiss you? We're almost publicly betrothed, aren't we?"

"Are we? You've never really asked for my hand."

"Miss Copeland—may I call you Dinah?—be mine. Be mine."

"I may not deny, Mr. Jernigham, that my sensibilities; nay, since I will not dissemble, my affections are touched by this declaration. I cannot hear you unmoved."

Henry kissed her and muttered in her ear that he loved her very much.

"All the same," said Dinah, "I do wonder why Mr. Alleyn wants us to go down to the hall to-night. I don't want to go. The place gives me the absolute horrors."

"Me, too. Dinah, I made such a fool of myself last night."

He told her how he had heard the three chords of the "Prelude" as he came through the storm.

"I would have died of it," said Dinah. "Henry, *why* do they want us to-night? Are they—are they going to arrest someone?"

"Who?" asked Henry.

They stared solemnly at each other.

"Who indeed," said Dinah.

III

"I tell you, Copeland, I'm pretty hard hit," said the squire, giving himself a whisky-and-soda. "It's so beastly uncomfortable. Have some more sherry? Nonsense, it'll do you good. You're not looking particularly happy yourself."

"It's the most dreadful thing has ever happened to any of us," said the rector. "How's Miss Prentice?"

"That's partly what I want to talk about. I ought to warn you——"

The rector listened with a steadily blanching face to Jocelyn's account of Miss Prentice.

"Poor soul," he said, "poor soul."

"Yes, I know, but it's damned inconvenient. I'm sorry, rector, but it—well, it's—it's—— Oh, God!"

"Would you like to tell me?" asked the rector, and if he spoke at all wearily Jocelyn did not notice it.

"No," said Jocelyn, "no. There's nothing to tell. I'm simply rather worried. What d'you suppose is the meaning of this meeting to-night?"

The rector looked curiously at him.

" I thought you probably knew. Your position, I mean——"

" As thé weapon happens to be my property, I felt it better to keep right out of the picture. Technically, I'm a suspect."

" Yes. Dear me, yes." The rector sipped his sherry. " So are we all, of course."

" I wonder," said the squire, " what Alleyn is up to."

" You don't think he's going to—to arrest anybody?" They stared at each other.

" Dinner is served, sir," said Taylor.

IV

" Good-night, dear," said Dr. Templett to his wife. " I expect you'll be asleep when I get home. I'm glad it's been a good day."

" It's been a splendid day," said that steadfastly gallant voice. " Good-night, my dear."

Templett shut the door softly. The telephone pealed in his dressing-room at the end of the landing. The hospital was to ring before eight. He went to his dressing-room and lifted the receiver.

" Hullo?"

" Is that you, Billy?"

He sat frozen, the receiver still at his ear.

" Billy? Hullo? Hullo?"

" Well?" said Dr. Templett.

" Then you are alive," said the voice.

" I haven't been arrested, after all."

" Nor, strangely enough, have I, in spite of the fact that I've been to Alleyn and taken the whole responsibility of the letter——"

" Selia! Not on the telephone!"

" I don't much care what happens to me now. You've let me down. Nothing else matters."

" What do you mean? No, don't tell me! It's not true."

" Very well. Good-bye, Billy."

" Wait! Have you been told to parade at the hall this evening?"

" Yes. Have you?"

" Yes." Dr. Templett brushed his hand across his eyes. He muttered hurriedly: " I'll call for you."

" What?"

" If you like I'll drive you there."

234

"I've got my own car. You needn't bother."

"I'll pick you up at nine."

"And drop me a few minutes later, I suppose?"

"That's not quite fair. What do you suppose I thought when——?"

"You obviously don't trust me. That's all."

"My God——!" began Dr. Templett. The voice cut in coolly:

"All right. At nine. Why do you suppose he wants us in the hall? Is he going to arrest someone?"

"I don't know. What do you think?"

"I don't know."

v

The church clock struck nine as the police car drew up outside the hall. Alleyn and Fox got out, followed by Detective-Sergeant Allison and two plain-clothes men. At the same moment, Nigel drove up in his own car with Sergeant Roper. They all went in through the back door. Alleyn switched on the stage lights and the supper-room light.

"You see the lie of the land, don't you," he said. "Two flights of steps from the supper-room to the stage. We'll have the curtain down, I think, Fox. You can stay on the stage. So can you, Bathgate, in the wings, and with not a word out of you. You know when to go down and what to do?"

"Yes," said Nigel nervously.

"Good. Allison, you'd better move to the front door, and you others can go into the dressing-rooms. They'll come straight through the supper-room and won't see you. Roper, you're to go outside and direct them to the back door. Then come in. But quietly, if you don't want me to tear your buttons off and half-kill you. The rest of you can stay in the dressing-rooms until the company's complete. When it is complete, I'll slam both doors at the top of the steps. You can then come into the supper-room and sit on the steps. The piano's in position, isn't it, Fox? And the screens? Yes. All right, down with the curtain."

The curtain came down in three noisy rushes, releasing a cloud of dust.

With the front of the hall shut out, the stage presented a more authentic appearance. Dinah's box set, patched and

235

contrived though it was, resembled any touring company's stock scenery, while Mrs. Ross's chairs and ornaments raised the interior to still greater distinction. The improvised lights shone bravely enough on chintz and china. The stage had taken on a sort of eerie half-life and an air of expectancy. On the round table Alleyn laid the anonymous letter, the "Prelude in C Minor," the "Venetian Suite," the pieces of rubber in their box, the onion, the soap-box and the teapot. He then covered this curious collection with a cloth.

Fox and Allison brought extra chairs from the dressing-rooms and put one of the paraffin lamps on the stage.

"Eight chairs," counted Alleyn. "That's right. Are we ready? I think so."

"Nothing else, sir?"

"Nothing. Remember your cue. Leave on the supper-room lights. Here he comes, I think. Away you go."

Fox walked over to the prompt corner. Nigel went through the opposite door and sat out of sight in the shadow of the proscenium. Allison went down to the auditorium, the two plain-clothes men disappeared into the dressing-rooms, and Roper, breathing stertorously, made for the back door.

"Shock tactics," muttered Alleyn. "Damn, I hate 'em. So infernally unfair, and they look like pure exhibitionism on the part of the police. Oh, well, can't be helped."

"I don't hear a car," whispered Nigel.

"It's coming."

They all listened. The wind howled and the rain drummed on the shutters.

"I'll never think of this place," said Nigel, "without hearing that noise."

"It's worse than ever," said Fox.

"Here it is," said Alleyn.

And now they all heard the car draw up in the lane. A door slammed. Boots crunched up the gravel path. Roper's voice could be heard. The back door opened. Roper, suddenly transformed into a sort of major-domo, said loudly:

"Mr. Jernigham senior, sir."

And the squire walked in.

CHAPTER TWENTY-SIX

Miss Prentice feels the Draught

"SO YOU SEE," said Alleyn, "I was led to wonder if, to speak frankly, the object of her visit was blackmail."

The squire's face was drained of all its normal colour, but now it flushed a painful crimson.

"I cannot believe it."

"In view of the record——"

The squire made a violent, clumsy gesture with his right hand. Standing in the centre of the stage under those uncompromising lights, he looked at once frightened and defiant. Alleyn watched him for a moment and then he said:

"You see, I think I know what she had to say to you." Jernigham's jaw dropped.

"I don't believe you," he said hoarsely.

"Then let me tell what I believe to be her hold on you." Alleyn's voice went on and on, quietly, dispassionately. Jernigham listened with his gaze on the floor. Once he looked up as though he would interrupt, but he seemed to think better of this impulse and fell to biting his nails.

"I give you this opportunity," said Alleyn. "If you care to tell me now——"

"There is nothing to tell you. It's not true."

"Mrs. Ross did not come this afternoon with this story. She did not make these very definite terms with you?"

"I cannot discuss the matter."

"Even," said Alleyn, "in view of this record?"

"I admit nothing."

"Very well. I was afraid you would take this line."

"In my position——"

"It was because of your position I gave you this opportunity. I can do no more."

"I can't see why you want this general interview."

"Shock tactics, sir," said Alleyn.

"I—I don't approve."

"If you wish, sir, I can hand my report in and you may make a formal complaint at the Yard."

"No."

"It would make no difference," said Alleyn. "I think the others have arrived. This is your last word?"

"I have nothing to say."

"Very well, sir."

Roper tapped at one of the supper-room doors.

"Hullo!" shouted Alleyn.

"Here they be, sir, every living soul, and all come together."

"All right, Roper. Show them in."

II

Miss Prentice came in first, followed by Dinah, the rector and Henry. Alleyn asked Miss Prentice to sit in the most comfortable chair, which he had placed on the prompt side of the table. When she dithered, he was so crisply polite that she was there before she realised it. She looked quickly towards the rector, who took the chair on her right. Dinah sat on her father's right with Henry beside her. The squire looked furtively at Alleyn.

"Will you sit down, sir?" invited Alleyn.

"What! Yes, yes," said the squire convulsively, and sat beside Henry.

Mrs. Ross came in. She was dressed in black and silver, a strange exotic figure in those surroundings. She said: "Good-evening," with her customary side-long smile, bowed rather more pointedly to Alleyn, and sat beside the squire. Templett, seeming ill at ease and shame-faced, followed her.

Miss Prentice drew in her breath and began to whisper:

"No, no, no! Never at the same table. I can't——!"

Alleyn sat on her left in the one chair remaining vacant and said, "Miss Prentice—please!"

His voice had sufficient edge to silence Miss Prentice and call the others to a sort of guarded alertness.

His long hands lay clasped before him on the table. He leant forward and looked with deliberation round the circle of attentive faces.

He said, "Ladies and gentlemen, I shall not apologise for calling you together to-night. I am sure that most— not all, but most—of you are only too anxious that this affair should be settled, and I may tell you that we have now collected enough evidence to make an arrest. Each of you in turn has provided evidence; each of you has withheld evidence. From the information you have given, and from the significance of your several reticences, has emerged a

238

pattern which, as we read it, has at its centre a single person: the murderer of Miss Idris Campanula."

They sat as still as figures in a tableau, and the only sound, when Alleyn paused, was the sound of rain and the uneasy stirring of the wind outside.

" From the beginning, this strange affair has presented one particularly unusual problem: the problem of the murderer's intention. Was it Miss Idris Campanula for whom this trap was set, or was it Miss Eleanor Prentice? If it was indeed Idris Campanula, then the number of possible suspects was very small. If it was Miss Prentice, the field was a great deal wider. During most of yesterday and part of to-day my colleague, Inspector Fox interviewed the people who have known and come into contact with both these ladies. He could find no motive for the murder of either of them, outside the circle of people we have found motive. Money, jealously, love and fear are the themes most usually found behind homicide. All four appeared in this case if Miss Campanula was the intended victim: the last three, if the intended victim was Miss Prentice. The fact that on Friday evening at five o'clock Mr. Henry Jernigham showed the automatic to all of you, except his father, who is the owner, was another circumstance that suggested one of you as the guilty person."

Henry rested his head on his hand, driving his fingers through his hair. Templett cleared his throat.

" At the inquest this morning you all heard the story of the water-pistol. The booby-trap was ready at 2.30 on Friday. The water-pistol was no longer in position at noon on Saturday when Miss Prentice used the soft pedal. Yet some time between Friday at 2.30 and noon on Saturday, somebody sat at the piano and used the soft pedal and the booby-trap worked."

Alleyn lifted the cloth from the table. Miss Prentice gave a nervous yelp. He took up the " Venetian Suite " and pointed to the circular blister and discoloured splashes on the back.

" Five hours after the catastrophe, this was still damp. So was the torn silk round the hole in the front of the piano. Miss Prentice has told us that her music was left on the piano earlier in the week. All Saturday morning the hall was occupied. It seems, therefore, that the water-pistol was removed before Saturday morning, and presumably by the guilty person, since an innocent person would not have kept

239

silent about the booby-trap. On Friday afternoon and evening the hall was deserted. At this stage I may say that Mr. Jernigham and Dr. Templett both have alibis for Friday afternoon, when they hunted up till a short time before the rehearsal-for-words at Pen Cuckoo. Dr. Templett has an alibi for Friday and well into Saturday morning, during which time he was occupied with professional duties. It is hardly conceivable that he would enter the hall in the small hours of Saturday morning to play the piano. The helpers arrived soon after nine o'clock on Saturday, and by that time the pistol had been removed.

"Now for the automatic. If, as we suppose, the water-pistol was discovered on Friday, it is of course possible that the automatic was substituted before Saturday. This possibility we consider unlikely. It was known that the helpers would be in the hall all Saturday morning, and the murderer would have run the risk of discovery. It was only necessary for someone to disarrange the rotten silk in the front of the piano to reveal the nozzle of the Colt. True, this piece of music was on the rack; but it might have been removed. Somebody might have dusted the piano. It is also true that nobody was likely to look in the top, as the person who removed the water-pistol had taken pains to re-fasten the bunting with drawing-pins and to cover the top with heavy pot plants. Still, there would have been considerable risk. It seems more probable that the murderer would leave the setting of the automatic until as late as possible. Say about four o'clock on Saturday afternoon."

Templett made a sudden movement, but said nothing.

"For four o'clock on Saturday afternoon," said Alleyn, "none of you has an alibi that would stand up to five minutes' cross-examination."

"But——"

"I've told you——"

"I explained yesterday——"

"Do you want me to go into this? Wait a little and listen. At about half-past three, Mrs. Ross arrived at the hall. Dr. Templett got there a few minutes later. She had come to complete the supper arrangements, he to put his acting clothes in his dressing-room. They had both called at Pen Cuckoo in the morning. Mrs. Ross tells us that while Dr. Templett went into the house she remained in the car. I imagine there is no need to remind you all of the french window into the study at Pen Cuckoo."

"I knew," whispered Miss Prentice. "I knew, I knew!"

"You're going beyond your duty, Mr. Alleyn," said Mrs. Ross.

"No," said Alleyn. "I merely pause here to point out how easy it would have been for any of you to come up Top Lane and slip into the study. To return to the 3.30 visit to the hall. Dr. Templett has given what I believe to be a true account of this visit. He has told us that he arrived to find Mrs. Ross already there and occupied with the supper arrangements. After a time they came here on to this stage. They noticed that the last window on the right, near the front door, was a few inches open. Mrs. Ross, who first noticed this, told Dr. Templett that she saw someone dodge down behind the sill. To reach the window this onlooker used a box."

He turned the cloth farther back and the dilapidated soap-box was revealed. Miss Prentice giggled and covered her mouth with her hand.

"This is the box. It fits into the marks under the window. Do you recognise it, Dr. Templett?"

"Yes," said Templett dully, "I remember that splash of white on the top. I saw it as I looked down."

"Exactly. I should explain that when Dr. Templett reached the window he looked out to see if he could discover anybody. He saw nobody, but he noticed the box. He tells me it was not there when he arrived. Now Mrs. Ross said that she did not recognise this person. But I have experimented, and have found that if one sees anybody at all under the conditions she has described, one stands a very good chance of recognising them. One would undoubtedly know, for instance, whether it was a man or a woman whose image showed for a moment and disappeared behind the sill. It will be urged by the police that Mrs. Ross did, in fact, recognise this person." Alleyn turned to Templett.

"Mrs. Ross did not tell you who it was?"

"I didn't know who it was," said Mrs. Ross.

"Dr. Templett?"

"I believe Mrs. Ross's statement."

Alleyn looked at the squire.

"When you saw Mrs. Ross alone this afternoon, sir, did she refer to this incident?"

"I can't answer that question, Alleyn," muttered the squire. Henry raised his head and looked at his father with a sort of wonder.

"Very well, sir," said Alleyn. "I must remind you all that you are free to refuse answers to any questions you may be asked. The police may not set traps, and it is my duty to tell you that we have established the identity of the eaves-dropper." He took the lid from a small box.

"One of these fragments of rubber," he said, "was found on the point of a nail on the inside of the box. The others were caught behind projecting splinters also on the inside of the box."

He opened an envelope and from it he shook a torn surgical finger-stall.

"The fragments of rubber," he said, "correspond with the holes in this stall."

Miss Prentice electrified the company by clapping her hands with great violence.

"Oh, inspector," she cried shrilly, "how perfectly, perfectly wonderful you are!"

III

Alleyn turned slowly and met her enraptured gaze. Her prominent eyes bulged, her mouth was open, and she nodded her head several times with an air of ecstasy.

"Then you acknowledge," he said, "that you put this box outside the window on Saturday afternoon?"

"Of course!"

"And that you stood on it in order to look through the window?"

"Alas, yes!"

"Miss Prentice, why did you do this?"

"I was guided."

"Why did you not admit you recognised the box when Inspector Fox asked you about it?"

With that unlovely air of girlishness she covered her face with her fingers.

"I was afraid he would ask me what I saw."

"This is absolute nonsense!" said Templett angrily.

"And why," continued Alleyn, "did you tell me you were indoors all Saturday afternoon?"

"I was afraid to say what I'd done."

"Afraid? Of whom?"

She seemed to draw herself inwards to a point of venomous concentration. She stretched out her arm across the table. The finger pointed at Mrs. Ross.

"Of *her*. She tried to murder me. She's a murderess. I can prove it. I can prove it."

242

" No! " cried the squire. " No! Good God, Alleyn———"

" Is there any doubt in your mind, Mr. Alleyn," said Mrs. Ross, " that this woman is mad?"

" I can prove it," repeated Miss Prentice.

" How?" asked Alleyn. " Please let this finish, Mr. Jernigham. We shall see daylight soon."

" She knew I saw her. She tried to kill me because she was afraid."

" You hear that, Mrs. Ross? It is a serious accusation. Do you feel inclined to answer it? I must warn you, first, that Dr. Templett has made a statement about this incident."

She looked quickly at Templett.

He said, " I thought you hadn't considered me over the other business. I told the truth."

" You fool," said Mrs. Ross. For the first time she looked really frightened. She raised her hands to her thin neck and touched it surreptitiously. Then she hid her hands in her lap.

" I do not particularly want to repeat the gist of Dr. Templett's statement," said Alleyn.

" Very well." Her voice cracked, she took a breath and then said evenly, " Very well. I recognised Miss Prentice. I've nothing whatever to fear. One doesn't kill old maids for eavesdropping."

" Mr. Jernigham," said Alleyn, " did Mrs. Ross tell you of this incident this afternoon?"

The squire was staring at Mrs. Ross as if she was a sort of Medusa. Without turning his eyes, he nodded.

" She suggested that Miss Prentice had come down to the hall with the intention of putting the automatic in the piano?"

" So she had. I'll swear," said Mrs. Ross.

" Mr. Jernigham?"

" Yes. Yes, she suggested that."

" She told you, perhaps, that you could trust her?"

" Oh, my God!" said the squire.

" I arrived too late at this place," said Mrs. Ross, " to be able to do anything to the piano." She looked at Dinah. " You know that."

" Yes," said Dinah.

" It was soon after that," said Miss Prentice abruptly, " that she began to set traps for me, you know. Then I saw it all in a flash. She must have seen me through a glass darkly, and because I witnessed the unpardonable sin she will destroy me. You understand, don't you, because

243

it is very important. She is in league with The Others, and it won't be long before one of them catches me."

Templett said, " Alleyn, you must see. This has gone on long enough. It's perfectly obvious what's wrong here."

" We will go on, if you please," said Alleyn. " Mr Copeland, you told me that on Friday night you expected Miss Prentice at the rectory."

The rector, very pale, said, " Yes."

" She didn't arrive?"

" No. I told you. She telephoned."

" At what time?"

" Not long after ten."

" From Pen Cuckoo?"

" It was my hand, you know," said Miss Prentice rapidly. " I wanted to rest my hand. It was so very naughty. The blood tramped up and down my arm. Thump, thump, thump. So I said I would stay at home."

" You rang from Pen Cuckoo?"

" I took the message, Mr. Alleyn," said Dinah. " I told you."

" And what do you say, Miss Copeland, if I tell you that on Friday night the Pen Cuckoo telephone was out of order from 8.20 until the following morning?"

" But—it couldn't have been."

" I'm afraid it was." He turned to Henry Jernigham. " You agree?"

" Yes," said Henry without raising his head.

" You can thank The Others for that," said Miss Prentice in a trembling voice.

" The Others?"

" The Others, yes. They are always doing these sort of tricks; and she's the worst of the lot, that woman over there."

" Well, Miss Copeland?"

" I took the message," repeated Dinah. " Miss Prentice said she was at home and would remain at home."

" This contradiction," said Alleyn, " takes us a step further. Mrs. Ross, on Friday night you drove down to Chipping by way of Church Lane?"

" Yes."

" You have told me that you saw a light in this hall."

" Yes."

" You think it was in Mr. Jernigham's dressing-room?"

" Yes."

" The telephone is in that room, Miss Dinah, isn't it?"

"Yes," whispered Dinah. "Oh, yes."

Alleyn took a card from his pocket and scribbled on it. He handed it over to Henry.

"Will you take Miss Dinah to the rectory?" he said. "In half an hour I want you to ring through to here on the extension. Show this card to the man at the door and he will let you out."

Henry looked fixedly at Alleyn.

"Very well, sir," he said. "Thank you."

Henry and Dinah went out.

IV

"Now," said Alleyn, "we come to the final scene. I must tell you—though I dare say you have heard it all by now —that at 6.30 Miss Gladys Wright used the piano and pressed down the soft pedal. Nothing untoward happened. Since it is inconceivable that anybody could remove the pot plants and rig the automatic after 6.30, we know that the automatic must have been already in position. The safety-catch, which Mr. Henry Jernigham showed to all of you, and particularly to Mrs. Ross, accounts for Gladys Wright's immunity. How, then, did the guilty person manage to release the safety-catch after Gladys Wright and her fellow-helpers were down in the front of the hall? I will show you how it could have been done."

He went down to the footlights.

"You notice that the curtain falls on the far side of the improvised footlights and just catches on the top of the piano. Now, if you'll look."

He stopped and pushed his hand under the curtain. The top of the piano, with its covering of green and yellow bunting, could be seen.

"This bunting is pinned down as it was on Saturday. It is stretched tight over the entire top of the piano. The lid is turned back, but of course that doesn't show. The pot plants stand on the inside of the lid. I take out the centre drawing-pin at the back and slide my hand under the bunting. I am hidden by the curtain, and the pot plants also serve as a mask for any slight movement that might appear from the front of the hall. My fingers have reached the space beyond the open lid. Inside the opening they encounter the cold, smooth surface of the Colt. Listen."

Above the sound of rain and wind they all heard a small click.

"I have pushed over the safety-catch," said Alleyn. "The automatic is now ready to shoot Miss Campanula between the eyes."

"Horrible," said the rector violently.

"There is one sequence of events about which we can be certain," said Alleyn. "We know that the first person to arrive was Gladys Wright. We know that she entered the hall at 6.30, and was in front of the curtain down there with her companions until and after the audience came in. We know that it would have been impossible for anybody to come down from the stage into the front of the hall unnoticed. Miss Wright is ready to swear that nobody did this. We know that Miss Dinah Copeland arrived with her father soon after Gladys Wright, and was here behind the scenes. We know Mr. Copeland sat on the stage until he made his announcement to the audience, only leaving it for a moment, to join the others at the telephone, and once again when he persuaded Miss Prentice not to play. Mr. Copeland, did you at any time see anybody stoop down to the curtain as I did just then?"

"No. No! I'm quite certain that I didn't. You see, my chair faced the exact spot."

"Yes, therefore we know that unless Mr. Copeland is the guilty person, the safety-catch must have been released during one of his two absences. But Mr. Copeland believed, up to the last moment, that Miss Prentice was to be the pianist. We are satisfied that Mr. Copeland is not the guilty person."

The rector raised one of his large hands in a gesture that seemed to repudiate immunity. The squire, Miss Prentice, Mrs. Ross and Templett kept their eyes fixed on Alleyn.

"Knowing the only means by which the safety-catch might be released, it seems evident that Miss Prentice was not the intended victim. Miss Prentice, you are cold. Do you feel a draught?"

Miss Prentice shook her head, but she trembled like a wet dog and looked not unlike one. There was a faint sound of movement behind the scenes. Alleyn went on:

"When you were all crowded round her and she gave in and consented to allow Miss Campanula to play, it would have been easy enough to come up here and put the safety-catch on again. Why run the risk of being arrested for the murder of the wrong person?"

Alleyn's level voice halted for a moment. He leant forward, and when he spoke again it was with extreme deliberation:

"No! The trap was set for Miss Campanula. It was set before Miss Prentice yielded her right to play, and it was set by someone who knew she would not play. The safety-catch was released at the only moment when the stage was empty. The moment when you were all crowded round the telephone. Then the murderer sat back and waited for the catastrophe to happen. Beyond the curtain at this moment someone is sitting at the piano. In a minute you will hear the opening chords of the 'Prelude' as you heard them on Saturday night. If you listen closely you will hear the click of the trigger when the soft pedal goes down. That will represent the report of the automatic. Imagine this guilty person. Imagine someone whose hand stole under the curtain while the hall was crowded and set that trap. Imagine someone who sat, as we sit now, and waited for those three fatal chords."

Alleyn paused.

As heavy as lead and as loud as ever the dead hand had struck them out, in the empty hall beyond the curtain, thumped the three chords of Miss Campanula's "Prelude."

"Pom. *Pom*. POM!"

And very slowly, in uneven jerks, the curtain began to rise.

As it rose, so did Miss Prentice. She might have been pulled up by an invisible hand in her hair. Her mouth was wide open, but the only sound she made was a sort of retching groan. She did not take her eyes from the rising curtain, but she pointed her hand at the rector and waved it up and down.

"*It was for you*," screamed Miss Prentice. "*I did it for you!*"

And Nigel, seated at the piano, saw Alleyn take her by the arm.

"Eleanor Prentice, I arrest you——"

CHAPTER TWENTY-SEVEN

Case Ends

HENRY AND DINAH sat by the fire in the rectory study and watched the clock.

" *Why* does he want us to ring up?" said Dinah for perhaps the sixth time. " I don't understand."

" I think I do. I think the telephoning's only an excuse. He wanted us out of the way."

" But why?"

Henry put his arm round her shoulders and pressed his cheek against her hair.

" Oh, Dinah," he said.

" What, darling?"

Dinah looked up. He sat on the arm of her chair and she had to move a little in his embrace before she could see his eyes.

" Henry! What is it?"

" I think we're in for a bad spin."

" But—isn't it Mrs. Ross?"

" I don't think so."

Without removing her gaze from his face she took his hand.

" I think it's Eleanor," said Henry.

" *Eleanor!* "

" It's the only answer. Don't you see that's what Alleyn was driving at all the time?"

" But she *wanted* to play. She made the most frightful scene over not playing."

" I know. But Templett said two days before that she'd never be able to do it. Don't you see, she worked it so that we should find her crying and moaning, and insist on her giving up?"

" Suppose we hadn't insisted."

" She'd have left the safety-catch on or not used the soft pedal, or perhaps she'd have ' discovered ' the automatic and accused Miss C. of putting it there. That would have made a glorious scene."

" I can't believe it."

" Can you believe it of anyone else?"

" Mrs. Ross," said Dinah promptly.

" No, darling. I rather think Mrs. Ross has merely tried

248

to blackmail my papa. It is my cousin who is a murderess. Shall you enjoy a husband of whom every one will say: ' Oh, yes, Henry Jernigham! Wasn't he the Pen Cuckoo murderess's nephew or son or something?'"

"I shall love my husband and I shan't hear what they say. Besides, you don't know. You're only guessing."

"I'm certain of it. There are all sorts of things that begin to fit in. Things that don't fit any other way. Dinah, I know she's the one."

"Anyway, my dear darling, she's mad."

"I hope so," said Henry. "God, it's awful, isn't it?"

He sprang up and began to walk nervously up and down.

"I can't stand this much longer," said Henry.

"It's time we rang up."

"I'll do it."

But as he reached the door they heard voices in the hall. The rector came in, followed by Alleyn and the squire.

"Dinah! Where's Dinah?" cried the rector.

"Here she is," said Henry. "Father!"

The squire turned a chalk-white face to his son.

"Come here, old boy," he said. "I want you."

"That chair," said Alleyn quickly.

Henry and Alleyn put the squire in the chair.

"Brandy, Dinah," said the rector. "He's fainted."

"No, I haven't," said Jocelyn. "Henry, old boy, I'd better tell you——"

"I know," said Henry. "It's Eleanor."

Alleyn moved back to the door and watched them. He was now a detached figure. The arrest came like a wall of glass between himself and the little group that hovered round Jocelyn. He knew that most of his colleagues accepted these moments of isolation. Perhaps they were scarcely aware of them. But, for himself, he always felt a little like a sort of Mephistopheles, who looked on at his own handiwork. He didn't enjoy the sensation. It was the one moment when his sense of detachment deserted him. Now, as they remembered him, he saw in the faces turned towards him the familiar guarded antagonism of herded animals.

He said, "If Mr. Jernigham would like to see Miss Prentice, it shall be arranged. Superintendent Blandish will be in charge."

He bowed, and was going when Jocelyn said loudly:

"Wait a minute."

"Yes, sir?" Alleyn moved quickly to the chair. The squire looked up at him.

"I know you tried to prepare me for this," he said. "You guessed that woman had told me. I couldn't stand that until—until it was all up—I wouldn't admit it. You understand that?"

"Yes."

"I'm all to blazes. Think what to do in the morning. Just wanted to say I appreciate the way you've handled things. Considerate."

"I would have avoided the final scene, sir, if I had seen any other way."

"I know that. Mustn't ask questions, of course. There are some things I don't understand—— Alleyn, you see she's out of her mind?"

Dr. Templett, I'm sure, will advise you about an alienist, sir."

"Yes. Thank you."

The squire blinked up at him and then suddenly held out his hand.

"Good-night."

"Good-night, sir."

Henry said, "I'll come out with you."

As they walked to the door, Alleyn thought there were points about being a Jernigham of Pen Cuckoo.

"It's queer," said Henry. "I suppose this must be a great shock to us; but at the moment I feel nothing at all. Nothing. I don't realise that she's—— Where is she?"

"The Yard car is on the way to Great Chipping. She'll need things from Pen Cuckoo. We'll let you know what they are."

Henry stopped dead at the rectory door. His voice turned to ice.

"Is she frightened?"

Alleyn remembered that face with the lips drawn back from the projecting teeth, the tearless bulging eyes, the hands that opened and closed as if they had let something fall.

"I don't think she is conscious of fear," he said. "She was quite composed. She didn't weep."

"She can't. Father often said she never cried as a child."

"I remembered your father told me that."

"I hated her," said Henry. "But that's nothing now; She's insane. It's strange, because there's no insanity in the family. What happens? I mean, when will they begin to try her. We—what ought we to do?"

Alleyn told him what they should do. It was the first time he had ever advised the relatives of a person accused of murder, and he said, " But you must ask your lawyer's advice first of all. That is really all I may tell you."

" Yes. Yes, of course. Thank you, sir." Henry peered at Alleyn. He saw him against rods of rain that glinted in the light from the open door.

" It's funny," said Henry jerkily. " Do you know, I was going to ask you about Scotland Yard—how one began."

" Did you think seriously of this?"

" Yes. I want a job. Hardly suitable for the cousin of the accused."

" There's no reason why you shouldn't try for the police."

" I've read your book. Good Lord, it's pretty queer to stand here and talk like this."

" You're more shocked than you realise. If I were you I should take your father home."

" Ever since yesterday, sir, I've had the impression I'd seen you before. I've just remembered. Agatha Troy did a portrait of you, didn't she?"

" Yes."

" It was very good, wasn't it? Rather a compliment to be painted by Troy. Is she pleasant or peculiar?"

" I think her very pleasant indeed," said Alleyn. " I have persuaded her to say she will marry me. Good-night."

He smiled, waved his hand and went out into the rain.

II

Nigel had driven his own car over to the rectory, and he took Alleyn to Great Chipping.

" The others have only just got away," said Nigel. " She fainted after you left, and Fox had to get Templett to deal with her. They're picking the wardress up at the sub-station."

" Fainted, did she?"

" Yes. She's completely dotty, isn't she?"

" I shouldn't say so. Not completely."

" Not?"

" The dottiness has only appeared since Saturday night. She's probably extremely neurotic. Unbalanced, hysterical, all that. In law, insanity is very closely defined. Her counsel will probably go for moral depravity, delusion, or hallucination. If he can prove a history of disturbances of the higher levels of thought, he may get away with it. I'm afraid poor old Copeland will have to relate his experiences. They'll give me fits for your performance on the piano, but I've covered myself by warning the listeners. I don't mind betting that even if lunacy is not proved, there'll be a recommendation for mercy. Of course, they may go all out for 'not guilty' and get it."

"You might give me an outline, Alleyn."

"All right. Where are we? It's as dark as hell."

"Just coming into Chipping. There's the police car ahead."

"Ah, yes. Well, here's the order of events as we see it. On Friday, by 2.40, Georgie had set the booby-trap. Miss Campanula tried to get into the hall before he left it. He hid while the chauffeur looked through the window. When the chauffeur had gone, Georgie re-pinned the bunting over the open top of the piano, replaced the aspidistras and decamped. At a minute or two after half-past two, Miss C. passed Miss P. in the church porch. Miss P. was seen by Gibson. She crossed Church Lane and would pass the hall on her way to Top Lane. In Top Lane she met Dinah Copeland and Henry Jernigham at three o'clock.

"Apparently she had taken half an hour to walk a quarter of a mile. We did it yesterday in five minutes. Our case is that she'd gone into the hall in a great state of upset because the rector had ticked her off at confession. She must have sat at the piano, worked the booby-trap and got the jet of water full in the face. She removed the pistol, and probably the first vague idea of her crime came into her head, because she kept quiet about the booby-trap. Perhaps she remembered the Colt and wondered if it would fit. We don't know. We only know that at three o'clock she had the scene in Top Lane with Henry and Dinah, the scene that was watched and overheard by that old stinker, Tranter. Tranter and Dinah noticed that the bosom of her dress was wet. That, with the lapse in time, are the only scraps of evidence we've got so far to give colour to this bit of our theory, but I'd like to know how else the front of her bodice got wet, if not from the pistol. It wasn't raining, and anyhow rain wouldn't behave like that. And I'd like to know how else you can account for her arrival, as late as three, at a spot five minutes away."

"Yes, it'll certainly take a bit of explaining."

"The butler remembered she got back at four. At five Henry explained the mechanism of the Colt to the assembled company, stressing and illustrating the action of the safety-

252

catch. Miss P. had told the rector she wanted to see him that evening. Of course, she wanted to give him a distorted and poisonous version of the meeting between Henry and his Dinah. She was to come to the rectory after the Reading Circle activities. About ten o'clock, that would be. Now, soon after ten, Miss C. flung herself into the rector's arms in the rectory study."

" Christopher!"

"Yes. I hope for his sake we won't have to bring this out; but it's a faint hope. The curtains were not drawn, and anybody on the path to the hall could have seen. Round about 10.15, Miss Dinah heard the gate into the wood give its customary piercing shriek. She thought somebody had gone out that way and believed it was Miss C. We contend it was Miss Prentice in for her appointment. We contend she stood inside the gate transfixed by the tableau beyond the window, that she put the obvious interpretation on what she saw, and fell a prey to whatever furies visit a woman whose ageing heart is set on one man and whose nerves, desires and thoughts have been concentrated on the achievement of her hope. We think she turned, passed through the post-stile and returned to Church Lane. To help this theory we've got two blurred heel-prints, the statements that nobody else used the gate that night, and the fact that Miss P. rang up shortly afterwards from the hall."

" How the devil d'you get that?"

"The telephone operator is prepared to swear nobody rang up the rectory. But Miss P. rang up and the old housemaid called Dinah Copeland, who went to the telephone. She evidently didn't notice it was an extension call. Miss P. said she was speaking from Pen Cuckoo. Miss P. has admitted she rang up. The hall telephone is an extension and doesn't register at the exchange. Mrs. Ross saw a light in the hall telephone room, at the right moment. It's the only explanation. Miss P. didn't know the Pen Cuckoo telephone was out of order and thought she was safe enough to establish a false alibi. She probably got the water-pistol that night and took it away with her to see if the Colt was the same length. It was an eleventh of an inch shorter, which meant that the nozzle would fit in the hole without projecting. Now we come to Saturday afternoon. She told me she was in her room. Mrs. Ross recognised her through the hall window, and we've got the scraps of rubber to prove that she handled the box. She looked through the hall window to see if the coast was clear. I imagine Templett was embracing his dubious love, who saw the onlooker over his shoulder. Miss P. took to cover, leaving the box. When they'd gone, she crept into the hall and put the Colt in position. She'd had four emotional shocks in twenty-six hours. The rector had given her fits. She'd seen Henry making ardent love to Dinah. She'd seen Idris Campanula, apparently victoriously happy, in the rector's arms, and she'd watched Templett and Mrs. Ross in what I imagine must have been an even more passionate encounter. And though I do *not* consider her insane in law, I do consider that these experiences drove her into an ecstasy of fury. Since it is the rector with whom she herself is madly and overwhelmingly in love, Idris Campanula was the object of her hatred. It was Idris who had robbed her of her hopes. Incidentally, it is Idris who left her a fortune. Georgie Biggins had shown her the way. It's worth noting here that she won a badge for tying knots, and taught the local Guides in this art. At half-past four she was back at Pen Cuckoo and waked the squire in time for tea. This account, too, sounds like conjecture, but the finger-stall proves she lied once, the telephone proves she lied twice, and the fingerprints in the teapot prove she lied three times."

"In the teapot?"

"I'll explain in a minute."

They reached the top of Great Chipping Rise, and the lights of the town swam brokenly beyond the rain.

"There's not much more," said Alleyn. "The prosecution will make the most of this last point. The only time the stage was deserted, after they arrived in the evening, was when all the others stood round the telephone trying to get through to Mrs. Ross and Dr. Templett. Only Miss Prentice was absent. She appeared for a moment, saw the squire in his under-pants, scuttled off to the stage and did her stunt with the safety-catch. Our case really rests on this. We can check and double-check the movements of every one of them from half-past six onwards. The rector sat on the stage, and will swear nobody touched the piano from that side. Gladys Wright and her helpers were in the hall and will swear nobody touched it from that side. The only time the catch could have been moved was when they were all round the telephone, and Miss P. was absent. She is literally the only person who could have moved the catch."

"By George," said Nigel, "she must be a cold-blooded creature! What a nerve!"

"It's given way a little since the event," said Alleyn

254

grimly. "I think she found she wasn't as steady as she expected to be, so she allowed her hysteria to mount into the semblance of insanity. Her nerve had gone at the shock of her dear friend's death, you see. Now she's going to work the demented stuff for all it's worth. I wonder when she first began to be afraid of me. I wonder if it was when I put the finger-stall in my pocket. Or was it at the first tender mention of the onion?"

"The onion!" shouted Nigel. "Where the devil does the onion come in?"

"Georgie Biggins put the onion in the teapot. We found it in a cardboard box in the corner of the supper-room. It had pinkish powder on it. There was pinkish powder on the table in Miss P.'s dressing-room. It smelt of onion. The dressing-rooms were locked while Georgie was in the hall, so he didn't drop the onion in Miss P.'s powder. My theory is that Miss P. found the onion in the teapot, which she had to use, took it to her dressing-room and put it down on the table amongst the spilt powder. The teapot has her prints on the inside, and hers and Georgie's on the outside."

"But what the suffering cats did she want with an onion? She wasn't going to make Irish stew."

"Haven't you heard that she has never been known to shed tears until Saturday night, when floods were induced by sheer pain and disappointment because she couldn't play the piano? She took a good sniff at the onion, opened her dressing-room door, swayed to and fro, moaned and wept and wept and wept until Dr. Templett heard her and behaved exactly as she knew he would behave. Later on she chucked the onion into the débris in the supper-room. She ought to have returned it to the teapot."

"I boggle at the onion."

"Boggle away, my boy. If it was an innocent onion, why didn't she own to it? There are her powder and her prints. Nobody else extracted it from the teapot. But it doesn't matter. It's only another corroborative detail."

"The whole thing sounds a bit like Pooh Bah."

"It's a beastly business. I detest it. She's a horrible woman, not a generous thought in her make-up; but that doesn't make much odds. If Georgie Biggins hadn't set his trap she'd have gone on to the end of her days, most likely, hating Miss C., scheming, scratching, adoring. Everybody will talk psychiatry and nonsense. Her *ideé fixe* will be pitchforked about the studios of the intelligentsia. That old fool Jernigham, who's a nice old fool, and his son, who's no fool at all, will go through hell. The rector, who supplied the *ideé fixe*, will blame himself; and God knows he's not to blame. Templett will hover on the brink of professional odium, but he'll be cured of Mrs. Ross."

"What of Mrs. Ross?"

"At least she's scored a miss in the Vale of Pen Cuckoo. No hope now of blackmailing old Jernigham into matrimony, or out of hard cash. We'll catch the Rosen sooner or later, please heaven, for she's a nasty bit of work, and that's a fact. She would have seen Templett in the dock before she'd have risked an eyelash to clear him, and yet I imagine she's very much attracted by Templett. As soon as she knew we thought him innocent, she was all for him. Here we are."

Nigel pulled up outside the police station.

"May I come in with you?" he asked.

"If you like, certainly."

Fox met Alleyn in the door.

"She's locked up," said Fox. "Making a great old rumpus. The doctor's gone for a strait-jacket. Here's a letter for you, Mr. Alleyn. It came this afternoon."

Alleyn looked at the letter and took it quickly. The firm small writing of the woman he loved brought the idea of her into his mind.

"It's from Troy," he said.

And before he went into the lighted building he looked at Nigel.

"If one could send every grand passion to the laboratory, do you suppose, in each resulting formula, we should find something of Dinah and Henry's young idyll, something of Templett's infatuation, something of Miss P.'s madness, and even something of old Jernigham's foolishness?"

"Who knows?" said Nigel.

"Not I," said Alleyn.